DATE DUE

D1084421

A LITTLE BADNESS

A LITTLE BADNESS

Josephine Cox

HEADLINE

First published in 1995 by
HEADLINE BOOK PUBLISHING

10 9 8 7 6 5 4 3 2

British Library Cataloguing in Publication Data

Cox, Josephine
   Little Badness
   I. Title
   823.914 [F]

Hardback ISBN 0–7472–1179–5
Royal Softback ISBN 0–7472–7804–0

Phototypeset by Intype, London
Printed and bound in Great Britain by
Mackays of Chatham PLC, Chatham, Kent

HEADLINE BOOK PUBLISHING
A division of Hodder Headline PLC
338 Euston Road
London NW1 3BH

Molly Irvine and her family have known me for many, many years.

Molly knew me as an urchin; she saw me courted and wed, and has followed my writing career with pride and joy.

God bless you, Molly sunshine.

Who couldn't love you!

CONTENTS

PART ONE

1900

Dreams Can . . .

CHAPTER ONE

Rita Blackthorn's heart was barren and hard. In all of her life she had never truly loved. *But she had hated.* She hated now, so deeply she could almost taste it. Beneath the loving gaze of her daughter's soft green eyes, her heart swelled with dark and dangerous emotions. 'Don't stare at me, child!' she snarled through gritted teeth. 'Get up from the floor, damn you.'

Curled up like a kitten, Cathy was a slim homely creature, with a nature as warm as her mother's was cold. She was barely sixteen years old. Since the day she was old enough to realise her mother hated her, she had yearned for one kind word, one affectionate glance. 'I love you, Mother,' she murmured. 'Don't turn me away.' The softly spoken words were uttered from the heart.

Rita made no move. She gave no answer. But Cathy's simple plea burned like fire in her brain. The emotions that swept her then should have been those of joy and belonging. Instead, her loathing clenched like a fist in her breast.

The girl's voice trembled as she dared to ask, 'Have I made you angry, Mother?'

Cold and aloof, the woman gave no answer.

Again the child entreated, 'Why don't you love me?' Beside her mother's chair, Cathy ached to touch those long slim fingers, to curl her fingers about them and to press them against her face. In the whole of her life, she had never experienced any loving response from her mother. Now, it had taken all of her courage to get out of her chair and bring herself this close. Her timid gaze swept the woman's face. As always, it was cold, forbidding. Her mother was so near, so tantalisingly near, yet Cathy dared not reach out.

3

Rita Blackthorn appeared not to have heard. Her handsome face was set like stone. Painfully aware that Cathy had come to kneel at her feet, she was almost overwhelmed by the desire to kill.

For a moment it seemed as though she might reply. But then she began rocking the chair in a frenzy, her long busy fingers moving skilfully over the embroidery in her lap. It was not a labour of love. The needle wove in and out with vicious rhythmic movements. For a while, the only sounds that could be heard were the muffled sigh of the rockers against the carpet, and the loud ticking of the mantelpiece clock.

Keeping her fingers clear of the rockers, Cathy studied her mother's beautiful face. Even now, she could not see the ugliness beneath.

Certainly, at forty years of age Rita Blackthorn was a vibrant, handsome woman. Having borne only one child, she had a firm, attractive figure and, with her flowing dark hair, magnificent green eyes and arrogant nature, she could have had any man she wanted. But she wanted none, not even her long-suffering husband, who cherished the ground she walked on. One quiet look, one soft word from her, and he was lost.

'Leave me now.' The movement of the chair was brought to an abrupt halt. Reaching down, she dropped her needle and silks into the sewing box. Savagely slamming shut the lid, she hissed, 'Get washed and away to your bed.'

On her feet now, Cathy resented being treated like a child. 'But I promised Margaret I would wait up for her.'

'You had no right to make such promises!' Getting up from the chair Rita said in a low trembling voice, 'Or do I have to fetch the stick?' She glanced at the door where, propped up in the corner, was a long willow stick. As a child, Cathy had been beaten with the stick many times.

'I'm not a child any longer.' The green eyes hardened.

'Don't defy me, girl! You may be sixteen years old, but you're not too old to be beaten.' With a grim expression on her face, Rita made a dash for the stick, but on hearing Cathy's footsteps and then the door closing softly behind her, paused, smiling with satisfaction. When she turned again, Cathy had gone. Softly laughing, she collected the sewing box, put the stocking inside and, with growing irritation, returned the box to the dresser.

Upstairs, Cathy sat at the window, her sad eyes scouring the countryside for a sight of her beloved Margaret. When it became clear that Margaret would be a while yet, she sighed and went about her preparations for bed. She washed at the basin, cleaned her teeth, then put on her nightgown before going to the dressing table to brush her hair. Perched on the edge of the stool, she swept the brush through her long, corn-coloured locks.

Afterwards, she sat on the window-seat, her knees to her chin, and her head resting on them. 'Hurry up, Margaret,' she pleaded aloud. But Margaret was nowhere in sight.

For what seemed an age she gazed forlornly out of the window, her heart missing a beat when she heard her mother climbing the stairs. For one awful minute, the footsteps paused outside her room.

'Don't let her come in,' Cathy whispered, her green eyes turned to the heavens. *'Please don't let her come in!'* She waited for the footsteps to carry her mother away. The silence was ominous.

Suddenly the door handle began to turn. Quickly now, the girl ran across the room on tiptoe and crawled into her bed. Turning on one side, she closed her eyes and pretended to be asleep.

Rita Blackthorn swept in. For a while she remained at the door, her hard gaze on the bed. She half-turned, satisfied that Cathy was sleeping. But then she changed her mind and, on stiff reluctant steps, came to the bed. Here, she leaned forward, staring at the long fine fingers that clutched the pillow, that pretty slim neck with its pink young skin, then the lovely face with its high cheekbones and perfect shape. 'You're too attractive for your own good,' she murmured bitterly. She wanted to tear herself away, but could not. Her envious gaze lingered, travelling the long corn-coloured hair and the thick dark lashes that fringed the closed eyelids. She imagined those striking green eyes beneath, eyes that were almost the mirror image of her own, and it was more than she could bear. 'You asked me if you had been bad,' she whispered. 'You were *always* bad. The badness is in your smile . . . it's in your laughter and your goodness. Since the day you took root in me, you've been bad.' Her features hardened. 'I wanted a son, and I got you!' Shivering with loathing, she rasped, 'I'll never forgive you for that.'

Incensed, she turned away. Her parting words cut the girl deep. 'As for "loving" you? *Never!* Not as long as I live.'

When the door was closed and she was alone again, Cathy was filled with sadness that permeated through and through. Confused and hurting, she returned to the window-seat.

Through a blur of tears she searched the countryside for another woman, one who was more of a mother than her own could ever be, a woman with a heart as big and warm as the summer sky, a dear and gentle soul who had loved her brother's child these past years, and was destined to be with her through all the years to come.

Burying her face in her hands, the girl pleaded, 'Please, Margaret . . . please come home.' The tears rolled down her face. Soon there were sobs which racked her body. Only the thought that Margaret would soon be home offered any consolation.

In that moment a sound made her look up. The squirrel had scurried up the tree outside her window and was almost near enough for her to touch. Cathy's face shone with delight. 'Oh, you lovely thing. I knew you'd be back.' Touching the window-pane she giggled when the squirrel sat staring at her, its mouth and nostrils working, almost as though it was trying to tell her something.

Softly now, Cathy slid open the window. 'Come for your tea, have you?' she asked. Taking a nut from a corner of the window-ledge, she held it loosely between finger and thumb. 'It's not very nice, but it's the best I can do.' Scolding the inquisitive creature, she explained, 'It's your own fault, because you haven't been to see me for a long time, and now they're all dried up.'

Creeping forward on the branch, the squirrel plucked at her hand until the nut was firmly grasped between his claws. He turned it over and over, his quick brown eyes examining every detail. At first he seemed not to want it. But then, with a little encouragement from the girl, he put it between his sharp teeth, split open the shell, and began nibbling at the contents.

'There!' she cried softly. 'It's still good.' Enchanted, her face shone with delight which deepened when she caught sight of a small familiar figure coming over the far hill. From the blue dress to the short fair hair glinting in the sunshine, there was no mistaking who it was. Margaret was on her way back.

Margaret Blackthorn paused for breath. It was a long walk to Nan Foster's cottage, and though she could have travelled on the tram from the end of the main road, she preferred to cut across the fields; especially on a day such as this, when the sun had shone gloriously down.

Shading her eyes with the flat of her hand, she squinted up at the sky. 'What a pity Cathy wasn't allowed to come with me,' she murmured, her brown eyes shadowed as she walked quickly on. There was still a way to go, and she knew the girl would be waiting for her. 'A woman like that should never have had a child in the first place!' she declared under her breath.

'They do say as how talking to yourself is the first sign of madness.' The man's voice was warm and kind, but it startled her.

'Good heavens!' Margaret reeled back as he came out of the woods and stood before her. 'Mr Leyton!' Relief flooded her face. 'You gave me a fright.'

'Sorry about that,' he apologised, then, holding up a large empty crate, he explained, 'I'm on me way back from the market, and this is all I have to show for me troubles.' Before she could express her curiosity about the crate, he pointed to the lane where his wagon and horse were waiting. 'That downpour last week opened up the potholes, and the lane's a shocking mess, I can tell you.'

Margaret smiled. 'You don't have to tell me,' she assured him. 'Why do you think I prefer to cross by way of the fields?' As always when she came into contact with Owen Leyton, she was struck by his handsome looks. He was not much taller than herself, but his figure was proud and upright, his muscles hard, and his shoulders broadened by labouring on the land. Owen Leyton caught the eye in a way she could never explain, and his manner was always most charming. With the sun streaming down on him, his brown hair gleamed, and his dark eyes twinkled as he spoke.

'You've still a way to go,' he pointed out. 'Why don't I give you a lift on the wagon?'

Margaret eyed the rickety wagon with suspicion. 'Are you

likely to hit any more potholes?' she asked wryly.

He laughed out loud. 'I'm offended,' he teased. 'You're talking to a man who was *born* on a wagon. What! I drove one almost as soon as I could walk. Me . . . hit a pothole? Whatever gave you that idea?'

'Shame on me,' Margaret responded with a grin. 'For ever thinking such a thing.'

'You'll travel with me then?'

Margaret nodded. 'Why not? My legs are aching, and I've the longest mile to go yet.' She began walking alongside him towards the lane. 'I've had a good day . . . spent an hour or two browsing in the Blackburn shops, then stopped off at Nan Foster's cottage on the way back.' Her gaze softened as she glanced to the big house in the distance. 'All the same, I'll not be sorry to get back. I expect Cathy's been watching for me all afternoon.'

He nodded as though agreeing with her. 'Aye. She's a lovely lass. An' if you don't mind me saying, Miss, I don't reckon I've ever known a mother and child to be so unalike. Oh, I know the girl has the stamp of her mother . . . and that's not a curse because the mother is a good-looking woman.' On seeing Margaret's curious glance, he quickly added, 'But their *natures* are as far apart as heaven from hell.' He kicked at the ground. 'I expect you know how your sister-in-law has a mind to put up the rents on all the tenant farms?'

Margaret should not have been shocked but she was. Trying hard not to show her anger, she merely answered, 'Is that so?'

'Aye.' His face was turned to hers and his eyes burned with a fury that almost matched her own. 'I'll not deny the prospect of finding more rent has caused me a deal of grief, especially as we've had a hard winter and the crops were recently beaten down by the rains.' Sensing he had said enough, he lowered his gaze.

It was on the tip of her tongue to reassure him that her sister-in-law had no legal right to make such threats. But she knew how devoted to Rita her misguided brother was, and how, if it pleased her, he would let her meddle in affairs that were none of her concern. So Margaret merely answered, 'My brother has said nothing of rent rises to me.' She gave a short laugh that lightened his dark expression. 'But then, like all women I don't have a head for business. Much better to leave such matters to the men.'

He eyed her with renewed interest, saying in a pleasant voice, 'Don't pretend you haven't a good head on your shoulders, Miss . . . we all know different.'

'Oh?' She was flattered.

'I'm talking about the way you step in whenever you think your brother is being too harsh. Like last year when it seemed he might levy a milk tax on us. If he'd gone ahead with that idea, I'd have been driven under for sure.' He nodded his head as though agreeing with some inner prompting. 'I've never really said thank you for putting a stop to it, but I'm thanking you now, Miss. There's no mistake about it, you saved my livelihood.'

'And if I said I know nothing about it?' She was astonished. How in God's name had he learned of her brother's plan? It was all exactly as he described and, for the first time since she and her twin brother had inherited the land and cottages, she had felt it morally right to oppose him on a business decision. But, as far as she knew, it had been discussed in private, and had not gone beyond the walls of the big house.

As though reading her mind, he answered cleverly, 'Walls have ears, Miss.'

'You mean the tale was carried out by someone from the house? Are you telling me it was Ruby?'

'Happen . . . and happen not.'

Her smile was friendly, forgiving. She found him wonderfully easy to talk to. 'Meaning?'

'If it *was* the housekeeper, you wouldn't tell your sister-in-law, would you?'

'What do *you* think?'

Grinning, he visibly relaxed. 'Well now, Miss. Taking into account the fact that Ruby Adams has no family but yours, and has served you well these many years, and knowing you have a gentle heart, I don't reckon you would punish her.'

'Ruby is in a position of trust, and she did wrong.' When she saw his expression fall, she quickly assured him, 'I intend to have words with her. But, no, I won't punish her, and neither will I speak to my brother about it.'

'Thank you for that, Miss.' His face hardened. 'If word of

Ruby's little indiscretion ever got to your sister-in-law's ears, she'd take great pleasure in making an example of her.' In his mind's eye he could see his landlord's spoilt wife, handsome, arrogant . . . *and immensely desirable.* Thrusting such dangerous images from his thoughts, he exclaimed, 'By! She's a hard one! I had a bull like that once . . . magnificent to look at, but get on his wrong side and he'd rip your heart out.' Suddenly he was trembling, whether from fury or desire he wasn't altogether certain. All he knew was that Rita Blackthorn had the power to shake his emotions like nothing he had ever experienced. And he hated himself for it.

Secretly amused by his comparison of Rita to a mad bull, Margaret let the matter lie. 'What's the crate for?' she asked brightly.

Momentarily surprised by her question and realising she wanted to change the subject, he answered gratefully, 'It's empty now, but it weren't an hour back.' Giving no more information than that, he strode along, swinging the heavy wooden crate as though it was no weight at all. 'Where in God's name has he got to?'

'Who?' she asked.

Pausing in his stride and turning his attention to the spinney, he didn't hear her question. 'It's no use him searching now,' he groaned. 'If I know anything at all, they'll be long gone.'

Margaret was intrigued. Standing some way behind, she watched him put down the crate. He then cupped his big hands round his mouth and emitted an ear-splitting whistle. It took her by surprise. Fascinated, she came to his side. Looking with him towards the spinney, she wondered what might suddenly emerge.

When only silence followed, he enacted the same procedure again. This time the whistle was so loud that Margaret was forced to press her hands over her ears, at the same time thinking she might have got home quicker if she hadn't accepted a ride in his wagon.

Suddenly the spinney came alive when two large birds burst from its cover. 'Well, I'm buggered! He found 'em after all.' Falling to his knees, he pulled her with him. 'Keep down, Miss,' he whispered. 'If they catch sight of us they'll be gone like the wind.'

The birds were in a panic. Flying a short distance then falling to the ground again, they flailed the air with their wings and nervously fluttered about.

'Is that what was in your crate?' Margaret recalled him saying he'd been to Blackburn Market.

'That's right,' he confirmed. 'Until we rumbled over the potholes and the blessed thing broke open.'

'Shouldn't you get after them?'

He shook his head. 'No. They're spooked enough. Best to stay put. I've taught him well. He knows what he's doing.' That said, he strained his eyes towards the spinney. 'There!' he whispered. 'D'you see?'

Margaret followed his gaze. Creeping from the spinney on all fours was a young man. Inch by inch he came up on the birds who were pecking at the ground one minute, and in the next squaring up to tear each other's eyes out. 'Careful now. Or it'll be *your* eyes they'll pluck out,' Owen whispered. Margaret remained silent, but watchful.

Suddenly there was a flurry of feathers as the birds went for each other, and in that same minute were grabbed by the young man. Wrenching them apart, he dropped each one into a separate sack before loosely tying the necks and setting towards the onlookers across the field. When he saw Owen, he grinned from ear to ear. 'I'd have bagged them in the spinney if your whistle hadn't scared 'em off.'

His father beamed with pride. 'I might have known he'd track the blighters down,' he laughed. 'Just as well too. They're valuable birds ... champion cockerels, that's what they are. And I don't mind telling you, they cost me a pretty penny.'

Together, Margaret and Owen followed the young man's progress across the field. At eighteen years of age, David was the elder of Owen's two children. The only son, he was the apple of his father's eye; the kind of son a man could boast of. Tall, well-built and incredibly handsome, he was also hard-working and possessed of a warm likeable nature. With his wild dark hair and smiling dark eyes, he had the makings of a heartbreaker.

'He's a fine young man,' Margaret declared as David strode towards them in that easy confident manner he had. 'And a good friend to Cathy.'

Owen snorted through his nose. 'Aye! And how long d'you reckon it'll be before *she* puts a stop to it?' Jerking his thumb towards the big house, he went on in a harsh voice, 'From what I know, your sister-in-law would rather wipe her boots on my son than have the girl speak to him.' He rolled his eyes to heaven. 'By! If she knew how her daughter was teaching David to read and write, there'd be hell to pay!'

'Then we'd best not let her find out,' Margaret said softly. 'What she doesn't know won't hurt her.'

'She'll not hear of it from *me*, that's for sure.' He rubbed his chin with the flat of his hand. 'All the same, I reckon it'll end in trouble.' As he dwelt on the possible consequences of the growing friendship between the two youngsters, a deep frown creased his forehead and he opened his mouth to say something else.

Margaret put up her hand and intervened. 'Do you want me to stop calling?'

''Course not.' The very idea would be like a slap in the face, for Margaret had brought great comfort to his poorly wife. 'What! Maria would never forgive me.'

'Do you want me to stop bringing the girl then?' Margaret was testing him, though she guessed he was made of sterner stuff than to let Rita Blackthorn dictate the pattern of his life.

'Then David would never forgive me.'

'I could always say it was my idea?'

'Then I'd never forgive myself!' Perceiving her little game, he shrugged his shoulders. 'Shame on you, Miss. You know well enough how I want our David to have the learning I never had. Cathy Blackthorn is the best thing that ever happened to him, and as for yourself, Miss, you must know how me and the missus appreciate your help.'

'That's very kind. But we're not talking about me in particular. What we're discussing is whether or not you still want things to carry on as they have these past few months? In other words, Owen Leyton . . . are you happy for me to go on visiting your wife? And is Cathy still welcome at your house?' She eyed him with serious brown eyes, the smallest suspicion of a smile appearing at the corners of her mouth. 'I must say, I never thought you were the kind of man to let a woman frighten you.

That's all she is, you know . . . just a woman.'

He was embarrassed then. 'She doesn't frighten me, Miss.' His hackles were up now, and his jawbone working in a fever. 'It's for *him*, isn't it? For David. And to hell with Rita Blackthorn!' His gaze went to the young man who was almost on them, and at once his eyes softened. 'Who am I to say he can't have his chance, eh? He's a good lad, and one day he'll make a better man than his father.'

There was regret in his voice, and something so painful that Margaret was obliged to comment. 'How can you say that?' she asked kindly. 'No son could wish for a better father.'

When he looked into her eyes, she was disturbed by his fleeting expression of guilt. 'You think so?' he murmured, dropping his gaze. 'Mebbe! But I wouldn't be much of a father if I robbed him of his chance to read and write now, would I, eh? David was always a loner, never one for mixing, especially with members of the opposite sex.' He chuckled knowingly. 'But that lovely girl of yours has opened up a whole new world for him. She's not only befriended him, she's taught him a love for words . . . given him the talent to write and read . . . something his father never could do.' He grimaced. 'It's the biggest shame of my life, not being able to read and write. All these years, I've felt only half a man. I don't want that for David. Until the girl came along, he still hadn't mastered the pen and page. Oh, it's not that he hasn't the brains because he has. He just didn't have the *heart*.' He chuckled. 'He hated every minute at school.'

'There's nothing wrong with wanting to be out in the fields instead of being squashed into a row of desks, with only the four walls to look at.' Margaret worried that Owen might see this as a flaw in his son's character. 'David is a bright intelligent young man, with a great love for God's wonderful creation.' She swept out her arms. 'And this is where he belongs, where he feels at home. It isn't surprising that he didn't enjoy his schooling.'

Soon they were all loaded on to the wagon; Margaret seated up front with Owen who had put on his cap and pulled the brim down over his forehead; David in the back, with the crate securely tied to the wagon rim. 'I'll have you home in no time,

13

Miss,' Owen declared as he gently tapped the whip against the horse's rump.

'I'm later now than if I'd walked,' she said, desperately hanging on as the cart lurched forward. With her free hand she dipped into her basket and drew out a scarf which she wrapped round her neck. Suddenly there was a light wind blowing and the sun was hiding behind a cloud.

'Looks like rain,' Owen remarked. Staring up at the sky, he drove the wagon on. The potholes were thick and fast, and with every turn of the wheels the wagon found them out.

'Miss Blackthorn?' David's voice cut through the air.

Not daring to glance round, Margaret replied, her voice vibrating as she was thrown from side to side, 'Yes? What is it, David?'

'Will Cathy be coming to the farm tomorrow?'

This time it was Owen who spoke. 'Talk sense, lad! It's Sunday tomorrow. Miss Blackthorn never visits on a Sunday.'

There followed an awkward silence. But then Margaret's warm voice answered, 'If the weather is as glorious tomorrow as it's been today, I have a mind to take Cathy on a long walk over the fields. I dare say we could make a detour to the farm.' She turned round then. Happiness shone in his face like a beacon. 'What's so special about tomorrow?' she asked.

His smile fell away. It was something secret between him and Cathy and, as much as he liked Miss Blackthorn, he had promised Cathy that no one would know about it until it was all finished. 'It doesn't matter,' he said quietly. 'It can wait till Monday.'

Margaret sensed his disappointment. 'I'm sure Cathy would be delighted to pay a visit tomorrow,' she said wisely. 'But, as I say, it's a Sunday so there'll be no reading or writing.' When she looked at him again, he was crouched before the crate, tenderly stroking the birds, a little smile on his face.

The short journey to Blackthorn House took only fifteen minutes during which the conversation embraced the Boer War, the assassination of the German Ambassador in Peking, and the opening of London Underground's central line.

'As you know, I was bitterly disappointed not to have joined the fighting force,' Owen lied.

'It wasn't your fault,' Margaret reassured him. She had heard the tale time and again, and knew it inside out.

'I should have been more careful. Two days before leaving, and I had to shoot myself in the knee with a shotgun!'

'It's no good blaming yourself, Dad.' David had remained quiet until now, just listening and enjoying the ride. But now he felt he had to defend his father. 'You have to be thankful you didn't lose your leg.'

Margaret sensed Owen's disgust at himself. 'Sometimes bad things happen and we just have to make the best of them,' she said softly. Her thoughts wandered. She thought of Cathy, and of how Rita had never deserved such a lovely child. She recalled how the girl had always craved her mother's affection but been constantly rejected, and she burned with shame at the way her own brother accepted the situation. In his eyes Rita could do no wrong. Some day, Margaret knew, he would regret the way she had twisted him round her little finger. But for now Frank Blackthorn could not see what was right before his eyes, and there wasn't a thing anyone could do about it.

'You're very easy to talk to,' Owen's voice interrupted her thoughts. 'You're a good woman with a sense of right and wrong.' Under his breath he added warily, 'The wife has always said you're a misfit in the big house.'

Margaret was made to wonder about this, and for some reason she was not too happy about it.

Fearing he had overstepped the mark, Owen quickly urged, 'Take no notice of me, Miss Blackthorn. Sometimes I let my tongue run away with my brains.' He blamed her too. Some people were so easygoing and kind that they made it too easy to be familiar.

Margaret smiled at him. He smiled back. But still he felt uneasy.

Conversation was at an end. Instead, he began softly whistling. Margaret thought about her aching feet and the few purchases she had made at the market. Behind them the young man lay on his back, stared up at the gathering clouds and dreamed of Cathy. So much separated them. So many things decreed that they could never be together as lovers. Yet he was determined: one day in the future, they *would* be lovers. One day in a far-off summer, when he was a man and Cathy was a woman, they would be man and wife. It seemed an impossible dream. Right now, the way things were, it *was* impossible, he knew that. But one day it must happen, or all of his life would count for nothing.

When the wagon drew up to the front door, two pairs of green eyes were watching from the house. Downstairs in the big front parlour, Rita was incensed that a tenant farmer should have the gall to drive his wagon right up to her front door; while upstairs, Cathy was delighted, her fond gaze going from David to Margaret, and back to David. He didn't see her at first. But when he looked up, his heart turned over and the smile on his face told its own tale.

Gathering up the hem of her dress with one hand, Margaret reached out with the other to take hold of Owen's outstretched fingers. 'Don't forget your basket, Miss,' he reminded her as she stepped to the ground. Sweeping the basket from the wagon, he handed it to her, afterwards tipping the neb of his cap and remarking that the clouds had darkened, and, 'It won't be long before the downpour.'

Almost before the words were out of his mouth, Rita's angry voice demanded, 'How dare you bring that filthy contraption to the front of the house?' Before he could answer, she rounded on her sister-in-law. 'As for *you*! I don't know what you're thinking of. I'm ashamed, that's what I am . . . *ashamed!*'

Brushing a cloud of dust from her dress, Margaret smiled sweetly. 'But there's nothing for you to be ashamed of, Rita, dear,' she remarked with feigned surprise. 'It wasn't *you* who rode home on the cart.'

Fuming, Rita turned to Owen Leyton. 'My husband will hear of this,' she warned. 'And when he does, I shouldn't be at all surprised if you and yours weren't thrown out on the streets where you belong!'

Owen stared at her for a moment, before saying in a soft persuasive voice, 'If I've offended you in any way, Ma'am, I'm sorry.' He thought her a splendid figure of a woman. Such was the effect she had on him, he gazed on her from top to toe, mentally ravaging her almost without realising it. He was acutely conscious of the shapely pair of ankles that showed from beneath the hem of her straight-skirted cream dress; the tiny waist and the long dark hair that was caught up on her crown with an expensive mother-of-pearl comb. He was aware of the soft creamy skin that showed at her neck, the exquisite ears and the hard set of her small square chin. He looked into those blazing green eyes and could hardly control his passion. He wanted her. He had wanted her from the first minute he'd seen her.

For a long moment Rita looked up at him, at those dark secretive eyes that seemed to touch her soul, and she couldn't tear her gaze away. She had seen Owen Leyton from a distance on many occasions. She had never been this close to him: never realised how devilishly handsome he was. Something stirred in her. Something deeply disturbing. It warned of shocking things to come; things that would alter the course of all their lives.

He smiled and the spell was broken. Her anger erupted. 'Be off,' she cried. 'And if you know what's good for you, you'll stay well away from this house.'

Without a word, he made a small bow with his head, touched his fingers to the brim of his cap, and swung into the wagon. In a minute he was gone. But his presence remained. And Rita was awed by it.

'Where's your sense of dignity?' she demanded of Margaret. 'You have a reputation to keep up.'

'There's no harm done to our reputation,' Margaret patiently assured her.

'We'll see what Frank has to say about this!' Rita brushed by, storming into the house and slamming shut the door.

'My! My!' Margaret tutted. 'What a sulk.'

After surreptitiously winking at Cathy, whom she had seen watching, Margaret went towards the house. Now a hundred years old, it made a pretty picture with its red-tiled roof, long stone-embrasured windows latticed with lead, and every inch of its brick walls festooned with climbers from which hung many colourful blooms. Her admiring eyes rested on the place that had been home for longer than she cared to remember.

In 1810, Edward Blackthorn, the love child of a country squire and his lowly mistress, came into a handsome legacy. When the house became available, together with some considerable acreage, he fought off all competition and paid a handsome price for it. A farm hand all his life, and possessing a great love for the land, he took on fellow labourers but worked himself into an early grave – and no doubt turned in it when Joshua Blackthorn, his only son and heir, vowed never to turn a shovel or darken his hands with the earth.

When Joshua's wife bore him twins, the boy, Frank, inherited his father's indifference to the land, while the girl, Margaret, shared her grandfather's love for it.

The house was many things to many people. To Rita it was a symbol of her higher status in the community. Her husband Frank was there merely because *she* was there; if she had lived in a pigsty, he would have grovelled in the dirt with her. To the tenant farmers, Blackthorn House was a formidable place, a place from which the 'Squire' presided over them, a place they were forbidden to enter. To Margaret and young Cathy, however, it was home; a place to come back to after a long walk across the fields, a place where they could hide away and tell each other their dearest dreams and wishes, a warm and welcoming sanctuary where they could shut out the hostility that surrounded them, and grow in the strength of each other's love.

As Margaret came into the hall from the front entrance, a small round figure with grey hair bustled in from the back kitchen. Ruby Adams was as much a part of this house as the foundations themselves. Now sixty years old, she had served the Blackthorns for over forty years. Hired by the infamous Joshua Blackthorn, she had cleaned his house, tended his wife, and, on a dark stormy night when the doctor couldn't get through the floods, she had brought the twins, Frank and Margaret, into the world. Less than a year later, deeply affected by her husband's blatant affairs with other women, Annette Blackthorn ran off and was never heard of again.

Afterwards Joshua Blackthorn brought one woman after another into the house. People came and people went. Money was scarce, then it was abundant. There was scandal and chaos; no servant ever stayed for more than a month – and throughout it all, caring for the children, protecting and loving them, Ruby remained ever constant. Even when, twenty years later, Joshua Blackthorn was found drowned in the river, she was there, a sane, familiar figure in a changing world; the same warm, kindly soul she was now.

Though older, and with the habit of speaking her mind to everyone but the arrogant Rita, for whom she had little time, Ruby was indispensable. Cathy and Margaret adored her. Frank had a lingering affection for her. And Rita tolerated her because she was a sort of family heirloom, handed down with their other possessions.

'Whatever have you been doing?' Ruby gently scolded. 'You've sent the mistress into a terrible rage.' While she talked, she collected the basket from Margaret's arm and walked through to the kitchen.

Leaning closer to the round grey-haired figure, Margaret looked into her eyes – pink because she had a liking for 'a drop o' the old stuff . . . for me poor old bones, you understand?'

'I rode home on Owen Leyton's wagon,' Margaret answered her question.

'You never did!' Ruby's pink eyes twinkled.

'Have you ever ridden on a wagon?' Margaret asked mischievously.

The old woman chuckled. 'If I have, I'm not about to tell you,' she said, blushing to the roots of her grey hair.

Margaret was intrigued. 'Why, Ruby Adams!' she teased. 'Whatever secrets are you keeping?'

'Not telling.' She grinned broadly, showing a row of baby-pink gums. 'And anyway, it were years back . . . when I were young and beautiful.'

Margaret burst out laughing. 'You were never young and beautiful.' It wasn't meant as an insult, and they knew each other well enough to understand that.

Ruby thought a while, then cocked her head to one side before replying wryly, 'Well . . . happen not "beautiful". But I wore the frilliest bloomers, and I walked off with the best-looking fella out the lot.' She shook her head and tutted. 'I'll never know why the bugger wed Alice Clegg when he could have had me!'

Margaret hugged her warmly. 'Because he was blind,' she declared.

'Aye. Well, good shuts to him, that's what I say.' With that she informed Margaret that there was a snack ready if she was hungry. Inclining her head towards the drawing room, she whispered, 'Her Highness just informed me that she don't want dinner served.'

'Why's that?'

'Because the master ain't home, and she's in a foul mood.'

'Has Cathy eaten?'

'Not yet. She's been sent to her bed. But I can fetch a tray up for the two of you, if you like?'

'That's a good idea, Ruby. Give me half an hour though. I need to wash the day off me first.' She also needed to have a word with Rita. 'Foul mood' or not, it was unfair of her to take it out on Cathy.

Impatient to see her niece, she went straight upstairs. A gentle tap and the door was flung open. Cathy threw herself straight into Margaret's arms. 'I'm so glad you're back!' she cried. 'I thought you were never coming home.'

'Well, you thought wrong. Not only am I home, but I've brought you a present.' Going into the room, she laid the small parcel on the bed. 'Open it,' she urged, sinking on to the bed beside it, and watching Cathy's excited face as the present was revealed. 'Do you like it?' she asked. But she already knew the answer. Cathy's face said it all.

'Oh, it's beautiful!' With great tenderness, Cathy cradled the brooch in the palms of her hands. An oval-shaped cameo set in silver filigree, it was the same brooch she had sighed over in Harpur's shop window the last time she and Margaret had gone into Blackburn town.

Going to the mirror, she pinned it to the neck of her nightgown. In the light from the window it shimmered and glowed. 'Oh, look!' she cried, glancing at Margaret in the mirror. 'The lady's smiling at me.' And, just for a moment, when she moved and the dying sunlight caught the cameo face, it did seem so.

'That's because she knows what a delightful creature you are.' Margaret came to her then, resting an arm around the girl's shoulders and gazing into the mirror at her. There was a world of love in her eyes.

Pressing one hand into Margaret's, and holding the brooch

against her throat with the other, Cathy told her softly, 'I do love you.'

Sensing the girl's dilemma, Margaret assured her, 'You don't have to tell me if you don't want to.'

The words tumbled out. 'She said she could never love me.' She believed her mother's words would haunt her forever. '*Why?* Why won't she love me? I've done nothing wrong, have I?'

'No, and don't think that.' She sought for a way to explain Rita's coldness towards her own daughter. It was hard. Instead, she gave Cathy a degree of hope. 'We're all different,' she began. 'Women are complex creatures ... some love their children even while they're carrying them. Others love them from the minute they're born. And there are those who simply don't have the capacity to love ... they can't open their hearts to *anyone*.'

'*She's* like that, isn't she?' Cathy stiffened in her arms. 'She meant what she said. For all my life, she'll never love me, will she?'

Margaret wanted to say the right thing, something that would help Cathy ... give her hope, but not too much, because there was no hope of Rita ever loving this precious girl ... no hope that her heart would soften with the passing of the years. It wasn't Rita she cared about now. It was Cathy. And the only solace she could offer was to say, 'Be patient, sweetheart. Give her time, and she might turn out to be the mother you want.'

'I wish you were my mother.'

'I'm not your mother, Cathy,' Margaret said regretfully. 'But, with the help of the Lord, I'll be here for as long as you need me.' They clung to each other then, and the world was right again.

'Anyway, you're not the only one who got on her wrong side.' Margaret chuckled at the way Rita had laid into her about riding on the wagon.

'Tell me all about it. How did you come to be on the wagon? And David? Did he ask after me? How soon are we visiting again?' The questions came thick and fast, and Margaret answered them as best she could. She outlined the sequence of events, and finished by assuring Cathy, 'I've promised we'll pay a visit tomorrow afternoon.' That brought a smile to her face.

So did the news that Ruby brought. 'I'm to tell you that dinner will be served after all, and you're *both* to be at the table. The master's home and roaring hungry,' she announced wryly. 'What's more, he's brought someone back from London with him ... though he must be a ghost, 'cause I ain't seen hide nor hair of the fella!'

On the stroke of eight o'clock, Cathy and Margaret came into the dining room; Cathy looking fresh and bright in a pale blue dress, and Margaret feeling just a little bit special after washing and changing into her favourite cream-coloured blouse and long straight skirt; scalloped at the hem, it showed more of her legs than her brother thought proper.

'Be quick! Be quick!' Frank Blackthorn was already seated at the table. A big man with a soft face, sad blue eyes and wild brown hair, he was normally a quiet and reserved soul. Tonight, though, he was greatly excited, and could hardly keep still.

The new maid, Milly, recently taken on because of Ruby's worsening gout, was standing ready to serve soup. As yet there was still no sign of Rita. 'Where on earth is she?' Agitated, Frank got up from his chair and proceeded to walk backwards and forwards, anxiously peering through the door whenever he came to it, and feverishly rubbing his hands together behind his back. 'He's like the rabbit in *Alice in Wonderland*,' Cathy whispered, but fell silent when Margaret shot her a warning glance.

It was ten minutes past eight when Rita arrived. The maid was nervously shifting from one foot to the other; Frank was beside himself with impatience; Margaret was toying with the idea of expressing her curiosity regarding the 'fella' Ruby had mentioned earlier; and Cathy was busy listening to the tune her hungry stomach was playing.

Rita swept in as though she was royalty about to meet her subjects. Bedecked in a crimson dress and matching shoes, and with her dark hair curled about her ears, she looked magnificent. 'My dear, you look wonderful!' As usual, Frank was besotted. Springing forward to lead her to her chair, he fussed over her all the way.

Looking about her as Frank returned to his own seat, she asked, 'Where is he?'

Frank gave a little secretive smile. 'Who, my dear?' He was obviously enjoying himself.

Impatient, Rita banged her fist on the table. 'Your guest, of course . . . the man you brought from London!'

'All in good time, my dear,' he replied, beckoning the thankful maid to serve the first course. 'Ruby should be attending to him now. I'm sure he'll join us soon enough.'

In fact, it was sooner than he had intended. They were half-way through the main course when screeches of horror were heard from the hall. Before Frank could get to his feet the doors had burst open and all hell was let loose. The fleeing dark shape flitted through the room, ducking and darting and letting out cries like a banshee. Behind him came Ruby, wearing a dirt-stained pinafore and looking flustered. 'He 'scaped from me!' she wailed above Rita's screams. 'The bugger took off when I were getting the soap!'

'Got you!' Frank lunged at the shape and hoisted it up for all to see. When it wriggled and squealed, Rita screamed the louder, Cathy giggled, and Margaret was astonished when she saw what Frank was holding. 'It's a *lad!*' she exclaimed, though she could hardly see its features beneath the layers of grime.

'A street urchin,' Frank corrected. 'It tried to pick my pocket outside the club in Piccadilly . . . would have been carted off and thrown in prison if I hadn't arranged for it to be brought here.' He seemed very proud of himself. In fact, there was much more to the young urchin than he intended revealing.

'You must be mad!' Rita yelled, wrapping her handkerchief over her nose. 'Get it out of here!'

Frank's reply was calm and sincere, and everyone there was silenced by it. 'No, my dear,' he answered. 'The boy stays. He'll be the son we never had.'

Lost for words, Rita stared at her husband as though he had lost his mind. Margaret was shocked to her roots. And Cathy could only watch with disbelief; she had always believed it was her *mother* who bitterly regretted never having a son. Now she realised it was her father also. She looked into his face, that big soft face that was now hard and unyielding. And, for the first time, she really despaired of ever winning her parents' love.

Margaret too saw the possessive look in her brother's eyes. She saw that Rita was reluctantly intrigued by the intruder. She looked at the boy, a surprisingly well-built creature, with dirt-encrusted hair hanging to his shoulders, the whites of his eyes staring out of a blackened face, and like Cathy she wondered what manner of chaos he would bring to Blackthorn House.

In those few moments before Ruby led the urchin away, no one there could ever begin to imagine the sequence of events that even now were being unleashed.

CHAPTER TWO

'Do you think he'll run away?' In spite of her generous nature, Cathy sounded hopeful.

'Who knows?' Margaret replied as they crossed the brook. 'Why? Do you *want* him to?'

Cathy thought for a while, then answered sincerely, 'At first I resented him. But now, I'm not sure how I feel.' She looked up with anxious green eyes. 'Mother said I was wicked. Maybe she's right.'

Stopping at the top of the bank, Margaret pulled her up short. 'Your mother's wrong,' she said softly. 'You're *not* wicked! Don't ever think that, sweetheart.' When Cathy seemed not to be convinced, she went on, 'When your father brought that boy into our lives, he gave us all something to think about. After all, we don't know anything at all about him ... who he is or where he's come from.'

'Do you want him to stay?'

'Like you, I'm not too sure.'

'What about Mother?'

Margaret's expression darkened. 'I'm sorry, sweetheart, I can't answer for her.' Sensing that the conversation might take a much more serious turn, she took hold of Cathy's hand and headed quickly towards the Leyton smallholding. Above them the sun shone out of a sapphire blue sky, and the sound of birds filled the air. It was a glorious day, and it was Margaret's intention that nothing would spoil it. Cathy was still smarting from her mother's treatment of her, and now there was the urchin to contend with. Not for the first time, she wondered where it would all end. 'Remember, it's Sunday,' she reminded Cathy. 'You're only visiting ... not working.'

25

Cathy's thoughts were still at Blackthorn House, with her mother and the boy. 'He seems to be worming his way into Mother's affections,' she recalled. 'When he spilled tea on the tablecloth at breakfast, she didn't even scold him.' Casting her gaze to the ground, she was quiet for a moment, before recalling an incident she would rather forget but could not. 'When *I* dropped my spoon on the floor last week, she slapped me really hard.' Subconsciously caressing the side of her face where Rita had struck her, she gave a small sigh. 'The other night, when she thought I was asleep, I heard her say I was bad ... and that she never wanted me. She only wanted a son.' Looking up at Margaret, she asked forlornly, 'Now they have a son, they won't want me any more, will they?'

They had come to a narrow lane. 'Come and sit here, sweetheart,' Margaret coaxed, pointing to a derelict cart. 'We deserve a breather, I think.' What she really wanted was to put Cathy's tortured mind at rest.

Easing herself up on to the shaft, Cathy sat alongside her aunt. 'As long as I've got you, I don't care,' she lied, but the despair in her voice betrayed the truth.

Taking a deep breath, Margaret smiled into her upturned face. 'You don't have to pretend with me,' she said, shaking her head in disapproval. 'I thought we always told each other the truth?'

Cathy was ashamed. 'I'm sorry.'

'I should think so too.' She put her arm round the girl's slim shoulders and drew her close. 'Now you listen to me, and listen carefully,' she began, and Cathy looked at her intently. 'First of all, you must never make hasty judgments ... sometimes people say things they really don't mean. Like you said just now, about not caring whether they loved you. Oh, I know it's hard, and I'm sorry you heard your mother say those things about wanting a son. But she didn't know you were listening, did she?'

'No.'

'Have you ever heard her say that before ... about wanting a son?'

Cathy thought hard. 'No, I've never heard her say that before,' she confessed.

'Have you ever heard your father say he doesn't want you?'

'No.'

'Well then! As far as I can tell, he loves you very much.'

'He never tells me that.'

'I know, and it's a great pity. But even if he doesn't tell you so, you know he loves you. In your heart, you know. Don't you, eh?'

'I suppose so,' she admitted in a brighter voice.

'Good. By the way, it might be wiser not to mention the boy to anyone. I think we'll let your father do the explaining, shall we?' She was amused by the idea . . . it would be a sort of punishment for what she believed to be his foolhardy action. When she spoke again, it was with a serious voice. 'After all, it was all his idea and, to tell you the truth, I'm afraid he may very well come to regret it.'

'I was going to tell David about him, but I won't.'

'Right then! Let's make our way, or it'll be dark before we get back.' She swung off the shaft and, with Cathy beside her, quickened her steps away from the lane.

Disappointed, Cathy glanced towards the cottage at the end of the lane. 'I thought we were calling on Nan Foster?'

'We are. But on the way back,' Margaret explained.

'Do you think he's a bad lot?'

'Who?'

'The urchin.'

'I think we should give him the chance to prove himself one way or the other.'

'He was picking Father's pockets.'

'I know, but from what your father told me, he has no home or family. Perhaps he was driven to it.'

Cathy thought on that for a time. Then, 'He has a nice face, don't you think?'

'Yes, I think he does.'

'Mother thinks he's handsome.' A shadow crossed Cathy's face.

'I suppose she's just pleased he looks more like a human being, now he's been washed and dressed like a little gentleman.'

'She'll probably dote on him.'

Margaret laughed. 'I don't think so. Tomorrow she'll probably throw him out on his ear.' In fact, Margaret too had been surprised when her sister-in-law made no objection to the boy's

27

remaining at the table throughout breakfast; though she made no effort to put him at his ease, she glanced his way occasionally when she thought no one was looking. 'Anyway, I have the feeling he would much rather be out on the streets, picking pockets.'

'He ate more than all of us put together.'

Margaret laughed. 'I expect that's because Ruby threatened him with all manner of horrors if he didn't eat her beautifully cooked food.'

'Would you say he's good-looking?'

'I suppose he is, yes.'

Like everyone else, she had been astonished at the change in the urchin. Ruby had scrubbed him until he glowed, then she cut his hair short and dressed him in the clothes which Frank had already bought from a shop in Blackburn. The result was astounding. Gone was the filthy bundle of rags, and in its place was revealed a young man who, though half-starved and pale, appeared to be about Cathy's age. With his thick mop of fair hair and light hazel eyes, he had a certain appeal – though there was nothing appealing about his manners or his speech. On being summoned to the breakfast table, he boldly warned his host, 'Don't think about callin' the rozzers, guv, cause I'll be long gone by the time they get 'ere!' However, once Frank assured him he was safe enough, he sat at the table and proceeded to fill himself with every morsel in sight.

'I'm a bit wary of him.' Cathy didn't care much for the way he stared at her, as though silently assessing her.

'No need to be,' Margaret assured her. 'He's probably more wary of you.' With that, she quickened her steps; over the hill, past the spinney, down through the valley, and it wasn't long before the Leyton smallholding was in sight. A tall red-brick house with square windows and a litter of farming implements outside, it was always untidy. But, nestling between the curve of a tree-lined river and the rising hills behind, it was situated in one of the loveliest spots around.

Cathy ran on ahead. By the time Margaret got to the back door, David and Cathy were already deep in conversation. Pausing to look on for a moment, Margaret saw the change in Cathy. Her eyes were sparkling and her face was alive with joy, as it always was when she was with David.

'Don't wander off,' Margaret warned. 'And mind what I said ... no working on the Sabbath!'

'Come in, Miss Blackthorn ... please.' The voice was weak and thin, like its owner. Maria Leyton was not yet fully recovered from a long and debilitating illness. Frail and painfully thin, with greying hair and tired blue eyes, she looked much older than her forty-one years. 'Our Teresa's about to put the kettle on.' Her smile was warm and genuine. 'You'll take a brew with me, won't you?'

Margaret followed her into the scullery; a cramped but cosy room, it contained a sofa, a straight-backed chair, an empty fire-grate, and a big earthenware sink. Above this was a large window through which sunshine flooded in, falling on the girl who stood there.

Eighteen next birthday, Teresa Leyton was only a year older than Cathy, but she could not have been more different. Thick-set, tall for her age and with staring blue eyes and shoulder-length brown hair, she was possessed of a devious mind and a quick temper. When the two women came into the room, she didn't turn round. Instead, she pumped the handle that much harder, and silently cursed when the water merely trickled out.

'Hello, Teresa,' Margaret said cheerily. 'If you want to go out in the sunshine, I can finish that.' She gestured to the kettle in the girl's hand.

'It's all right,' came the sullen reply, 'Dad said I wasn't to leave until the kettle was boiling on the stove.' With that she rammed the spout of the kettle beneath the tap and stood stiffly while it began to fill.

'Sit yourself down, Miss,' urged Maria Leyton. Embarrassed by her daughter's open hostility to their visitor, the woman made a mental note to scold her later.

When Margaret sat herself in the upright chair, Maria smiled with relief. Easing on to the sofa, she said, 'You've just missed Owen. He's off over the fields ... after a fat juicy rabbit to fill the pot, y'see.' Chuckling, she pointed to the wood-stove. 'He's lit the stove all ready, so he'll not be long afore he's back, an' I know he'll be glad to see you.'

'It's you I've come to visit,' Margaret assured her. 'How are you feeling, Maria?'

'Oh, up and down. Getting stronger by the day.' She tugged

at the embroidered bed-jacket given to her by Margaret on a previous visit. 'I've been real glad o' this,' she said. 'I can't keep the warmth inside me bones, y'see. But this jacket's been a real godsend.' Her voice fell to a whisper. 'These past months... you've been that good to me, Miss. As God's me judge, I don't know what I'd have done without you...' Her eyes swam with tears of gratitude.

'I'm a neighbour, Maria,' Margaret murmured, 'I'm sure you would do the very same for me.'

'Oh, I would!'

Another voice intervened then, a hard and spiteful voice. 'No, you wouldn't!' Teresa swung round to address her mother, her blue eyes brilliant with hatred. 'Folks like us can't hardly help ourselves, let alone help others.' Casting a derisory glance at Margaret, she declared in a harsh voice, 'It's easy for the likes of you, Miss Blackthorn, because you don't know what it's like to go without. Up there in your warm house, what would you know, eh?' Tossing her head, she snapped, 'Me dad might be easily fooled by a pretty smile, and me mam might be glad of you with your presents and your do-gooding. But not me! I can see right through your kind, and I don't want you here! Do you understand what I'm saying? You're not wanted here!'

'Teresa!' White-faced and shocked to the core, Maria struggled from the chair. 'Your father would flay the skin off your bones if he could hear what you're saying. Miss Blackthorn has been a real good friend to this family, and well you know it!' Having worked herself up, she fell back on the sofa, coughing and gasping. 'Shame on you,' she spluttered, and as Margaret rushed to the woman's aid, the girl made haste towards the door.

'It's the truth!' she cried from the doorway. 'She might seem to be helping us, but she ain't no better than the rest of 'em who live up at the house!' Staring with contempt at her mother, she sneered, 'She makes me sick... coming here in her fine frocks and fetching basketfuls of goodies. And what about the *other* witch who threatens to put us out of house and home?'

Though deeply hurt, Margaret addressed the girl in a cool voice that betrayed nothing of what she was feeling. 'My sister-in-law and I may live under the same roof, but that doesn't make us the same in nature.' She paused a moment, not wanting to say it, but knowing she should. 'Any more than it makes you and your brother of the same nature.' It pleased her that the girl was brought up sharp by the remark. 'As far as being put out of house and home is concerned, all I can promise is that it won't happen if I can help it.'

Choosing to ignore what she knew to be the truth, the girl claimed viciously, 'You come here to spy, don't you, eh? Spying and taking tales back to that sister-in-law of yours. You're all in it together: wanting to make life harder and harder for us, threatening this and that, wanting to take the bread from our mouths, making us live in fear. You and the high and mighty Rita Blackthorn ... you're all the same. You've got money and we ain't. But it don't make you any better than us!' White-faced with rage, she stormed out, slamming the door behind her.

'God help us, what have I raised?' Maria was in tears. 'You surely don't believe anything she said, do you?' she entreated. 'I'll not deny we've no liking for your sister-in-law. But you must know that me and Owen value you as being somebody special. What! If it hadn't been for you, I don't think I'd ever have made it through the winter.' She clung to Margaret. 'I'm sorry, lass,' she groaned, 'I don't know what came over her to say such dreadful things.'

Margaret too had been taken aback by the assault on her. But she saw that the other woman was making herself ill and was quick to reassure her. 'It's all right, Maria,' she murmured, 'you're not to worry.' She recalled the girl's words and saw a vestige of truth in her accusations. 'To some extent it's right what she said. After all, my sister-in-law *has* threatened to put you out of house and home – for no other reason than that she's a selfish and spiteful woman – and has gone out of her way to make life difficult for you ... for Nan Foster too! What's more, perhaps it's wrong of me to think I can give my help without being asked for it.'

'Oh, no! You mustn't believe that.' Maria sat up straight, her gaze downcast as she ruminated on what she was about to reveal. 'No mother should have to say this, but ... well, Teresa is not a very nice person. When I were taken badly, so ill I could hardly move from me bed ...' She gave a deep sigh and raised her head to look straight into Margaret's clear brown

31

eyes. 'What I'm trying to say is that some folk can't abide illness. They turn away, fearing it might strike them down.'

Margaret had not realised but she saw it all now and it came as a shock. 'Are you saying Teresa turned away?'

'Aye. That's exactly what I'm saying, lass. When I were too ill to put one foot afore the other, Teresa showed her true nature. All the time when Owen thought she were tending me whenever he were out, it were our David who fetched and carried for his poor old mam. It were him who fed and washed me. Teresa kept out of the way, with never a word of comfort in passing and hardly a glance to see how I were faring. It were as though she couldn't care whether I lived or died.'

'No, that can't be right, Maria.' Margaret was loth to believe such a thing.

'Oh, it's right,' she declared sadly. 'Our Teresa has shown her true colours. And now, by saying what she's said to you, she's made me ashamed.' Suddenly she squared her shoulders and announced in a firm voice, 'I shall have to tell her father this time! He'll tan her arse good and proper, that he will!' She blushed to the roots of her hair. 'I'm sorry, Miss! I should never have used such language in front of a lady.'

'Away with you, Maria Leyton. Do you think I've never heard a bad word before?' Margaret's hearty chuckle put the woman at her ease, 'Anyway, you're as much as a lady as I'll ever be.'

'By!' Maria shook her head. 'You're a tonic, that's what you are. God knows how I'll ever repay you for the friend you've been to this family. Aye! Even to our Teresa, though she ain't got the sense to see it.'

'There *is* one little thing you can do, Maria.'

'Name it.'

'Do you really mean to tell Owen about Teresa's outburst?'

'What! Just see if I don't!'

'I'd rather you didn't.'

'Whyever not? That young madam has earned herself a leathering.'

'I'm sure she didn't mean half the things she said. What's more, I wonder about the reason she didn't help you when you were at your worst. She was probably more upset than you realised, afraid she might lose you and unsure how to deal with it all.'

Maria was made to think. 'Aye, happen you're right. Happen I'm being too harsh on her.' Her eyes crinkled into a smile. 'What you're saying is, you don't want to see her get a leathering from her dad?'

'I don't think *you* want to see it either. Isn't that so?' Margaret believed that, in spite of Teresa's behaviour, Maria loved her deeply.

Maria was quiet for a while. She needed to think. Presently she answered, 'I'll not tell her father this time.'

'Thank you, Maria.'

In a more relaxed atmosphere, Margaret poured the tea and they chatted a while longer. They talked of the beautiful weather and of how Maria had sat outdoors yesterday. 'Owen wanted me to see how his new cockerels strutted amongst the hens,' she laughed. They discussed the manner in which the birds had escaped from the wagon, and Maria giggled at Margaret's account of what followed. They spoke proudly of David and his learning, and how quickly he had mastered the arts of reading and writing. 'It's all because of your lovely niece,' Maria said. And Margaret replied by telling her how a teacher was only as good as the scholar. Then they parted affectionately.

Cathy and David were seated on the bank of the river. 'Your aunt's coming for you,' he said, catching sight of Margaret as she made her way towards them. 'I wish you didn't have to go.'

'So do I,' Cathy said wistfully.

They had spent these precious minutes together, laughing and talking, and delighting in each other's company. Suddenly, they were painfully shy. David gazed at her sweet face, at the stunning green eyes and full half-smiling mouth which he had wanted to kiss for ever and dared not. He resisted the urge to stroke the flowing corn-coloured hair and had a desperate need to hold the small hand that rested near to his. All these urges rose up inside him like a tidal wave, threatening to overwhelm him. In a rush he whispered her name. 'Cathy?' The word was a caress. His heart was thumping and his mouth was painfully dry as he wondered how he might begin; how he might tell her that one day he meant to wed her.

She had turned her eyes from him to watch the ducks on the river. But she was always aware of his closeness, his strength and dark good looks, and now, when he murmured her name, she brought her gaze to his face. In that moment, like so many times before, she was confused by her own feelings. 'Yes, David?'

He took a deep breath. It would need all of his courage to say what was in his young heart. He even began, 'There's something I have to . . .' Hesitating, he squared his wide shoulders and gulped hard. 'Something I want to tell you.' He felt hot and cold all at the same time, and the palms of his hands were sweating.

'Yes?' She shifted closer. And his courage was gone.

'It's nothing.' Astonished that he could not bring himself to say what was in his overflowing heart, he felt a rush of anger. 'You'd better go.' Stretching out his long legs, he stood up, addressing Margaret now. 'Hello, Miss Blackthorn. Did Mam tell you she sat out in the sunshine yesterday?' When he spoke of his mother his eyes shone with pride.

Margaret said how pleased she was that Maria was making such good progress, and after a brief and friendly exchange they said their farewells.

As they came to the gate, Margaret asked the girl, 'Did you and David have an argument?'

'No.' Cathy was surprised. 'We had a lovely time.'

'Oh, well, if you're sure.' Margaret wasn't altogether convinced. She had sensed the atmosphere between those two, and it made her curious. 'I had a lovely time too,' she declared. 'David's mother is much stronger today.' She made no mention of Teresa's bitter words. There was nothing to be gained by Cathy knowing how the girl felt.

She was also greatly relieved that Teresa would not be punished. 'It's a pity you and Teresa can't get on,' she remarked casually. 'She doesn't appear to have many friends, does she?' In fact, Margaret couldn't recall any time when she had seen Teresa in the company of others.

'That's because she doesn't *want* friends!' Cathy replied. 'I've tried to be nice to her, but she won't let me. And I know she doesn't like me teaching David to read and write.'

Margaret thought it wisest to make no comment. Instead she turned her mind to the malice in Teresa's attack. All the way

34

to Nan Foster's the incident dominated her thoughts. She thought about the way in which Teresa had neglected her ill mother, and wondered what David must have thought about that. She knew the sorry situation had cut Maria deep, and her heart went out to the unfortunate woman.

Alone with her own troubled thoughts, Maria knew her husband would not be home for hours yet. Bitter and unforgiving, she made him a promise: 'One of these days, Owen Leyton, you'll pay for your womanising.' Disturbed and unhappy, she fell asleep.

Teresa stayed in the barn. From there she had watched the visitors depart. She had seen how her own brother longed for the Blackthorn girl, and was charged with such a loathing that she could hardly breathe. Unable to resolve the turmoil within her, she took to the fields, sometimes running, sometimes walking. It would be many hours before she returned home, and even then it would be with great reluctance.

Standing on the very spot where Cathy had left him, David continued to stare after the disappearing figures. Angry with himself, he kicked at the earth. 'What a fool you are, David Leyton!' he chided himself. 'You lost your opportunity.' He thrust his hands into the pockets of his trousers and stared up at the sky. Suddenly he laughed at the way he had hesitated, amused now at the manner in which he had lost his tongue when he needed it most. 'Not to worry,' he consoled himself. 'There'll be another day.'

The thought brought a smile to his dark eyes and a merry tune to his lips. With a lighter heart, he went into the house to see if he was needed.

At the bottom of the lane where they had previously rested stood the ancient cottage. Now, recovering from the long walk, Cathy and Margaret took a moment to gaze on it. An old thatched place of diminutive proportions, the cottage had once been picturesque and desirable; surrounded by lovingly kept gardens profuse with many coloured blooms whose fragrance mingled with the song of birds. Now the garden was overgrown, and birds were seldom seen there. Once the cottage had housed a family of twelve. Its walls and grounds echoed to the laughter of ten children. But they were long gone and in their place rested one lonely soul by the name of Nan Foster.

As they approached the front door, it was opened to them by a woman of some seventy years; though she stooped slightly from the shoulders and her mouth trembled as she spoke, she still carried a certain grace and beauty. Her hair was now white and her eyes the most wonderful shade of violet, though the once beautiful face was lined with the cruel ravages of time. She wore a long grey dress that had seen better days yet she remained a proud, independent woman. 'I saw you pass by,' she told Margaret in a curiously refined voice, 'and I was afraid you might not find the time to come and see me.' When she smiled, her eyes were lit from within and the lines on her face simply melted away.

'You know we would never miss an opportunity to see you,' Margaret told her.

The old lady led them into the cottage. Though it was a mess outside, it was meticulously neat inside. The curtains were sparkling clean, and the fire-range was polished until it reflected every corner of the living room. The furniture, however, was of poor quality and the rugs were threadbare. A smell of damp permeated the air. 'I wish you'd let me talk to my brother,' Margaret protested. 'This place needs a great deal of work done on it.' Time and again she had argued with the old lady, but Nan would not be budged.

She wasn't now. 'Sit down,' she said, and as always it sounded more like an order than a request. Cathy and Margaret sat on the wooden-framed sofa with their hostess opposite, looking regal and dignified in a high-backed chair with straight legs and curved arms. 'Please don't fuss, dear. I'm happy the way things are.' A shadow darkened her face. 'Besides, it would mean noise and dust, and people trampling all over.' She stared at the glass-fronted display cabinet and was momentarily lost in a world of her own. 'Strangers touching my precious belongings . . . I couldn't bear that.'

'We wouldn't let that happen,' Cathy promised. 'Aunt Margaret could arrange for all of your belongings to be stored, and while the work was going on, you could come and stay with us at Blackthorn House.'

The old lady looked at her for a moment and there was a strange kind of sadness in her eyes. 'I know you mean well, and I thank you for that, dear,' she said through trembling lips, 'but you're asking too much. We've been through all this before, and the answer is still the same.' She smiled serenely. 'Oh, I know the cottage has seen better days. It's everything you say . . . poky and draughty . . . riddled with woodworm and warped with age.' She laughed aloud. 'But then, so am I!'

'No, you're not!' Cathy was appalled.

'Oh, but I am. I'm old and withered and past my prime.' Nan laughed and in a more serious voice continued, 'This little cottage has been my home for too long now. I've seen out seven winters in it . . . two of them the hardest I can ever recall in my lifetime . . . and here I am, still healthy and strong. I have enough for my needs. A larder full of food, logs to make a fire when the wind howls, and all manner of God's tiny creatures coming to call.' Something from the past touched her memory. It was like a knife through her heart. Shaking the melancholy from her, she told Cathy in a brighter voice, 'When I saw you both earlier, I got the sarsaparilla ready. It's on the tray in the scullery. Save an old woman's legs, dear. Pour three glasses, would you?'

Before she'd finished speaking Cathy was on her way to the tiny scullery, leaving the old lady and Margaret together. It was exactly what Nan Foster wanted.

'Please, Margaret, don't think I'm not grateful for your offer,' she said. 'It's just that, well—' She hesitated before going on, 'I've never spoken to you about my past life . . . where I come from, that sort of thing. But if you knew the turmoil, the heartache . . .'

Margaret stopped her there. 'You don't owe me any explanation. You needn't worry because, as far as I'm concerned, the cottage will stay exactly as you want it, unless you tell me otherwise. Will that do?'

The old lady reached out to touch her hand. 'You're a good soul,' she said softly. 'And, yes, that will do.' She gazed round the room, at the thick oak beams and crooked windows, and was astonished that she had remained here for so long. 'I won't deny I've lived in grander places . . . known better times. But now, I'm happy to end my days here.'

'I understand.' In a strange way, Margaret really did understand.

The old lady studied the younger woman and was strangely moved. 'In all this time you've never asked anything of me,' she said. 'You've given of your friendship and wanted nothing in return.'

'What should I want?'

'I can't say. But it seems so unfair that I know a great deal about you, while you know nothing at all about me.'

'I know more than you think,' Margaret teased. 'Let's see.' She turned her eyes to heaven. 'I know you came to this area seven years ago, and in all that time you have rented this cottage from my brother.' She met the old lady's fond gaze with a smile. 'I assume you pay your rent on time, or my sister-in-law would have shouted it from the rooftops. I know we have a good relationship, you and I. Cathy adores you. And, though you keep the cottage beautifully clean and tidy, I can see you hate gardening.' She clapped her hands together. 'You're intelligent, articulate, and so graceful that you make me feel positively clumsy. There! What do you think to that?'

'I think you know more about me than is good for you.'

'What a strange thing to say.'

'You didn't describe me as being lonely.' The old lady skilfully avoided responding to Margaret's comment. 'Here am I, some seventy years old, living on my own, with not even a dog or cat to keep me company. I shy away from people and could count on one hand the number of times I've travelled into Blackburn town. Indeed, in seven years I've hardly set food outside this cottage, except to walk around it on a summer's day. I have almost all my needs delivered in cardboard boxes. As you can see I live well, dress well, and though I have no visible means of support, am not without money. Does that not make you curious, my dear?'

'Material things never make me curious.'

'Ah! That's because you think with your soul.'

'If that means I believe there are more valuable things on this earth than material possessions, then yes, I think you must be right.' Margaret sensed there was much more to this conver-

38

sation than the old lady would admit. She felt the strangest impulse to leave. In fact, for one awkward minute, she was tempted to call Cathy and draw short their visit. Instead she warned, 'Your past is your own. Like I said, I know all I need to know.'

The old lady was silent for a time. When she spoke, it was almost to herself. 'There are things about me you really should know,' she murmured. 'Precious things . . . close to my heart.'

Before Margaret could comment, Cathy was back. Setting the tray down on the table, she handed out the tumblers of dark liquid.

The old lady took a delicate sip from her own glass and settled back in the chair, seemingly content. 'Now then,' she said at length, 'who's going to tell me all the gossip?'

In a furtive whisper, Cathy suggested to Margaret, 'I'm sure it would be all right for Nan to know about the urchin.' Taking up her glass she told them, 'I'm going outside in the sunshine.' What she really wanted was to sit on the back doorstep, think about David and wonder what it was he had almost confided in her.

'What's all this about an urchin?' Nan was intrigued.

After Margaret had finished telling her all about how Frank had caught the boy picking his pockets and had decided to bring him home, telling Rita he would be the son they never had, Nan was horrified. 'Whatever does your sister-in-law say?'

'Strangely enough, she seems to have taken to him. At least that's what Cathy thinks, and I'm inclined to agree. Though of course it's early days yet.'

'It's a very dangerous thing your brother has done.'

'I'm inclined to agree with that too.'

'What possessed him then?'

Margaret shrugged her shoulders. 'Who knows? It's true they've always wanted a son, and though Rita is the dominant partner, he can sometimes rebel in a most unpredictable manner. But, to be honest, Nan, I think he must have had a brainstorm this time.'

Nan seemed to brood then. 'Goodness knows what will come of such a thing,' she muttered presently. 'It changes everything. No! I won't allow it!'

'Sorry, Nan, I didn't quite hear.' Not certain whether the old lady was addressing her or talking to herself, Margaret leaned forward. 'Or was it not meant for my ears?' she asked with a smile.

At once the older woman was on her guard. 'Oh, I'm sorry, my dear,' she apologised. 'I suppose I was thinking out loud.' She laughed nervously. 'At my age you begin to do silly things like that.' Eager to allay any suspicions, she quickly added, 'It was only an echo of your own anxieties though. An urchin off the streets! It's bound to turn everything upside down, wouldn't you say?' She glanced towards the door, not wanting Cathy to hear her next words. 'And what about Cathy? It must have come as quite a shock when her father arrived home with this boy. Is she *really* expected to accept him as her new brother?'

'I've been very concerned about that, Nan.' Margaret had spent a sleepless night worrying over that very issue, and what she had decided was this: 'I honestly don't think my brother has thought this business through. He did it on the spur of the moment, and I think... *hope* ... he will come to regret it and send the boy packing. Oh, not just for Cathy's sake, you understand? There are other issues at stake here, not least of which is his own well-being.'

'You mean, if the boy turns out to be a bad one?'

'I don't really know *what* I mean,' Margaret admitted. 'It's true the lad is a pickpocket, but does that make him "a bad one"? Why not merely a desperate character? More importantly, who exactly has Frank brought into the household? He intends to raise the boy as a gentleman ... the son he and Rita never had. But who is this lad? Where does he come from? Has he any family? Will they come looking for him?' She ended on a sigh. 'I've made light of it for Cathy's sake, but I don't mind admitting I'm uneasy about the whole incident.'

'Well then, let's hope that's all it is ... an incident. Have you talked out your fears with your brother?'

'I mean to do just that when I get back.'

'I should if I were you, my dear.'

The conversation ended when Cathy returned.

Rising from her chair, the old lady told her, 'I have something very special to show you.' Taking Cathy by the hand, she led

40

her to a small oak sideboard. Here she turned to address Margaret. 'It might be as well if you hear what I have to say,' she pleaded, and there was a strange excitement in her violet eyes.

With Margaret standing to one side of her and Cathy to the other, she opened the drawer. Like every corner of that tiny cottage it was astonishingly neat inside; containing a batch of old yellowing letters, a long slim case whose contents were not visible, and a soft round bag that tied at the top with a pretty blue ribbon. 'I've been wanting to show you this for a very long time,' she told Cathy. 'I thought it could wait a while longer, but I see now it can't.' Fearful they might guess her real reasons, she said with a wry little laugh, 'You see, I'm very old . . . seventy-one this year. If I don't make my wishes plain to you now, I may never again get the chance.'

Margaret had seen a certain look in the old lady's eyes, a look that spoke of regrets and sorrow. It moved her deeply. 'Are you sure you wouldn't rather leave this business for another day. It troubles you, I know.'

The old lady shook her head. 'The only thing that troubles me is my great age. Oh, not that I'm afraid of dying or anything like that. In fact, there are times when I truly believe it would be preferable to living.'

'What then?'

'Oh, how shall I put it? The past? The future? Sins and forgiveness?' Her smile was beautiful. 'One day I might find the courage to confide in you. Until then, there is still so much to be done, and time is running out for me.' She turned to reach into the drawer. Withdrawing the round silken pouch, she placed it on top of the sideboard and opened it. Inside, jewels shimmered and sparkled: a gold ring with a huge emerald stone; a pair of diamond earrings with platinum clasps; a silver latticed bracelet; and, nestling on top, a magnificent wedding ring. 'Mementoes,' the old lady whispered. 'Nearly all gone now.'

'Are you saying you've been *selling* them to stay alive?' It was all clear to Margaret now.

'It's ironic, isn't it? In a different way these beautiful trinkets carried me through my youth. Now they're carrying me through my old age.' Touching the tip of her finger against the wedding ring, she said softly, 'There was a time when this above all else meant everything to me. Now it means nothing. Even the touch of it makes me cringe.' She shivered as though icy water flowed through her veins.

'Cathy?'

'Yes, Nan?'

'I want you to listen very closely to what I'm about to say.' With trembling fingers, the old lady plucked a fold of silk from the back of the pouch. 'Come to the table, child,' she requested, beckoning Margaret as she turned. When they were all three seated round the table, the fold of silk was put between them. 'Of all the things I've sold and all the things I've kept, this is the most beautiful.' Opening the fold of silk, she laid bare its contents. The tiny heart-shaped box was fashioned in gold and platinum and inlaid with vivid rubies. No more than three inches in diameter, it was a work of art.

'Why! It's exquisite!' Margaret was stunned. Never before had she seen such a delicate thing.

'Is it a box?' Cathy wanted to know.

The old lady's answer was to click the lid open and let her have a brief glimpse inside. 'It's a very special one,' she said. 'While I'm alive I can't let it be parted from me. But one day, Cathy dear, it will be yours.'

Reaching up to kiss the old lady's face, Cathy assured her, 'I want you to stay alive forever, Nan. But if the box ever comes into my keeping, I promise I'll take very good care of it for you.'

Margaret had remained silent, but she spoke now. 'The box must be worth a small fortune. Are you sure you want to do this?'

'It's already done, my dear. The wheels have been set in motion.'

They said their goodbyes and, concerned about the darkening sky and the threat of rain, hastened on their way. 'It's getting late,' Cathy remarked. 'Ruby will be wondering where we are.'

The old lady stood at the window until they were no longer in sight. 'This urchin troubles me,' she murmured. Returning to the trinket box, she took from it a small faded portrait. Raising this to the light, she stared at it through a blur of tears.

Two pairs of eyes gazed back at her. Two tiny faces that almost broke her heart. All these years she had carried the crippling guilt with her. Now, though, her heart was more tranquil. Old age had a way of quieting the heart and easing the mind. Yet still she couldn't rest. Not yet. Soon maybe, but not yet.

She took a while to remember how it was all those years ago. She kissed the two small faces. 'All these years I've watched over you,' she said brokenly. 'When I'm gone, you'll be given into the safe keeping of your daughter.' Pressing the portrait to her breast she sat in the rocking chair and rocked gently back and forth, until sleep came over her, lulling her old heart and taking her back over the lonely years.

CHAPTER THREE

'You'll take his land only over my dead body!'

'Calm yourself, Margaret.' Frank was caught between his wife and his sister and, on this occasion, had to admit his sister was in the right. Rising from his comfortable armchair, he crossed to the sideboard. 'I'm sure the three of us can talk this through in a civilised manner, over a glass of sherry.'

'Thank you, but no.' Margaret rarely showed her temper but when she had learned of his plans to recall four acres of land from Owen Leyton she had realised she would have to take a very firm stand. 'I won't allow it, Frank. Time and again I've stood by you while you've made plans without consulting me. I see now that was very foolish.' She glanced meaningfully at Rita who, until now, had remained silent.

'It's only four acres, for heaven's sake.' Sensing that her husband was weakening, Rita felt she must intervene.

'Four acres is almost half the land he rents from us,' Margaret persisted. 'It's difficult enough for him to make a living as it is.'

'How others fare is not our problem.' Rita took the sherry her husband offered and gulped it down. 'Frank and I are decided. We need to recall that land and, make no mistake, we shall have it.' If she had seen the warning expression on Frank's face she might have guarded her tongue.

'I think you're forgetting something, aren't you?' Margaret was only made the more determined by Rita's arrogance.

'Oh? And what might that be?'

'Though it doesn't amount to a fortune, Father left everything equally divided between me and Frank.'

'What are you saying?'

'I'm saying what I should have said long ago. Frank has no

right to make decisions without consulting me. It was a mistake to leave the running of Blackthorn Estate to him.' Addressing herself to Frank she said calmly, 'I'm sorry, but if you persist in this, I'll have to fight you.'

'Good grief! Whatever's the matter with you? *Fight me?*' Falling into the chair, he stared at her as though she was out of her mind.

'If you ask me, she's gone completely mad!' Sitting bolt upright in her chair Rita slammed her empty glass on to a side table. 'It's all this mixing with lesser people. It's affecting her reason.'

'I don't know what you mean by "lesser" people,' Margaret declared. 'What makes you think we're any better than they are? We may own this house, two dilapidated cottages and a few acres of second-grade land, but that only means we don't have to tend the earth to make a living. It certainly doesn't mean we can look down on our neighbours!'

'They're not neighbours.' Rita stared defiantly. 'They're tenants... *our* tenants. It's right that we hold ourselves above them.' Turning to Frank, she pleaded, 'Your sister is undermining our authority. Look how that insolent fellow drove his filthy wagon right up to our front door. It wasn't bad enough that a member of this family actually travelled home in the contraption, but he had the nerve actually to speak to me... to *me*! Filthy, he was! Looked like he hadn't had a wash in weeks.'

Margaret sprang to Owen's defence. 'The man had only just returned from a day at the market... on top of which he'd been in the spinny. Owen Leyton is a respectable working man, as clean and proud as any of us.'

Rita was made to recall the incident more closely. The memory of his dark eyes on her was more than she could bear. Since that day she had felt a strange kind of longing, and it frightened her. Clutching at her throat, she rasped, 'You'll have to speak to him, Frank.' Scowling at Margaret, she added vehemently, 'Moreover, you must forbid your sister from visiting these people.'

Frank looked from one to the other and felt out of his depth. 'I'm not really in a position to insist on that,' he said lamely.

'Why not? You're the head of this house. The man who makes all the decisions.'

It was Margaret who answered. 'I think what Frank is trying to explain is that he isn't the elder. *I* am. By twenty minutes.' Her implication was plain as she now addressed him in a softer tone. 'No doubt you're thankful I was born a woman?'

Glancing sheepishly at the plush red carpet, he fingered his waistcoat buttons then toyed with a stray thread on the arm of the chair. Without looking at her, he replied, 'I'm sorry, but I have to agree with my wife. The fact is I have taken on the role of head of the house, and for some long time you have trusted me to do what's right for us all. I really think you're being a little too protective of our tenants. After all, we don't owe them anything, do we? If they were to leave, no doubt there would be a queue of others waiting to take their place.' Suddenly filled with a sense of his own importance and encouraged by Rita's curt nod of the head, he squared his shoulders and announced smugly, 'About recalling the four acres. I think you should give my little plan some further thought.'

'Think what you will, but I won't allow Owen Leyton and his family to be impoverished. That land is his livelihood.'

Rita smiled at her. 'Anyone would think you had a soft spot for him,' she suggested wickedly.

Frank was horrified. 'Now now, Rita. I won't have that.'

Returning his gaze to his sister, he urged, 'Be reasonable. After all, four acres isn't a great area.'

'Is it your intention to sell the land?'

'Of course not. No self-respecting landowner would ever *sell* his land.'

'I think you mean *our* land?'

'Of course.' He seemed to blush. Or it could have been a drop too much sherry that made him suddenly go a bright shade of pink.

'Do you intend to work the land then?'

The suggestion made him laugh. 'Are you trying to kill me off?'

'You're right. A spell of hard work probably would kill you off.' She stood up, preparing to depart. 'I'm well aware of what you mean to do with the land. You and Rita have made no secret of it. First you bring a street urchin into the house. Then you begin grooming him to be the "son you never had". You shamefully neglect your own daughter, denying her the pony

47

she's always craved, yet you plan to buy this urchin an expensive animal the cost of which would keep us all fed for the best part of a year. And now you mean to lay out four acres of farmed land so your new "son" can practise the pursuits of a gentleman.'

Rita eyed her with glee. 'You sound almost envious,' she purred. 'Is that what all this is about? Do you see Jack as taking your place in Frank's affections?'

The idea gave her immense satisfaction. In fact, she had been all for sending the boy back where he came from, but had thought better of it. The more Margaret and the girl were hurt by the boy's presence here, the more she meant to pamper him.

Margaret rounded on her then. 'As far as I'm concerned, you and Frank are free to do as you please with regard to the boy. It's just a great pity you can't lavish a measure of love and attention on your own daughter.'

Frank took offence at that. 'What a wicked thing to say,' he said sullenly.

'Really?' Margaret stared him out. 'I suggest you think about it, Frank.' Addressing her sister-in-law, who was still smiling, she said coldly, 'I suggest you *both* think about it.'

As she walked across the room, Frank asked, 'So you won't reconsider . . . about the four acres?'

'No.'

Rita's voice dripped with malice. 'Is there something between you and Owen Leyton?'

Margaret swung round, her face chalk-white. Inside she was burning with rage. Outside she was astonishingly calm. 'How clever of you!' she answered, and Rita's eyes grew wide with surprise. 'You're right. There *is* something between me and Owen Leyton. But it isn't what you would like to think, Rita dear. What Mr Leyton and I share is a love for the land, that's all. But then, I can't expect someone like you to understand that.'

An awkward silence followed, during which Margaret made her way to the door. If she didn't get out of here as quickly as her feet would take her, she might forget she was a lady and stuff Rita's malicious words down her throat.

'Margaret?' Frank had been stunned by his wife's suggestion

that Margaret was having an affair with Owen Leyton.

'It's no good arguing, Frank. I won't change my mind.'

'I can see that.' He straightened his back and assumed his most authoritative expression. 'No. It's something else that makes me curious.' Clearing his throat, he glanced nervously at his wife before going on, 'There have been some very harsh things said here, and I'm saddened by them.'

'Then I suggest you speak to your good wife.'

Rita sniffed. 'I never take back what I've said.'

'*Please!*' Frank sighed aloud. When his wife merely smiled triumphantly he continued his appeal to Margaret. 'You've taken a dislike to Jack, haven't you?'

'I don't know him well enough to take a dislike to him.' He had hit on a sore point with her. 'However, I do feel the pair of you should be more cautious.'

'In what way?'

'Just now you said you wondered if I had lost my mind. Well, I must admit there have been times over these past weeks when I've wondered that about *you*!' He had asked her, and she meant to tell him. 'This boy . . .'

'Jack!' Frank grew impatient. 'His name is Jack.'

'That's the name *you* christened him,' Margaret retorted, 'because he refused to give you his *real* name! And what else is he keeping from you, I wonder?'

'Explain yourself.'

'I wouldn't have thought it needed any explaining. Who is he, Frank? Where does he come from, and what's he doing here? You know nothing at all about him.'

'I know enough.' In fact he knew a great deal more than he was prepared to divulge, and if the truth ever came out all hell would be let loose.

'What? *What* do you know? That he was picking your pockets? That he lived on the streets . . . earning a living by using his wits? Does he have friends, I wonder? And are they likely to turn up here? And if they do, are you prepared to take them in as well?'

'I can't believe I'm hearing this!' Springing out of his chair, Frank took a step towards her. 'I expected you of all people to understand.' He was pleading now. 'You were always the tender one ... the one who championed the underdog, the one who abhorred everything harsh and unfair in this world. The boy has had a hard life. Surely he deserves to be loved and pampered now?'

It was a moment before Margaret replied. When she did it was with a harshness that shocked them both. 'And what about your own daughter? Don't you think it's time *she* was loved and pampered?'

'But she *is* loved!'

'Then tell her.'

He bowed his head. 'You know I can't speak of such things.'

'Then *show* her!'

'How do you mean?'

'In the same way you show this boy your affection.'

'I wasn't aware I did.' He stared from Margaret to his wife, then back to Margaret again. Suddenly he felt as though he was greatly in the wrong, but didn't know why.

'Oh, but you do, Frank.' Her voice softened. 'You take him to town and buy him clothes. You walk the fields with him, and spend hours talking with him.' She choked on the words. 'And there is a special softness in your voice when you speak to him.' She glanced at Rita who was intrigued and delighted by Margaret's distress. 'You *both* pander to his every need while denying your own child's. Do you really think Cathy doesn't see all this? Do you believe she isn't deeply hurt by it?'

Rita stamped her foot. 'That girl wants for nothing! Her wardrobe is filled with clothes. She has a shelf crammed with books, and each year she's allowed to take a holiday with you. What more does she want?'

Margaret shook her head. 'If you can't see, then I'm just wasting my time.'

Frank hated the way his wife and sister seemed to bring about the worst in each other. Appealing to Margaret's better nature, he explained, 'It's in a man's nature to want a son. Rita and I have been denied that.' He gave his wife a tender glance. 'Now here is a boy without family or home ... an orphan driven to desperation through no fault of his own. He's strong and healthy, with an attractive appearance. He's already proved his determination to break from his unsavoury past, and has it in him to be a good citizen. I intend to give him every opportunity.'

Margaret dwelt on his words for a moment, realising how deeply he felt about the project he had taken on. There was no doubt that he had become strongly attached to the boy. In that light, she questioned her own right to interfere. It was not in her nature to be hard or disagreeable and, for one moment, she might have relented. But then she remembered her own greatest love. 'What about Cathy?'

'I don't understand. We're discussing the boy! A son for Rita and me.' Frank shook his head in frustration. 'For heaven's sake, Margaret, you haven't understood anything I've said.'

'No, Frank.' She gazed at him sadly. 'It's you who haven't understood anything I've said.'

Spreading his hand before his face as though to blot out her presence, he interrupted, 'There's clearly no point in discussing it any further. The boy stays. He has been here almost four weeks now, and never put a foot wrong. In fact, with the exception of the first few days, his good behaviour has only strengthened our belief in him.' He looked at Rita and beamed, not realising how his intimate smile sent a shudder through her.

'I can see the two of you are very proud of yourselves,' Margaret observed dryly. With that she went smartly out of the room.

Rita's voice followed her through the open door. 'You really should be nicer to Jack,' she called arrogantly. 'It won't be long before you're his aunt, because we're already planning adoption. Being our son will also give him certain rights. In fact, I shouldn't be at all surprised if his rights proved to be greater than his little sister's.' Slightly intoxicated by the sherry, she began laughing.

Frank brought her up sharply with a stern warning. 'Careful, my dear! It isn't wise to make enemies.'

It was midnight. Ruby woke in a sweat. 'Who's there?' Sitting up on her elbows, she squinted into the gloom. 'Is somebody there?'

When there was no answer, she clambered from the bed, lit the lamp and threw her dressing gown about her shoulders. 'You old fool!' she chided herself. 'What would anyone want to come in here for? There ain't no jewels nor money, and I don't know any man who'd want to spend the night with an old crow like you.' The idea was so outlandish that she burst out laughing.

Taking up the lamp, she crept up on the door and snatched it open. There was no one in sight and she was puzzled. 'I were sure I heard a noise,' she muttered, glancing up at the ceiling. 'Bleedin' rats I shouldn't wonder.'

The sound of a door closing startled her. 'I'm buggered if there really ain't somebody larking about!' she whispered furtively. Leaning over the banisters, she stared down into the tiny hallway; no one there either. Still not convinced, she went cautiously down the narrow stairs, in and out of the scullery, through the parlour, searching everywhere, and still there was neither sound nor sight of what might have caused her to wake. 'Must'a been them pickled onions I ate at supper,' she chuckled. 'Should'a known I'd suffer for it.'

Before returning to her bed, she gingerly inched open the door which led from her own humble quarters to the big house. All was quiet and in darkness, everyone sleeping, she thought.

Nodding with satisfaction, she closed the door and went back upstairs. Here she crossed the room to stare out of the window at a beautiful moonlit night. 'Even the owls are fast asleep,' she muttered, yawning and stretching her podgy arms. 'Got more sense than folks like you, Ruby, you daft old bugger!' With that she hoisted herself into bed and was soon snoring.

Margaret remained at her window a moment longer. She too had been woken by strange sounds. But, when she could see nothing untoward, she got back between the warm sheets and lay there awake, her mind in turmoil after the day's events. Soon, overcome by weariness, she closed her eyes and slept. But it wasn't a restful sleep. Instead she tossed and turned, and in her worst nightmares feared for young Cathy's future.

Two rooms away, Rita feigned sleep. It wasn't sounds that had woken her, but the urgent needs of her husband. Pushing his naked body against her, he grew with excitement. 'I want you so much,' he murmured in her ear. 'I've wanted you all day.'

'I don't want you.' His breath was warm and nauseating on her face. His weakness made her bold. 'Go back to sleep.'

'How can I?' he wailed. 'You've roused me now.' Stroking

her face with his fingers, he muttered impatiently, 'I'll only sleep after I'm satisfied.'

Inwardly groaning, Rita mentally prepared herself for yet another bout of what she considered to be an undignified and loathsome act. She knew from experience that he would not leave her be until she had succumbed. 'All right,' she snapped, rolling on to her back. 'But be quick!'

While he fumbled at her nightgown, she lay like a corpse, cold and unyielding, her eyes fixed on the ceiling, arms pressed to her sides as though to restrict his embrace. She had no intention of helping him to invade her. In fact, she turned her mind to other matters. 'What will you do about your sister?' she asked coolly. 'Surely you don't mean to let her dictate to you?'

'For God's sake, woman!' Gripping her nightgown with both hands, he thrust it above her waist. 'I don't want to talk about that *now!*'

She knew then he would not assert himself over Margaret. And she despised him. 'Be quick, I tell you.' Even the touch of his skin against hers was nauseating. When he slid his fingers into the crevice of her thighs, it was all she could do not to leap from the bed and flee the room.

But she stayed. Like so many times before she stayed, because it was her duty, and because it was the one thing that gave her power over him, the one thing above all others that made him like clay in her hands.

'Love me,' he moaned. Easing her legs apart, he mounted her.

She made no reply, gave no encouragement. She wanted no more than that it should soon be over. *But then a strange and unpredictable thing happened.* When he probed inside her with the tip of his erect member, she held herself rigid as always, setting her mind against the tedious ordeal to come. She amused herself by wondering how such a big-built man could have such a small penis; reminding herself at the same time that she had no means of comparing it because she had never seen another man in the flesh. But then, without warning, her mind was filled with the image of a man who had looked at her and seen something of her soul.

Owen Leyton rose up in her mind like a physical presence.

Recalling the intimate look that had passed between them, she remembered how handsome he was, those brooding dark eyes and the strong squareness of his chin, the high cheekbones, the brown hair that fell lazily below his ears, and those broad ox-like shoulders.

She wondered about Owen Leyton. He was a big man yet not in the same way as her husband, because one was flabby and the other hardened by hard work. Her husband's hands were soft and white, while the younger man's were coarse and brown. Frank was always meticulously attired in silk cravats and fancy waistcoats while Owen had worn little better than rags.

She had used every argument to discredit him in front of her husband and sister-in-law. Yet her instincts told her that Owen was a better man than her own husband. Rough and ready, one with nature, exactly as Margaret had described him, he intrigued her. Never before had she looked into the eyes of such a man. Normally she would look away, walk on the other side of the road, disown the very idea that they might share the same thought. But this man was different. She had met him in a rage, and he had seen right inside her. It was a frightening thing. Yet it was exhilarating.

The more she thought of him, the more he intrigued her. Even his name sounded right. 'Owen,' she whispered aloud. 'Owen.'

Lost in his own delight, her husband didn't hear the name she called. He heard only the sound, a sigh of contentment that sent shivers down his spine. 'Come on,' he pleaded. 'Show you love me.'

She heard him coaxing but her heart was like stone. When he now pushed rhythmically in and out, licking her lips with his long wet tongue and stroking her private parts with frantic fingers, she wondered how *he* might do it. Would Owen Leyton cover her in the same manner? Was every man the same? Was the act of lovemaking all for the *man's* satisfaction? Did Owen Leyton have a different way? Could he persuade her to give of herself? Actually to enjoy it? She was immensely curious, imagining the younger man unclothed and wondering how they would differ, he and her husband.

One thought loomed in her mind to overshadow all others.

Owen Leyton had fathered a *son*. That one splendid achievement raised him in her esteem. Some small fragment of her fevered mind wanted it to be Owen Leyton who was using her body now. Loathing seeped back.

Her husband became frantic, lunging into her again and again, uncontrollably excited. She knew how it would end, how it always ended, and this time was no different. With a long shivering groan he gave one almighty thrust and crumpled in a heap on top of her, his weight crushing her. After a moment he rolled away and she turned from him with contempt. She had never hated him more.

Long after her husband was contentedly sleeping, Rita Blackthorn paced the floor, driven by a demon, unable to rid herself of the feeling that *he* too was pacing the floor, thinking of her just as she was thinking of him. 'I don't know if I'll see you again, Owen Leyton,' she whispered. 'It might be wisest to stay clear of you.'

Outside, the wind blew stronger, cutting through the trees with a whistling sound. 'Sounds like the banshees have been let loose, don't it?' The woman looked to be in her late thirties, of slim build and clothed in a long dark skirt and brown-fringed shawl. Her face was partly hidden by the shawl which she had drawn tightly about herself, but her eyes were visible: very beautiful, large childish eyes of deepest blue. Desperate now, she pleaded, 'You must come back!' She glanced about, crouching fearfully, as though suspecting someone might be watching. 'If he finds out, he'll flay me alive!'

Her pleas left the boy unmoved. 'How did you track me down?'

'It took me an age. But I were determined, that's all.'

'I'm not coming back, so you can forget it. As for *him*, I couldn't care less.'

'And what about me?'

'I'm not coming back.'

'I swear he'll kill me!'

'Let him kill you then.' Lashing out with a spiteful push, he sent her staggering backwards.

'How can you do it?' Tears swam up in her beautiful sad

eyes. 'I've never done you no harm.'

'Get away from here.' Being the same height as the woman, he could look her straight in the eyes. Putting his face closer to hers, he whispered a warning. 'If I ever see you round here again, I'll set the dogs on you.' Certain that she would leave without a fuss, he made his way back to the house.

By the time he had stealthily entered his bedroom, the woman had climbed on to the cart and seated herself on the hard wooden bench. With one last look at the house, she dug in her heels, took up the reins and urged the old horse: 'Home, boy. We've a long way to go, God help us.'

The morning arrived in a blaze of sunshine. Raising her eyes to the blue sky outside her window, Ruby moaned, 'Can't see what you've got to smile about. Some of us ain't had no sleep at all.'

She glanced anxiously at the kitchen clock. 'Six of a morning,' she tutted. 'I've been up nigh on an hour already, and since that useless maid cleared off, I still can't seem to get meself on a right footing.' With renewed determination, she went quietly about her duties. There was the range to be lit, a mile of floor to be scrubbed, the breakfast table waiting to be laid, and she had a head that felt the size of four. 'Bugger it!' she said, slamming shut the range door. 'One o' these days I'll take up the life of a gypsy and wander the roads.'

She peeped through the back door; though the sun was rising gloriously, the howling wind was bending the trees and rattling the buckets against the outer wall. 'On second thoughts,' she grimaced, 'I don't reckon I'd be well suited to the outdoors.'

In spite of Ruby's misgivings, breakfast was ready on time. The routine had not changed since she first came into service at Blackthorn House. Eggs, bacon, sausages, kippers and porridge were all served in rose-coloured tureens which were set out on the sideboard. Tea and toast were brought on request, and Ruby was then free to go about her other duties. It was a good system all round. Everyone could have as much or as little of what they fancied, and there was no standing on ceremony. Rita would have dearly liked to be surrounded by servants, but this household didn't have the money for such luxuries.

'Something smells good.' As usual Frank was the first down. Going to the tureens he piled his plate with scrambled eggs and streaky bacon. 'Nothing like a good breakfast,' he declared with a broad smile. After having one appetite satisfied last night, he was now assuaging the other. 'Tea for me, Ruby,' he told her. 'No toast.' When she hurried out, he began softly whistling until he gathered a mound of scrambled egg on to his fork and thrust it into his mouth. After that he wolfed down everything on his plate, drank four cups of tea, and was still seated there, mopping his face with a napkin, when his wife came in. 'Oh, there you are, dear.' Leaping from his place, he ran to pull out her chair. 'Sleep well, did you?' he asked meaningfully, winking and watching her as she reluctantly joined him.

'Say what you want and I'll get it for you. Eggs? Bacon? Maybe a little helping of porridge?'

Rita was not impressed. 'Don't be absurd.'

Ruby emerged with a fresh pot of tea. 'Get me some toast, and be quick about it,' she was told. The order was given with a scowl.

' "Get me some toast" ... "Get me some toast," ' Ruby mimicked all the way to the kitchen. 'That bugger thinks her arse don't stink.'

'You were a bit harsh on Ruby, weren't you?' Frank complained half-heartedly.

Rita's answer was to glare at him in the hope that he might leave the room.

Much to her annoyance, he inched his chair closer to hers. 'Last night was wonderful,' he murmured. 'There was something...' He thought hard. 'Oh, I don't know... something different about you.' He reached out and touched her hand, which she instantly withdrew. 'You were kinder... softer, somehow.'

His words struck fear into her. Had she allowed her thoughts of Owen Leyton to convey emotion to this odious man who was her husband? If so, she was a fool. 'Have you finished your breakfast?' she asked coldly.

'Yes, and a very good breakfast it was too.' He irritated her by smacking his lips. 'You don't appreciate Ruby, I know, but she really is a treasure.'

'If you've finished your breakfast, I suggest you leave and let others enjoy theirs.'

He sat back as though slapped in the face, but still couldn't believe he was being dismissed. When she ignored him, he sighed and said in a little boy's voice, 'You're being rather cruel this morning.'

'And you are being obnoxious.'

'Did last night mean nothing to you?'

'I refuse to discuss it.'

'Will you stroll with me after breakfast?'

'I would rather not.'

'Will you ride with me later then?' He frowned. 'I have the onerous job of collecting rent from the tenants.'

'If you hate it so much, why don't you employ a rent collector?'

'You know very well why. I don't employ a rent collector for the same reason I haven't filled the house with servants.'

'You're always pleading poverty. It's embarrassing.'

'Not half as embarrassing as it would be if we took them on and couldn't pay their wages.'

'The answer is simple, then.'

'Oh?'

'Raise the rents.'

He bowed his head and thought a while, then stood up, clenched his fist and hit it gently against the table. 'You know very well it isn't always easy.'

Ruby returned with tea and toast. 'There you are, Ma'am,' she said cheerily. All she got for her trouble was a hard look. Sensing the bad atmosphere, she quickly collected Frank's dirty plate and departed. 'Sour buggers!' she muttered, thankful when she came into the sanctuary of her beloved kitchen.

Margaret and Cathy came down together. Cathy ate heartily, but Margaret had little appetite. After nibbling at a spoonful of scrambled egg, she prepared to leave. 'I'll be in the sitting room when you've finished,' she told Cathy. 'I thought we might get started on your schooling early this morning.' She looked at the girl and saw a woman. 'Soon you won't need me as an instructor any more, then how will I fill my hours?' Before anyone could answer, she hurried away.

'I'll always need you,' Cathy murmured. Apart from Ruby, Margaret was all she had.

At the bottom of the stairs, Margaret met Frank and the boy.

'What do you think?' Frank asked, pushing Jack forward for Margaret's inspection. 'A fine-looking fellow in his Monday suit, isn't he?'

It was courtesy rather than curiosity that prompted her to run her gaze over the young man. He was dressed in a blue serge suit, white shirt and black polished shoes. His thick fair hair was combed back, and she had to admit he looked smart. 'He's very presentable,' she agreed. 'Now, if you'll excuse me, I have to get ready for Cathy's lessons.'

Barring her way to the sitting room, Frank stood his ground. He grunted and sighed and finally declared in a foolish voice, 'As you know, I've been grooming Jack in the manners of a gentleman.' He slapped his hand on the boy's shoulder. 'You must agree he's made admirable progress.'

'Without a doubt.' Margaret had no idea what her brother was leading up to, but knew he must have something in mind. 'You've done a good job.' Moving forward, she told him with a hint of impatience, 'I really must get ready for Cathy's lessons.'

He coughed and smiled and grew a little pink in the face. Addressing the boy he said, 'Off you go and get your breakfast. Remember what I told you. Don't leave the breakfast table until you're sent for.' Once the young fellow was out of earshot, he told Margaret, 'Give him time enough before you collect him.'

'What do you mean?' Margaret had hoped she needn't play a part in the boy's upbringing. 'Are you asking me to school him?'

Frank beamed with relief. 'Yes! That's exactly what I'm asking.'

'But I thought you had it in mind to engage a male tutor?'

'Well, yes, and so I will . . . next season. For now, though, I want you to train him in the rudiments of reading and writing.'

'What you really mean is you don't want to be embarrassed by the fact that here is your son . . . fifteen years of age if he's telling the truth . . . who still can't read or write.'

Frank was indignant. 'Hiring a male tutor is a very expensive business. More so if he has to start right at the beginning.'

'Frank Blackthorn, you're a hypocrite.' He was an easy man to see through. 'This isn't a matter of money, you and I both know it.'

59

'What are you getting at?' The colour drained from his face. Fearing she had somehow discovered the awful truth about the boy, he visibly trembled. 'Come on. Out with it! What are you saying?'

Margaret mistook his anxiety for rage. 'It's no good you getting angry or trying to bully me. I have a mind of my own, you should know that by now.' She waited a moment, half expecting he would yell and shout. When he didn't, she answered, 'What I am saying is this . . . you should be ashamed! You obviously don't want the world to know you're about to adopt a boy who can't read or write.'

Relieved she knew nothing that could threaten him, he hung his head, saying sheepishly, 'Such a thing might cause tittle-tattle in the village, and I would rather avoid that if possible.'

'It isn't the boy's fault he can't read or write.' Margaret was astounded to find herself defending him. 'He obviously comes from the sort of background where it's more profitable to learn the art of pickpocketing than to know how to write his own name. In that respect, he has an excuse for being illiterate.'

'I knew you would understand, and because of the way you feel about my having brought Jack here, I realise I'm asking a lot of you. Especially as I can't pay you, and you already tutor Cathy without a penny reward.'

'I have no need of your money, Frank.' Margaret was insulted. 'Even if you offered me wages for teaching Cathy, I wouldn't accept them. Seeing her grow intellectually is my reward. And, after all, I am a trained teacher, or have you forgotten?'

'No, my dear. In fact that's the very reason I know you'll do a good job with the boy. Moreover, he's family now, and you might as well accept it.' Playing on her professional pride, he urged, 'Please. Take him on for a while. All I ask is that you send him to his new tutor with at least the basic rudiments of education.'

Margaret began to see it as a challenge. 'All right. But I would much rather put aside another time, when I can give him all my attention.' Though she couldn't refuse to teach the boy, Margaret saw him as being a possible distraction to Cathy. 'Your daughter is nearing the end of her schooling, while this fellow is only beginning.'

'I've already told him he's to start lessons this morning. Surely it's more expedient to teach two pupils at the same time?'

Reluctantly, she agreed. 'Very well, Frank. But if I'm to be responsible for his learning, I won't have you interfering.'

'I wouldn't dream of it.' His face broke into a triumphant grin. 'I knew you wouldn't let me down.'

Hating the way she had been manipulated, Margaret told him sharply, 'I'm taking him on a week's trial. If in that time he displeases me in any way, that's an end to it.'

The grin vanished and in its place came a penitent expression. 'Of course.'

'Tell him to report to the sitting room in half an hour.' Pushing by him, she continued on her way, hoping she might never come to regret the decision she had just made.

The morning went swiftly. Cathy was surprised to find herself seated at the same table as Jack, though Margaret had been wise enough to put them at separate ends. While Cathy kept her head down to her advanced studies, Margaret went through the alphabet with the boy. She wrote the letters down and he copied them. She spoke each one out and he repeated after her. By the end of the first lesson, he was scrawling his name. 'J . . . a . . . c . . . k'. As he wrote, he spelled the name out. When it was done, he stared at it for what seemed an age. 'I've written my own name,' he muttered with delight. 'I've written my own name.'

Cathy was also delighted. 'David can write his name now,' she said with pride. 'He can read too.'

'Who's David?' Though he tried hard not to show it, the boy was jealous.

'Work now, talk later,' Margaret intervened. She sensed more than curiosity in Jack's voice, and it only deepened her reservations about him.

At midday the lessons were over. Cathy walked out in the sunshine and Jack followed. From the window, Margaret saw them together, seated on the bench by the apple tree. 'How can I keep them apart?' she murmured.

'You can't!' Rita had come into the room unheard.

Startled, Margaret swung round. 'What do you want here?'

'Only to ask how the boy fared with his lessons.' She was too sweet, too smiling.

'And if I said he was a poor scholar?'

'I would blame the teacher.'

Margaret nodded. 'Of course you would.' Coming from the window she took up the pile of books from the table and leisurely stacked them in the cupboard. Her deliberately methodical movements annoyed Rita beyond endurance.

'How *did* he fare?' She struggled to keep her composure.

'As a matter of fact, he fared very well. He wrote his own name for the first time.' In spite of her coolness, she couldn't stop the pride from creeping into her voice. 'You say you would blame the teacher if the boy stumbled at his lessons,' she prodded. 'So now, you may praise the teacher for a job well done.'

Rita stiffened. 'It's the boy who deserves the credit. He obviously has intelligence.'

'I won't argue with that.'

'Just now . . . when I came in?' Rita seated herself at the table, her green eyes glittering and hostile as they raked the other woman's face. 'You were watching them.'

'And if I was?'

'You don't like the boy, do you?' Her handsome features were wreathed in a devious smile. 'You'd prefer him to be thrown back on to the streets, wouldn't you?'

Margaret knew from old that she was being drawn into a trap. But she could not be less than honest. 'You're wrong,' she confessed. 'I don't dislike the boy.'

'You'd rather he hadn't been brought here though, wouldn't you?'

'I can't deny that.'

'You're afraid he'll steal Cathy's rightful place in this house?'

'Hasn't he already done that?'

'I hope so.' Her smile deepened. 'The girl should know she must take second place.'

For the first time, Margaret could see through the whole charade. 'My God!' She dropped the pile of books on to the table, her face openly astonished as she accused Rita, 'You don't want the boy at all, do you?'

Rita outstared her. 'What a thing to say.' She cursed herself for having almost given the game away. 'Why should I take the boy on if I don't want him?'

'To hurt Cathy. That would be reason enough for you.'

Margaret rounded the table and, for one frightening minute, Rita feared she would be attacked. 'You've always treated Cathy with contempt!' There was no stopping her now. 'Why do you think I gave up my career to care for her? You took me on as nanny, but I've been mother and father to that lovely child. I've loved her like she was my own, and now you expect me to stand by and see her totally humiliated.'

'You're hysterical.' Secure in the knowledge that her sister-in-law was too much of a lady to hit out, Rita dared to torment her further. 'Frank and I have a son now, and he must be our first priority. Cathy will be taken care of, I dare say.' She was feeling smug, capable of anything.

'Oh, she'll be taken care of all right, you can be sure of that.' Incensed, Margaret slapped her hand on Rita's shoulder. 'Now get out!'

Standing up, Rita casually brushed down her skirt and adjusted her waistband. Smiling once more, she said with malice, 'You won't be able to keep them apart. They're brother and sister now.' She said something then that made Margaret's heart grow cold. 'Unfortunately, however much Frank and I would want it, the boy is not our flesh and blood. It's to be hoped that Jack and Cathy don't become *too* close. After all, she's fast becoming a very attractive young woman.' She gave a small laugh. 'But I expect you were thinking of that when I saw you at the window just now.' In a harder voice she added, 'You do right to be concerned. But human nature being what it is, I shouldn't try too hard to keep them apart. Your efforts may have just the opposite effect.'

Margaret could see it all now. 'You're a witch!'

'And you are a thorn in my side.' With that Rita swept out.

When Margaret returned to the window, she was dismayed to see Cathy and the boy laughing together, he with his arm resting on her shoulders and Cathy looking up at him with affection. Pushing open the window she called out, 'Cathy!' Jack turned and looked, but Cathy appeared not to have heard. She called again, louder, 'CATHY!'

This time Cathy heard and came running, leaving the boy smiling after her. 'He seems nice enough,' she told Margaret. 'He's been asking about David . . . wants to meet him.'

63

Margaret knew she had to be very careful. 'I'm not sure we should take a stranger to Mrs Leyton's house, certainly not without asking permission first.'

Cathy chatted on and it soon became obvious to Margaret that the boy was already worming his way into Cathy's affections. She recalled the two of them just now, the way he had draped his arm round Cathy's shoulders and the possessive manner in which he was looking at her. Moreover, it was disturbing the way he had chosen to ignore her call for Cathy to return indoors.

It was almost as though Rita had set a serpent loose in the house, a viper to charm and destroy her trusting daughter. It was all a plan, she could see that now. An evil and vindictive plan, to punish Cathy for not being the son Rita had yearned for. 'She'll ruin you over my dead body,' Margaret promised softly. And vowed to watch over Cathy as never before.

Unnerved and excited by her encounter with Margaret, Rita strode through the streets of Langho, nodding a greeting to others as they passed, and enjoying the admiring glances of plain and uninteresting women. There was a defiant spring in her step as she went along by the post office and down through the rows of terraced cottages, despising the people who resided there and thinking herself above them.

'Mornin', Ma'am.' The old cobbler sat outside his shop, his cap drawn down to protect his eyes from the sun, and a pipe of baccy jutting from his thin-lipped mouth. 'Off for a stroll, I see.' A man of a simple nature, he spoke to everyone in the same friendly manner.

As Rita glared at him with open hostility, he visibly cringed, at the same time making a mental note to keep his mouth firmly shut whenever she crossed his path.

'Snooty cow!' Ada Long from number ten was never one to pick and choose her words. 'Who the bleedin' hell does she think she is, eh?' She held a squealing child in one hand and a stick in the other. When the child struggled to be free, she whacked it hard with the length of the stick. 'Keep still, yer bugger!' she chided. 'Yer to come in for a wash an' that's an end to it.' The other three, all aged under six and daring her to take them in, suddenly realised she was not in a mood to be tampered with. In a matter of minutes they were all walking sedately beside her as she marched them back to the house. 'Yer little sods!' she yelled, clipping the biggest round the ear. 'Next time I shout for you to get inside, happen you'll move yerself a bit quicker.'

After she had ushered the last one into the house, she sneaked an envious glance towards Rita. ''Tain't fair the way some folks have it all an' are never satisfied,' she sighed. Then she sighed again and followed Rita out of sight. 'She's a looker, I'll give 'er that,' she muttered grudgingly.

Though not many people cared for her, Rita certainly attracted attention. She wore a long beige-coloured skirt and matching jacket, small low-heeled shoes and a white beret over her flowing dark hair. She felt beautiful. As she came away from the houses, she let her thoughts run free. She thought of Frank and hated him. She recalled the confrontation with her sister-in-law and her face hardened. When she remembered how she had gone along with Frank's outrageous plan to adopt a complete stranger, she felt a tinge of regret. But the regret was soon swamped by an immense surge of satisfaction. Things would turn out exactly as she planned. Moreover, the boy was making a handsome addition to the Blackthorn family. Margaret had confirmed his intelligence. He had shown a healthy appetite to learn and, much to her own surprise, Rita found herself being drawn to him. A son was what she had always wanted. *Someone else's* son had at first seemed daunting. Now, though, she was warming to the idea; especially when Margaret had so set herself against it. And even more so when it was becoming increasingly obvious how Cathy's life might be turned upside down by the arrangement. The whole situation appealed to her wickedness; so much so that revenge blinded her reason. As she climbed over the stile and into the open fields, she actually laughed out loud.

An hour later, her laughter had turned to tears. As she pushed her way through the spinney, she was suddenly startled by the screech of a bird. When she looked up, it was to stare straight into the glassy eyes of two dead rabbits; strung across the fork of a tree, their heads were dangling almost to her shoulder.

Fresh blood from their wounds dripped on to her neck and sent her into a frenzy. In that moment there was the sound of a gun being fired, followed by a man yelling. It was all too much. With a piercing scream, she took to her heels, breathless and panic-stricken as she scrambled towards the edge of the spinney. Flailing branches tore at her clothes as she ran, and jagged thorns rent her skin.

Driven by fear and seeing the open fields so close, she didn't notice how the ground fell away beneath her. By the time she realised, it was too late. With a cry of horror, she plunged sideways, crashing to the bottom of a steep bank where she rolled against a tree trunk and lay bruised and unconscious.

Owen Leyton had been rabbiting in the spinney. Having already bagged two and just shot another, he was celebrating his good fortune when he heard the scream. Slinging both rabbit and shotgun over his shoulder, he ran towards the spinney, just in time to see Rita tumble over.

At first he made no move to lift her. Instead he stood over her, his dark eyes drinking in her beauty. Taking the gun from his shoulder he laid it on the grass next to her; the rabbit was dropped at her feet. Kneeling down beside her, he tenderly raised her in his arms, his gaze softening as he looked into her face. 'You're even more handsome close to,' he murmured. Her long hair fell over his hands and he could feel the trim curves of her body beneath his fingers. Beads of perspiration stood out on his forehead.

Rita couldn't recall how she had come to be lying there, dazed and hurt. Her eyes closed, but she heard his voice, felt his arms round her, and for just one brief, wonderful moment she felt safe. Slowly she moved, wincing as the torn skin twisted. With confused green eyes she looked up at his face.

'It's all right,' he told her softly. 'You slipped down the bank, but you're safe now.' When she seemed confused, he whispered, 'You're very beautiful.'

His smile mesmerised her. When she looked into those dark brooding eyes she knew where she had seen him before. Rage gathered in her. But something else, something far more powerful, took hold of her. 'Leave me be,' she told him weakly. 'I can make my own way home.' She struggled, before falling back exhausted into his arms, her gaze meeting with his.

Fired by her beauty, he could contain himself no longer. Leaning over he kissed her hard on the mouth, astonished when she seemed to enjoy it. 'You want me, don't you?' He smiled, stroking her face with the tips of his fingers. 'I saw it in your eyes the first time I looked at you.'

'You filth!' With a vicious sweep of her hand she caught him hard on the side of the face. 'What makes you think I could want *you*?'

Though his cheek throbbed and his first instinct was to slap her hard, his voice was soft with admiration. 'No use denying it,' he said arrogantly. 'You want me every bit as much as I want you.'

She stared at him long and hard. Then she softly laughed. 'I want no man,' she scoffed. 'Least of all you.'

Sensing a weakness in her, he boldly opened the neck of her blouse. Without a word he bent his mouth to her nipple, gently sucking like a child, sensuously playing his tongue against the hardening mound.

Never before had she experienced such feelings. He was like an animal, wild and frenzied, filled with an urgency that intoxicated her. Shivering with delight, she made a show of pushing him away. 'No,' he murmured in her ear. 'It had to happen, you know that.' And she could not refuse him.

By the time she was delivered safely home, Frank was beside himself with worry. He thanked Owen profusely, and ordered Ruby to take care of her mistress at once.

He saw the unguarded look that passed between Owen and Rita but, not realising its significance, paid no mind to it. Yet one day in the not too distant future, when a price must be paid for pleasure enjoyed, he would live to remember that day with burning regret.

CHAPTER FOUR

'Mind you behave while I'm gone.' About to depart for London, Frank loathed the idea of leaving Rita behind. 'Won't you come with me?' he begged for the umpteenth time. He couldn't understand her reluctance. In the past whenever he'd had call to visit the city she always insisted on accompanying him.

'I'm not pleasant company at the moment,' Rita told him, pressing a handkerchief to her nose. 'I have a cold coming on.' She gave a little cough.

'I've a good mind to stay.' He took her in his arms, offended when she pushed him away.

Alarmed he might change his plans, she reminded him, 'I thought you needed to see your financial adviser?'

'Well, yes, I do. These six-monthly meetings are essential, to keep the house in order so to speak, and I want to know whether or not we can afford to send Jack away to a fine school.' He smiled grandly. 'I'm proud of that boy!'

Ignoring his comment, she gave another little cough. 'I think I'll go back to my bed.'

'I really *should* go to London, my dear. But it will mean me staying overnight. I can postpone it if you want?'

'No.' In a move which both surprised and delighted him, she threaded her arm through his and escorted him to the front door. 'I'll be fine,' she insisted. 'Your precious Ruby will see to that.' She allowed him a brief peck on the cheek. 'You'd better go or you'll miss your train.'

'It's *you* I'll miss.' He fussed over her all the way across the hall and on to the doorstep. The keen October wind took his breath away. 'Get back inside, before you catch your death.' He gently pushed her into the vestibule. Blowing a kiss, he got inside the carriage and hung out of the window, waving frantically until he was out of sight.

Thankful that he was gone at last, Rita put on her coat and hat and prepared to leave. As she opened the front door, Margaret came out of the sitting room. 'Spying on me, are you?' Rita demanded angrily.

'I have better things to do with my time.' Margaret had heard certain rumours which deeply troubled her. 'I was hoping to have a word with you.' Going across the hall, she stood before the other woman, wondering how she should broach the subject, or even whether she had a right to.

'What can we possibly have to talk about?'

'Has my brother gone yet?'

Rita's answer was short and sharp. 'If you've something to say, get on with it. I can't stand here all day.'

Margaret took a deep breath. 'There are rumours...'

'Rumours?' Rita's face turned a shade of grey and she seemed visibly to shrink. '*What* rumours?'

'I think you know.' She saw the guilt in Rita's face and was shocked. 'You and Owen Leyton. It's true, isn't it? I couldn't bring myself to believe it, but now I'm not so sure.'

Rita laughed in her face. 'Me and Owen Leyton!' She was a mistress of deception. 'You must be out of your mind.' Straightening to her full height, she set her shoulders and declared haughtily, 'If I were you, I should be very careful what you say.' Before Margaret could answer, she was out of the house and striding down the path.

'Where's she going?' Jack had come out of the sitting room and was staring out of the open doorway. 'Have you two had an argument?' The corners of his mouth curled into a smile. The idea of everyone at each other's throats amused him.

'Go back to your lessons.' Hurrying across the hallway, Margaret closed the door and escorted him to the sitting room.

Cathy, too, was curious. 'Has Father gone?' She knew it was too much to expect him to say goodbye. Why should he change the habit of a lifetime?

'I believe so, sweetheart.'

Jack butted in. 'He's gone to see his financial adviser and won't be home till tomorrow.'

Margaret stared at him with astonishment. 'You seem to be very well informed, young man.' Even she didn't know Frank's plans.

'That's because it has to do with me.' He was very pleased with himself. 'Father says you've taught me well but I have to move up soon, so he has to see this man in London... about finances and everything.' Coming to where Cathy sat, he stroked her long fair hair. 'Don't worry about Father,' he said. 'You've got me, haven't you? If you like we can go down to the brook after lessons?'

'We have other plans,' Margaret quickly told him. 'Now, please sit back at your work. I want the essays completed before we break in an hour.' She glanced up at the mantelpiece clock. It was five minutes to one. Nan Foster was expecting them by three. She had arranged a little tea party to celebrate her seventy-first birthday, and was baking a cake especially.

'Am *I* invited?' Jack enquired boldly.

It was the last thing Margaret wanted. 'I think not,' she answered.

Seeing his disappointment, Cathy felt for him. 'I'm sure Nan wouldn't mind.'

Margaret considered for a moment. 'All right.' With Frank away and Rita in one of her moods, it might be wise to keep the boy where she could watch him. 'But I hope Nan doesn't mind.'

These past four months she'd worked hard to keep Cathy and the boy apart. But it was proving to be an impossibility. He always seemed to be there and, while she had every reason to resent his presence in her parents' house, and though Jack was too secretive for Margaret's liking, Cathy sought the good in him.

In view of her acceptance of him, Margaret reluctantly decided to give Jack the benefit of the doubt. But her vow to watch him closely was stronger than ever. There was something very mysterious about the boy, and she couldn't help but feel he was not all he seemed to be. Time and again she had discreetly quizzed him about his background but, apart from telling her what she already knew, he was suspiciously secretive.

Coming to the end of the lane, Rita turned left, towards the community of Langho, and Dickens Street. She hated Dickens Street. It ran like a vein right through the heart of Langho, a long meandering street of back-to-back houses, everything she despised. There was poverty in Dickens Street, with the men earning a pittance from the cotton mills and factories here-abouts, and the women raising hordes of children; ragged snotty-nosed children, who filled the street with their laughter and sat on the kerbstones with their feet dangling in the gutter. The women wore turbans and white-stoned their front doorsteps. In the evening the men stood about on the street corners or went to the Red Lion pub, where they sat and supped their beer and afterwards stumbled home with pickled brains and a hankering to enjoy their wife and make another child.

There was no other route to the doctor's surgery so, while she wended her way along the pavements of Dickens Street, Rita Blackthorn tried not to think too much about the people who lived here. Instead, she quickened her footsteps and was soon crossing the market square towards the big red house that stood on the corner. In a minute she was knocking on the door, impatient to be let in.

'I'm sorry, Mrs Blackthorn, but the surgery is already finished and the doctor is on his way to the hospital. I can make an appointment for him to call on you though?'

'Just tell him I'm here. He'll see me.'

'I've already turned away two people, Ma'am.'

'I am not "people"!' Rita thumped her clenched fists on the wooden counter. 'Do as you're told, girl. Tell him I'm here, and I have no intention of leaving until he's seen me.' That said, she sat herself on the nearest chair and kept her stony glare on the girl.

'Very well, Ma'am. I'll tell him.' The girl had never liked Rita Blackthorn. She liked her even less now. 'But he's in a hurry and I know he won't see anyone else,' she said boldly.

Almost at once the doctor emerged. Unlike his receptionist he had always admired Rita Blackthorn as a woman of beauty and determination. 'Come with me,' he said softly, leading the way into his consulting room.

Rita smiled serenely as she followed him in. As they went into the consulting room she glanced at the girl with a smirk of satisfaction.

Some minutes later, the doctor's words wiped the smile from her face. 'I think congratulations are in order.' He beamed. 'You are definitely with child.'

He was surprised by her reaction. She seemed neither pleased nor disappointed. But she was in a great hurry to leave, and he assumed she couldn't wait to relay the news to her husband. 'I'll make another appointment,' he said. 'If I remember rightly, you had complications during your previous pregnancy.' He rubbed his hand against his chin, thinking hard and recalling aloud, 'Threatened miscarriage, wasn't it?' He nodded and made a note in his pad. 'I shall have to keep a closer eye on you this time.'

Outside on the pavement, she couldn't decide which way to go. In the end she walked to the market square and there flagged down a cab. 'Brook Lane,' she said, climbing in and making herself comfortable. As they drove away from the houses and out into the countryside, she thought on the doctor's words. 'If I remember rightly, you had a difficult pregnancy last time.' She thought of Cathy and her mood darkened. 'Pity the brat ever drew first breath.'

Settling back in the soft leather seat, she mused aloud. 'If I'd given birth to a boy, things would have been different.' Rubbing her stomach, she whispered lovingly, 'Owen's child will be a boy, I'm sure of it.'

During the short journey, she convinced herself that she was carrying a son. In strange mood, she was both thrilled and afraid. What if Frank found out? He was a man of mild and gentle manner but where she was concerned, he was madly possessive. Yet even the fear of Frank's finding out was itself exciting to her. 'What do I care if the whole world knows!' she muttered defiantly. 'I've been clever enough to hoard a nest of money, and Frank would have to make a decent settlement on me. Yes, Owen and I will move away . . . we'll make a new life together.' The more she thought on it, the more like reality it became. She was convinced that all she had to do was tell Owen she was carrying his child, and everything would be just as she had planned.

'Do you want me to wait, Ma'am?'

Dropping the fare into the driver's grubby hand, she told him sharply, 'No. Be off with you.' Fastening her coat tighter about her, she hurried away, head down against the wind as she went towards the house where Owen lived with his family.

It was Owen himself who opened the door. 'What the devil are you doing *here*?' Quickly, before his wife might grow curious, he closed the door and spoke with her on the step. 'I told you never to come here.'

'I had to.' Rita wanted to throw her arms round him, but something about his manner made her nervous. 'I've just come from the doc—' Suddenly the door was opened and there stood Owen's wife. She didn't speak, but looked from one to the other with quizzical eyes.

'It's Mrs Blackthorn.' Owen quickly stepped back. 'She's come to discuss a business matter.' He smiled at Rita as though she was little more than a stranger. 'Isn't that so?' he urged, widening his eyes in a warning.

Rita rose to the deceit magnificently. 'You're looking well, Mrs Leyton,' she remarked casually, thinking how much better it would be if the woman was suddenly to drop dead. 'My husband has been rushed away on business and he asked me to speak to Mr Leyton here . . . about the fencing alongside the lane.' The excuse just popped into her mind. 'We've had one or two complaints, you see.'

'Complaints?' Maria was puzzled. Turning to her husband she asked, 'Didn't you repair that fencing only last week?'

'That's right, I did. The wind must have brought it down again.' When he saw how she shivered from the cold, drawing her shawl over her bony frame as she stepped deeper into the hall, he put his hands on her shoulders and took her back inside. 'You've no business standing in a draught,' he scolded. Easing her into a big armchair, he wrapped a blanket round her legs. 'You're doing so well, I'll not have you making yourself ill again.' When she looked up, he kissed her on the forehead. 'What would I do without you, eh?' he asked fondly.

'Oh, you'd do all right, I dare say.'

'Don't you believe it.' Lately he had come to know the value of Maria.

Jerking her head towards the door, she said meaningfully, 'I expect *she* feels the cold too. You'll either have to fetch her in and give her a brew, or send her on her way.' Chuckling, she leaned forward to whisper. 'To be honest, I'd sooner you sent her on her way. She's a right uppity bugger ... not like Miss Margaret at all.' Screwing her face up, she added, 'On second thoughts, get rid of her.'

'Right then.' He got his jacket from the back of the door. 'I'll send her away, then I'll go and take a look at the fencing. When Teresa comes in, tell her to start the tea for you. I'll not be gone long.'

He laughed when she said she was capable of getting their tea without Teresa's help. 'And eat it too if you're not back,' she joked.

Ushering Rita away from the house, he thrust her angrily into the barn. 'What the hell d'you think you're playing at?' he hissed. 'Do you want her to find out? Is that what you're after?'

Rita was thrown by his manner. She knew he would be angry at her going to the house, but she hadn't expected him to be so hostile. 'I had to see you.'

'We arranged to meet tonight. What's so important it couldn't wait?' Whenever he was near her she swamped his senses. It was like that now. 'Never mind ... just don't do it again.' Taking her roughly by the shoulders, he jerked her towards him, raining kisses on her face, neck and every inch of skin that was visible. 'You drive me crazy,' he groaned. He stripped away her hat to let her long hair tumble through his fingers. Now he took off her coat and pawed at her breasts. 'You're poison to me,' he murmured in her ear. 'The pity of it is, I can't get you out of my blood.'

Desperate for him now, the news she had brought him could wait. He still wanted her, that was all she needed to know. 'Take me,' she moaned. And he did, with the same wild lust as before, biting and bruising her, bringing her to a fulfilment she had never found with Frank.

Later, when passion was spent and they sat together in that cold draughty barn, he told her grimly, 'If you ever knock on Maria's door again, I swear I'll kill you.'

She laughed at his threat. 'Anyone would think you loved her.' Though she laughed at the idea, she was mortally afraid it might be true. 'You *don't*, do you?'

Standing up to fasten his trousers, he grew anxious that David would soon be home. If he was to see his father here, with another woman! The idea didn't bear thinking about.

Suddenly Rita was there before him, her fingers gripping his arm. 'Did you hear what I said?'

He looked down to see her green eyes blazing with anger. There was a vindictiveness about her that struck fear into his heart. 'Sorry,' he said. 'I was just thinking.' Glancing towards the big doors, his nervousness increased. 'You'd better go. David could arrive back any minute.' Looking towards the far corner and the empty stable there, he explained, 'He's only as far as the spinney... setting rabbit snares.'

'I'll go when I'm ready.'

'You'll go when *I* say.' He realised now he'd been a fool ever to have tangled with her. She was trouble he could well do without.

'Do you love her?'

'What are you talking about?'

'*Her*!' She snuggled up to him. 'Your wife. I couldn't stand it if you loved her.'

'I don't know what you want me to say.' He had on his jacket now, and was ready to go. 'Maria has nothing to do with what's between us.' He shrugged her off. 'Leave her out of it.'

'Tell me you don't love her!' She stiffened against him, drawing her head back to look into his face.

His instincts told him to be wary. Gripping her arms, he dug his fingers into the flesh. He wanted to hit her, to let her know that he was already eaten up with regrets. 'Bitch!' Intoxicated by her beauty, he bent his head and kissed her hard. 'Does that answer your question?'

She seemed satisfied. 'It's just as well you don't love her,' she said with a cunning smile, '*because I'm expecting your child.*' She saw the colour ebb from his face, and still she didn't realise the way he felt. 'I know it's a boy... a son for me at last.'

'God Almighty!' He saw his whole life turning upside down. 'With child? Are you sure?'

She laughed. 'I came straight from the doctor to you.' She was so full of the news she couldn't see how devastated he was. 'What's the matter, Owen? Aren't you thrilled?'

His voice shook with emotion. 'How do you know it isn't

your husband's?' He clung to a glimmer of hope.

'Don't worry, my love.' She actually believed he would have been disappointed if the child was Frank's. 'It can't be his. Since you and I have been together, I've used every excuse to turn him away.' She was lying. In fact she had given in to Frank on two occasions since that day when she and Owen made love. 'In any case, this is a boy.' She took his hand and stroked it over her stomach. 'Frank was never man enough to make a son,' she said bitterly.

Startled by the sound of someone pushing open the big doors, he put his finger to his lips and ushered her out by the back way. 'Make your way home before dark falls,' he warned softly. 'And remember . . . you must never come to this house again.'

Angered because he hadn't offered to see her home, she demanded, 'You *are* thrilled about the baby, aren't you?'

'You know I am,' he lied. 'Now get off home.'

Still she resisted. 'I have a certain amount of money, and Frank will be made to see me all right. You say you don't love Maria, so you see how easy it all is? There's nothing at all to stop us making a life together.'

The big doors were open now, letting the light in. 'For God's sake, Rita!' He pushed her out. 'Don't worry . . . I'll make plans.' The 'plans' he had in mind did not include her, but he mustn't let her know that. 'It'll take time. It must be done right. Meanwhile, this is our little secret. Do you understand what I'm saying?' He was frantic in case she was foolish enough to confront her husband with the information.

She smiled then. 'I won't tell a soul, I swear,' she assured him. The smile fell away and her face darkened. 'You won't let me down though, will you?'

Not for the first time, he saw the bad side of her and knew she would make a dangerous enemy. 'Trust me,' he pleaded. Later, he would have to consider moving away. For now, though, he had no choice but to play along. 'Not a word to anyone or it could ruin everything.'

'I'll do as you say,' she agreed. 'And anyway, who would I tell?'

The silhouette of a young man leading a horse could clearly be seen entering the barn at the other end. 'Dad? Is that you?'

David peered deeper into the barn, coming closer with every step.

'Go! Quickly. Keep to the high ground.' Mortified that his son might see her, Owen thrust Rita out of the barn. 'Wait for me to contact you.'

'Don't make it too long,' she replied softly. Then she was gone.

Almost as soon as she emerged from the rear of the barn, Rita saw a face staring down. It was Jack! Leaning against the trunk of an oak tree, he was smiling at her, a sly knowing grin that made her heart turn cold. Quickly now she ran the other way, across the valley and along by the brook. But she couldn't get his expression out of her mind. 'He knows! He saw us!' The idea that he might tell Frank before she was ready spurred her on. 'Perhaps he didn't see us after all,' she hoped aloud. 'We'll see.'

Unaware that they might have been seen, Owen breathed a sigh of relief. But it wasn't over yet, he reminded himself. Rita Blackthorn was carrying his child! The thought filled him with dread.

'How come you're home so early? Have you set all the traps?' Once he'd made his presence known to his son, Owen forced himself to talk about mundane matters.

'Every one of 'em,' David replied with a grin. 'And I'm home early because I've been invited to a party.'

'A party?'

'Nan Foster saw me making for the spinney and came after me. It's her birthday and she's having a party.' A soft blush spread over his handsome face. 'Cathy will be there,' he said. The touch of her name on his lips was warmer than a summer's day.

Relieved that David had not seen Rita Blackthorn, Owen shook his head and tutted. 'By! A party, eh? Some folk do have grand ideas and that's a fact.'

'That's because Nan Foster is a grand lady.'

'I'll not deny that. Though how she came to be living alone in a dilapidated cottage is a mystery to me.'

His thoughts flew back to another 'lady'. The one who lived up at Blackthorn House. The one he'd been unwise enough to become involved with. Some women knew when an affair was over. Some women could take no for an answer, but not Rita Blackthorn. This time he had made a mistake, but he would put it right. Somehow he would put it right.

As he and David walked back to the house, Maria watched from the window. There was something about her husband ... But she wasn't sure. It was always worse when she wasn't sure.

'Come in! Come in!' Nan Foster had on her best dress, a fancy cream creation, with beads at the neck and hem, and a cameo clasp at the throat. In her white hair she wore a headband of blue. 'I'm so glad you're here.' She looked from Margaret to Cathy and then noticed the boy. Studying him for a moment, she frowned deeply. He was everything Margaret had described, handsome and mature for his fifteen years. His fair hair was superbly cut and his sturdy figure seemed at ease in the expensive clothes his new 'father' had provided.

While she studied him, he appraised her through bold hazel eyes. 'Am I right in thinking you're Jack?' she said in a curious voice. Her greeting was neither friendly nor hostile.

Cathy stood alongside him, her pretty face troubled. 'You don't mind our bringing him, do you, Nan?' she asked worriedly.

The old lady merely smiled and continued to regard the boy, grateful that none of them could read her thoughts. She glanced at Margaret and saw her own reservations echoed in those serious brown eyes, but it was to Cathy she spoke. 'I expect there's room at my table for one more.' This was her birthday treat. She had here the two people she loved most in all the world, and she was determined that nothing should be allowed to spoil it all.

As she led the trio into the tiny sitting room, the old lady softly sang her favourite lullaby. Margaret had heard it so many times before, she felt as though she had known it all her life.

'There! What do you think?' Standing proudly before the small square table, Nan waved her hands in an extravagant gesture. 'Have I done you proud?' The table was covered in a white lace cloth, and the cloth was covered in porcelain dishes filled with fish and meat and fancy titbits to whet the appetite. Set about the edge of the table were four small white plates with dainty blue borders, knife, fork and spoon beside. 'I've only set four places, but it won't take a minute to put out another one.' Nan glanced meaningfully at the boy. A part of her wished he hadn't come here. Yet another, greater part of her was glad. Better to know the enemy than to be taken by surprise, she thought.

'Who else is invited?' Margaret had been led to believe it was just herself and Cathy.

'That nice young David Leyton,' the old lady explained. 'He's always been very good to me ... cutting logs for the fire and fetching the odd rabbit to make a fine stew.' She went out to the scullery and brought another setting. Laying it on the table, she shifted everyone along a place. 'There! Now we can all be comfortable.'

'What do you want me to do?' Cathy asked. 'We're here to help as well, you know.'

'Thank you, dear, but I've been up since the crack of dawn, and everything's ready.' She smiled graciously. 'I've made my first cake in years, and I must say I'm very pleased with myself.' She sighed wistfully and in a softer voice appeared to be addressing herself. 'It's been so long since I really entertained.'

Cathy was about to make a comment, but the knock on the front door interrupted her. 'Shall I answer it?' she asked.

'You'll do no such thing!' Nan chided. 'You can take off your coat and see these two do the same.'

Hurrying to the front door she began softly singing the lullaby. It was a strange plaintive melody that never failed to touch Margaret deeply.

By the time Nan returned, Cathy and Jack were seated comfortably on the settee, and Margaret was putting a chunky log on the fire. 'Thank you, dear,' Nan said. 'It wouldn't do if we were to have our tea in front of a dying fire.' She pushed David forward. 'Here we are,' she said grandly. 'Another handsome fellow.'

David's dark eyes surveyed the little group. They lit up on seeing Cathy, but grew hard at the sight of Jack. The whole village had heard about this new addition to the Blackthorn family, but few people had actually seen him. Frank Blackthorn kept him close. 'Hiding him away' was how some put it.

The two young men regarded each other for what seemed a
long awkward time but was in fact only seconds, with David
inwardly flinching at the sight of Cathy and Jack sitting so
close and Jack staring at David with a half-cunning grin. The
atmosphere struck cold and, for some reason she couldn't
fathom, Margaret thought the old lady was studying the two
with some degree of satisfaction.

'Come and sit here,' Cathy invited as David came deeper into
the room. She too had felt the coldness between the two young
men, and wasn't quite sure what to make of it. She thought
David might be jealous of Jack, but hoped not. After all, he
was to be her brother. The growing affection she felt for him was
altogether different from the deeper emotions that David raised
in her. She had no experience of love between a man and a
woman, but often wondered if that was what she felt for David.
Certainly he made her feel warm and wanted whenever he was
near, and when they were apart she was incredibly lonely.

Nan intervened. 'You can all sit at the table now,' she
announced. 'The tea's ready and I can't wait to show off the
cake I've made.' As they went to the table, she went to the scullery. 'Sit where you like,' she called. 'It doesn't matter.'

With the chill of the outdoors still on her, Margaret chose to
sit closer to the fire. Cathy sat to her right, Jack placed himself
beside Cathy, and David, wishing he hadn't come, hating the
idea of sitting next to Jack, made his way to the place on
Margaret's left side, leaving a seat vacant for Nan between
himself and Jack.

It was only a minute before she returned, carrying a wonderful
cake, her face wreathed in a glowing smile. 'Made of fruit and
brandy, spread with marzipan and iced by my very own hands.'
Setting it in the centre of the table, she gazed at it and sighed.
'I can't thank you all enough for coming,' she said warmly. But
when she looked at the faces round her table, she deliberately
avoided looking at Jack.

Margaret said it seemed a shame to cut the cake, but everyone
had a slice and remarked on how good it was. As the time sped
by, they chatted and laughed; Jack and David avoided each
other, and Cathy exchanged intimate glances with David.

Finally, Nan opened the presents they had brought. A pair of patchwork cushion-covers from Margaret and Cathy, sewn from odd pieces of material which they had carefully saved and sorted especially for Nan's birthday. Jack presented her with an expensive porcelain vase, and there was a large fruit bowl from David, crafted by his own hands from a small beech log. 'They're all lovely. Thank you so much,' Nan cried. She hugged Margaret and Cathy, and smiled at the two young men; though the smile she gave David told him she valued his present above that of Jack. Later she was to tell Margaret, 'The porcelain vase brought by Jack might well have cost a deal of money but what David gave, and you and Cathy also, was precious time and skill, and a measure of love.'

When the tea was finished, Margaret and Cathy offered to help with the dishes. 'You'll do no such thing,' Nan objected. 'You're my guests, and anyway, there'll be plenty of time for that after you've gone. I've got little else to do.'

She did set the young men a task though. 'Jack, would you kindly have a look at the window fastener in the bedroom? It won't hold tightly, and I'm afraid the hinge might be broken.' She suspected he wouldn't have a clue about what to do, but it would keep him busy for a while, giving Cathy and David a chance to talk.

'What can *I* do?' Cathy was eager to help.

'You can go with David and draw two buckets of water from the outside pump. Oh, and while you're at it, David, could you clear the fallen leaves out of the trough, or the water won't be able to drain away.'

'I did offer to fell that tree for you,' he reminded her. 'Being close to the pump, it'll always cause you trouble. And anyway, it's on its last legs.'

'So am I,' Nan chuckled. 'Does that mean I should be done away with too?'

'Sorry.' He grinned. 'I didn't mean it like that.'

'I should hope not!' Nan was grateful for his offer. 'All the same, you're right. Come and see me tomorrow, and we'll discuss a lesser punishment for the tree. It was here when I came and I hope it will be here long after I've gone.' A fleeting sadness shadowed her face. She had a lot to do before that day ever came. 'Perhaps we can just cut back some of the overhanging branches?'

'Whatever you say.' Ever since he was a young boy, the old lady had lived in the cottage. She had put him in mind of an angel, with her gentle smile and snow-white hair. 'Just tell me what you want and it's done,' he promised. Stepping back, he allowed Cathy to go before him.

As they left the house, the two were happy enough to be in each other's company at last. Jack however, glowered at them through the upstairs window, slamming and banging at the window fastener, until Nan was forced to call up the stairs, 'Be careful, young man. I want it mended, not broken altogether!'

She made a fresh brew of tea and sat with Margaret in front of the cheery fire. 'What do you make of him?' she asked, jerking a thumb towards the ceiling.

'I'm amazed by the way he's settled in, and he's so quick at learning there soon won't be very much more I can teach him. Still, I understand Frank intends to have him tutored by better than me.'

'Don't belittle yourself.' Nan knew how talented Margaret was. 'And, anyway, I wasn't referring to how clever the boy is. What I wanted to know was what you thought about him, now you've got to know him better?'

'That's just it, Nan. I *don't* know him better.'

'How do you mean?'

'I've tried to talk about his background with him, but he's very secretive and gives nothing away. All I know is what Frank has told me. He's an orphan, made by circumstances to wander the streets, stealing and doing goodness knows what, until Frank came across him and gave him a better life.'

Nan thought on this a while. 'It's very little to know about someone who shares your house, don't you think . . . a stranger who stands to inherit everything your brother owns?'

Margaret smiled wryly. 'Of course I would rather know more about him. In fact . . .' she leaned forward and spoke more intimately '. . . lately I've been toying with the idea of hiring a private investigator to find out what he can. But there is precious little to go on.' She drew back. 'I'm torn in so many ways about the whole business, Nan. I think Frank was foolish to do what he did, yes. But he and Rita have craved a son for so long that they can't see clearly any more.' She had agonised over the situation, and now Nan was echoing all the fears she herself felt ... for Cathy and Frank ... even Rita, because what hurt his wife hurt Frank more.

'David doesn't like him.'

Margaret peered out of the window. The greyness of a late-October day made the little cottage seem like a haven. 'David is a fine young man. Like me, he senses the badness in Jack.'

'Ah! So you do think he's bad then?'

'Maybe "bad" isn't the right word. I don't know.' She tried to rationalise her suspicions. 'All I do know is he makes me feel uncomfortable, as though he's waiting ... keeping secrets.'

'He seems to have an eye for Cathy. That spells trouble.'

Margaret nodded. It was uncanny how the old lady could read her thoughts. So many answers raged through her mind in that moment, but all she said was, 'I wish he hadn't come into our lives.'

Nan leaned back in her chair and began softly humming that lilting lullaby, her thoughts reaching back over the years. It was a long moment before she spoke again. 'Life is a trial,' she said softly. 'Sometimes we have to do things we're ashamed of.' She lowered her gaze to the floor and was silent a moment longer. Presently she declared in a brighter tone, 'But you mustn't be too concerned, because Cathy will be fine.' Her face set and her hands, which were resting in her lap, clenched into fists. 'I would never let anything harm either you or the child,' she said grimly.

Momentarily taken aback by the old lady's manner, Margaret was lost for a reply. Laughter from outside caused her to peer through the window to see David and Cathy flicking water at each other. 'Look at them, Nan,' she urged. 'I know they're very young, and still have a lifetime of experience to be lived, but if ever two people were made for each other, it's those two.' There was something beautiful about their relationship. She had seen it time and again, and it never failed to move her.

'If the hearts are together, age doesn't matter,' the old lady murmured. 'But a bad marriage can ruin your life forever.' All the awful memories came rushing back, overwhelming her. Should she tell Margaret? Could she bring herself to say: 'I am the mother who walked out on you all those years ago?' Margaret would be shocked. It could mean the end of their relationship. She couldn't risk it. For now, at least, she must keep her secret close. One day her daughter would know. They would *all* know. Until then, she had to keep them safe, protect Margaret and Cathy from events that might overtake them.

Cathy sat on the edge of the trough, her collar turned up about her ears and her hands thrust deep into her pockets. She watched David lift the second bucket. 'I don't want to go in yet,' she said. 'I want to stay with you a while longer.' She was always happiest in his company.

'Aren't you cold?' David swung the bucket on to the ground and sat beside her. Pulling her two hands into his, he rubbed them with his own. 'Your hands are like frogs' backs,' he said.

She loved the feel of his hands on hers. She smiled up at him and in his dark eyes could see a reflection of herself. It made her feel closer to him somehow. 'I'm glad you're here,' she said. 'You made Nan's party even more special.'

He looked into that sweet uplifted face with its heart shape and stunning green eyes, and trembled inside. She made him feel like a man, creating emotions in him that left him shaken. 'Do you ever think about the future?' he asked softly.

His hands lay still and warm over hers. Whenever he was near she could think about nothing but him. Yet there were times like now when the intensity of her own emotions confused her. Bending her head she stared into the bottom of the trough, where the spilled water lay blackly. It looked dark and deep and she couldn't see through it. That was how she felt about her future. 'That isn't up to me,' she said in a small voice. Suddenly he had made her sad.

'If it was up to me, I'd carry you away and spend my life making you happy.' He felt her hands trembling in his and loved her more than she could ever know.

'What a lovely thing to say.' Her eyes sparkled with pleasure as she brought her gaze up to his handsome face. 'Would you really want to spend your whole life with me?' The prospect excited her.

'Every minute of every day.' He stroked her face. 'Do you know what I mean?'

Her response thrilled him. 'I feel the same as you.'

'Do you like being with *him*?' His expression darkened as he glanced towards the house.

'Do you mean Jack?'

'That isn't his real name, is it?'

'I'm not sure.'

'Who is he, Cathy? I mean . . . where does he come from?'

She studied David's face, wishing she could put his mind at rest. 'You don't like Jack, do you?'

Evading her question, he remarked, 'You're shivering. I think we'd best go in.'

'I'm not ready to go in yet. Besides, you didn't answer my question.'

'I won't lie. The truth is, no, I don't like him.' He put one hand on the handle of a bucket, preparing to lift it. 'Now are you ready to go in?'

She grinned and squeezed his free hand. 'You're not jealous, are you?' she teased.

'A little, I suppose.'

'Oh, David! That's silly. I feel sorry for him. He has no family but us, and sometimes he's very lonely.'

'*He* told you that, did he?' There was resentment in his voice.

'It would be nice if we could all be friends.' All afternoon Cathy had sensed the distrust between these two and it was painful to her. 'Won't you please try?'

'If that's what you really want.' How could he refuse her?

Her answer was to snuggle up to him. 'I love you,' she whispered.

It was on the tip of his tongue to ask in what way did she love him? But the time wasn't right yet, and it was enough for him to know that she cared. He had often argued with himself that they were too young for real love, yet what he felt for Cathy burned in him day and night. There had been a time when he felt as she did, when he could say he loved her and think nothing more of it. But that day was long gone, vanished with his childhood. All he could hope was that the same thing would happen with Cathy; that one day she would wake and realise she could not face life without him. In his heart he knew this moment was not too far away. And he could wait. If it was for Cathy, he could wait for ever. He must be patient, bide his time, and all would be well.

Jack's calling voice interrupted his thoughts. 'Cathy! It's time we were going.' He sauntered up to them. 'Are you ready?' He stared at David. 'You shouldn't have kept her out so long. Can't you see she's freezing?'

'He didn't keep me out,' Cathy corrected him. 'I wasn't ready to go in yet.'

Grabbing up both buckets, David looked Jack straight in the eye. 'Since when have you been Cathy's keeper anyway?' he said angrily. Already he was regretting the promise he'd made. He could never be friends with this sly fellow.

'What's a brother for?' came the arrogant reply.

'Don't argue, you two.' Fearing a confrontation, Cathy stepped between them. 'We'd better get back. I expect Margaret will be wondering where we are.' Turning to David she said, 'The buckets must be heavy, filled to the brim. Jack can carry one.' In fact she was disappointed he hadn't already offered.

Jack seemed taken aback by her remark. The last thing he wanted to do was to carry a bucket filled with freezing cold water. On the other hand, he was determined to make a good impression in front of Cathy. More than that, he intended to make David look like a fool. 'Only be too pleased,' he scoffed. 'After all, we can't let poor David carry them both, now can we?' With a deliberately rough action, he wrenched at the bucket. David was taken unawares, and Cathy cried out as a deluge of cold water drenched her legs and feet.

Secretly delighted, Jack made a show of being outraged that such a thing could have happened. 'You did that on purpose!' he yelled, throwing himself at David and lashing out with his fists.

Taken by surprise, David staggered backwards, dropping the buckets and trying to fend off Jack at the same time. The water spilled out over the ground and soon the two of them were rolling about in the mud.

'Stop it!' Cathy tried to intervene, but they were hell-bent on hurting each other. Going like the wind, she ran into the cottage where Margaret and the old lady were deep in conversation. 'They're fighting!' she cried. 'David and Jack are fighting.'

At first there was no stopping them. Locked together in hatred, they drove into each other with clenched fists. 'You need to be taught a lesson!' Jack cried, at the same time kicking out with his feet and catching David hard in the stomach. 'Living on the streets teaches a fellow how to handle himself,' he gloated when David reeled back in pain. His triumphant cry turned to agony as David lifted him off his feet by the scruff of his neck and slammed him effortlessly into the side of the cottage.

'That's enough!' Rushing over, Margaret pressed her hands into David's chest. It was like holding back a bull elephant. 'I know how you feel,' she whispered. 'But he's not worth it.'

Behind them, Jack had recovered enough to snatch up a large piece of timber, and was silently creeping up on the unsuspecting pair. Raising his arm to strike, he would have brought the timber down on David's head. But just in time Margaret spun round and caught him in the act. 'Shame on you!' she snapped. 'What kind of coward are you?'

David eyed him with contempt. 'The worst kind,' he answered. His dark eyes sought Cathy, who had defied the old lady and come rushing from the cottage. A fond look passed between them before he turned back to Margaret. 'He's a bad 'un,' he warned. 'And if I were you, I'd watch him closely.' Without another word, he strode away, his blood boiling with rage.

Rita was ashamed when Jack returned home with a bloody nose and his clothes caked in mud. 'Why did you let him do that to you?' she demanded.

'If he hadn't run off, I'd have laid him out!'

All the way home, Jack boasted about how he could have beaten David to a pulp. 'If you hadn't stopped me, I'd have taught him a real lesson,' he told Margaret. His bragging made no impact on her, other than making her see him for the despicable character he was.

Cathy remained silent until they reached the back door of the house, where she told the astonished Ruby, 'He picked a fight with David.'

'Good God above!' Ruby declared, stifling her giggles. 'I'm surprised he's still walking upright.'

Now he was washed and changed, and standing before Rita. 'You'd best go to your room and don't come down until breakfast,' she decided. Later that evening she told Margaret, 'If Frank was to find out about this, he'd throw the Leyton family out on their ear.' She was in a dilemma, and too involved with Owen for such a thing to happen.

'Anybody would think you actually cared what happened to them.' Margaret eyed her suspiciously. 'I should have thought it suited you to have them thrown out?'

'So it would.' Regretting her earlier remark, Rita chose her words carefully. 'But in *my* good time, not theirs.' Turning away, she smiled at her little secret. Once she and Owen had carefully laid their plans, he would be leaving the area anyway. What happened to the rest of his family was no concern of hers.

'So you agree that Frank should not be told about the incident?' Margaret had argued for that since arriving home. She never imagined that Rita would be so easily convinced.

'In this instance, yes, I think it would be wisest to say nothing.'

'I see.' She didn't 'see' at all, but was thankful for small mercies. 'I'll speak to all concerned and make sure they understand that.' Not wishing to stay in Rita's company any longer than was necessary, Margaret took her leave. She was relieved that Frank was not to be told. On the other hand, she couldn't help but wonder at Rita's peculiar change of heart.

The following evening, two things happened that gave Margaret even more food for thought. She and Cathy had gone to the Leyton house where Teresa answered the door. 'What do you want?' Surly as usual, she obviously had no intention of letting them in.

'I would like to speak with your mother about the fight between the two young men.' Margaret felt she needed to apologise on behalf of Jack. After all, he was now a Blackthorn in all but blood. She'd suggested he should make his own apologies but, true to form, he had merely laughed at the idea.

'I knew you'd be here.' Teresa glared at her. 'I warned our mam that David would get the blame.' Giving Margaret no time to explain, she went on, 'I was right an' all. Well, you can clear off. We don't want you here. Mam don't want you visiting, and David don't want no more reading lessons from *her*.' Staring at Cathy, she was pleased when her words seemed to wound.

'You're wrong.' Margaret had half expected Maria to be unnerved by the incident and was anxious to put matters right. 'No one's blaming David. In fact, I've come here to apologise.'

'I've just told you. We don't want your sort round here any more.'

'If that's what your mother wants, then of course I'll leave and won't intrude again.' She stared the girl out. 'But I would rather hear it from her.'

With a half-smile, the girl pushed open the door. Keeping a wily gaze on Cathy, she yelled into the house, 'Mam . . . it's the Blackthorn woman and the girl. Tell 'em what you told me.'

The voice was shaky, but unmistakably that of Maria Leyton. 'Go away!' she called out. 'Teresa's right. You lot up at the house have too much over us.'

'Satisfied?' Closing the door, Teresa couldn't hide her delight. 'We don't want none of you here.' Casting a dark look in Cathy's direction, she told her, 'Especially you. You've caused our David enough trouble.'

'Is he here?' Cathy was only concerned that she might never see David again.

'No, he's not. And even if he was, he would only tell you what I'm telling you now. He doesn't want nothing more to do with you lot.' When she realised her words were getting through at last, she drove the point home with a softer voice. 'I'm really sorry, but that's what he said, and after what happened, you can't really blame him, can you?'

Dejected, the two of them made their way back to Blackthorn House. 'She's right, you know,' Margaret mused aloud. 'You *can't* really blame them for not wanting us in their home. Maria Leyton has always been a little nervous about us visiting, but she needed help when she was ill, and when you started teaching David to read and write, she was so proud . . . she didn't have the heart to put a stop to it.' She gave a little smile. 'I know how fond you are of David,' she said kindly, 'but we have to abide by their wishes.'

'I wish Jack hadn't caused all that trouble.' Cathy's heart felt like a lead weight inside her; especially now, when she truly realised how much David meant to her.

'It seems he has a way of causing trouble.' Margaret had tried but could not feel any affection for Frank's protégé. Not wanting to transmit her true feelings to Cathy, she said brightly, 'Still, I expect your father will soon be packing him off to some fancy school, and we'll see less of him.'

'I wouldn't like to be packed off.' In spite of her mother's indifference and her father's neglect of her, Cathy would never want to be too far from Margaret. And the idea of leaving David behind was unthinkable.

'You're not likely to be packed off, sweetheart,' Margaret assured her. 'It's different with young men though . . . important for them to be well educated in all subjects. Like it or not, women don't command the same importance.'

Cathy's thoughts strayed. 'Do you think David will avoid me now?'

'I honestly don't know.' She sensed the girl's pain, but had no way of easing it. 'David doesn't seem like a young man who would bear a grudge, though of course his mother may have given him an ultimatum.' Taking hold of Cathy's hand, she urged her on with the encouraging words, 'If he wants to remain close to you, I'm sure he'll find a way. You'll just have to wait and see.'

Teresa rubbed her hands at the fire. 'It's bitter cold out there,' she said. 'Our David should have got more logs in before he and Dad went across the fields.' She took another log from the laden basket and thrust it into the flames.

Maria rocked back and forth in her chair, all the while regarding the girl through narrowed eyes. 'The lad filled the basket to bursting,' she replied sharply. 'There's enough to keep us warm till they come home.'

Pleased with herself, Teresa seated herself opposite her mother. 'I sent 'em packing, didn't I?'

'Aye. Yer did that right enough.' She studied the girl closely. Teresa was a handsome young woman, and Maria should have been proud. But there was a terrible hardness about her daughter, a bitterness beyond her years. 'Enjoyed it an' all, didn't yer, eh?'

'I only said what you told me.'

'You had no right to speak for David.'

'And he has no right making eyes at the landlord's brat!' She leaned forward, her blue eyes bold as she demanded, 'You won't tell him, will you?'

'Serve you right if I did. What! He'd skin yer alive if he knew yer'd sent that nice young lass packing.' She liked Cathy. In fact she owed the girl a great deal, because hadn't she taught her

son to read and write? Maria sighed heavily, lowering her gaze
to stare into the flames. 'Still. Happen it's just as well you've
driven a wedge between her and David. He's grown too fond
of her by half.' David was a sincere young man, and he would
never easily commit his affections. These past months, though,
she'd seen her son and Cathy growing closer, and to her regret
had ignored the danger signs. 'Don't worry,' she told the anxious
girl, 'I'll not tell him. If he doesn't see the Blackthorn lass again,
it'll suit me just fine.'

'I can't understand why you ever had them here in the first
place.'

'They were good to this family, and don't you ever forget that.'

'Then why did you turn them away?'

Impatient now, Maria snapped, 'Enough questions! There's
work to do about the house . . . the chickens want feeding and
there's room for a few more logs in that basket. Get on with it.'

Sulking, Teresa sprang out of the chair and slammed the back
door as she went out.

'Yer surly little bugger!' Maria's voice sailed after her. When
only silence greeted her, she fell back into the chair, filled with
regrets at having turned friends away from her door. Getting
out of the chair, she went to the window. In the far distance
two small figures could be seen going in the direction of Blackthorn House. 'It were a bad way to repay you for all your
kindness,' she murmured sadly. 'But it's all for the best.' When
a chilling breeze found its way in through the old window
frames, she drew her shawl tight about her. 'It ain't your fault,'
she said. 'It's *his*.' Her expression grew sad. 'Some women have
lazy husbands . . . others have them as gamble away their money.
Me? I've got one that can't keep his hands off other women!'

She returned to her chair and rocked silently for a while,
weighing the consequences of things. 'You're a fool, Owen
Leyton,' she growled. 'Do you think I haven't known when
you've bedded other women? I've known every time, and kept
me peace 'cause I knew yer'd allus come back to me once yer'd
had yer fun. But this time?' She pondered awhile. 'This time
I'm frightened. Yer've picked a rotten apple outta the barrel
an' it's sticking to yer fingers. *You're* the reason I've sent two
good friends away.' She shook her head forlornly. 'Being Black-

thorns is the only crime them two have committed.'

She stared towards the sideboard, at a photograph of her and her husband on their wedding day. 'I turned them away, an' it ain't their fault. It's yours, yer bloody fool! *Your* fault. Yer brewing up more trouble than you can handle, an' if I'm not careful we shall *all* be dragged under!'

She'd been angry, then afraid. Now a little smile brightened her face. 'You've had your fun, an' it don't matter to you who suffers for it. But it won't be me and the young 'uns, I can tell yer that. Not if I have *my* way, it won't.'

'Goodbye, Mr Blackthorn. Have a pleasant journey, sir.' The hotel clerk handed over the receipt, his smile becoming a frown when Frank returned only the smallest coin for his trouble.

The porter led Frank out into the night. It had rained all day, but now the air was calm and the sky speckled with stars. 'Right you are then, guv.' Throwing Frank's portmanteau in beside him, the porter held out his hand, astonished when he received twice the tip given to the clerk. 'Gawd bless yer!' he said, reverently touching his cap as the cab pulled away. 'Though yer might have found an extra sixpence if yer'd dug a bit deeper!'

At King's Cross station Frank checked the timetable, cursing when he realised he had just missed the eight o'clock train for Blackburn. 'You've a fair old wait 'til the next one,' he was told. 'The tea-bar's open though, and they do a tasty bacon sarnie.' The ticket clerk grinned like a Cheshire cat. 'An' I should know, 'cause it's my old woman as makes 'em.'

Tired, and with his head still aching from the meeting with his accountant, Frank picked up his case and trudged along the platform. The clerk was wrong. The tea-bar was closed. 'Hmph! His missus obviously doesn't tell him everything,' he groaned.

Whether it was the prospect of a tasty bacon sarnie or a refreshing cup of tea, Frank couldn't tell, but he was suddenly stricken with the need for refreshment. Realising he had time to kill, he decided to go back to the streets in search of a public house or a café of sorts.

Half a mile from King's Cross station, he found what looked like a respectable public house. Inside it was warm and cosy, and a few minutes after giving his order he was seated at a table. In no time at all he was brought a meat pie and a jug of ale with a deep measure of froth on top. 'That should warm the cockles of yer 'eart,' the waitress laughed. She said exactly the same ten minutes later, when Frank ordered a second helping.

Halfway through his second jug of ale, he was convinced someone was watching him. When he glanced up, his heart stood still. Some short distance away, a couple stood by the bar: the man was a big burly fellow with a shock of red hair and a loud mouth; the woman with him was a pretty little thing, with long brown hair and big sad eyes. She was looking straight at him! He knew her at once. How could he forget?

Flustered, he grabbed his case and fled into the night. The woman followed him. 'I only have to raise my finger and he'll tear you apart,' she threatened.

Instinctively drawing her into the shadows, Frank gave his own warning. 'If he knew the truth, it would be *you* he'd tear apart.'

'What makes you think he doesn't know?'

In spite of her bravado he knew she was lying. 'Because if he did, you wouldn't be here to tell the tale.'

She had no reply to that, except to hang her head in shame.

'So! You haven't told him. I knew you'd have more sense.' It was the first time he had come face to face with the man, and he didn't particularly like what he saw. 'He's an uncouth sort. You deserve better than him,' he remarked kindly.

'Who then?' Her sad eyes mocked him. 'You, maybe? Do I deserve *you*?'

He looked at the ground, absent-mindedly studying the puddles which had gathered in the cracks between flagstones. He couldn't answer. She should have known better than to ask such a thing.

Sensing his embarrassment, she laughed gently. 'After all this time, it hasn't changed, has it? I'll never be good enough for you, will I? Even if I was you'd never leave that wife o' yourn . . . tied to her for life, ain't you?' She looked into his face. She didn't hate him. She didn't even know him all that well, but in spite of everything, she believed he was a good man. 'By! I've never known a man so besotted with his own wife.'

'You knew that all along. I never kept the truth from you.'

'No, you didn't,' she admitted. 'You turned my life upside down. But you never lied to me.'

'If it's money you want...?'

'No, it ain't money, Frank.' She raised her eyes to the dark sky and gave a sigh that sent a shiver through him. 'Though God knows he spends it faster than I can earn it.' Inclining her head to one side, she glanced meaningfully towards the public house.

Frank was horrified. 'Are you telling me he's spent all the money I gave you?'

Her sad eyes looked him up and down as though she was seeing him for the first time. 'You've got a short memory, Frank,' she chided. 'You didn't *give* me anything.' The impact of what she'd said struck her as being ironic. 'Well... apart from the boy. You gave me him sure enough!' Her blue eyes hardened. 'Then you took him away.' Her voice broke. 'That was cruel, Frank. Oh, it was so cruel.'

'It was all meant to be, can't you see that?'

'No, I can't.' In the cold of the evening, she trembled a little. Recalling something he had told her in one unguarded moment, she thought to use it for her own ends. 'You have a daughter... Cathy, isn't it?'

He seemed surprised she should remember that much about him. 'What of it?'

'Have you considered her? If you mean the boy to have your name, won't he be able to take everything that should rightfully be hers?'

'Every man needs a son. What use is a daughter?' Only now did he fully realise the contempt he felt for Cathy.

'Don't punish me for one mistake,' she pleaded. 'It was only one night, Frank... just one night. He'd thrown me out, and you were so kind.'

'I was *drunk*! That's what I was.' Disgusted with himself, he spat the words out. 'Rita and I were going through a really bad patch and I felt lonely.' He groaned at the memory. 'God Almighty! If she should ever find out what happened, I'd lose her forever. I couldn't bear that.'

'What if I was to tell her?'

Grabbing her by the wrist, he made her cry out. 'You do that and I'll make sure your man in there knows every detail of that night . . . how we made a child . . . how you gave birth to a boy he thought was his. What would he say, I wonder, if he knew how you came to me for money soon after the boy was born? We made an agreement, you and I.'

'I should never have promised you the boy.' She was crying now.

'But you *did*! And I paid you a handsome sum twice over. Then you ran out on me. I searched high and low and it was as though you'd vanished from the face of the earth.' He took a deep breath, a sigh of satisfaction. 'No doubt you cursed the fate that made the boy pick my pocket . . . his own father's pocket.'

'Yes, I curse that night. And I curse ever having come to the police station. I should have let him take the consequences of his own action. Instead of that, I rushed to help him.' She shook her head and rolled her eyes in anguish. 'You could have knocked me down when I saw the "kindly gentleman" who was reluctant to press charges.'

'I was even more shocked when it was you who turned up to collect the boy. It was very wise of you not to block my generous gesture of offering him a good home. If you'd gone against me, I would have pressed charges and had him locked away for a very long time.' He regarded her with a deal of admiration. 'I must say you behaved very well in front of the officers present . . . never once letting the truth be known.' An unpleasant thought occurred to him. 'When you and the boy were allowed a minute together, you didn't tell him he was my son, did you?'

'I'm not altogether stupid.' She glanced nervously towards the public house. 'All these years that brute in there believed the boy to be his. If he knew I'd slept with another man . . . that he'd raised one of the gentry's kids.' She closed her eyes in anguish. 'You don't know him, Frank. He can be murderous.' There were tears in her eyes. 'The boy's run away before when they've rowed, so he's not suspicious.' A shadow washed over her face. 'But he's never stayed away too long, you see.' She appealed to Frank's good nature. 'I want the boy back. He's my only comfort.' His silence made her bold enough to threaten him one more time. 'I'm sure if your wife knew how the boy was got, he'd be shown the door right enough.' She trembled again, but this time it wasn't the cold that got to her, it was fear. Fear of the man she had deceived for so long. 'And if you should tell *him* . . .' Her round blue eyes stared defiantly. 'I suppose I could always take the boy where he'll never find us.'

'*I'll* find you though.' In the darkness his eyes glinted like broken glass. He was a gentle soul but when it came to the threat of losing Rita, he was prepared to do anything . . . even murder. He sensed her horror and forced himself to smile. 'Be sensible, my dear. And besides, what makes you think the boy would come with you?'

She had to be careful because he had no inkling that she had already been to his house, seeking to lure the boy home. His harsh words still haunted her dreams. 'He'd have no choice if he was thrown out.'

'I advise you to forget the whole idea.' His voice was cold as the night. 'The boy is my son . . . all my wife and I have ever craved. I really couldn't allow you to ruin everything.' Digging into his pocket, he withdrew a wallet. 'What will it take for you to forget he ever existed?'

She lashed out with her fist, sending the wallet flying to the pavement. 'I've told you! I don't want your filthy money!'

'What the bleedin' 'ell's going on?' The burly fellow had come in search of his mate. Unsteady from the booze, he studied the situation before squaring himself up to Frank. 'Why was this bastard offering you money?' Giving Frank a hefty push that sent him staggering back against the wall, he demanded, 'There's summat funny going on 'ere. What's your game, matey?' He drew a knife from his pocket and held it to Frank's throat. 'Out with it! Why were you offering my good woman money?'

'Leave him be!' Desperately afraid the truth might come out, she got between them. 'He was mistaken, that's all. The poor sod thought I was a prostitute.'

Far from calming him, her words appeared to enrage him. Swinging round, he caught her by the hair, twisting it over and over in his fist until she screamed for mercy. 'Thought you were a prostitute, eh?' he sneered. 'Why would he think that?' His

97

face was almost touching hers, his bloodshot eyeballs protruding from his head as he shook her like a rag doll. 'A man ain't likely to think a woman's a prostitute unless she gives him good cause. Is that what you did, you bitch? Did you give him good cause?' Raising his fist he brought it crashing down into the woman's face. 'Slag! Answer me! What made this bastard think you were a prostitute?'

'I don't know!' Kicking out with her foot, she tried desperately to throw him off balance. There was a fierce scuffle and the two of them fell to the ground. In the awful silence that followed, the woman stirred beneath the burly fellow, her sad blue eyes turned towards Frank. 'Make a little gentleman of him,' she whispered. Her head lolled to one side, she gave a sad smile and all was silent.

Stunned, Frank remained like a statue, unable to take his gaze from her face. A tiny trickle of blood oozed from her neck and dripped to the pavement. 'God above!' He couldn't believe what his own eyes told him. 'You've killed her!'

The burly fellow lay beside his woman, his head bleeding where it had come into contact with the wall. Barely conscious and groaning in pain, he made a valiant effort to stand up. But his strength gave out and he fell back with a thud.

While Frank made good his escape, a group of men came out of the public house. There was a cry of 'Murder!' and the sound of running footsteps. Frank didn't look back. 'I've done nothing wrong,' he told himself, and by the time he arrived at Blackburn station he was totally convinced it had all been a tragic nightmare.

CHAPTER FIVE

The small headline caught his attention and he froze:

WOMAN STABBED IN LONDON STREET

The account told of a lover's tiff, describing how the woman had been taken to hospital, where she remained in a very serious condition . . . 'not expected to survive'. The man with her was arrested and charged with the attack. His claim that another man was involved was being investigated but, according to witnesses who arrived on the scene before police, there was no sign of this other man. Another witness who knew the couple said this was not the first time the woman had been subjected to a violent attack by her husband.

'Thank God nobody saw me!' Tearing the newspaper into shreds, Frank stuffed it into his wastepaper basket. 'Cancel all newspapers from today,' he told Ruby at breakfast. 'They're an unnecessary expense.' He smiled at Jack across the table. 'Now that we've found you a suitable tutor, we mustn't waste money. Isn't that so, son?' He frowned, dabbing at his mouth with the napkin and seeming suddenly irritable. 'Though why you don't want to attend a fine school like Harlington, I will never know.'

'I would rather stay here with you and Mother.' Jack was wily. Here he could keep an eye on things and, more importantly, worm his way deeper into the Blackthorns' affections. He wasn't satisfied to share things with Cathy. He wanted it all.

Frank beamed with pride. Looking at Rita, he announced, 'Aren't you pleased, my dear? The boy would rather stay here with us. Why! I might have saved myself the bother of going to London after all.' He grew agitated. 'Rita dear . . . you haven't heard a word that's been said. Is anything the matter?'

Fearing he might come and actually put his big paws on her, she made herself smile. 'I heard every word,' she lied.

'And don't you agree, the boy is a treasure?'

'He is.' She bestowed a half smile on Jack. Lately she had lost all interest in him, not caring whether he went or stayed. In fact she cared for nothing but Owen and being with him for all time. Frank's interruption into her thoughts aggravated her. She felt unwell, acutely aware of the child growing inside her. Her nights were sleepless and she had been sick every morning for a week. Her only consolation was knowing that Owen was making plans for them to be together, and that at long last she would have a son of her own.

'The boy is quite the little gentleman now, wouldn't you say?' Frank insisted. 'Not at all like the wild thing that first burst into this dining room.' He laughed at the memory.

Glowering at Cathy, who had remained silent throughout, Rita answered deliberately, 'I believe he could teach the girl a few social graces.'

'How do you mean?' Up until then Frank had hardly noticed Cathy. He noticed her now and, like his wife, stared disapprovingly at her.

'Can't you see?' Pointing to Cathy's full plate, she said angrily, 'Good food . . . all wasted!'

It didn't matter to Frank whether Cathy had eaten her meal or not but he felt duty bound to chastise her. 'Really, young lady! I've only this minute explained to Jack that we should not waste money, and here you are, turning your nose up at Ruby's excellent food.' Leaning over the table he demanded, 'What have you to say for yourself, eh?'

Cathy had very little to say for herself, except, 'Sorry, Father. I'm not hungry.'

'Hmph! Sorry indeed. I should think so too.' He glanced at his wife, who was stony-faced. 'You've managed to offend your mother yet again,' he complained angrily. 'Leave the table this instant.'

As Cathy left the room, Margaret also excused herself. 'I have a great deal to do,' she said. In fact the truth was that these past few days since Jack had been taken out of her care, she had more time to call her own.

Cathy made straight for the kitchen, where Ruby was having a welcome cup of tea while she waited for the family to finish their meal. 'I'm sorry I didn't eat anything,' she told the homely soul. Sitting down at the big pine table she looked very lonely.

Ruby felt cheered at the sight of her. 'Aw, lass, yer don't have to apologise for not eating what I cook,' she gently chided. 'There's plenty folk round here who'll be glad of a few titbits.' Pointing to a large white bowl covered with muslin, she explained. 'There's bacon strips and plump sausages in there . . . all left over from yesterday.' Wiping her hands on her pinnie, she poured out another cup of tea. 'There! I'm sure you can manage that,' she said with a grin.

Taking up the cup, Cathy took a big sip. 'Thank you, Ruby.' She looked at the white bowl. 'What will you do with the bacon and sausages?'

'I shan't throw it in the midden, that's for sure,' Ruby declared, shaking her head indignantly and sinking her chin into her neck. 'Not while there's worse off than you and me. No indeed. Them's for the coalman. It's his day today, and he's got six childer who'll polish that lot off afore you can see the whites of their eyes.' She chuckled. 'They shall have a deal more an' all,' she promised.

Margaret had been concerned when she couldn't find Cathy upstairs in her room. 'Here you are,' she said, 'I've been looking everywhere for you.'

'The lass is having a cup o' tea.' Ruby quickly poured another from the big brown teapot. 'Sit yourself down, Miss,' she invited, pushing the teacup and saucer across the table. 'If you'll excuse me, I'd better go and see if they've finished.' With that she bustled away to see what was left for the coalman's brood.

Cathy was so quiet that Margaret was prompted to ask, 'Are you ill?'

'No.'

'What then?'

'I'm frightened.'

'Whatever do you mean?'

Cathy shrugged her shoulders. How could she explain to Margaret when she didn't even understand it herself? Lately, all manner of feelings had plagued her. 'Everything's changing,' she admitted sadly. 'Jack's going to a new tutor. Mother doesn't talk

101

to me at all any more except to rant and rave, and David's turned his back on me.' That was the hardest of all.

Without a word, Margaret took the girl in her arms. For a few precious minutes they stayed like that, shutting out the world. Presently, Margaret told her, 'Some things *have* changed, sweetheart. The world turns and things are bound to change. But some things remain the same. *I* haven't changed, and neither has Ruby. More than that, I really don't believe David has turned his back on you.'

'Why hasn't he been in touch then?' Teresa's words had cut deep. Even now Cathy believed them to have come from David himself. 'Why doesn't he wait by the stile like he used to?'

'I don't know for sure.' Margaret, too, had noticed how David was never at the stile when she and Cathy went on their frequent walks. 'Oh, I'm not saying he isn't angry about what happened with Jack. And I'm not saying he isn't just the teeniest bit jealous. On the other hand, he might be taking time to think about what happened ... to assess his relationship with this family. Then, of course, we have to remember he may be under pressure from his mother to keep a distance. Or it could be because of work. After all, there's the late potato crop to be got in and taken to market ... cabbages and brussels to be set. And after that, the land needs to be got ready for the next planting. When you realise there's only David and his father to do the work, it's not too surprising if he can't find the time for anything else.'

Cathy's spirits lightened. 'Do you think he'll get in touch when all the work's done?'

'I shouldn't be at all surprised.'

When Ruby came back, loaded with plates and dishes, Cathy offered to help her. 'My! You've cheered up an' no mistake,' she exclaimed. A few minutes later, she chased the two of them out of her kitchen. 'So I can get on with me duties, you understand,' she declared, blushing pleasantly when Cathy treated her to a big hug.

At twelve noon, after she had finished her lessons, Cathy accompanied Margaret to the drapers. The November day was bitter cold, so the two of them wrapped up well; Cathy in her ankle-length blue coat and matching beret, and Margaret in a brown cape with a hood. 'I don't intend to stay out long today,' she said. The sky was heavy with the threat of snow, and the icy wind cut right through a body's bones.

Teresa was just coming out of the butcher's. She would have gone on without speaking, but Margaret wanted to know, 'How is your mother?'

'She's all right.' As usual, Teresa was scowling. The threadbare coat she wore was no protection against the cold. 'We're *all* well,' she insisted.

'And David?' Margaret asked only for Cathy's sake. 'Is he still angry?'

'No. He ain't angry. But he don't want nothing to do with any of you.' She eyed Cathy with hidden malice. 'In fact, he said if I saw you, I was to say how he was very sorry about what happened. But it were only to be expected, and it's best if he don't have no more truck with you.'

'He really said *that*?' For Cathy's sake, Margaret had hoped there would be something left of the friendship between them. Now, though, it seemed David had chosen to sever all ties.

'I've just told you.' Teresa had seen how Cathy's face clouded over with disappointment, and she was in her element. 'Our mam was sick with worry when David told her he'd been fighting with the lad from Blackthorn House. She were convinced we'd be thrown out. The fact that we only got a warning letter from Mr Blackthorn himself don't make no difference. Next time it could be notice to quit. David should never have let himself get caught up in a fight with a Blackthorn. Not when they own the very roof over our heads! He knows his mistake now, and he has to put his own family first.' She glanced at Cathy. 'You do understand that, don't you?'

In spite of everything, she tried to understand. 'It was as much my fault as David's,' she said. 'But, yes, I do understand, and I'm sorry.' She was more than that. She was devastated.

'Should I go and see him?' she asked Margaret on the way back.

'No, sweetheart. I imagine David must have thought long and hard before coming to his decision, and however much it hurts, I want you to promise you'll abide by it.'

'I will,' Cathy murmured. As she looked up she was smiling. But the thought of never seeing David again, never sitting on the bank of the river with him, never laughing together or sharing little secrets, weighed heavy on her young heart.

Teresa chuckled all the way home. She was still chuckling when she passed the big barn. David saw her and came out. 'Have you been to the shops?' he asked. He had been mending the tractor and was covered in grease.

'What's it to you?'

'I just wondered, that's all.' Cathy was never out of his mind.

'What you mean is, did I see any of the Blackthorns?'

'Well, did you?'

'I saw the one who used to visit our mam.' She paused, making him suffer. 'She had the girl with her.'

'*Cathy*!' He could hardly contain himself. 'Did you speak to her?'

'I wasn't going to, but she spoke to me.'

'What did she say?'

'Only that you'd caused a lot of trouble by fighting with that other one. She said you should be ashamed, and hoped you would never speak to her again.' She delivered the torrent of lies without any sense of shame, or even the slightest tremor in her voice. She even feigned sympathy. 'I know I didn't always see eye to eye with you about the Blackthorns coming here,' she said softly, 'but I know how you liked the girl, and I'm really sorry.'

Turning away, he felt a great anger rising in him. 'Happen I should have known better,' he said harshly. If Cathy could throw aside their friendship just like that, maybe he'd been a fool all along. Telling himself that didn't help though. He still loved her. Whatever she did and however much distance she put between them, he would always love her.

CHAPTER SIX

Cathy loved the snow. For six days now it had poured relentlessly from the skies. She and Margaret had built four wonderful snowmen; there was one with a twisted nose and a loose mouth dressed with a twig for a cigar, another merry-faced, round-bellied fellow wearing one of Frank's discarded waistcoats and a pair of furry mittens, a third lumpy character who had fallen all to one side and resembled a drunk. And the latest, created on this Friday morning, and Cathy's favourite: small and chubby, with a toothless grin and bright round eyes made of black coal. It was dressed in one of Ruby's old shawls. On its head it wore a vivid pink home-made turban tied with an extravagant bow; Cathy had stuck various bits of bracken all round the edges of the turban, giving the illusion of a full head of hair beneath. The result was almost lifelike. 'By! You've used me for a model without me knowing,' Ruby chuckled. When she saw the three snowmen and one snowwoman all lined up outside the back door like visitors waiting to be let in, she screeched with feigned horror. 'It's no use you scraggy lot thinking yer can sit at my table, 'cause I'm particular who sits in my chairs. Be off!' Shaking the broom, she ran at them. 'Off with yer!' she yelled. 'Yer not getting in ol' Ruby's kitchen, an' that's a fact.'

She only stopped when Margaret and Cathy laughed out loud at her antics. 'Come away in, you two.' Breathless and full of fun, she gave her orders. 'Get in, I say. It's enough to freeze the nose off a parker out 'ere. I've a fresh brew o' tea made that'll warm yer blood rosy.'

'You two go in,' Margaret said. 'Thanks to Cathy dragging me outside, I still haven't put the school-books away.' She went one way and they went the other. 'Keep the tea hot, Ruby. I'll be along in a minute.'

Inside, sitting round the big friendly table, with her coat hanging over the hook in the kitchen door and the smell of meat pie emanating from the cooking range, Cathy felt warm and cosy. 'Did you ever make snowmen when you were young?' she asked Ruby, who was seated opposite. With her two hands wrapped round the cup Ruby had given her, she slowly sipped at the steaming hot tea, her face growing pinker by the minute.

'Did I make snowmen?' Ruby peered at her from beneath bushy eyebrows. 'Happen I did, and happen I didn't,' she said with a twinkle in her eye. 'It ain't one o' the things I recall most.'

Cathy grew curious. 'I can't imagine you being a girl,' she said truthfully.

'Well, I can promise you, I *were!*' Ruby winked, tossing her head with a little burst of pride. 'I weren't quite as pretty as yerself, mind. But I were slim and tidy, and I expect I did fancy meself just a bit.' She waited for the next question, and when it came it stunned her to silence.

'When you were my age, Ruby . . . did your mother and father love you?' Though she had wisely come to terms with her parents' indifference, it was something Cathy would never understand. Margaret had taught her to accept it, but it didn't make it any easier.

Ruby floundered. 'What a strange thing to say, child.' She knew well enough what Cathy meant, for wasn't it common knowledge in this household how Frank and Rita Blackthorn shamefully neglected their own daughter?

Lost in thought, Cathy spoke softly. 'I suppose they did love you, because parents *are* supposed to love their children, aren't they?' The whisper of a smile lit her features. 'When I had David I didn't mind so much. Now, I only have you and Margaret.'

'Aw, lass. You do miss that young fellow, don't you, eh?' Ruby chose not to comment on the disturbing subject of Cathy's parents. Lord knew they were a strange pair and, after all these years, she didn't understand them any better than Cathy did herself.

'David was special.'

'Ain't yer Aunt Margaret special?'

'Yes, but David was different.' She had often wondered about her feelings for him. 'I love Margaret more than I love my own parents.' She felt ashamed to admit such a thing, but was sure that Ruby would understand. 'With David, it was another kind of love, I think.'

'How do you mean, child?' Like Margaret, Ruby felt it was always best to let a niggling worry out into the open. She sensed that Cathy needed to talk, and so made time to listen. 'Is it because David and you are nearer each other's ages?'

Cathy thought on that. Feeling the need to put the record straight, she answered, 'No, it's more than that.'

'Hmh.' From what Ruby could tell, Cathy was in love. 'You're neither of you children any more, are you? What! When I were your age, I'd been in service for two years, and looking after the master's three young 'uns.' She shook her greying head at the memory. 'By! They were a handful an' no mistake.' Realising she had wandered off the point, she prompted, 'What were so special about David then?'

Cathy smiled and she was never more lovely. 'David seemed to know everything I was thinking,' she said. 'It was strange, Ruby . . . but when I was with him, it was like there was no one else in the whole world.' Her voice broke a little and she bent her head to take a sip of her tea. Using the moment to compose herself, she continued, 'Now he doesn't want to talk to me any more.' Suddenly she was conscious of how she had opened her heart. She blushed deeply and her brighter smile would have fooled anyone who didn't know her.

Ruby studied Cathy's pretty face for a while, before saying smartly, 'Shall I tell you what *I* think?'

'I'd like that.' Having known Ruby all her young life, Cathy trusted her implicitly.

'*I* think he's a fool to turn his back on a darling like yerself . . . especially when you've spent so much time teaching him to read and write an' all.'

'I really enjoyed doing that, Ruby, and you'd be surprised how quickly he learned.' Pride surged up in her. 'He was a natural scholar.' Being close to David, with their heads almost touching as they pored over the books, was a memory she would keep forever.

'Aye, well . . . I reckon he couldn't have been the friend you thought he was. What's more, I believe he'll want you long afore you want him, an' that's a fact.' Taking the empty cups she walked over to the sink. 'Men can be so ungrateful, an' ain't it true that he's a man in the making?'

'Did you mean what you said? About him wanting me before I want him?'

Coming back to the table with a cloth to wipe the spills, Ruby affirmed, 'Well, o' course! It's allus the same, lass. These men go off at the deep end, then soon enough they realise their mistake.' While she spoke she flicked the cloth over the table top before ambling back to the sink. 'The trick is to let 'em get on with it.'

'I thought I might go and see him, but Margaret says I ought not to.'

'What! I should think not, lass.' Turning to look at Cathy through knowing old eyes, she said softly, 'You were a fine friend to David Leyton. Either he values you or he don't. An' if he don't, then you're best off without him.' With that she began peeling the vegetables, thinking of all her regrets. Still, she had known the love of good parents, while this lovely girl had been hurt time and again. She thought of how David had hurt her now, and had to have her say. 'No, lass. If David Leyton don't want yer near, then stay well away. That's my advice if yer want it.'

It was bitter advice. 'I'd better go. Thank you for the tea, Ruby.'

'Aw, yer welcome, lass.' When she smiled her old face crinkled into a thousand lines. 'Think of what I've said now. But don't go telling that Jack I've entertained yer in the kitchen, 'cause I don't want him sitting at me table.' She gave one of her cheeky winks. 'What's more he got a right ticking off from your mam while you were out making your snowmen. He's been sulking in his room ever since, an' as far as I'm concerned he can stay there, 'cause I don't want him fetching his sour face down here, an' that's a fact!' She didn't say it in so many words, but she had never cared for the boy.

Cathy was surprised. As a rule, Jack was in favour with her mother. 'Why was he told off?'

'Too much to say for himself as usual,' Ruby retorted. 'I don't know it all, but for some reason known only to herself, your mam seems to have taken against him . . . wants him to go away to school after all, an' she's told your father the same.' Nodding her head in the direction of the door, she added softly, 'Yer mam and dad are in the study talking it over.'

'She really *likes* Jack.' Cathy was puzzled. 'Why would she want him to go away?'

'If you ask me, he's been getting above himself, that's why.' Ruby reminded herself to guard her tongue. Jack wasn't the only one Rita had been getting at lately. Only the other day she herself had got the length of Rita's tongue for nothing at all. 'If you ask me, I don't think yer mam's well.' She had seen the changes in Rita Blackthorn these past weeks. She had also been the one to clear up the morning sickness, and now she would stake her life on her mistress's being with child.

'What's wrong with her?' Cathy hadn't noticed anything. But then she was never allowed to stay in her mother's presence long enough to know whether she was ill or in the pink.

Ruby shrugged her shoulders. It was time to clam up, she thought. 'Don't ask me, lass,' she said innocently, 'I keep meself to meself, then I'm not likely to get in no bother.' Giving Cathy a sideways glance, she suggested, 'Happen it'd be best if you asked her yerself, eh? Now off you go, lass. Leave old Ruby to get on with her chores.'

On her way to the sitting room, Cathy paused outside her father's study. She could hear her parents, still arguing. On tiptoe she moved away.

Margaret bent to her work. 'Give me an hour,' she told Cathy. 'If I don't mark this work before dinner, I'll regret it later.' On seeing Cathy's thoughtful expression she put down her pen. 'What is it, sweetheart?'

'They're rowing . . . about Jack.'

Margaret nodded. 'I know,' she said. 'But it's nothing for you to worry about. It's just a question of whether he is sent away to school or not.'

'But he doesn't want to go.'

'Your father doesn't want him to go either. Your mother does, and they can't agree on it.' Putting an arm round Cathy's shoulders, she advised, 'Whatever you or I say, they'll make

109

their own minds up on the matter.'

Cathy was angry. She had suffered her parents' neglect long enough to know how they could hurt others. 'They don't care about people's feelings,' she declared. Casting her gaze to the table she saw the pile of correspondence there. Having taken up enough of Margaret's time, she was mortally sorry to have put her way behind on her work. 'I'll go and talk to Jack,' she said. 'He must be feeling miserable.' Before Margaret could object, she was out of the room and going up the stairs two at a time.

Jack was hopping mad. All his best laid plans were going out of the window. Having been fairly confident that he'd secured a worthy inheritance, he now sensed something going wrong. Lately there had been a definite lessening of Rita's affections. There was something about her that worried him, and he couldn't quite put his finger on the reason. 'Who is it?' The knock on the door startled him.

'It's Cathy.'

'Come to gloat, have you? Glad to see the back of me, are you?' At first he hadn't minded being sent to school. It seemed a laugh. Now, he felt he was losing control of the situation. He didn't want that at all.

'I've come to see if you're all right?'

'I'll be all right when people stop pushing me around. Now clear off and let me think.' He heard her run down the stairs, and for a minute he wondered whether he'd done the right thing in sending her away. After all, wasn't she one of the prizes?

Going to the mirror, he stared into it, admiring his reflection and thinking what a good-looking fellow he was. 'Don't forget she's the daughter of a landowner, and the prettiest thing you've ever seen ... yours for the taking, if you're very cunning.' And he prided himself on being the most cunning fellow there ever was. Sometimes, though, he longed for the streets again, ducking and diving and keeping an eye out for the richest pickings. The more he thought on it, the harder it was to keep up the identity he had adopted. In his mind he was back on the streets, and it felt good. 'Yer a bleedin' fool. 'Course she's a pretty little thing, an' there's no doubt she fancies yer.' He fancied himself too, swaggering a little and winking at the mirror. 'But she ain't what you come 'ere for. Why don't yer stuff yer pockets with all yer can carry an' make off?' The thought amused him. 'Ah! But then you'd lose it all, wouldn't yer, eh? The land, this big house, the cottage where the old lady lives . . .' He recalled the fight with David and a dark hatred rose in him. 'And think what a pleasure it would be to turf the Leytons out of house and home.'

There was something else too. Something he had kept to himself for too long. 'What about the precious Rita Blackthorn?' he asked himself; several times he had seen her and Owen Leyton, and each time had been an eye-opener. 'What would her old man say if he knew she'd been larking about with one of the peasants, eh? Skin her alive, like as not.' Falling on the bed, he stretched himself full-length. 'That's a card I've not played yet. I mean . . . it wouldn't be clever to rock the boat that's carrying me to a fortune. Oh, but let her talk him into sending me away and I just might be forced to make things very unpleasant for her.' He softly laughed at the idea.

He was still laughing to himself when suddenly there was pandemonium from downstairs. Panic-stricken, Frank's voice carried to every corner of the house as he ran into the hall. 'Margaret! Come quick. It's Rita!' He sounded frantic. 'Dear God above, I think she's dead!'

Rita wasn't dead, but according to the doctor, who was fetched to the house in no time at all, 'She's totally exhausted . . . in a state of anxiety.' He made sure she was recovered enough to sit up in bed before telling Frank, who was waiting outside the bedroom, 'You'll have to make certain she doesn't overdo things.'

'Oh, I won't!' Frank had suffered the fright of his life. Rita was everything to him, and he would be only half a man without her. 'Just tell me what I'm to do,' he pleaded. 'It was all my fault. We had an argument . . . Rita got excited and lost her temper.' He laughed nervously. 'You know how it is with these women.'

Looking sternly at Frank, the doctor chided, 'You should know better. I've already told your wife to take things easy and now it looks as if I'll have to confine her to bed for the duration of her pregnancy.' He saw the colour drain from Frank's face. 'You mean your wife hasn't told you?'

Frank couldn't believe his ears. 'Are you saying, she's . . . with child?'

'That's exactly what I'm saying. I'm sorry to have spoiled the surprise, but you would have known soon enough. Better now, when you can keep an eye on her.' He found himself talking to thin air as Frank rushed back into the bedroom. Shaking his head, the doctor went downstairs smiling. Margaret, equally astonished to discover that Rita was expecting, was waiting at the bottom with Ruby. 'See Mrs Blackthorn gets these as prescribed.' Handing a prescription to Ruby, he spoke briefly to Margaret before bidding them good day.

Upstairs, Frank caught hold of Rita's hand, his eyes sparkling with tears and his face aglow with love. 'You don't know how happy you've made me,' he said brokenly. 'Carrying my child . . .' He shook his head in disbelief. 'And you never even told me.' His trusting gaze roved his wife's handsome face, and he was stricken with such ferocious love that it frightened him. 'Oh, Rita! Rita! Why didn't you tell me?'

She wanted to tell him. But not the things he wanted to hear. She longed to say how it wasn't *his* child growing in her belly. She ached to belittle him by describing how she and Owen Leyton had made wild passionate love . . . the kind of love he could never give her. Love that he could never understand. But it was too early for the truth. She and Owen would be gone from here soon enough. When the plans were made and Owen came for her, she would tell Frank everything, and enjoy every minute of it. For now she had to play the game, however obnoxious. 'I suppose I should have told you, but no matter. You know now.' Pretending to be weak, she languished deeper into the bed. Draping her arm across her face, she whispered, 'I'm tired. Let me sleep.' All she wanted was to be rid of him. The touch of his hands on hers made her shrivel inside.

Bending to kiss her, he didn't realise how she cringed from him. 'Thank you, my darling,' he murmured. 'You've made me a very happy man.' His eyes lit up as he dreamed aloud. 'A son maybe. Who knows?'

Thoughts of Jack prompted her to speak. At first she had

allowed that dirty urchin into the house only to spite Cathy. Later she had come to believe he really could be a son to her. Now she wasn't sure whether he knew about her and Owen. Certainly he must have seen her leaving the barn that day. Then again, maybe he hadn't seen her at all. She might have imagined it, because he had never mentioned the incident. All the same, she could no longer abide being in the same house with him. 'Promise me you'll send the boy away.'

Even now, Frank was loth to do so. 'The doctor says you're not to worry or exert yourself.' He was greatly attached to Jack, which wasn't so surprising when the boy was his own flesh and blood. However, if Rita was to give him a son, he might find himself swayed by her wishes. Until then he must be careful not to upset her. Being evasive, he pleaded cautiously, 'Rest now, and I promise we'll talk about it when you're stronger.'

It would be weeks before Rita felt stronger. Meantime she was confined to her bed, growing more frustrated and bitter by the day. News of her condition quickly spread, the townspeople gossiped, and Owen, who still hadn't planned a way out of the awful situation, thanked his lucky stars that he had been temporarily reprieved. Then the snows came in earnest and many of the roads were cut off.

'When will it end?' Frank insisted on bringing her tray each morning. He brought it on this Friday and his smile was as loving as ever. 'I'll have to get a message to Owen Leyton,' he said. 'The timber yard has had to close, and as far as I know Leyton's the only one with a sizeable stock pile of logs. He'll fetch us a load, I'm sure of it.'

Rita could hardly hide her excitement. The thought of seeing Owen after all these weeks, even from a distance, was something to look forward to. 'You must ask him at once,' she urged. 'Ride over yourself if needs be.'

That was exactly what Frank did. From her bed, Rita craned her neck to look through the window. She watched him go and she watched him return. An hour later, just when she had given up hope and was lying miserably in her bed, she heard the scrunch of wheels in the snow.

Putting on her robe, she went to the window. It was him! Handsome as ever, Owen sat up front, his son directly behind him, and the logs piled so high they were in danger of rolling over the sides of the cart.

Eager to catch his attention she pressed herself close to the pane, waving her hand and softly calling his name. Concentrating on his work, he was oblivious to her. In a moment, though, her chance came. Jumping off the wagon to clear a way through to the outer yard, David left his father to check the horse, which had seemed to be limping. Rita held her breath. Owen was directly beneath her window. Seeing him so close and yet not being able to touch him was more than she could bear. Throwing caution to the winds, she began knocking on the window. At last he looked up, his eyes widening with fear when he saw it was Rita trying desperately to catch his attention. He would have turned away, pretending not to see her, but he knew if he did she would only persist. Suddenly Frank was alongside him, looking up too, waving and smiling, making silent words with his mouth. For the briefest moment she disappeared from their view, hiding behind the curtains until she felt sure that Frank had applied his attentions to other matters. When she peeped out again, he was standing back; never one for too much labour he was happy now to leave it all to others.

In that split second before Owen drove the cart on, he glanced up. When she blew a kiss, he seemed highly nervous, flicking his gaze from Frank to her. For one angry moment she thought he would leave without acknowledging her. An unreasonable rage took hold of her. But then he winked, and was instantly forgiven. In her joy, she couldn't know that he too was playing a game; the same kind of cruel game she was playing with Frank.

Cathy had seen the horse and cart arrive. From the scullery window she watched David help his father offload the logs. 'Do you think I should talk to him?' she asked Ruby.

'No, I don't!' Ruby was adamant. 'A lady would never run after a man.' She had been bending over the oven and her face was raspberry red. 'Let the men come after you,' she declared stoutly.

Disillusioned, Cathy put on her hat, coat and mittens and stood by the back door. She kept watch until all the logs were off and the empty cart pulled away. As it swung round towards her, David's gaze met hers. For one heart-stopping minute it seemed he would say something. Until he remembered how she had told Teresa she never wanted to speak with him again. Hurt and bewildered, he deliberately looked the other way.

'See that?' Ruby also had witnessed it. 'He ain't worth a second thought, lass.' Reluctantly, Cathy had to concede that Ruby might be right.

'What's up with you, son?' Even though Owen was steeped in his own problems, he couldn't help but notice how despondent David was. Easing the wagon along the snowbound lane, he glanced sideways at the young man. 'Something playing on your mind, is it?' Plagued with guilt, he was afraid David might have guessed at his affair with Rita Blackthorn.

'I'm all right.' That was all he said, but what he felt was far from it. He was heart-broken, and nothing would console him. Since losing Cathy, he had thrown his whole self into his work. At the end of the day he would come into the house dripping with sweat and bone tired; he washed and ate and did all the things that made a day pass quickly. In the evening he read the books which Cathy had brought to the house, going over the exercises and mastering the most difficult texts. But it didn't help. Nothing did.

Owen and his son continued the journey in silence, each heavy with his own heartache and each wondering how it had been allowed to come about. At the end of the journey, when the horse was unharnessed and the wagon upended against the barn wall, Owen strode through the snow to the house, while David sat for a while in the barn. Stony-faced and racked with regrets, he let Cathy swamp his thoughts.

The snows fell relentlessly over the next few weeks. It was well into December before the streets of Langho were clear and folk could move about in relative ease. The doctor visited Rita several times, and each time he was more pleased with her progress. 'Keep it up,' he told her, 'and it's possible I could let you sit downstairs of a morning.'

It wasn't enough for Rita. She wanted to go out. She needed to visit Owen, to persuade him that the time was right for them to go. She didn't want to have the baby here, nor did she want to spend one minute longer with Frank. She felt trapped, and all of her scheming wasn't enough to free her. She was even frustrated in her desire to have Jack sent away. On her first morning allowed downstairs, Frank made her comfortable in the drawing room before leaving to collect the tenants' rents. A few moments later, Jack came to see her.

'Thought I should come and see how you are,' he said. When he'd tapped on her door she hadn't realised who it was. If she had, he would never have gained admittance.

'I'm not well enough for visitors.' She was impatient and it showed.

'Just want a word with you, that's all.' He made no move towards her. Instead he closed the door and remained there, leaning against the wall, hands in pockets and looking every inch a cunning scoundrel. When he spoke again, his voice conveyed a threat. 'It's about me being sent to school.'

'What about it?'

'I'm not ready to leave yet.' He grinned. 'Same as you, eh? Biding my time . . . enjoying the things that keep me here.'

'What are you trying to say?' Her face grew red with anger. She knew well enough what he was getting at.

'That's just it. I don't want to say anything,' he replied meaningfully. 'Besides, I reckon it would be a real pity if you and me couldn't keep a secret, wouldn't it, eh? You and me . . . and Owen Leyton.' His sly grin left nothing to her imagination.

Incensed, she stared at him, her green eyes narrowed to dark glittering slits. 'You'll rue the day you ever threatened me!' she hissed.

He didn't reply but smiled a little then departed, leaving Rita shaking with rage. 'I won't let *anyone* spoil things,' she whispered after him, and there was murder in her heart.

Just as suddenly as the snows had started, they stopped. Two days before Christmas, the roads were clear and it was as if there had been no snow at all. Feeling cooped up, Jack decided to go for a walk across the fields. Cathy went with Margaret into Manchester, where they planned to buy all their Christmas presents. 'I wonder if David will send me a card?' she said when they climbed off the tram at the boulevard. 'I really miss him.'

'I thought you said he ignored you when he and his father brought those logs to the house?'

'He did.' For days she had thought about it, and even now it hurt to remember.

Margaret smiled at her. 'In that case, don't you think you should forget all about him?' She was secretly hurt by the way the Leytons had treated them both ... David deliberately ignoring Cathy, and Maria passing her in the street without a word of greeting. 'It doesn't do to dwell on what's gone.'

For a while Cathy lapsed into a deep and thoughtful silence. 'What's gone' Margaret had said, and it was true. David didn't want her any more and she must accept that. But it was the hardest thing she had ever been made to do.

The shops were full to bursting with Christmas cheer, presents and toys for even the most discerning buyer and, grateful that they were no longer trapped in their homes by the deluge of snow, people had poured out of their homes. For two hours, Cathy accompanied Margaret round the shops, wide-eyed and excited by the wonder of Christmas: the organ players lining the streets, the hot chestnut barrow and the vendors shouting their wares from the shop fronts.

'Fancy a rest?' Cathy's attention had been caught by the corner café from where the aroma of hot pies and fresh baked barm-cakes filled her nostrils. 'I'm starving,' she said. More than that, her arms ached from carrying all the things she'd bought. The meagre allowance she received from her father had been carefully put away until today. She had no need of money generally, so it was all kept for birthdays and Christmas. Giving brought more pleasure than receiving, she always thought.

'I shan't be sorry to rest my feet.' Margaret had spied the café and was already making for it. 'We'll have a cup of tea and a bite to eat, then we'll catch the next tram home. How's that?' With a grateful sigh she sat herself in the nearest chair and dropped her bags to the floor. Cathy sat opposite, her gaze drawn to the counter and the range of delicious cakes there.

'Yes, ma'am?' The waitress was a thin little thing, with wispy hair and two front teeth missing. 'Can I help you?' Taking the pen from behind her ear and the notepad from her pocket, she waited, impatiently tapping her foot against the floor tiles.

Cathy ordered a cup of tea and a custard slice, while Margaret was gasping for 'Just a big pot of tea, dear.' When the waitress had gone, she remarked, 'A bit surly, wasn't she?'

'I expect her feet ache,' Cathy said. She'd noticed how the waitress hobbled away, as though she had a marble under each shoe. Margaret agreed the poor thing must have been on her feet all day, and gave her a shilling tip. That brought the smile back to her sulky features.

On the homeward journey, Cathy made mention of something else that was on her mind. 'I think Mother's taken against Jack.'

'What makes you say that?' Margaret too had noticed the very same, but had kept the observation to herself.

'Just a feeling, that's all. She snaps at him all the time, and can't seem to bear him near her.' Something else had played on her mind and she had to mention it or burst. 'Margaret?'

'Yes?'

Cathy hesitated, but only for the briefest minute. 'Do you think Jack looks like Father?' Now that the words were out in the open, she felt curiously afraid.

Margaret stared at her, then shook her head and softly laughed. 'My! You do have a vivid imagination. No, I can't say I've noticed a likeness. But then, as the boy is no way blood-related to the family, I wouldn't expect to, would I?' Even so, Cathy had set her thinking. *Was* there a likeness between the boy and Frank? Could it be remotely possible that the boy was his? After all, he often spent time away in London, and Frank was no more resistant to temptation than any other man. Though he adored Rita, she was a cold and forbidding soul. A man like Frank needed warmth and affection. If he couldn't get it from his own wife, then he may well have fallen for the passing charms of some other woman; no doubt bitterly regretting it later. The idea grew in her mind. If he really *was* the boy's father, it would explain so many things . . . not least why he had brought a stranger into his home and taken him for adoption. It was certainly a fascinating and awful idea. Also, if it were true, Cathy would never see her father's money. Nor could she ever hope to win his favour because, when all was said and done, a man valued his son above all else; although where Frank was concerned, it was Rita who owned his soul.

The next day was Christmas Eve. Jack was in good spirits after being told he was not going away to school for at least another year. Margaret found herself studying him at every opportunity, searching for a likeness yet not being altogether certain. Rita stayed in her bed all morning. Ruby was 'Run off me feet!' preparing for Christmas Day. Frank bustled about getting ready to collect the weekly rents and, in the hope of seeing David, Cathy had no intention of letting her father go without her.

'Surely you're not collecting rents on Christmas Eve?' Margaret was appalled. 'Especially when they're not due until the end of the month.'

'If I left it till then they'd have spent the lot.' Putting on his warmest overcoat, he then grabbed a flat tweed cap from the hallstand and rammed it over his ears; next came a long brown scarf which he wrapped several times round his neck before peeling on a pair of thick kid gloves. 'Christmas Eve or not, I mean to have what's mine.' Slamming out of the door, he hurried to the barn, where he put the horse to the trap and led the ensemble out into the open.

'You don't mind if I come along, do you?' Cathy had followed him out. Dressed in boots and long coat with a blue beret pulled over her long fair hair, she was not prepared to take no for an answer. Before he'd opened his mouth to reply she had climbed on to the trap. 'I can hold the horse while you go in for your rents,' she offered brightly.

Exasperated, he climbed in alongside her. 'Damn and blast! I hadn't counted on taking a passenger.'

'Please, Father.'

Glancing sideways at her, he was momentarily shaken by her beauty. The girl is grown into a woman, he thought, and I never even noticed.

'You have a look of your mother,' he said, his voice filled with wonder. 'The same wonderful green eyes.' Cathy, however, had something Rita did not . . . a softness, a gentle quality that shone from her face and threw into the shade everything around her. For a time he was dazzled, unable to take his eyes off her. He had neglected her shamefully, but it was of no consequence. All the same, a huge surge of guilt fired his anger. 'You should have been a boy!' he snapped.

Though his words cut deep, Cathy made no comment. Her

silence only compounded his guilt. 'Hold on, dammit! If you fall off, I'll not stop to pick you up.' Grabbing the crop from its cradle, he snatched the reins and flicked them across the horse's rump. With a jolt it lurched forward, taking them at a frenzied pace along the winding lanes. If there had been anything coming in the opposite direction the two would have collided head on.

With her two hands clutching the bars either side of her, Cathy hung on for grim death. Only when they came in sight of the Leyton house did she begin to relax. The trap skidded to a halt. 'Stay where you are,' Frank ordered, jumping to the ground. 'And don't excite the horse.' Without a backward glance he went straight to the front door, where he banged his clenched fist loudly against the wood panel.

Getting down from her seat, Cathy stood by the horse's head. White foam was oozing out of its mouth and its back was sleek with sweat. 'And he told *me* not to excite you!' she remarked, tutting in disgust. Taking off her glove, she first wiped the foam away then ran the clean side along the animal's back. 'There, that must feel better,' she murmured. Her reward was a soft nuzzle and a wet face pressed into her hand. 'You stand still and behave,' she said, 'while I see if I can find you a bite to eat.'

She hoped David might be in the barn, but he wasn't. Disappointed, yet wondering whether he might have snubbed her yet again, she took a handful of hay from the stable and carried it out to the horse. 'Here were are.' Pushing a small handful towards him, she watched him greedily devour it. Soon the hay was gone and her father was striding down the path from the house, muttering to himself all the way.

'Damn tenants!' he snarled, climbing into the seat beside her. 'They never want to pay their way.'

As they passed the far field, David caught a glimpse of them. He mentioned it to Teresa on his return to the house. 'Happen if I'd been here, Cathy and I could have patched up our differences,' he said hopefully.

'I don't think so,' she answered, shaking her head and deliberately dashing his hopes. 'Her father was here demanding the rent early . . . got quite upset when he had to wait while Mam fetched her purse. As for the girl, well, I should put her right out of your mind if I were you.' She spoke quietly, hiding the malice that dwelt in her heart. 'She's no better than the rest of them. At least her father lowered himself to set foot in the house. Not her though. Oh, no. *She*'d rather stay out in the cold keeping the horse company.'

'Happen she thought she wouldn't be welcome.' He was clutching at straws.

'Don't you believe it.' Keeping her voice deliberately soft, she went on, 'I even went out to invite her in for a cup of tea. "Warm your bones it will," I said. But she wasn't having it. She simply shook her head and that was that.' She made a noise that sounded like a sigh. 'I'm sorry, David, but I did try my best to make friends, I really did.'

'No need for you to be sorry, sis,' he said bitterly. 'I reckon we'd best forget Miss Cathy Blackthorn.' His dark eyes blazed. 'It's plain to me now ... we're not good enough for her any more.'

'Isn't that what I've been saying all along,' Maria declared, coming into the room. 'Her sort will allus think they have a God-given right to insult the likes of us.' She was thinking more of Rita Blackthorn, her husband's latest plaything. For days now she had toyed with the idea of confronting him, but it would cause uproar and she didn't want the children to know. It was too shameful, and besides they had no idea their father could be capable of such badness. The time was close though when she would have to say something, for she had suffered in silence long enough.

Nan Foster met them at the door. 'Come in, do,' she said, ushering them inside and smiling graciously. 'I expect you've come for the rent?'

Frank was taken aback. 'How did you know that?' he mused aloud. 'It's not due for another week.'

'Oh, I'm not such an old fool as you might think,' she answered through a bright smile. 'You're a businessman. It would make sense to collect your money today ... before folks could spend it on Christmas foolishness.'

Taking off his cap he returned her smile. He and this gentle old lady hardly ever exchanged words, perhaps once a week, during the few minutes it took to sign her rent book and take her money. But the strangest thing happened to him whenever he was near her. He felt humbled somehow, inferior to her yet without knowing why. She had a peculiarly calming effect on him. Just now he had arrived in a sour mood and banged on her door every bit as hard as he had banged on the Leytons'. But the mere sight of the old lady standing there, with her serene face and quiet manner, had sobered him again. 'I do apologise for collecting the rent on Christmas Eve,' he told her. 'But, as you say, if I left it till next week there may well be none to collect.'

'I have it ready,' she declared. Going to the sideboard she opened a drawer and took out her rent book; inside was a small envelope, and inside that were a number of coins. She gave the book and envelope to him, and while he counted the coins into the palm of his hand she asked, 'How is your wife?'

After scribbling his signature into the rent book, he looked up. 'Why, she's much better, thank you.'

'Are you going away for Christmas, Nan?' Cathy had stood patiently by, but now she felt it was right to intervene.

'Away?' She shook her head. 'Where would I go? Who in their right mind would want an old woman like me at their Christmas table?'

'*I* would!' Cathy declared.

'And so would I!' Frank would never know what prompted him to offer such an invitation, but having blurted it out he felt obliged to follow it through. 'In fact, Mrs Foster, my wife and I would be pleased to have you as our Christmas guest.'

Cathy beamed from ear to ear, while Nan could only stare at her landlord with amazement. 'Oh, no. I couldn't impose. I didn't mean . . .'

'Please, Nan, do come.' Now that her father had done such an unpredictable thing, Cathy couldn't let it go. 'Father wouldn't have asked you if he didn't really want you to come.' Turning to Frank, she left him no way out. 'You do want her to come, don't you, Father?'

Wondering what possessed him, he stammered and coughed and finally remarked, 'Of course. Why else would I ask?' Suddenly the prospect didn't seem so daunting. 'Besides, isn't it the custom to share your dinner with those less fortunate than yourself?' His own words embarrassed him and he blushed to the roots of his hair. 'Do forgive me,' he pleaded. 'There are times when my tongue tends to run away with me.'

Nan smiled at that. 'As it did just now, when you asked me to sit at your table?' Before he could respond, she raised her long slim hand. 'I'm sorry, that was very ungracious of me. Of course I would be honoured to accept your kind invitation.' Her smile was telling. 'Though I'm not sure I agree with you ... about me being less fortunate than yourself.'

As he chivvied the horse and trap along the lanes, Frank still couldn't believe he had done such a foolhardy thing. 'Your mother will not be pleased.' Glancing at Cathy as though by some miracle she might rectify the situation, he wiped his hand over the sweat on his brow. 'What in God's name made me ask a complete stranger to Christmas dinner?'

'She's not a stranger.' In fact Cathy knew the old lady better even than she knew her own mother. 'Nan has impeccable manners and Mother will like her, I know.'

Rita was furious. 'I won't have that old woman at my table!'

'Be reasonable, dear.' Her grim face lowered Frank's spirits. 'All right, all right!' Thinking a compromise would pacify her, he said, 'My invitation had extended to the whole day, but I can restrict it to the evening meal only. Will that do?'

'I don't want her here at all. You must have been out of your mind. How dare you invite one of your tenants to sit at my table?' Frustrated because she had not heard one word from Owen, and suspecting he may have grown cold towards her, she took her temper out on the nearest person: Frank. 'If you insist on bringing that woman into this house, I shall remain in my room for the entire Christmas period.'

'It will be a happier Christmas without her,' Margaret quipped. But he didn't see it that way. Instead, he waited for Christmas Day like a man waiting for the gallows.

That night Cathy sat by her bedroom window counting the stars. Then she was counting the happy times she and David had spent together, and after a while, when the memories grew painful, she began counting the hours to when Nan would arrive.

Morning came and with it a clear bright day that chased away the deeper shadows of winter. 'Can I come with you to fetch Nan?' Cathy bombarded her father at breakfast. 'What time are you going for her? How long will she stay? Have you talked Mother round?'

'For goodness' sake!' Frank passed his hands over his closed eyes and bowed his head to the table. Looking up with hang-dog eyes, he said in slow deliberate tones, 'No, I have not talked your mother round. I have not yet decided the exact hour when I shall have to drag myself out in the cold to bring Mrs Foster here, nor have I an exact hour when I shall drive her home again. And, no! You may not come with me.' He glanced fondly at Jack, who was pretending to keep out of it all. 'As it happens, I've already promised Jack he can come for a ride.'

Jack couldn't resist a sly little smile. 'Sorry about that, Cathy,' he said. 'How was I to know you wanted to go?'

Sighing heavily, Frank addressed Cathy in a harsher voice. 'I hope that answers all your questions. Now kindly eat your breakfast, and don't say another word on the matter. I wish to God I had never invited the wretched woman in the first place.' His nerves were still jangling from Rita's tantrum when he'd taken up her tray just now.

Cathy wasn't finished though. All through breakfast she forced herself to keep quiet. But later, when her father strode across the hall towards the stairs, she waylaid him. 'Why won't Mother let me and Margaret put up a Christmas tree in the hall?'

'Because your mother is poorly, and if she is not in the mood for Christmas, then that's the end of that.' Glaring at her, he insisted, 'There will be no tree in this house, and no further argument on the matter. Is that clear?'

'If you say so.' Yet again he had managed to dampen her spirits.

She stood at the bottom of the stairs watching him climb every step as though it was the side of a mountain. At the top, he squared his shoulders and went at a smarter pace towards Rita's bedroom. From where she stood, Cathy heard him open the door and his voice as he called out, 'Hello, sweetheart. Here I am come to see you.'

The door closed and Rita's voice carried through it. 'Do you still mean to bring that woman here?' Frank must have answered yes, because in the next minute she was screeching like a fishwife, 'Damn you! Get out!'

On hearing the door flung open and her father's footsteps hurrying along the landing, Cathy wisely withdrew to the sitting room, where Margaret was putting out the presents. 'Are you sure you don't want to open yours now?' she asked as Cathy came in.

'No.' Cathy had already explained, 'I want us all to open our presents after dinner, when Nan's here.' The thought gave her a cosy feeling. 'Because Father hasn't allowed a tree, we'll have to set them out in the hearth. But it'll look nice, won't it?' She was more disappointed about the absence of a tree than she was prepared to admit. However, Margaret assured her that it would not take away the spirit of Christmas, and that Cathy was to 'Enjoy every minute of it.' And that was exactly what she decided to do.

The day rushed by; lunch was a brief affair, with only Margaret and Cathy at the table. 'Thank Gawd for that,' Ruby sighed, clearing away afterwards. 'I'm tuckered out. Lord knows I've enough to keep me busy, what with the house to clean and the washing to be done whether it rains or shines. On top of that I've been baking till I'm cross-eyed.' Staring at them both, she shook her head. 'There's enough mince pies, sausage rolls an' biscuits in that larder to feed a blessed army.' Waving her hand over the crockery on the table, she moaned, 'There's this lot to be washed and put away, the turkey to keep on basting, vegetables to be peeled and got ready, and on top of all that I've now got an extra guest to wait on at dinner.' She groaned as though someone had trodden on her bunions. 'What's a poor old soul to do, eh?' she asked, rolling her eyes to heaven and loudly tutting. 'I don't know.'

'I'll help you, Ruby.' Getting out of her chair, Cathy began gathering up the plates. No sooner had she collected two than they were snatched from her grasp.

'The very idea!' Ruby was bristling. 'You'll do no such thing, my girl. What! If I let you clear away the dishes, you'd be washing them up next. After that you'd want to make the beds and hang out the laundry. And what would Ruby do then, eh? She'd be out of a job and twiddling her thumbs, that's what.' Collecting the remaining plates she waddled out of the room, complaining all the way: 'The very idea! Ruby loves her work, that she does.'

At the door she flung them a challenging glance. 'And don't go telling folks I'm in a bad mood, because I ain't. Once the meal's ready and I'm ready to serve dinner, I shall have on me best pinnie, *and* me best smile. So don't forget *that*!'

With Ruby out of the room, Margaret couldn't help but laugh out loud. 'I think we'd better stay on the right side of Ruby,' she suggested. 'She's certainly got a bee in her bonnet today.'

'Do you think she's angry because Nan's coming to dinner?' Cathy couldn't recall Ruby ever being so annoyed.

'No. Of course not.' When she thought about it though, Margaret wasn't so sure. After all, Ruby was a proud little soul and she might take offence at having to wait on someone the mistress clearly didn't want at her table.

At precisely four o'clock, Frank and his son left for Nan Foster's cottage. Cathy watched them go. 'Nan won't be very comfortable squashed between those two,' she remarked.

Margaret came to the sitting-room window in time to see the trap turning the corner. 'I don't know why Jack wanted to go in the first place,' she commented. 'He doesn't even like Nan.'

'I don't think she's too fond of him either.' Frustration rose in Cathy. 'Do you think they'll be long before they're back?'

'Oh, about an hour, I should think. The snow deepened the potholes and with Nan aboard your father will have to drive more carefully than usual.'

Nan Foster was waiting for him. 'I'm not coming,' she said, before inviting the man and the boy inside. She was still wearing the same clothes she had worn the day before, her hair was very slightly dishevelled and there were dark rings beneath her eyes that suggested she had suffered a bad night.

'Are you ill?' Frank could barely hide his relief at her change of heart.

'No, I'm not ill,' she replied. 'Though I must admit I've had a sleepless night.' Taking a deep breath, she invited the man to be seated, but not the boy. Instead, she made a request. 'I would be very grateful if you could perhaps go for a short walk along the lanes? I have something very private to discuss with Mr Blackthorn.' Anxiously she glanced from one to the other. 'I assumed you would be alone,' she told Frank. Addressing Jack, she said, 'I'm sorry, but it shouldn't take too long.'

Frank was intrigued, but irritated. 'And *I'm* sorry if you're about to ask for a rent reduction, because the answer must be a resounding no.'

'It has nothing to do with the rent,' she assured him, beginning to relax. It was good to know that she had him at a disadvantage.

'And it can't wait? This "private" discussion?'

'It's waited too long already.' All night she had listened to her conscience and it told her she must reveal the truth before it was too late. She saw how the situation was developing between the boy and the man, and sensed that it must be now or never.

'Off you go then, Jack.' Reluctantly Frank dismissed his son. 'Don't wander too far though. I'm sure this little matter won't keep me.'

But it did keep him. More than that, he was shocked to the core when Nan Foster told him what was on her mind. First, though, she made him as comfortable as possible, and then she began her story. It was an astonishing one, a tale of adultery and unhappiness, of two people going their separate ways; it was a harrowing account of innocent children and desertion, of regrets and heartbreaking secrets. 'Please hear me out before you say anything,' she begged. 'I want you to know that I'm telling you all of this not for gain or spite, but to right a wrong. After it's done, I'll go away and never come back, if that's what you want.'

While she told her tale, Frank listened in silence, gasping now and then with horror and reeling back in the chair with astonishment. 'I was young and naive when I married Joshua Blackthorn. If you have learned anything at all about your father, you must know he was the laziest man on God's earth, a philanderer who gambled away most of your inheritance, a womaniser who broke my heart time and again. I stood it all, until one evening he arrived home drunk, in a foul and fighting mood after having lost a great deal of money. I knew I couldn't stand it much longer, and so I planned to leave him.'

'Are you telling me...' Frank swallowed hard, unable for a minute to mouth the words that pounded his brain. Shaking his head slowly from side to side, he spoke in a low choking voice. 'Are you saying... you're my... *mother*?' Convinced he was in the throes of a dream, he actually smiled.

She hesitated, lowering her gaze to the floor as it all came flooding back. 'I wanted to take you and Margaret with me, but he wouldn't allow it. He threatened to track me down and punish me if I took you away. And I have no doubt that's exactly what he would have done. If I believed for one minute that he might have hurt you or your sister, I would never have left you there. But, for all his failings, he adored his children... especially you, Frank, his only son.' She wrung her hands in despair as the guilt that had haunted her all these years bore down on her. 'I loved you too, but so help me, I could not stay one minute longer with a man who beat me so much that the child I carried was lost.' She saw the growing horror on Frank's face and had to assure him, 'Oh, yes, but for him you might have had another sister, or even a brother. Oh, I'm not saying there weren't times when he could be a good man, but as he grew older the other times became more and more frequent until I didn't even know him any more.'

As he listened to her story, all manner of emotions assailed him. He suspected his father had been everything she said. But he and Margaret had grown up hating the mother who had deserted them. If this was she, if this woman was his mother, he wanted to hurt her as she had hurt him. 'How do I know you're telling me the truth!' Springing out of the chair, he stood over her. 'For all I know you're an imposter, out for what you can get. Do you plan to lay claim to the estate? Is that what this is all about? Because I'm warning you now, I'll fight you all the way.'

'I'm telling you the truth.' Her voice was calm, her manner gracious. Going to the dresser drawer, she took out a sheaf of papers. 'It's all there,' she told him softly. 'The marriage certificate, birth certificates and other proof.' When he snatched them up and pored upon their every word, she went on softly, 'I've never stopped loving you. Wherever I went, you and Margaret were in my heart.'

In a rage he threw the papers at her. 'All right!' He had seen for himself that she was indeed the same woman who had deserted them long ago, and hatred burned in him like a beacon. 'So you're who you say you are . . . Joshua's wife . . . my mother.' His voice broke on a sob. 'What do you expect me to do? Would you like me to fall at your feet and thank the good Lord for bringing you back? Well, I can't! I WON'T!' The tears rolled down his face. 'How can I ever forgive you? And Margaret? What do you expect of us? Tell me, dammit!'

'I don't expect anything at all.' The old lady knew she had hurt him, but it had to be done. 'Not for myself anyway.' She could feel herself trembling all over. The ordeal had been too much, yet she had to go on. For Cathy's sake, she must see it through. 'Your father and I were never divorced. After he died I could have stepped in and claimed his estate, but I didn't. And I won't now.' Soberly regarding him, she went on in a calm deliberate voice, 'I won't make a nuisance of myself. Unless, of course, you mean to cheat Cathy out of her rightful inheritance.'

'Explain yourself.' He was so chilled with loathing he could hardly speak.

'This boy . . . Jack. If you have a mind to place him above Cathy, to make him sole beneficiary of your will, I can't stand by and see that happen.' She smiled then, a smile that told him to be cautious. 'Of course you could assure me that was not the case, but I would never be sure. To that end, I have taken the liberty of making an appointment with my solicitor in Blackburn. No doubt he can produce a watertight and legal document that will safeguard Cathy's rights.'

'You won't get a penny out of me!'

She rose from the chair, her manner every bit that of a hostess seeing off her guest. 'Goodbye, Frank,' she said a little sadly. 'What a pity you've chosen the hard way. You've seen the documents, and you know I have a substantial claim. As I said, I don't want anything for myself, but I will not allow that urchin to rob my grand-daughter.' With that, she went to the door and opened it wide. 'So kind of you to invite me to dinner,' she said in a matter-of-fact voice, 'but you can see now why I really could not accept.'

Storming past her, he paused, glowering down on her through

rage-filled eyes. 'I want you out of here tonight. This is *my* property.'

'Are you sure?' she asked, and her smile infuriated him.

Curious, Jack had hidden himself beneath the window. He had heard every word and was fascinated. When the door was opened, he quickly scurried round the back, emerging only when his name was called. As he sauntered to the trap, he looked back at the old lady and a hardness came into his voice as he murmured, 'So, you reckon you'll undo everything I've done so far, do you?' He chuckled. ''Fraid not, lady. The day ain't 'ere when an old woman can get the better o' me.'

'Look at that! It's a crying shame, that's what it is.' Ruby stood at the head of the table with her hands on her hips and a look of frustration on her face. 'What's going on? Where is everybody? And what's the matter with you two? Lost yer appetite, 'ave yer, eh?' Having slaved all day in the kitchen and set out the most beautiful Christmas table, she was deeply upset to see only Margaret and Cathy attend for dinner, and neither of them in good spirits. 'Is it me food? 'Ave I disappointed yer?' She looked from one to the other, waiting for some kind of explanation.

Cathy had been lost in thought, but at Ruby's hurt tones she looked up with a quick smile. 'Please don't take offence, Ruby,' she pleaded. 'It's nothing to do with you. The food is lovely and I'm sure you've set the best Christmas table in the whole of Lancashire.' She hated seeing that dear soul so upset.

'If that's the case, why ain't yer eating yer dinner?'

'I'm not all that hungry at the moment,' Cathy admitted. 'But I intend to have a little of everything.' Taking up her plate she collected a slice of plump white turkey, two roasted potatoes, half a dozen small round brussels, and a measure of cranberry sauce. 'I'll eat it all,' she promised. 'Afterwards I mean to have a helping of your delicious pudding and a mince pie.' Picking up her knife and fork she ate the first mouthful, and, though it was beautifully cooked, it stuck in her throat like a piece of wood. She'd had visions of everyone enjoying their Christmas dinner together . . . like a real family. Now, it was all spoiled.

Ruby watched her for a minute then, coming to where she

sat, put her hand on Cathy's head, saying fondly, 'Aw, it don't matter, lass. You don't have to force it down just to please old Ruby. I know how disappointed you are that the old lady couldn't come to dinner, and I know yer'd rather ye mam and dad were seated at the table with yer.' She didn't mention Jack because she still saw him as an intruder in this household. She had been here many long years and had learned to ride the storms. But that boy was unnatural. It didn't matter to Ruby that her master was besotted with his 'son'. He didn't belong, that was all, and as far as she was concerned, he never would.

Glancing at Margaret who as yet had said nothing, she apologised softly. 'I'm sorry, Miss. The both of yer 'ave allus been good friends to me, and if there's summat on yer minds that teks away yer appetites, well, what I mean is, I ain't got no right to make yer feel guilty.'

'It's us who should apologise,' Margaret insisted. 'We know how hard you've worked, and honestly, Ruby, it really is a lovely spread.' She looked regretfully at the table. 'But I'm afraid you're right. We *do* seem to have lost our appetites.' Since Frank returned from Nan Foster's there had been a very disturbing atmosphere in this house. It had seemed to affect all of them, with the exception of Ruby, who was no doubt too busy preparing this feast to sense anything unusual.

'Aye, well, happen everyone will feel peckish enough to finish the lot before you go to bed, eh?' Ruby was living in hope.

'Ruby?' Cathy reached up to touch her hand.

'What is it, lass?'

'Has Father said anything to you?'

'What about?'

'About why Nan Foster didn't come to dinner?' She had been waiting at the door when he returned. But when she ran out to ask why Nan wasn't with him, he impatiently brushed past her and went into his study. He hadn't been out since.

Ruby shook her grey head. 'He ain't said a blessed word. 'Course I noticed the Foster woman weren't here, an' I wondered whether I should set a place for her at the table.' Her irritation was betrayed when she looked fiercely towards the door. 'Twice I tapped on the study door to ask what I should do, an' all I got for me trouble was the order to "Go away, damn you!" ' She looked at Cathy, then she looked at Margaret, and her face tightened. 'I ask you, Miss, is that the way to speak to folks as is just trying to help?'

'It's no way to speak at all, Ruby,' Margaret agreed. 'You're quite right to be angry.' Something puzzled her. 'Have you seen Jack since he and Mr Blackthorn returned?'

'Ain't seen hide nor hair of 'im.' She didn't want to neither.

'And Mrs Blackthorn?'

'She won't even let me take a tray up.' Her little round body stiffened. 'What's more, she sent me off with the length of her tongue. Humph! Seems manners are a thing o' the past.' Looking down at Jack's place, she added haughtily, 'And that boy is just as rude. Where is he, eh? Why isn't he at the table, that's what I'd like to know.' Thinking she might overstep the mark, or that the master would suddenly appear and give her what for, she thought it time to excuse herself. 'Eat what you fancy,' she told them. 'The rest will allus keep.'

When she had disappeared into the kitchen, Cathy's curiosity got the better of her. 'Where *is* Jack, do you think?'

Margaret had no idea. 'I saw him only briefly when your father returned.' As she recalled, the boy had been deep in thought, almost colliding with her when she crossed the hall. 'I expect he's gone to his room.' She dabbed the napkin at each corner of her mouth. 'I mean to have words with him at the first opportunity. If he had no intention of joining us for dinner, he might have had the common courtesy to let Ruby know.'

'He's not in his room.'

'Oh? How do you know that?'

'Because when I came past just now, the door was wide open.'

'Well, he can't have gone far.' Margaret glanced at the mantelpiece clock which told her it was five minutes to eight. A glimpse through the window prompted the remark, 'It's dark outside, so I should imagine he must be in the study with your father.' She recalled Frank's red face and obvious rage when he returned from Nan's. The boy, too, had been in a strange mood. 'He may well have incurred your father's displeasure for some reason or another,' she deduced. 'He's probably getting a ticking off right this minute.'

Cathy thought about that and was forced to reply, 'If he is, it's a very quiet ticking off, because I haven't heard a sound since Father went into his study.' All the same it wasn't important enough for her to dwell on it. 'I think I'll go and see if Mother wants a tray.'

'Rather you than me.' Margaret was always humbled by the manner in which Cathy refused to be shut out of her mother's life. 'It's a kind idea,' she encouraged. 'It isn't healthy for her to go without food in her condition. By now I should imagine she must be starving, though I don't expect she'll admit it.'

Cathy tapped gently on the door. 'Mother, would you like me to fetch you a tray? Ruby's cooked a wonderful Christmas dinner. I know she'd be pleased if I brought you a few titbits?'

The answer was a harsh one. 'Get away from my door. I want nothing, do you understand? I want *nothing!*' Taking a paperweight from the dresser, Rita flung it with all her strength against the door. She heard a small cry as Cathy reeled back from the almighty thud, then the sound of footsteps as her daughter reluctantly retreated.

Laughing aloud Rita threw herself on the bed, her laughter turning to tears as the pain pierced her side. Gripping her stomach with both hands she rocked herself back and forth. 'I'm hurt,' she moaned. Her voice rose to a higher pitch as she surveyed the dent in the wood-panelled door, beneath which the paperweight lay. 'Why can't you all leave me alone... knocking on my door, worrying me about this or that? Now see what you've done!' Writhing from side to side in a frenzy, she whispered hoarsely, 'I want none of you. Only Owen. *He's* all that matters to me now.'

Rising from the bed she hobbled to the dressing table, where she studied herself in the mirror. 'Where is he?' she asked in anguish. 'He must know I'm house-bound. Why hasn't he found a way to let me know what he's planned?' Groaning from the depths of her soul, she ran her hands distractedly through her hair, wincing when it caused her pain.

Agitated beyond endurance, she dropped into the chair and bent her head into her hands. 'I can't stand being cooped up in this house any longer!' Looking up with wild eyes, she stared into the mirror, examining her every feature as though she was examining a stranger. 'You're very beautiful, Rita,' she murmured deviously. 'Any man would want you for his own, and Owen is no exception.' She regarded herself carefully; smiling into the cat-green eyes, tenderly touching the wonderful high cheekbones and caressing the long dark hair that hung round her shoulders like the spill of midnight.

'Tomorrow morning, Owen,' she whispered, and the smile slid from her face. The pain was shooting all over her body, but she was determined. 'You've had enough time to get in touch with me. Now I must come and find you. I need you to tell me you have a plan now, a plan to get us away from here, to set us up somewhere together, you and me and our son.' She touched her fingers against the mound beneath her robe. 'It's growing inside me, Owen,' she muttered. 'Your seed is growing inside me.'

Suddenly she was ripping the clothes from her back. In a frantic moment she was stark naked. Turning sideways she regarded the mound of pink skin, a swollen tight mass that was pushing out from her slim form. 'You've made me ugly,' she whispered bitterly. 'I was never made for carrying children. But this is your son, Owen, yours and mine, and you have to take us away from here.' Swinging round to see herself full on, she said softly, 'In the morning, Owen.' The thought gave her a deal of pleasure. 'You've had time enough.'

Downstairs, Frank paced his study like a caged animal. 'I can't tell Margaret,' he moaned to himself. 'How can I tell her the woman we thought was dead so long ago is here, renting our cottage ... waiting to rob us of everything we own?' His eyes glittered as a thought struck home. 'My God! It wouldn't surprise me if Margaret didn't know already. Of course! That's why she's befriended the old witch. And Margaret has never taken to Jack ... wanted him out the minute he set foot across the threshold. It all becomes clear now ... the pair of them are in on it!' He was so astounded by his thoughts that he had to sit down.

His mind was racing ahead, telling him this, telling him that. 'NO!' Common sense prevailed. 'Margaret is too honest. If she'd known who that woman was, she would have told me long ago. The truth is more likely to be that the cunning Foster woman is out to rob Margaret as well.' He began pacing again. 'Should I tell her?' He shook his head. 'No. Think, Frank. Think hard about what happened after she ran out on you. Remember how your sister cried for her mother ... how, when she was old enough she searched long and hard, until Father was forced to say that Mother had died? Remember how Margaret ached for her ... yearned for her? My God! If I was to tell her what was told me this very day, she'd likely throw herself into the arms of that old witch ... rejoicing at the return of her long-lost mother.' The idea was unthinkable.

Going to the desk, he leaned his hands on it and straightened his back, his head bent forward and his eyes closed. 'I can't tell her, and I can't let any of them dictate my life. I *won't!*'

Beating his fist on the desk, he opened his eyes just a little, lost in a trance as he stared at the brass ink-holder. 'If that witch thinks I'm just going to stand back and let her tell me what to do, she couldn't be more wrong. *I'll see her dead first!*'

Margaret was coming across the hall when Frank came bursting out of the study, almost careering into her as he rushed to the front door. He was further irritated when she dared to question him. 'Where on earth are you going at this time of night?'

'Out!' he snapped. 'I have to get some fresh air.'

'Oh, you'll get that all right.' She smiled. 'It's bitter cold out there.' Glancing at his attire, she remarked thankfully, 'At least you're dressed for the night air.' He had on his cap and coat, and was even wearing gloves.

Affording her a withering glance, he advised, 'Don't concern yourself about where I'm going. Or when I'm likely to be back.' With that he stormed out, slamming the door behind him.

When Margaret turned round it was to see Cathy approaching. 'That's funny,' Cathy remarked thoughtfully.

'Oh? What's that?'

'Ruby said Jack was in with Father. Getting a ticking off, she said.' Cathy looked from the study door to the foot of the stairs, and finally brought her gaze to rest on the door through which her father had just departed. 'If he was in the study with Father, where is he now?'

Shrugging her shoulders, Margaret suggested, 'He probably went straight up to his room after your father was finished with him.' A little smile curled the corners of her mouth. 'And from

135

what I've just seen of my dear brother, I can imagine Jack got more than a ticking off. In fact, it wouldn't surprise me if we didn't see him until tomorrow morning.' Draping her arm around Cathy's shoulders, she suggested, 'How about you and me sewing some more squares for Nan's eiderdown?'

'I'd like that,' Cathy replied. It was to be a surprise for Nan's next birthday, a beautiful chequered eiderdown to match her pretty cushions. It was a slow tedious job, and they would need every spare minute to have it finished in time.

As the two of them walked to the drawing room, they chatted about all the things that had recently touched them ... Rita's continuing foul moods, Frank's obsession with her, and Jack. He was the apple of Frank's eye, the apple that had upset the cart. Margaret couldn't really forgive him for that, but she kept that particular thought to herself. And, though Cathy had cause to resent him more than most, she had gone out of her way to accept him. Albeit in different ways, she saw in him a soul as lonely and deprived as herself, though she still hadn't altogether forgiven him for having picked a fight with David and ruining what had been a beautiful friendship.

'If there's time enough, I thought we might perhaps sew two pillow-cases to match the eiderdown.' Going up the stairs to her bedroom where the sewing was kept, Margaret glanced at Cathy. 'What do you think, sweetheart?' Cathy hadn't heard. She seemed a million miles away. 'Cathy? Did you hear what I said?'

Talking about Jack had raised thoughts of David. She thought of him often. She was thinking of him now. And she missed him so much.

'Sorry, yes, I heard what you said,' she apologised. 'I think it's a lovely idea and if we're going to get it all done, we'll have to work extra hard.' In fact it occurred to her that the eiderdown and pillow-cases might be a blessing in disguise, for if the sewing took up her every spare minute it might ease the loneliness of being without David.

Nan Foster felt unusually disquieted. Ever since her confrontation with Frank, she had been swamped with guilt. 'You did right though.' Rocking back and forth in the old wooden chair, she chided herself, 'No one can blame you for what you did all those years ago.'

All the same she wished it hadn't come to this, threatening her own son. 'I came here to be close to my children,' she murmured regretfully. 'Margaret is everything I hoped she would be, and Frank is blinded only by his obsession for that wife of his. As for the boy, he's rotten at the core. I feel in my bones he has no real affection for Frank. He's out to get what he can, even at the expense of Cathy.'

Her eyes softened at the mention of Cathy's name. 'What a darling creature she is,' she whispered lovingly. 'No wonder Margaret adores her. And how can I stand by and see her robbed?' Her determination had not wavered.

Tired out by events which had overtaken her, she closed her eyes and rocked a while. The warmth of the fire was soothing, lulling her thoughts and bringing a glow to her face. She slumbered awhile, her dreams uneasy.

She didn't hear the intruder creeping up on her. The log came crashing down against her temple and she fell sideways, her eyes still open, still staring. It took a few frantic minutes to search for valuables, then there was a burst of soft laughter as the intruder fled, leaving the door wide open and the cold dark night rushing in.

'I tell you, I don't want a doctor. He'll only make me stay in bed. I'll go mad if I don't soon get out of this house.' Rita was in a shocking state, clutching her side and crying in agony. 'It was *her* . . . that daughter of yours. *She* did this!'

Frank was a man in torment. 'What do you mean? How could Cathy do this to you?' When he'd returned home late, Rita was waiting for him at the bedroom door. She had replaced the paperweight on the dresser, and as yet he hadn't seen the dent in the door-panel, so when she accused Cathy he was concerned and curious all at the same time.

'By getting me all riled up, that's how!' came the retort. 'All I want is a drink . . . something stronger than tea.' Rolling on to the bed, she gave a little cry of pain.

'You'll have a doctor, that's what you'll have,' he said, easing her into the bed. And no amount of bullying from Rita could change his mind.

When the doctor arrived, Cathy was wide awake. After looking out of the window and seeing whose trap had come to the house, she went into Margaret's room. 'The doctor's here,' she whispered. Together the two of them went out on to the landing. Jack was there. Bleary-eyed and dishevelled, he lazily tied the belt of his robe. 'What's going on?'

When told it was the doctor, come to see Rita, he yawned. 'Oh, that's all right then.' He seemed relieved. A minute later he was back in his bed, with the door closed against the world.

Rita's bedroom door opened and Frank came out. His face was a ghastly shade of grey and there were bags under his eyes. 'I should have been here,' he moaned. Rubbing his hand over his face, he peered at them through his fingers. 'God almighty, I should have been here. If she loses that child ... if anything happens to my Rita, I'll never forgive myself.'

The three of them waited and waited, and it seemed an age before the doctor emerged. 'She'll be fine,' he promised. Taking Frank by the arm, he walked with him to the foot of the stairs. 'She's twisted a muscle, that's all, though of course she can be forgiven for thinking it might be much worse.' He smiled reassuringly. 'Women easily frighten when they're with child.'

Frank nearly fainted with relief. 'She'll be all right then? Her and the child?'

'She's stronger than when I last saw her, and yes, they'll be all right, Mr Blackthorn. However, just to be on the safe side, I've confined her to bed for at least another week.' He saw the look on Frank's face, and patted him on the shoulder. 'I know she doesn't like it, but doctor knows best, I think.' He went then, leaving Frank to face the bitter end of his wife's tongue.

The strange thing was, Rita had very little to say. After relaying the doctor's diagnosis to Margaret and Cathy, who had been anxiously waiting, Frank returned to his wife's bedroom. 'Please be patient, my dear,' he begged, closing the door. 'I know how you loathe being shut up, but it won't be for long, and it is for your own good after all ...' He would have gone on, but her stillness silenced him. 'Rita?' Creeping up to the bed, he was fearful of what he might find.

What he found was Rita seemingly fast asleep, so he drew the blankets over her shoulders, kissed her on the forehead and tiptoed out. 'Good night, my dear,' he whispered from the door. 'I'll see you in the morning.'

When the door was closed, her eyes instantly opened, and they were alive with hatred.

In the morning, the whole house was rudely awakened by the sound of Ruby hammering on her master's door. 'Come quickly, Sir,' she cried. 'It's the authorities to see you. Real urgent, they said.'

Cathy was the first one out on the landing. Running across the carpet in bare feet, she asked breathlessly, 'What is it, Ruby? What's the matter?'

Before she could reply, Frank flung open his door. 'Have you all gone mad? What do you mean by hammering on my door at this time of morning? I've had no sleep . . . no sleep at all, dammit!' All night long he had drifted in and out of sleep, waking with a sweat on him, his every nerve-ending crying out to lie with his wife, to feel the warmth of her body against his. And now to be jolted out of his first few minutes of real sleep was more than he could stand. 'Out with it, woman! What is so important that you have to knock down my door?'

Her manner somewhat subdued by the sight of him with his hair standing on end and his robe flung wide open, Ruby stepped back a pace. 'I know it's only seven o'clock,' she answered. 'I'm really sorry, Sir, but it's the authorities, you see.'

'The authorities? What in God's name do they want with me?'

'They didn't say exactly, only that I was to wake you as it was urgent.'

He pursed his lips and thought hard before briskly ordering, 'Very well. Inform them I'll be right down. Oh, and wake Miss Margaret, would you?'

Margaret was already awake. She and Cathy were washed, dressed and only five minutes behind him. When they arrived in the drawing room, it was to find Frank seated in a chair. There were two constables standing by the door, and seated opposite Frank was a thin balding man in a dark blue suit. On Margaret and Cathy's arrival, he stood up and greeted them. 'Good morning. Forgive me for getting you from your beds at this hour.' Addressing Margaret, he declared, 'I assume you must be Miss Margaret Blackthorn?'

'That's right.' Drawing Cathy closer, she explained, 'And this is my niece, Cathy Blackthorn.'

'I am Inspector Collins, and these are my colleagues.' Pointing to the uniformed men, he told them sharply, 'It might be better if you waited outside in the hall.'

Frank spoke in a low serious voice. 'The girl.' Glancing at Cathy, he flicked a hand to dismiss her. 'There is no need for her to stay.'

Margaret instinctively knew it was the right decision. 'It might be best if you go and talk to Ruby,' she suggested.

Reluctantly, but with little choice, Cathy went without delay. As she closed the door behind her, she heard her father relating the awful news to Margaret, and his words struck horror to her young heart.

'It's that friend of yours and Cathy's ... Mrs Foster.' There was a slight pause, then, 'Young David Leyton was making a delivery of logs early this morning when he found the door wide open and the old lady still in her rocking chair.' Another pause, while Cathy lingered with her heart in her mouth. '*Murdered!*'

Unable to believe what she was hearing, Cathy fled to the kitchen where she fell sobbing into Ruby's arms, pouring out what she had overheard. 'It's not true, Ruby,' she begged. 'It can't be true.'

Ruby held her close, crying with her. 'Aw, lass, I'm sorry,' she said brokenly. 'I know you thought the world of the old lady. Take heart, lass.' Clutching Cathy tight, she promised, 'Old Ruby's 'ere, and she won't let go of yer no how.'

CHAPTER SEVEN

On 8 January 1901, Annette Rosalind Foster was laid to rest. Never having been divorced from Joshua Blackthorn she could have kept his name, but in order to hide her true identity had adopted the name Foster. Right up to the day she was savagely murdered, she kept her anonymity.

There were few mourners. The only representatives of the Langho community were two traders who'd delivered her supplies over the years; though, as the grocer remarked afterwards, 'None of us really knew her.' Owen and his son David attended, as did Margaret and Cathy. Frank was there in his capacity as landlord to the unfortunate woman. Throughout the service he bowed his head and prayed. Only once did he glance at the coffin. Not for one moment throughout did he regard its contents as being the remains of his own mother. She had been a tenant of his, that was all.

Cathy quietly sobbed. Seated some way behind, David longed to hold and comfort her. At the end, when she walked past him, he lowered his gaze, afraid she would hurt him again. Cathy saw this and took it as yet another sign that he had finished with her. Margaret saw it too, and hurried Cathy out to the trap where Frank was impatiently waiting to be away. 'Thank God that's over,' he muttered as they climbed in. 'The whole business is damned inconvenient though, because now the cottage has to be cleared. After that I've got to find a new tenant.'

Unsure as to what evidence the old lady had left behind, Frank took it on himself to visit the cottage that very afternoon. In the sideboard he found a quantity of old porcelain figures. 'They should fetch a good price at auction,' he remarked, turning

141

the beautiful figurines over in his grasping hands. 'I dare say I'm entitled to have first call on anything of value.' Probing into every corner, he chuckled wickedly. 'Especially if I make it known that she was badly in arrears with her rent.'

There were two framed paintings of modest value, he thought, and a rather old but attractive wicker chair in the bedroom. A more thorough search gave up a small treasure trove, skilfully hidden in a locked compartment at the back of a drawer. It took only a moment to prise the compartment open. Inside was a cash box containing a number of letters and official-looking documents. Beside the cash box was a blue velvet wallet.

'What's this, I wonder?' he whispered, gingerly opening the wallet. When the brooch was laid bare, his eyes almost popped out of his head. 'Good God!' Taking it out, he laid it in the palm of his hand, a feeling of wonder washing over him. 'Good God!' The brooch was delicately crafted of sapphires and platinum. 'It's exactly the same as the necklace at the house.' He stared at it for what seemed an age, turning it over in his hands as though he was handling something too precious to see daylight. 'Of course! It's a set. She must have taken the brooch when she ran off.' If he needed more proof that the old lady really was his mother, it was here in the palm of his hand.

He knew he dared not keep it. 'Can't show it to Rita, or she would accuse me of having kept it from her all these years. Can't sell it either,' he mused aloud, 'or it might be traced back, and how would I explain it?' He sat in the very chair where Nan had been found. 'Oh, but it *is* splendid,' he groaned, continuing to stare at the brooch. 'I haven't the heart to destroy it. What am I to do then?' He thought a while, debating on the best course of action. 'Left her husband and two children behind, but stayed long enough to pack the brooch, eh?' His face darkened. 'Well, it's mine now, and this little trinket is worth a pretty shilling. After all, with the old lady gone and the cottage empty, there's no rent coming in. Because I'm bound to suffer, I have a right to compensation where I can find it.' He chewed on his bottom lip as he had a manner of doing when faced with a dilemma. 'I can't afford not to be careful though,' he reminded himself. 'Don't want folks knowing the old biddy was related.'

He began pacing the floor. 'What to do? What to do?' He

stopped and gazed out of the window, his face growing red with frustration. 'Let me think! I can't think straight here ... with all this round me.' He shifted his eyes round the room, visibly shivering when they came to rest on the chair where Nan had been bludgeoned to death. 'She's still here ... watching me.' His lips moved but no words would come. They moved again, and this time he heard himself saying what he had not said for too many years: 'Mother ... my mother.'

Overcome with emotion, he sank into the nearest chair, bent his head and was silent for a moment. Then he sat up straight, threw back his shoulders and laughed like a man tormented. 'My mother!' His laughter turned to tears. The years fled away and he was a child again, a child deserted, a child whose innocent heart was racked by sobs, just as his guilty heart was racked by sobs now.

He had tasted the word 'Mother' on his lips. It had been a bitter taste and, for the remainder of his life, he would never utter that word again.

When his emotions were drained, he took one more lingering look at the brooch. Then he slipped it into his pocket and turned his attention to the cash box. The letters were written in the most beautiful copperplate by his mother, addressed to his father Joshua, but never posted. For one crippling minute he fought within himself; should he open them, or would he live to regret it? 'I've done many things I regret,' he said wryly, 'one more won't matter either way.' Opening the first letter he started to read:

Dear Joshua,

I know you must hate me for what I have done. Yet, I could not stay with you. There is nothing to be gained by going into the reasons for my leaving. Let it be sufficient for me to say you have changed beyond recognition from the man I married. Or perhaps you never changed, I just didn't see you as you really were.

I can't regret leaving you, but with all my heart I regret leaving my children. I know what you said when I left, that you would never allow me to have them, and that you would move heaven and earth to keep them from me. I know you can do that. I know only too well what cruelty you are capable of.

I beg of you, Joshua, don't be so heartless. Send me word that I may return for them. I shall wait at the address above for the next week only. After that, I leave the area, with no plans to return.

Annette

The letter was nigh on forty years old, almost as old as Frank himself. It had yellowed round the edges and the blue ribbon that bound it to the others was frayed with age.

Frank read it again and again, and each time he wondered why she had never posted it. 'WHY DIDN'T YOU POST IT?' His cry rang from the heart. 'Was it because you were so afraid of him? Or could it be that you never posted it because you changed your mind!' He was beside himself with rage. 'Whatever the reason, you left without us, and I for one will not forgive you.'

He was screaming at the letter, twisting it over and over in his fist. 'Damn you! Damn you!' Long-buried emotions overwhelmed him and it was all too much. Desperate, he thrust the whole batch of letters into the fire-grate, where he set light to them.

When the papers were curled and blackened beyond recognition, he put his mind to the official papers. They amounted to nothing more than domestic bills, circulars, invoices, and a brief acknowledgement from a local solicitor which read:

Dear Mrs Foster,

In answer to your letter, I would be pleased to see you on 2 January at 10 am as requested.

It would have been helpful if you had briefly explained what you require. However, on the last point, the making of your will, I will be able to advise you better on the day. To that end, I look forward to seeing you.

Yours sincerely,

Bartholomew Wright

Frank breathed a sigh of relief. 'Had it all in hand, didn't you, Mrs Foster?' he said through clenched teeth. 'Well now, it's just as well for me and mine that you couldn't keep the appointment with your solicitor.'

Tearing off the address at the top of the letter, he crumpled the remainder in his hand. Throwing it into the grate he watched it follow the same fate as his mother's personal letters to his father. 'Annette and Joshua Blackthorn, I commit your ashes to eternity,' he said savagely. 'And I hope the pair of you burn in hell!' He grew quiet, observing an odd kind of reverence as the evidence crumbled away. 'One way or another you're both to blame,' he murmured. 'If I'm weak and selfish, it's your fault. If I'm only half the man I should be, who else is there to blame but you two? Joshua Blackthorn, whose wild ways drove you away, and *you*, a woman who deserted all her responsibilities. For years after you left, I felt so very lonely, a lost soul, without purpose or sense of belonging.' His eyes filled with tears. 'Until Rita came along.' There was great joy in his voice now. 'She gave me what you took away, and now she's *everything* to me. Why should I mourn your loss, either of you? I don't need you. As long as I have my Rita, I don't need any of you.'

His emotions deeply stirred, he began shouting, oblivious to the fact that he might be overheard. Even here, miles away from anywhere, a voice might carry, a secret might be lost. 'Ssh, Frank!' he whispered. 'Don't lose your mind. Not now. Not when there is so much at stake.'

The following week he arranged a date when a band of men would clean out the cottage and make it ready for the next tenant. On the day before they were due to start work, Cathy asked Margaret, 'Could we have one last look before they go in?' The idea of strangers in hobnail boots treading over Nan's pretty rugs and poking about in that delightful place was distressing to her.

Margaret had much the same idea. 'Why not? It is Sunday after all.' She glanced out of the window at a clear January morning. 'It's a perfect day for a walk.' Getting up from the chair where she had been sewing, she warned Cathy, 'However, it's still very cold out, so mind you put on your boots and beret.'

Well wrapped up against the cold, with Margaret in long coat and fur hat, and Cathy looking exceptionally lovely in her blue beret and matching coat, wearing leather gloves and a pretty white scarf tucked round her throat, the two of them left the house. 'Can we go by way of the streets?' Cathy loved to see the people chatting in the streets, and the children playing hop-scotch on the pavements. She liked to see the babies in their prams and, whenever the opportunity presented itself, would stop and chat to the old folk, who smiled back through toothless gums. Old and wise they were, happily minding the children and singing their praises; full of the kind of love she had never known from her own parents.

Margaret agreed, and soon they were walking down the narrow cobbled street. Though it was chilly and the children wore little more than rags, they ran and played and hopped to their games, the dogs ran in and out of their legs and the street was alive with laughter.

From one end of the street to the other, women in turbans were on their knees, white-stoning their steps and mopping the area immediately round their front doors. Men of all ages stood about, leaning on the walls, hands in pockets and voices raised in light-hearted banter as they argued about the state of the world. One mother had braved the cold to sit on a chair in the fresh air and openly breast-feed her baby. Poor they were, and no doubt hungry from time to time, but there was a carefree air about this street, a special bonding of souls, a will to survive as long as they pulled together. These were good people. This was a street filled with love. And Cathy thought it a world away from the sorry house where she lived.

'Mornin', luv. Off fer a walk, are you?' The old woman had passed the time of day with Cathy before.

Recognising her at once, Cathy guided Margaret over to where the old woman was seated. 'We're going to see Nan Foster's cottage before the workmen move in,' she explained sadly.

'I see.' The old woman's red-rimmed eyes looked from Cathy to Margaret, and it was Margaret she addressed. 'Dreadful business that. By! What's the world coming to when an old woman can't sit by her own fireside without having her brains bashed out?' She saw how her words were cutting Cathy and quickly asked, 'Did the old lady leave any next-of-kin?'

A younger woman might have thought twice about questioning a Blackthorn, but age had made her bold. Age, poverty and a sense of survival had chipped away at the niceties of her existence, until now she saw only the *faces* of people. The expensive cut of a dress or the silk ribbon round a bonnet didn't bother her. Not any more. Not since she had suckled her last child and fought with dogs on the pavement for a meaty bone when her husband was out of work.

Margaret had already talked to Frank about the possibility of Nan's having relatives. 'As far as we can tell she had no kin.' Her mind wandered back over the many pleasant conversations she and Nan had shared, and not once could she recall Nan's ever having mentioned family. The old lady's kind gentle face came to mind, and with it a bitter-sweet sensation. 'She was such a loving soul,' she said wistfully, thinking how a woman like Nan was made to have a family. Glancing at Cathy, she said softly, 'We shall miss her.'

'Poor bugger.' The old woman shook her grey head. 'We're all here today and gone tomorrow, an' that's a fact. Still, from what I hear the old lady weren't badly off . . . paid her bills on time by all accounts and never asked for credit. Then, o' course, she had a nice little home, didn't she, eh?' Without waiting for an answer, she rushed on, lost in her own thoughts and not talking to anyone in particular, 'I expect there's another tenant already lined up to fill her shoes, ain't there? I mean . . . the cottage wouldn't be my idea of heaven, but there's plenty who'd love it.'

Seeming mentally to shake herself and realise she was conversing with them from the big house, she screwed herself into a tight little ball, like a hedgehog might do when faced with danger. 'No, I couldn't stand living out there amongst the wind and the trees, with nary a soul in sight.' Squinting up at Cathy, she smiled warmly. 'Me, I like the sound o' childer around me arse, an' the smell of a man's pipe up me nostrils. I like to see the babbies at their mams' titties, an' listen at night through the walls when a fella demands his rights.' She laughed raucously. 'Shame yer, do I?' Grinning sheepishly at Cathy, she apologised. 'I ain't as bad as I sound, me beauty. But I'm a street woman an' there ain't nothing in the world to change me.'

'I understand,' Cathy replied, and she did.

The old woman smiled. "Course yer do, dearie. A cottage is fine fer them as can stand the loneliness, an' like I say, there's plenty folk who'd be glad of a little place like that.' Cocking her head to look at Margaret, she studied her a moment before asking boldly, 'Got a tenant already, 'ave yer?'

'To tell you the truth, I don't know,' Margaret answered. 'My brother deals with all of that.'

"Course he does, me dear,' came the retort. 'Ain't men allus the same? Like to think they're in charge, ain't that the case, eh? Lost my old fella many year ago ... a drunken ol' bugger he were.'

Margaret bade her good day. 'We have much to do yet,' she explained.

'Yer should be like me then,' replied the harmless old soul. 'If yer ain't got no money nor property, then yer ain't got nothing to worry about.'

'Do you think she's very old?' Cathy asked as they went down the lane towards the cottage.

'Ancient, I'd say.' Margaret laughed softly at the old woman's wise philosophy. 'I certainly believe she could teach us a thing or two.'

With the key that Margaret had brought, Cathy opened the cottage door. The scene that greeted them was utter mayhem. Cathy stood there dumbfounded. 'Someone's ransacked it!' she cried. They had no idea it was Frank who had turned the place upside down. Every room told the same story; cupboard doors flung open, drawers thrown to the floor and their contents strewn over the rugs. There were remnants of burnt paper littering the hearth, and several of Nan's precious ornaments had been swiped from the dresser shelves and left in fragments on the floor.

'Who could have done such a terrible thing?' Like Cathy, Margaret was close to tears.

It took almost an hour for them to clean up the mess, but the things that were broken could never be mended. 'And even if we could repair them, who would they belong to? What would we do with them?' Cathy asked. 'Father said Nan didn't leave a will, and he hasn't been able to trace any relatives.' She lovingly caressed a small plate that had been one of Nan's favourites. Darkest blue with a pattern of flowers round the brim, it had hung over the mantelpiece all these years. 'Isn't it beautiful?' she whispered, looking at Margaret with tearful eyes. 'Like *all* her pretty things. And now someone has been in here and destroyed them.'

'People can be very cruel, sweetheart,' Margaret consoled her. 'Take the plate and keep it safe. I'm sure Nan would like that.' She remembered something else and her eyes went straight to the sideboard. 'The box,' she said. 'The one Nan so wanted you to have.' Going to the dresser she pulled out the small top drawer which only a minute ago Cathy had carefully replaced. The box wasn't there. It wasn't anywhere to be found. 'Whoever came in here must have taken it.'

'It doesn't matter,' Cathy said wistfully. 'It was very lovely, and I know Nan wanted me to have it,' – she pressed the plate close to her heart – 'but I'll be happy just to have this. Nan loved it so, and it will always remind me of her.' She couldn't stand to be in that room where she and Margaret had enjoyed the old lady's company. It wasn't the same any more.

On the way home they talked about Nan. 'What will happen to her furniture?' Cathy wondered. When Margaret explained how she herself would organise either a sale for charity, or even a gift to a poor family in Langho, she was partly comforted. 'Nan would be pleased to know she was helping others,' she replied. One thing she was sure of – never again did she want to enter that cottage. Nan had lived and been brutally killed there. Now she was gone, and with her all of the gentleness that had filled that little place. 'Do you think they'll find the person who killed her?' She daren't even think about what kind of monster he must be.

'Who knows, sweetheart?' Margaret had been thinking the very same. 'He may be long gone from the area by now. My thinking is it must have been a stranger ... someone who couldn't have known Nan.'

Glancing back to the cottage, Cathy was filled with rage. 'Someone evil,' she said harshly, 'or totally insane.' It had to be a stranger, she reasoned, because anyone who knew of that delightful soul would never have hurt her. 'I hope they do catch him, but as you say, he's probably long gone.'

Time passed and the police still hadn't caught the murderer. Much to Frank's dismay, people seemed wary of living in a place that had seen such horror. 'I've spent good money on having it cleared out and repainted,' he moaned to Rita. 'I didn't even get the chance to sell the furniture because Margaret snatched it from under my nose and gave it away to one of her wretched families. I've paid out a large sum of money on advertising for tenants, and I've dropped the rent by sixpence. And still I haven't found anyone willing to take it on.'

'I'm not interested.' Still frail but now allowed out of bed and enjoying the run of the house, Rita had more important matters on her mind. She was toying with the idea of paying a visit to Owen's house. Not to see him, but to confront his wife with the truth. Lately there had been a growing suspicion in her mind, and it had caused her many a sleepless night. Only yesterday she had seen Owen pass by at the bottom of the lane. He and David were carting a load of logs to Langho. Filled with excitement at the sight of him, she had waved from the window, expecting him to look towards the house, hoping he was missing her as much as she was missing him. Instead he kept his gaze averted, apparently engaged in deep conversation with his son. Not once did he glance her way.

The incident had unnerved her, and from it the seed of doubt was sown. Had Owen grown cold towards her? Was he preparing to turn his back on her? Would he leave her carrying his child and not lay claim to it? No! Not if she had her way. Before she would let that happen, she would see him ruined.

'Did you hear what I said?' Frank bent to her, a gentler expression on his face. 'Would *you* like to live in the cottage, my dear? We could sell this place and have an extra room or two built on the cottage if you like.'

Already disturbed by her own thoughts, Rita laughed in his face. 'You must be mad!'

'Not mad, my dear,' he said, straightening his back and looking down at her with disappointment. 'Sensible, perhaps? It would help our finances, do you see? As you know we've never been what you might call rich. I'm already paying out a crippling fee for Jack's schooling, and now we've lost the rent from the cottage.' Anticipating an argument, he went on, 'Oh, I know what you're going to say. You're about to remind me that Margaret owns half of this house, *and* the cottage. I've thought of that, and I'm sure she'll agree. After all, I do believe she's had enough of residing under the same roof as the two of us . . . especially since we took Jack under our wing. And she wouldn't be going away empty-handed because this house would fetch a fine profit.'

'Are you saying we're desperate for money?' Rita was not altogether astonished. Frank had a way of letting money run through his fingers like water with his frequent trips to London, his weakness for a game of cards and his liking for best whisky and cigars. Then there was the boy . . . expensive shopping trips, extravagant gifts, and now the tutor's crippling fees. It wasn't surprising the money went out faster than it came in. No, she wasn't altogether astonished.

But she was glad of something else, and that was her own astuteness where money was concerned, because now she was comfortably off in her own right. Since the day they were married, she had carefully put away every shilling that had come into her own hands. She had jewellery that was worth a small fortune, and a dazzling sapphire necklace left by Joshua Blackthorn. That alone would keep her in luxury if she chose to sell it.

'I have no intention of living in that cottage.' In fact she had no intention of living *anywhere* with him. She too had plans, but they did not include Frank Blackthorn.

'Don't dismiss the idea out of hand, my dear,' he pleaded. 'Think about it while I'm gone to collect my one remaining rent.'

He had her attention now. 'Are you going to the Leytons'?' Her green eyes were shining as she got from the chair and walked with him to the door. 'Would you give Mrs Leyton my regards?'

'Really?' He was surprised and it showed. 'I hope you're not developing Margaret's tiresome trait of compassion for your neighbours.'

'No, but I think you should ask . . .' Frowning, she pretended: 'Goodness, I've forgotten his name.' Putting her arm through her husband's, she smiled up at him. 'Well, anyway, I think it might be a good idea if you asked Mr Leyton to deliver a load of his logs to the house.'

Frank was delighted she could not recall the man's name. After all, Owen Leyton was a fine figure of a man, with a certain look that would turn any woman's head. Oh, but not Rita's, he thought. Rita has eyes for no one but me. 'His name is Owen, my dear,' he said, kissing her on the forehead. 'It isn't like you to forget a thing like that. But of course you would have no reason to remember it.'

She shivered, not because she was cold – though it served her purpose for him to think that – but because the wetness of his kiss disgusted her. 'The house is so chilly. I would hate us to run out of logs.'

He was mortified. Looking towards the fire he was pleased to see a pile of logs blazing cheerily away. 'I'll get Ruby to keep the fire piled up, my dear,' he promised. 'We do have a good stock of logs, but seeing as you're still not well and feel the cold more than most, I'll have Owen Leyton deliver another load. Will that suit you?'

'You're a good man,' she purred, thinking what a fool he was. 'Hurry now, or he won't be able to get here before dark.'

Jack was in the kitchen, stuffing his face with what was left of an apple pie. It was the first place Frank looked. 'I need a hand, son,' he said, beckoning him out. 'Get the trap ready while I fetch my rent-ledger from the study.'

'If you're going to the Leytons', can I come with you?' What with one thing and another, Jack had felt neglected lately, and it peeved him.

'Why not? You'll need to know how to conduct a gentleman's business once the estate comes to you.' Frank's smile was all embracing, 'Meantime it behoves me to keep it profitable, wouldn't you say?'

'Too true!' And the sooner it comes to me the better, Jack thought. Even now, with the old lady gone . . . and with her the threat of being ousted, he still didn't feel altogether secure. On top of that he was missing the excitement of the streets. Langho was a quaint mixture of town and countryside and, though he had tried, he felt his face didn't really fit there. But London town? Now *there* was a place! Alive with vendors and reeking with the smell of hot chestnuts, villains round every corner and painted dolls selling their bodies for a few shillings. Carriages taking the gentry to their posh clubs; pockets to pick when their owners had swallowed a few bevvies; fist-fights in the alleys and rozzers on the beat. Alive and throbbing, that's what London was, and he was sore at heart to be parted from it.

Jack had long known the familiar streets were calling him back, and suspected there might be a day when he would return. But not yet. Oh, no, not until he had got what he came here for. He had suffered the starched collars and the discipline; he had sat through hours of being tutored; endured mealtimes when he was a spectacle; and felt the hostility of Margaret Blackthorn. There was a woman with a quick and suspicious mind, a woman he would have to watch if he was to fulfil his plans. There was no doubt he had been tempted many times, occasions when he could quite happily have rammed his pockets full of valuable trinkets and made his way back to London town. But it wasn't enough. When he had properties and land to sell, a fat balance in the bank and money in his pocket, now that would be another matter altogether . . .

He chuckled inwardly at the idea of turning up at his mam's door in a hansom cab, stepping out of it dressed in a toff's clobber and flaunting his newfound wealth to all and sundry. His mam might be reproachful at his having left her to the mercies of that awful fellow who slept alongside her. But, oh, just wait until she saw what he'd made of himself! Wait until he pushed a wad of notes into her grubby hand. She would have a change of heart then, no doubt. But it was still a long way off. And he had a great many cunning plans to undertake before he saw the light of that day.

When the trap was ready, Frank emerged from the house. 'By! It's a cutting breeze,' he exclaimed, climbing on to the seat. Though he was wrapped up warm in a woollen muffler and cap, with his long coat tucked round his legs, he felt the wind go right through his bones. 'Are you warm enough, son?' he asked, noting Jack's short jacket and bare head.

'Warm as a toasted muffin,' came the reply. There was nothing like the promise of an inheritance to make a body feel rosy, he thought.

Teasing the horse off to a careful start on the slippery ground,

Frank chuckled. 'You young blighters don't feel the cold. What it's like to be young, eh?' Shaking his head, he silently congratulated himself for providing a better childhood for his own son Jack than his parents had ever done for him. It never occurred to him that he was sorely guilty of neglecting Cathy, in the same way he himself had been neglected as a child.

As they passed the end of the lane which led to Nan Foster's cottage, Jack remarked, 'Shame about the old biddy.'

'*Lady*,' Frank corrected. 'Mrs Foster was always a *lady*. With her fine features and genteel manner, she could have been an aristocrat.' He felt a pang of guilt at having ransacked her home.

'Give you a shock, did it, when she were killed like that?'

Frank was quiet for a moment before answering in a low voice, 'She didn't deserve to be killed in that way. And, yes, it was a shock.'

The journey continued in silence. When they got to Owen's house there was another shock in store.

'I'm giving a month's notice,' Owen told Frank. 'It's time I moved on to pastures new.'

He didn't reveal that Maria had given him an ultimatum. She knew about him and Rita, and was adamant: 'Either you take me and the children miles away from here, or I'll have words with Frank Blackthorn. I'm sure he'll have something to say about the way you and his wife have been carrying on!'

Now Frank was taken aback. 'You can't leave!' Slamming the rent-ledger down on to the table, he glared at Owen. 'You've got a good thing going on here, Leyton. . . . prime land at a reasonable rent, a solid house for your family, and a landlord who doesn't interfere. What makes you think you can do better elsewhere?'

'It's just time I spread me wings, Mr Blackthorn.' Owen could feel his wife's presence at the back of the room, and his hair stood up on end. Terrified she might blurt out the truth, he gabbled on, 'Me and the wife . . . we've already made the decision, and there's no going back. In a month's time I'll be leaving the area altogether. Don't worry, the rent will be paid up, and I'll take nothing that isn't mine.'

'You're damn right you'll take nothing that isn't yours!' Seeing yet another source of revenue disappear was almost too much for Frank. Thumping his fist on the table, he shouted, 'It's a damned inconvenience, that's what it is. A damned inconvenience.' It was more than that. It was a further squeezing of the purse strings, and Rita wouldn't take kindly to it.

'If I've caused you a problem, then I'm sorry.' Owen was more sorry for himself. He loved this land, and if it wasn't for the mess he'd got himself into, he would be content for his bones to be laid here. He was a weak man where attractive women were concerned. Maria knew that, and so far had turned a blind eye. This time it was different. Oh, there would be temptation again, he was in no doubt about that. But with Rita Blackthorn he'd been too careless, and now she was carrying his child. Because of it, he was having to leave this place, to tramp the roads looking for work and hoping to earn a roof over their heads. What a bloody fool he'd been!

When Frank and the boy were gone, with Frank sending the horse down the lane at a furious pace, Maria told her husband the same. 'You've been a bloody fool, Owen Leyton.'

'I've done what you want.' Irritated, he stared her out. 'Let it go, Maria. We'll be leaving here soon enough. I just hope you don't come to regret it.'

'And if I do . . . if we have to rough it and live in the hedge-rows, if I die from lack of warmth and food, whose fault will that be, eh?' Exhausted and weakened by her long illness, she sat in the chair and hung her head. 'I'm sorry.' She had never been a vindictive woman.

Owen came to her then. 'No, Maria, it's *me* who should be sorry,' he murmured. 'We both know it's time to move on, and you're right about its being my fault.'

Looking up with tear-stained face, she spoke to him in a softer voice. 'In many ways you're a strong man,' she told him, 'but you have a weakness for women. I've known it all along, but it hasn't really bothered me. You've always come back to me.' She wiped her eyes and sighed. 'This time it's different.'

'How different, Maria?' He knew she was right, but wanted her to spell it out.

'Rita Blackthorn is a dangerous woman. She won't let you go as easily as the others.' Squaring herself up to him, she studied him for a while, the handsome face with its strong square chin and dark eyes; eyes that held a fear she had never seen before. In a soft voice that held a world of conviction, she declared, 'You meant to leave us, didn't you? You really meant to set up home with that woman?'

The question rocked him on his feet. Yet he couldn't deny it. Instead he lovingly stroked her hair and remained silent for what seemed an age. Then he sighed deeply and turned away. 'How could you know that?'

She reached up to grasp his hand. 'Look at me, Owen Leyton,' she said, and when he turned there was a smile on her face.

'I know because I'm a woman,' she whispered. 'Women have a way of sensing such things. Call it instinct, or mebbe fear. All I know is what I feel here.' She tapped her breast.

'Can you forgive me?'

'Haven't I always?'

'You're a good woman, Maria Leyton, and I don't deserve you.'

There was no answer to this. She smiled and squeezed his hand, and he was satisfied.

Teresa heard the entire conversation. Having returned from the barn where David was sawing logs, she remained in the scullery, hidden from view but able to see her parents through the crack in the door. Still undetected, she crept out again, returning with a bucket in hand and clattering it to make sure she was heard. 'David!' Owen's voice rang out. 'Is that you?'

As he came towards the scullery, Teresa showed herself. 'David's sawing logs in the barn,' she told him. 'Is everything all right?'

'You'd better call him in. There's something he should know, something you should *both* know.'

A few minutes later, the family were gathered in the tiny parlour. Maria and her daughter were seated at the table. David stood behind them, his face clouded with anxiety. Owen stood with his back to the fireplace, desperately thinking of the best way to break the news to them. His first remark was addressed to his son, whose dark eyes were intent on him. 'No doubt you saw the landlord pass the barn on his way here?'

David looked at Teresa and nodded. 'Yes. We saw him . . . come to collect the rent, I expect?'

'That's right, son. He collected something else too.'

'Oh?' Sensing trouble, David stiffened, his hand going involuntarily to his mother's shoulder.

'I gave him a month's notice.'

'What? You mean to leave here?' David couldn't believe his ears. 'Why? What's happened?' Foremost in his mind was Cathy, and the awful knowledge that if they were to leave here he might never see her again.

'Nothing's happened.' Owen had no intention of revealing the truth to his own son: that he was to blame for having bedded Frank Blackthorn's wife. 'We've been here long enough, that's all you need to know. Your mam and I have decided it's time to leave.'

'But you can't!' Stepping forward, David confronted his father. 'You love this place. Your heart's in it . . . and so is mine! When we came here the land was fit for nothing. Now it's rich and fertile. Why would you want to leave? WHY?'

'The decision is made.' Owen felt the despair in his son, and his guilt was tenfold. 'Don't question it.'

During this exchange, Maria and the girl remained silent. They were still silent when David swung round and strode out of the house. 'I'll go after him.' Teresa rose from the chair. 'He's bound to be bitter.'

'What about you?' Maria had been astonished when her daughter took the news calmly.

Shrugging, Teresa thought for a moment then said, 'I think you're right, and I for one won't be sorry to see the last of this place.' Having successfully ruined the relationship between her brother and Cathy, she was growing restless. Besides, now she knew what had been going on between her father and Rita Blackthorn, it was best they should make tracks, and the sooner the better.

Owen was relieved. 'Happen you can persuade your brother to think the same way?'

'Don't worry about David. I'll go and talk to him now.'

'No. Leave him be.' Owen knew how shaken David was by the news. More than that, he had not forgotten how devoted to Cathy his son was. There were times when a man needed to be alone, and he sensed this was one of them. 'Just see where he's gone.'

Teresa was in and out in no time. 'He's making his way to

the top field,' she said. 'He always goes there when he wants to think.'

For the first time, Maria wondered whether they were doing the right thing. 'It's hard on him,' she murmured. 'He's given his heart to this land, and he's known such happiness here.'

Ignoring her mother's remark, Teresa sullenly declared, 'If you ask me, he was getting too pally with that Blackthorn girl.' Eyeing Owen through spiteful eyes she said meaningfully, 'No good can come of things like that.'

Disturbed, yet not really knowing why, Owen snapped at her, 'Seeing as David's made himself scarce and I have the tractor to mend, do you think you're capable of delivering a load of logs?'

''Course I am!'

'Good. Then you'll need a warm coat and a pair of stout boots.'

He waited while she disappeared into the scullery, a moment later showing herself at the door, wearing her boots and carrying a long coat. 'I'm ready.'

Squaring his shoulders, he led the way to the barn. Here the two of them got ready the horse and cart, and in a surprisingly short time it was loaded high with freshly sawn logs. 'Take your time, and watch out for potholes in the road,' he warned.

Climbing into the hard seat, she asked for the umpteenth time, 'Where am I delivering?'

Beads of sweat ran down his temples as he stared up at her. His back ached and his heart even more. He had been all kinds of a fool and now he was paying the worst price. 'Blackthorn House. He brought the order with him this morning.' He gave a strange little laugh. 'In his temper, he forgot to pay for them, but never mind. I'll stop it out of next week's rent.' To tell the truth he was already toying with the idea of leaving before the rent could be collected. Now the hardest decision was made, he had a hankering to put it all behind him.

When the girl was gone, Owen looked round the barn with sad eyes. 'David's right,' he whispered. 'It's going to be a heart-breaking wrench. We've put a lot of years and back-breaking work into this place, and it's part of us now.' Every word was like a stab to his heart.

The familiar sights and smells overwhelmed him: the high pitched roof which he and David had mended so many times he'd lost count; the timber rails that divided the bays; the stable and the hay loft with its long narrow ladder ... all lovingly created by himself and his son. Groaning, he wiped the palms of his hands over his face. Through the gaps between his fingers, he peered out in anguish. 'What will we do? Where will we go?' His voice trembled with emotion. With shoulders drooping, he bent his head and gave vent to his feelings. The sobs shook his body, and the soft sound of his crying echoed from the walls. 'You've gone too far this time, Leyton,' he whispered. 'For the sake of a fling with Rita Blackthorn, you've lost it all, and damned well serve you right!'

Frank was still in a fury. On his return, he found Rita in the drawing room. Desperate to see Owen, she had positioned herself by the window, eagerly awaiting the sound of his horse and wagon. On the chair beside her lay a long dark shawl; she was wearing a burgundy high-necked dress and neat ankle boots. Her face was flushed with excitement as she turned to greet her husband. 'You look angry,' she remarked. 'What's wrong?' Not that she cared. But she wondered whether his sour mood had anything to do with Owen.

Instead of answering he made a remark of his own. 'Good heavens, look at you, my dear.' He saw how she was dressed and was both irritated and curious. 'Anyone would think you were ready to go out.' Rushing across the room he urged, 'Come away from the window, my dear, you know how draughty these old frames are. I don't want you to catch your death of cold.'

'Stop fussing!' Pushing his hand from her shoulder, she rounded on him angrily. 'You suffocate me,' she snapped. 'Why can't you leave me alone?' His stern features and turned-down mouth alerted her. 'What's the matter?' she demanded, keeping her distance. 'Something bad has happened. Tell me at once. Is it Owen Leyton? Has he angered you in some way? Speak up, can't you?'

He grimaced and clenched his fist, his next words making her heart sink. 'Yes, I'm afraid something *has* happened, my dear. And, yes, it *has* to do with the Leyton fellow.' Forcing himself to smile, he assured her, 'However, you're not to worry. I have it all in hand.'

'But I do worry, and I want to know.'

He sighed, a long breathy noise that repelled her. 'I'm afraid we'll have to be careful about the money we spend . . . at least until we've secured new tenants.'

'You're not making sense. I already know you're looking for tenants to take the cottage.' She looked curiously at him. 'It isn't the cottage though, is it? Tell me, Frank. I need to know.'

'It's that damned Leyton fellow.' He clenched his fists and punched one hard against his thigh. 'Would you believe he's had the gall to give me a month's notice?' When she was too surprised to answer, he began pacing the room. 'If I didn't want every penny I can squeeze from him, I'd throw him out here and now . . . but, of course, apart from the rent, I need the time to find a new tenant, and God knows I'm having no luck at all with the cottage. If I have *both* properties left vacant, it will mean a considerable loss of income.' He paused to look at her anxious face. 'But, like I said, my dear, you're not to worry. I won't have it.'

She was too busy thinking about this new turn of events to worry about his loss of income. 'Why is he leaving? Where does he mean to go? Has he explained?' At first she had been enraged, but now she was beginning to wonder if it wasn't all for her sake.

He laughed aloud. 'Explained? Not a word of it. All I'm told is that he's leaving, and that's as much as I know.'

Hope rose in her, bringing a smile to her face. 'I expect our Mr Owen Leyton has plans.' Certain that these plans included her, she could afford to be pleasant. 'A man like that, well, I suppose he likes to be secretive about what he means to do. No doubt he's been making these plans a long time, so you'll just have to accept it, I'm afraid.'

'You sound almost pleased?' He was staring at her with interest.

'Not at all.' Owen would be here soon, she told herself, and when he asked her, she would go with him to the ends of the earth.

'He should be here shortly with the logs I ordered.' Frank

glanced out of the window. 'I'm not in the mood to deal with him. I have other problems to think about.' As he left, he told her kindly, 'Do stay away from that draughty window, my dear, and remember what I said . . . you're not to worry. If you want me, I'll be in my study.' With that he went out of the room and down the hallway; leaving Rita smiling triumphantly to herself as she waited for Owen to arrive.

Her smile widened when she saw the horse and wagon approaching. It faded when she realised it was not Owen who drove it, but his daughter. Throwing the shawl over her shoulders, she met the wagon at the rear of the house. 'I was told your father would deliver the logs.' Though she tried hard not to show her disappointment it was easily evident to the girl.

Clambering down from the lofty seat, Teresa set about unloading the logs. 'As you can see, he's not here,' she answered sourly.

'Where is he then?'

'Working.'

'You're a very surly young woman.'

Teresa made a little bow. 'Sorry, Ma'am,' she said with a sly lilt to her voice. 'And I'm sorry if you're disappointed not to see my father. You'll just have to put up with me.'

Rita was instinctively cautious. 'I beg your pardon?' Sounding suitably offended, she demanded, 'What are you implying?'

This time the girl stopped in her work to look up. 'I know what the pair of you have been up to, and it's no use you denying it. But it's over. We're leaving the area and he'll never see you again.' She took delight in every word.

As the truth sank in, Rita turned a deathly shade of grey. 'What are you saying?' Faltering, she reached out and steadied herself against the wall of the house. 'Who told you these things?'

'It don't matter who told me. The plain truth is we're leaving, and he wants nothing more to do with you.'

'Liar!'

'Oh?' Stepping closer, Teresa pushed her face into the other woman's face. 'If I'm a liar, why is he running away with our mam instead of with you?' She turned her attention to Rita's swollen stomach. 'I wonder what your husband would say if he knew the brat you're carrying ain't his?'

The remark was too much for Rita. With a scream, she lunged forward. 'You liar!' Lashing out, she scored her sharp nails down the girl's face. Teresa struck out in defence and soon the two of them were fighting like wildcats.

When the horrified Ruby pulled them apart, the girl was laughing hysterically. 'You little vixen!' Ruby gasped. 'The master will have your hide for this.'

'I don't think so.' Tearing herself from Ruby's grasp, she stared at Rita with crafty eyes. 'I won't say anything if you don't.'

It was a form of blackmail and Rita was not ready for the truth to come out. Not yet. 'Let her go,' she told Ruby through bruised lips.

Triumphant, the girl clambered on to the half-emptied wagon. As she careered out of the yard at hair-raising speed, the remaining logs spewed from all sides and at one point, when the wheels became entangled in the rolling debris, it seemed as though the whole equipage would topple over. 'Good Lord above! She's mad as a hatter,' Ruby remarked. 'Whatever's got into the creature?'

'Forget it, Ruby,' Rita ordered. 'And you're not to say a word to the master.'

'Whatever you say, Ma'am.' But Ruby was immensely curious, believing there was more here than met the eye.

As she led Rita back to the house, she said nothing more. At times like these it was best to keep your mouth shut and mind your own business. She had her suspicions, though, and they included Owen Leyton.

In the peace of her own room, Rita sat impatiently while Ruby dabbed at the bruises and cuts to her face. Ruby worked silently, her mind going over what had taken place in the yard. She still couldn't believe the mistress had allowed the Leyton girl to get away with attacking her. 'The hoyden,' she remarked angrily. 'She deserves a whipping.'

Pushing Ruby away, Rita reminded her, 'You're to say nothing about this, not to the master, nor to anyone else. Do you understand?'

Ruby shook her head. 'No, Ma'am, I don't,' she said with the boldness of age. 'But you've told me not to say anything and I won't.' Gathering her bowl and towel, she asked, 'Is there anything else I can do for you, Ma'am? Happen a nice hot cup of tea to steady yer nerves?'

Realising Ruby was confused by her decision not to have the girl punished, and not wanting to mystify her any further, Rita decided to humour her. In a kinder voice she replied, 'Thank you, Ruby. A cup of tea would be nice.'

'Don't worry about the bruises, Ma'am,' Ruby assured her. 'A cold-water swab and they're gone in no time.' Her chest swelled with pride. 'I'm a good nurse if I do say so myself.'

Rita was not in the mood for chit-chat. 'Miss Margaret and the girl. Where are they?'

'Gone to Langho. Madge Penny's old man did a runner last week and her eighth bairn is due any minute.' Ruby chuckled. 'You know how Miss Margaret likes to help. She had me sorting out the linen cupboard at the crack of dawn. Her and Miss Cathy left the house some time back, loaded down with all manner of things. Sheets and pillow-cases, towels, nightdresses, and goodness knows what else.'

'And the boy?'

'I ain't seen him since breakfast, Ma'am. I expect he's gone off on one of his little secret missions.' She smiled, but it was without humour. 'The master's still in his study. Do you want me to fetch him?'

'No. I just want to be left alone. In fact, if he shows himself, tell him I'm very tired and don't want to be disturbed.'

'I'll fetch your tea, then I'll see no one comes near.'

When Ruby had gone, Rita sat in the pink wicker chair, her mind on fire from what the girl had told her. 'You lied,' she muttered through clenched teeth. 'Owen wants *me*. I'm carrying his child. I know he would never leave without me.'

Rising from the chair, she went to the window and looked out. Angry tears ran down her face. 'He does love me,' she told a cloudy sky, 'but he *is* leaving. Frank told me he was leaving.' The idea that he might go without her was unbearable. The longer she thought on it, the more confused her mind grew. 'No! He would never leave without me!' A crafty smile transformed her face. 'He's probably waiting for me right now.' A kind of madness took hold of her. Turning on the spot she spun

163

faster and faster until she fell into the chair, dizzy with joy. 'Of course! He daren't come to me, so I have to go to him.' She laughed aloud until Ruby knocked on the door and she was forced to reply in a more serious voice: 'Come in.'

'Here you are, Ma'am.' Ruby had heard her laughing, but thought it best to say nothing. These days she had seen a strangeness in Rita Blackthorn, but to tell the truth she wasn't altogether surprised. Placing the tray on the small table, she quickly withdrew to the quietness of her own kitchen.

Sipping the tea and collecting her thoughts, Rita knew what must be done. 'I'll go to him this very night,' she told herself in the mirror. 'We'll be together for all time.' Softly singing, she lay down on her bed and dreamed of how it would be.

Madge Penny made a loud noise when she made love, and she made a frightening noise when giving birth. Her eighth labour was no exception. The ear-splitting screams could be heard from one end of the street to the other. 'Lord help us!' she cried, squeezing Margaret's hand until it grew numb. 'Where's Widow Carter?'

'She'll be here any minute.' Margaret would never admit it but she was frightened by Madge's awful wailing.

Clutching wildly at her sleeve, Madge writhed on the bed, her plump face contorted with agony. 'For God's sake, get her here . . . tell her I've started and it's bad.' A long crippling pain set her off in a howl that shook the room.

Margaret was beside herself with worry. Never having delivered a child, she was fraught with all manner of doubts as to her own ability. 'Hold on if you can,' she pleaded. 'I've sent for the widow and I'm sure it won't be long before she's here.' She wiped the wet flannel over the woman's face and coaxed her to be quiet. 'Cathy will go with the boy again. Don't worry now.'

'I'm sorry, luv.' Madge Penny was a good soul at heart, but it peeved her to have the gentry woman at her bedside instead of the widow who had given birth to nine of her own and knew what a woman had to endure. 'I've been through it all afore and happen I should know better than to scream and shout,' she said with a little chuckle, 'but it helps, y'see. The louder I shout the easier it is, so don't fear it means I'm dying.'

'I don't fear that.'

'To look at you, anybody would think it were *you* who were giving birth.' Margaret's kindly face was bathed in sweat, and she intermittently paced the room, staring out of the window in search of the widow's homely figure.

'I've never attended a birthing before,' Margaret confessed. 'But you can rely on me. I'll stay until help comes. Meanwhile, just tell me what I have to do.'

The older woman sat up in bed, her long mouse-coloured hair matted with sweat and her face red from exertion. 'The little sod's resting now,' she explained, 'but it won't be long afore it kicks up again with a vengeance.' She rubbed both hands across her stomach and groaned. 'Let's hope the widow's here by then.' Patting at Margaret's hand, she thanked her for all her kindness. 'I reckon we've time for a brew,' she suggested. 'Make it hot and black . . . oh, and put a drop o' booze in it. You'll find it hidden behind the sideboard.' Laughing aloud, she pointed to her stomach. 'That should shift the bugger!'

Margaret was relieved and it showed. 'I could do with a cup of tea myself,' she revealed. 'I'll be as quick as I can. But first, let me make sure you're comfortable.'

Downstairs in the parlour, Cathy waited with Madge's seven children. The room was tiny, no bigger than the shed at the foot of her father's garden. But it was more of a home than Cathy's own. In spite of the poverty that surrounded her, Madge Penny had made the old house into a cosy refuge. The parlour walls were painted green, the black iron fire-range was brightly polished and the long window was covered with respectable lace curtains. The square table was spread with a serviceable green chenille cloth, and in the centre stood a pot plant, green and thriving, making the place surprisingly cheery.

Cathy was seated in the big horse-hair armchair by the fire. Every now and then she would gaze round at the faces of the children. At eleven years of age John was the eldest; small-boned and quiet, he sat in the chair opposite Cathy. The four girls sat round the table, one of the smaller boys sat by Cathy's feet sucking his shirt, and the youngest, a boy not yet two, lay asleep in his makeshift cot under the window. For over an hour they had suffered the howls and wails that issued from upstairs, and now the ensuing silence was unnerving. 'Is she dead?' John stared at Cathy with great big frightened eyes.

Suppressing her own fears, she smiled. 'No, sweetheart. She's having a rest, that's all,' she answered wisely.

'Why's it gone all quiet then?' His voice trembled with emotion.

'She doesn't have to shout *all* the time, silly!' At nine years of age Jessie was the eldest girl. She believed she knew everything, and her brother's questions appeared to amuse and irritate her. 'Honestly, John Penny!' she chided, 'Don't you remember how Mam said she would shout a bit, then be quiet a bit?' She tutted and shook her head like a little old woman. 'Boys are softies,' she told Cathy with a frown. '*You're* not frightened, are you?'

Cathy was honest. 'Just a bit,' she said apologetically.

'Have you heard a baby being born before?'

'No.'

'That's all right then. When our mam had her,' she pointed to the smaller girl beside her, 'I was frightened too.' She cast a glance of derision at her brother John. '*He* shouldn't be frightened though, 'cause he's heard our mam have *all* her babies and she ain't dead yet!'

Cathy smiled. 'Do you want it to be a boy or a girl?' she asked. The idea of a new baby enthralled her.

The girl shrugged her shoulders. 'Don't much care,' she remarked casually. 'They're all the same anyway... shit themselves and scream all night they do. Our mam says she wished she'd drowned us all at birth.'

John gave her an angry stare. 'She never meant that and you know it!'

Sensing a row brewing, the smallest child at the table began crying. 'I don't want to be drowned,' she wailed, looking up at her big sister with appealing eyes. When the older girl put an arm round her and promised, 'Not you, Peg. Our mam didn't want to drown *you*,' she spread her little fingers on the table and began proudly entertaining everyone by counting up to four.

At that point Margaret returned to the parlour to tell them, 'Your mother's fine. It won't be long before you have a baby

166

brother or sister.' Her words were greeted with a smile from Jessie, a confused look from John and a bevy of questions from the smaller children. 'In a minute,' Margaret answered patiently. Addressing herself to John, she said, 'Run to Widow Carter's ... tell her your mother needs her right away, that she's close to birthing.' When he jumped from the chair and thankfully headed for the door, she told Cathy, 'Go with him. Make sure the widow knows it's urgent.' That said, and the two of them gone at a run down the street, she turned her attention to Jessie. 'I'd be grateful if you could make a pot of tea while I talk to the young ones.'

'That's our mam,' the girl replied with a grin. 'Always wanting her brew.' While she set about making it, Margaret couldn't help but think how mature she seemed, when in fact she was only a bairn.

As Jessie came back in through the scullery door with a mug of tea for her mam, Widow Carter came rushing in through the other door, with John and Cathy hurrying behind. 'I couldn't come afore,' she explained in a slurred voice. 'Got into a deep sleep and couldn't find me way out of it.' She grinned through numerous gaps between her blackened teeth. 'Truth is I sank a few too many bevvies last night.'

Margaret hurried down the narrow stairs when she heard Widow Carter arrive.

'I'm sure Mrs Penny will be glad you're here now,' Margaret said with relief. She went on to explain that they had arrived earlier to find the poor woman already in the throes of labour.

'Right then!' Rolling up her sleeves, Widow Carter demanded in a sergeant-major voice, 'Plenty of hot water and towels ... and keep that lot out of me way.' Pointing to the children, she wagged a finger. 'You behave yerselves down here. If I know yer mam I'll have enough to do keeping her quiet.'

She laughed as she made for the stairs. Cathy followed with the mug of tea. 'Old Madge ain't the easiest in the world,' the widow called out to her as she went. 'All women is different when it comes to birthing. What! I've heard the buggers scream blue murder, and I've seen 'em cry like babbies ... I've had to hold 'em down and fight with 'em till I'm black and blue. Then there's them as sees it all as something wonderful and can't wait to hold the little 'un in their arms. But Madge!' She chortled, almost losing her footing as she began her way up the stairs. 'What! She'll scream like a banshee from beginning to end.' Poking a gnarled finger in her ear, she complained wryly, 'I've delivered every one o' Madge's, and now I'm nearly deaf for me thanks.'

Once inside the bedroom, the widow took charge. Giving Madge a scolding, she said, 'You might have waited till I felt capable. I've a head on me like three, and me tongue's stuck to the roof o' me mouth. I'm tired and sick, and it ain't fair yer should wake an old 'un from her bed.'

Madge replied that if she felt ill, it served her right for boozing, and if she didn't soon get on with it, the babby would be here and there'd be no need for her services. 'Miss Blackthorn here's done a wonderful job,' she said, taking great gulps from the mug of tea which Cathy handed her.

'I'm sure she has.' The widow smiled at Margaret, who asked if there was anything more she could do. 'Not a thing,' came the reply. 'In fact, if yer want to make yer way home, I'll say goodnight to yer.' It was clearly a dismissal, and Margaret was quick to realise she was no longer required.

She said her goodbyes and assured Madge that if she needed anything she must send one of the children to Blackthorn House. Madge thanked her profusely, and within minutes Cathy and Margaret had left the house and were on their way down the street. As they reached the corner, Madge's dreadful howls brought them to a halt. 'Is it always like that?' asked Cathy.

Margaret shook her head. 'No,' she replied kindly. 'According to Widow Carter, Madge is unique. Never having had a child myself I'm no expert, but it seems every woman deals with childbirth in a different way. I remember when your mother had you, she was in labour for only two hours and never uttered a sound.'

Cathy dwelt on these words for a long time. Deep in her heart she had hoped that she and David would marry and have children. Now that dream was gone, and she was left with an emptiness that nothing could fill. 'I thought it was so lovely in that house ... all the children, I mean.' She glanced back down the street. 'When you have brothers and sisters you're never lonely, are you?' Not like *she* was lonely, she thought. Even though she had her beloved Margaret, there were still times when she felt all alone in the world.

In the lamplight Margaret looked into her face, and it struck her that at sixteen Cathy was already a woman, with a woman's heart. It was evident in those strong green eyes and that lovely heart-shaped face whose expression was now thoughtful. 'I think you were made to be a wife and mother,' she said softly. 'And it will happen, I know. One day it will happen, sweetheart.'

'But it won't be with David will it?' Cathy's voice trembled, betraying her most private fears. And if it couldn't happen with David, she didn't want it to happen at all.

Margaret's answer was to put her arm round Cathy's shoulders and draw her close. As they walked on, the silence was soothing to them both.

Behind them a child was brought into the world. 'What in God's name were yer thinking of?' Widow Carter had kept her opinions to herself until mother and bairn were safe. 'Fancy letting the gentry near yer ... especially at a time like this!' Apart from a fervent belief that gentry and ordinary folk should be kept miles apart, Widow Carter had a natural suspicion of anyone who lived in a big house.

'She's no different from you nor me,' Madge retaliated. 'Miss Blackthorn and that young niece of hers have been good to me and mine, and I'll not hear a word agin 'em.'

'Oh aye!' Widow Carter hadn't forgotten the shocking fate of someone else who had got too close to Margaret and Cathy Blackthorn. 'An' weren't she good to poor Nan Foster? An' didn't that poor soul have 'er brains bashed in?' She washed Madge, then she washed the bairn, and all the time she grumbled through the wide gaps between her blackened teeth. 'Yer want to be careful o' the company yer keep, Madge Penny,' she warned. 'Or yer might rue the day.'

As they approached the house, Cathy's attention was caught by a flurry of movement against the far hedge. Glancing across, she saw a dark hurrying figure. 'There's someone there,' she whispered, drawing Margaret to a halt. 'Did you see?'

Margaret peered through the darkness. There was nothing. 'A trick of the moonlight,' she suggested. 'Unless of course it's Jack. I wouldn't be at all surprised to see *him* sneaking about at all hours.'

'There *was* someone there, I'm certain of it!' Linking her arm through Margaret's, Cathy quickened her steps towards the house.

Ruby was waiting for them. 'Wherever have yer been till now?' she demanded. When told the whole story, she made them each a mug of cocoa and saw them off to bed. 'Everyone else has been asleep long since,' she declared. 'And now that the two of you are home, I'll not be long afore I'm off to me own bed.'

What with the excitement at Madge Penny's and then the conviction that she had seen someone skulking about as they approached the big house, Cathy couldn't sleep. For a long time she wandered about her bedroom, restless and disturbed but not knowing why. She thought about David and suffered the same painful regrets. She cried a little and chided herself for doing so. She sat by the window and looked over the darkened gardens below, and finally, when a thirst came on her, she put her robe round her shoulders and crept down to the kitchen – almost jumping out of her skin when Jack opened the door just as she had her hand on the door-knob. 'Goodness! You gave me a fright,' she gasped. 'I didn't think anyone would be down here.'

Putting his hands on her arms he drew her inside the kitchen. 'I was on my way to bed,' he said, 'but I'd rather stay and keep you company. I can't sleep anyway.'

Whether Cathy wanted his company or not didn't bother him. 'You were late coming in,' he recalled. 'And you've been gone for most of the day.' He followed her to the pantry. 'You're very quiet. Is anything wrong?'

Pouring the sarsaparilla, she lifted her eyes to stare at him. 'Does it look as though there's something wrong?'

Thrusting his hands into his pockets he warned himself to be careful. If he questioned her, she might feel obliged to question him. That would never do, because his secrets were his own. 'No. I just wondered, that's all.' Pointing to the sarsaparilla he said, 'You can pour me one while you're at it.'

When they were sitting at either end of the table, it was Cathy's turn to ask a question. 'What time did you get in?'

'Ages ago. I've been cooped up and needed a breath of fresh air, so I went for a walk across the fields.' Already he was on his guard. 'Why do you ask?'

Cathy didn't answer straight away. Instead she took her time while recalling the furtive figure she had seen hurrying from the house. 'Did someone visit tonight?'

He shrugged his shoulders. 'Not sure.'

'How long has Father been in bed?'

'He was in the study when I got back. A short time later he went upstairs and there was one hell of a row. He came rushing down again and told Ruby he was feeling ill and going to his bed . . . said he didn't want her disturbing him till tomorrow morning.' He leaned back in his chair and studied her. 'As far as I know he's been in his room since, and no, I don't think he's had any visitors.'

'What about Mother?'

'Been in bed for most of the day . . . sulking as usual.' He rolled his eyes to the ceiling. 'I heard Ruby knock on the door to tell her she'd brought a tray of refreshments. Next minute she was going down the stairs in a bad mood after being sent packing, tray and all.' He eyed Cathy curiously. 'What's all this about?'

'Nothing. Just that when we came back from Mrs Penny's, I thought I saw someone leaving the house.'

'Mrs Penny, eh?' he sneered. 'Who's that? One of your poor folk?'

Cathy didn't like the way he put the question, so she chose not to answer it. Instead she quickly drank her sarsaparilla and bade him good night.

'You're not leaving me here on my own, are you?' He got to the door before her. 'I don't want you to go,' he murmured, deliberately barring her way.

'I'm tired.'

'You weren't tired a minute ago.'

'Well, I am now.' She had welcomed Jack into this house and been a friend to him, but, since he had deliberately picked a fight with David and spoiled their relationship, her feelings towards him had begun to change. 'Let me pass.' Though she felt threatened, her voice was low and calm. 'I don't feel like talking any more.'

He gazed at her lovely face and a kind of anger surged through him. 'You haven't forgiven me, have you?' he remarked bitterly.

She could have evaded the subject, pretending she didn't understand what he meant. But she *did* understand and now that he had raised the matter she had to reply. 'No, I haven't forgiven you. What you did in goading David into a fight was petty and unnecessary, and because of you, he and I are strangers.'

'All the more reason for you and me to be closer.' Sensing an opportunity he was quick to grasp it. Reaching out he caught her by the back of the neck. 'After all, we're not *really* brother and sister, are we?' Pressing his mouth to hers, he kissed her long and hard.

Taken completely by surprise, Cathy was shocked rigid for a minute, but then rage flowed through her. Lifting her hands, she grabbed his ears and twisted them until he cried out, 'Bitch!' Stumbling in pain he backed away, clutching his ears and staring at her in disbelief. 'What did you do that for?'

'I'm surprised you have to ask.' As she stared at him indignantly her face was set like stone. 'It saddened me that Aunt Margaret could never take to you. I see now she had good reason.'

Enraged and humiliated, he grabbed her by the arm. 'I don't give tuppence for what anybody thinks of me, least of all her. But *you're* different. Your precious Margaret might not have taken to *me*, but I took to you right from the start.' He would have stroked her face but she backed away. Her action further infuriated him. Darting to the door, he slammed it shut.

Up to that point, Cathy had felt all kinds of emotion towards him: anger, indignation, even a touch of loathing. But she had not felt fear until the moment when he slammed shut the door. 'Get out of my way!' she snapped. 'NOW!' Suddenly he was not the brother who had been foisted on her, the waif she had pitied and gone out of her way to befriend. Instead he was a dangerous creature.

He smiled at her words, shaking his head as though it was inconceivable that she should ask him to go. 'You're forgetting, I have as much right in this house as you now.' Taking hold of her by the shoulders, he stared at her long and hard, his smiling eyes boring into hers, making her turn away with disgust. When he tugged her forward she struggled like a wildcat. But he was the stronger. 'Don't want to kiss me, eh?' he murmured. 'Think I'm not good enough for you, is that it?' His voice took on a hard edge. 'Oh, but you'd kiss *him* right enough, wouldn't you, eh? You'd let David Leyton put his hands on you?' Bringing his leg up, he pushed his knee between her legs. 'How many times have you done it with him, eh? You can tell me, Cathy.' When she struggled fiercely, he shook her hard. 'HOW MANY TIMES?'

Unyielding she stared him out, at the same time frantically wondering how she could be rid of him. She could scream and wake the entire household, but deep down she realised there were those who would blame her and not him. Besides, even though he was being cruel and unpleasant, she couldn't believe he meant to harm her, not really. She decided to remain calm and be dignified. Surely he would respond similarly. In a quiet voice she told him, 'David is worth ten of you, and you know it.'

Her words seem to surprise him. Softly laughing, he said incredulously, 'It's plain as a pikestaff you'd want him above me.' Squeezing her shoulders, he enjoyed it when she winced. 'You love him, don't you?'

'That's my business. Now get out of my way.' Burning with shame and anger she pushed her hands against his chest, but she was no match for his brute strength.

Suddenly he released her, sending her off balance. 'Go on then!' he urged, opening the door. 'Get back to your bed and dream of your precious David.' He wanted her more than he had ever wanted anything. The want rose in him like a black tide, swamping every other emotion. Now, as she brushed past him, it was all he could do not to take her.

When she left him there, he remained by the door, watching her as she walked along the hallway, his lascivious eyes following her as she went towards the staircase. She had a special kind of grace and a loveliness of nature that he had never before encountered. 'You're beautiful,' he whispered, and the want was overwhelming, spreading through him unchecked, firing his veins and smothering his reason.

On soft footsteps he followed her like a shadow, only a heartbeat behind. Soon he would be leaving this house. He couldn't go without first tasting of Cathy's loveliness.

Unaware that she was being pursued, but deeply unnerved by the incident, she sped along the upper landing towards her bedroom, her soft bare feet making no sound against the carpet. Like a breath of air, David came into her mind, into her heart, warming her senses, making her happy, making her sad. 'Oh, David,' she murmured, coming quietly into her room, 'I wish you were here now.'

As she half turned to close the door, Jack was on her. Fired by lust and hating her because she would always be good and he would always be bad, he clamped his hand over her mouth and pushed her to the floor. The more she struggled, the more brutal he became. In the half-light he saw the terror in her eyes. 'I won't hurt you,' he said. 'But you shouldn't have said those things to me.' Nuzzling his face against hers, he groaned, 'You've made me wild, y'see. And I've always been a bad lot when I'm wild.'

With her arms pinned down and the weight of him on top, she couldn't move. Her heart was beating as though it would burst and when he tore at her nightgown the fear in her was tenfold. As he ravaged her, the fear became horror, then immense pain, and then it was a strange and shocking numbness.

After he moved away, she lay like a stone at his feet. 'Happen you'd like to tell your precious David about that,' he snarled. When she didn't answer or look at him, he kicked her. 'No doubt he'll come after me. Well, let him. Life on the streets taught me how to look after myself. You'd be surprised how good I am with a knife.'

Still she didn't look up, nor did she move. For one awful minute he thought she might be dead. But then he saw the shocked green eyes blink and the tears roll down her face. He sighed with relief. 'You tell him to come after me if you like,' he bragged. 'But be warned . . . I'll be waiting. One dark night when he least expects it, I'll jump on him from some alley.' He

grinned, and in the moonlight he looked half crazy. 'I can promise you this, my lovely. If he comes after me, he won't walk
away.' Bending his face to hers, he whispered, 'Best if you're
sensible, eh? If I were you, I wouldn't tell *anybody* ... not
David, and certainly not your precious Margaret. Because if you
did, I would have to hurt them, and then you'd never forgive
yourself, would you, eh?' Prodding her with his foot, he
demanded, 'You can hear me, can't you? You do know I mean
what I say?'

Cathy heard his every word. Torn and hurting, she waited,
silently biding her time. Her first instinct was to kill him. In her
pain and confusion, she wondered why the good Lord had not
struck him down in front of her. That would be a fitting punishment for what he had done.

'Remember what I said,' he warned grimly. 'Tell whoever you
like. But *I* won't be the one to pay ... it'll be them. O' course,
there's always the chance I might be caught and made to answer
for what's happened. But that wouldn't do you no good neither,
because I'd only deny it till I'm blue in the face.' He chuckled.
'Though I say it meself, I'm a good liar. It wouldn't take much
to convince them that it was your precious David who came
here and attacked you. What! I even saw the fella with me own
eyes ... ran off like the coward he was. Oh, yes, I'll tell a good
story, and it'll see him thrown inside for a very long time, I
reckon.' He pressed his face against hers. 'You know they'd
believe me. After all, anyone could see the way you two felt
about each other.'

Grabbing a hank of her long hair, he said with a moan, 'Don't
make the mistake of thinking I wouldn't do it. Oh, I've sat
across the table from you. I've eaten from your mother's dainty
plates and I've studied the ways of a gentleman. But here where
it matters' – he dug his thumb into his chest – 'I'm a chancer,
a rogue made hard and cruel from living on his wits. You don't
really know me. None of you do. Open your mouth, say one
word about this to anybody, and I swear you'll rue the day. It
won't be me who faces the consequences. It'll be the others ...
them you think the world of. I'll see they suffer one way or
another.' His voice trembled with hatred. 'If I can't promise you
anything else, I can promise you that.'

Like the shadow that had followed her in, he left, silent and unseen by her, a creature with badness born in him.

When the door closed behind him, Cathy lay where she was, dazed and bleeding, tears streaming down her face. After a while she struggled up. Going to the washbowl she bathed herself from head to toe time and again, until the water was all gone and the towel stained with her blood. Taking it and the torn nightgown she put them into the pillow-case and pushed them under the bed. She went to the drawer and took out a clean nightgown which she put on, shivering with cold and tainted by the awful memory of what had taken place here in this very room where she had always felt safe. She didn't feel safe now. She might never feel safe again. The thought was nauseating.

For a while she was lost, not knowing what to do. She paced the floor then sat on the edge of the bed, thinking, not thinking, hardly alive inside.

After an hour she sat in the wicker chair and stared out of the window. The night was very beautiful and the moon was high in a clear dark sky; stars twinkled like tiny jewels and she knew the Maker was watching. 'Help me,' she pleaded. 'Forgive me.' In some way she blamed herself, yet couldn't see why. Folding her arms across her breast, she began rocking back and forth. The clock on the mantelpiece ticked and the hours went by. Soon the dawn was rising and his last words echoed over and over in her tortured mind. She whispered them now and every one etched itself in her heart. 'The others ... them you think the world of. I'll see they suffer one way or another. If I can't promise you anything else, I can promise you that.'

Going to the window, she pressed her face close to the pane. It was cold and hard. The tears came again, bitter painful tears that tore her in two. 'I can't tell,' she cried softly. 'He knows I can never tell.'

The burden of what had happened would be her secret, hers and the fiend who had violated her. For all her life she would have to live with it, and never be able to take comfort from confiding in those who loved her. It was a daunting prospect. Yet Cathy knew in her heart that she would be strong enough. To be weak now would put others in danger, and she could never bring herself to do such a thing.

At long last, emotionally scarred and mentally exhausted, she curled up in bed and sank into a fretful sleep.

Out on the landing, another creature of the night emerged. Twice Rita had inched open her door to peer out. The first time she had seen Jack enter her daughter's room; she had seen how he pushed her inside and suspected his intention. But she did not intervene. To intervene might have jeopardised her own plans and she couldn't have that. And anyway, what did she care about Cathy's fate? Or even Jack's for that matter?

The second time she looked out, it was to see Jack creeping away. From his wicked secretive smile she suspected something awful had taken place in Cathy's room. But her concern was only fleeting. She had other more important matters to attend to. Matters that concerned her and Owen, their future, their child, and she was excited beyond endurance. She waited a while longer until she was certain Jack wouldn't see her; though she was curious when, instead of going in the direction of his room, he went down the stairs. But again, she had neither time nor inclination to dwell on it.

She waited again to see if he might return. He didn't. Convinced he must either be in the kitchen or the sitting room, she carefully ventured out.

Fully dressed and with a hooded cloak hiding her, she went quickly down the stairs and out of the house. 'Be ready, Owen,' she muttered lovingly. The thought of being with him made her quicken her steps.

As she hurried away, Rita was unaware of the young man who watched. Fascinated to see the mistress of the house wandering the fields at night, Jack took up pursuit. Two dark hearts, bent on their own gratification, without remorse or conscience, and with not one saving grace between them.

The night was dark outside, but here in the house she had made cozy Maria sat by a cheery fire. In the light from the blazing logs, she studied her husband's face. 'You're still a handsome man, Owen Leyton,' she said proudly. 'Happen that's the trouble . . . happen if you'd been an ugly old bugger the women wouldn't fall head over heels for you.' She shook her head. 'But they do. And you, like the fool you are, can't refuse the temptation offered you.' She sighed and smiled a little. But then the smile slipped away and a look of concern replaced it. 'If our David knew the things you'd done, he'd have you out that door afore your feet could touch the ground.'

That was the one thing Owen was afraid of. 'David must never know,' he pleaded. 'Teresa neither. If you were to tell them, I couldn't forgive you.'

She laughed at that. 'Oh, I see! If I were to tell our children how you've bedded one woman after another, made a nonsense of our marriage vows and caused us to move on because of your shameful behaviour ... you'd never forgive me? Is that what you're saying?' Her eyes popped out of her head and her mouth hung open with astonishment.

'I know I have no right to ask anything of you.'

'Well, at least you're man enough to admit that.'

'You won't tell them then?'

She studied him before assuring in a warmer voice, 'No, I'll not tell 'em. You can rely on it.' Settling back into her chair she stared into the flames. 'I must be getting soft in the head in me old age.'

'You're far from old, Maria.' He had never seen her as old and never would. 'And you're certainly not soft in the head.'

'Hmph!' She smiled at him. 'I must be, because you've given me a great deal of heartache over the years, and still I've stood by you.' A deep and weary sigh issued from her. 'Any other woman would hate you for what you've done. But so help me, I must be as big a fool as you, because I can't do without you.'

Suddenly he was on his knees before her. 'And I can't do without you, Maria,' he confessed. 'Why do you think I want us away from here? Why haven't I gone off with Rita Blackthorn? I'll tell you why. Because it's *you* I want. Other women tempt me like you said, and yes I'm weak ... and stupid, and I don't deserve someone like you. But in spite of everything, I can't see a life without you. I couldn't survive that, and you know it.' Only when it seemed he might lose her, did he realise how much she really meant to him.

But Maria knew. 'You don't have to tell me,' she said, touching her fingers against his face. 'I've always known we belong together. Oh, the women came and they went, you cheated me time and again, but I always knew it wouldn't last with them. You and me, we're a pair. That's the way it is.' A cold hand took hold of her heart. 'There was only ever one woman who frightened me. One woman who I thought would take you from me.' She visibly shivered. 'I don't have to say her name, do I?'

He shook his head. 'I was afraid too,' he revealed. 'Rita Blackthorn is a witch like no other. I found myself being suffocated ... wondering what life with her would be like.' He closed his eyes and groaned. 'I never wanted that.'

'Then the sooner we're gone from here, the better.' She shivered again. 'Is there a window open?' She looked round, searching for the means by which a chill could enter the room; she wasn't aware that the chill was in their thoughts.

'Not unless David's left a window open in his bedroom again.'

'Go and look, will you? The cold's crept right through me bones.'

Going to the fireplace he took two logs from the basket. Wedging them into the grate, he waited for them to catch alight. When they did he turned to her and said softly, 'It's been a while since we made love in front of the fire, Maria.'

'Has it?'

'The other two won't be back till early light. You know what they're like ... especially David. He won't come home without something to show for a night's poaching.'

'You're right. It *has* been a long time, and to tell the truth I don't know if I could ... not tonight.' She had never felt right making love on the floor. It didn't seem proper. The look on his face prompted her to remark cynically, 'All the same, if I refuse I've no doubt you'll find somebody else only too willing, eh?' Not so long ago she wouldn't have minded even that. But now, since Rita Blackthorn, she saw the risk and didn't want to lose him. 'All right, yer bugger,' she whispered, staring round the room as though afraid someone might overhear. 'But we'll have to be quick. I don't want the children surprising us.'

He came to her and cupped her face in his hands. 'I do love you, Maria.'

'So you should!'

'You have the loveliest blue eyes.'

'Pity you didn't notice 'em when you were gallivanting about.'

'I *always* noticed them.'

'And did you notice the sallow skin and the bags under me eyes?'

'Never!'

'Liar.'

'Don't talk, Maria. Let's enjoy each other.'

'You mean let *you* enjoy me.'

'Shh. Just hold me.' Reaching down he plucked away her shawl and dropped it on the rug. 'Remember how it used to be, before you were took ill,' he urged softly. Raising her skirt, he fondled her soft thighs, then after undoing his trousers he placed his hands beneath and drew her to the edge of the chair. He was kissing her full on the mouth when he entered her, and he knew from her long contented sigh that she was remembering. 'I need you, Maria,' he whispered against her face. 'I will always need you.'

It seemed like a lifetime since she had felt the warmth of his bare skin against her. The warmth invaded her senses and, like a young woman in love for the first time, she clung to him, her legs wide apart and he between them. In that fevered moment there was no other woman, no regrets; only joy of a kind she had almost forgotten.

Rita Blackthorn emerged from the darkness and made her way towards the house. Her hair was dishevelled and the hem of her dress torn where it had tangled in the brambles; her feet ached and her body was wet with sweat. She had trudged a long way and was weary. The only thought that spurred her on was that soon she and Owen would leave this place for good.

Like the bold creature she was, she went straight to the front door and knocked on it. When there was no answer she knocked again. Still no answer. Resting for a moment against the wall she recovered her breath and tidied the straying strands of her hair. A moment later she was creeping softly around the house, towards the one lighted window she had seen on her approach. She thought it odd that the house was so quiet, especially when a family of four lived within its walls.

Light from the window shafted into the night. The curtains

were not closed and so she peered in. She could see only half the room. It looked warm and cosy, the logs danced and crackled in the fireplace, throwing flickering shadows on the walls and lighting up the pretty pictures that hung there.

In the cold night air, balancing on a mound of dry earth in order to see inside, she felt impatient and uncomfortable. Seeing no one, and assuming the room was empty, she was about to move away when a sound caught her attention; it was a strange noise, a grated sigh, the guttural moan of a wounded animal – or like the sound she knew Owen made when he was in the throes of love.

Shifting position so it was easier to see the entire room, she craned her neck and looked to the right of the fireplace. At first she didn't understand. But then, as her senses took it in, her eyes grew round with horror. She saw it all; Maria, naked from the waist down, half-sitting, half-lying in the chair, her arms stretched wide with fingers gripping the chair-arm. Owen too was half-naked, on his knees, with his trousers round his ankles; his whole body rose and fell as he feverishly thrust forward. Then, in the moment when Rita reeled away, he fell on his wife's body, his face bathed with a look of ecstasy.

Insane with jealousy and fired by it, Rita ran to the front door and slammed her fists against it. 'BASTARD!' Her voice cut viciously through the night air. The door was flung open and there stood Maria, white-faced and angry. '*You!*' Momentarily taken aback, she stared open-mouthed.

Rita used the moment to push her way past. 'It's not you I want,' she snapped. 'You know that!' Made insane by what she had seen through the window, she still intended that nothing would stand in the way of her and Owen being together.

Fearful that everything she had achieved was in danger of being spoiled, Maria followed her. 'You won't have him!' she yelled. 'He doesn't want you, can't you understand that? Get out of here! Who the devil do you think you are . . . barging your way into my home?'

Suddenly Owen was there, his face dark with rage. 'She's right,' he said in a firm low voice. 'I *don't* want you. I never really wanted you . . . not in the way you thought.'

Something about his calm manner stilled her, though inside

181

she was bubbling with such hatred she could have strangled him with her bare hands. For what seemed an age she didn't speak. Instead she stared at him, stared *through* him, her eyes dark with rage as they raked his handsome face. 'I could kill you,' she whispered harshly, and as she spoke her fists clenched and unclenched, twisting the sides of her dress until it tore.

'I want her out!' Maria stumbled against the sideboard, her breathing hard and shallow, her cold blue gaze going from one to the other. 'Tell her it's finished. Tell her if she doesn't leave, *I'll* be the one to do the killing.'

Owen didn't look at his wife. His eyes were on Rita, and even now he was stunned by her beauty. 'You heard what my wife said,' he told her. 'She wants you to leave.'

Rita had seen the fleeting admiration in his eyes. She sensed his dilemma. Her smile was triumphant as she slyly regarded him. 'You still want me, I can see.'

'You're mad.' The assurance in his voice belied the awful truth, for he did still want her. Even now, after having made love to his wife, his loins burned for this woman.

Rita shook her head. 'I saw you ...' She glanced at Maria, who appeared to be struggling for breath, her face drawn and pale. 'You and her.' There was disgust in her face. 'How could you?' she asked, her voice darkening. 'How could you couple with her, when I'm here for the asking?'

'Because I love her.' Owen was desperately struggling. In that minute, even with Maria looking on, he could hardly hide his need for Rita. His weakness was shocking, making him wish he had never been born. But it was there and Rita knew it. Worse ... Maria knew it too.

'You can't love her. It's me you really want ... me and the child.' She glanced at Maria once more and her mouth twisted in a wicked smile. Then she was addressing Owen again. 'I should hate you for what you've done, but I can't. Nor can I leave here without you.'

Coming forward, Maria stood between them. Her voice trembled as she addressed Owen. 'What does she mean ... she said her and *the child*. What child, Owen?'

'Please, Maria.' He looked sadly at her before dropping his gaze to the floor. 'Can't you see she means to break up this marriage?'

This time Maria would not be pacified. 'What child, Owen? I want to know the truth.'

Rita was delighted. 'Tell her, Owen.' She pressed the flat of her hand to her stomach. 'Tell her I'm carrying our love child.'

Maria's action took them both by surprise. Launching herself at Rita, she got her by the throat, shaking with a strength that amazed even her. Before Owen could separate them, the two women had fallen to the floor. With a sickening thud, Rita's head hit the corner of the fender. 'Leave her, Maria!' cried Owen, grabbing her by the shoulders and pulling her away. 'For God's sake, do you want to kill her?'

Maria herself was ill, weakened by the struggle and heart-broken by what Rita had told. 'Yes, I want to kill her,' she replied, watching him as he lifted Rita to her feet. 'Just tell me . . . is it true? Is she carrying your child?' All the time she spoke she was aware that his arm was round Rita, that Rita was staring at her, hating her. Maria told herself it wouldn't have mattered if she *had* killed the witch.

Owen turned his face from Rita's. 'It's all right,' he said, easing her into a chair. 'She isn't badly hurt.' Rita was dazed and there was a trickle of blood coming from the back of her head. But she was recovered, and enjoying the friction between husband and wife.

'Answer me, Owen. Is she carrying your child?'

'I was going to tell you.' He was frantic. 'Once we were away from here, I meant to tell you everything.'

'You're a liar. I've forgiven you for your womanising,' she said in a chillingly flat voice, 'I've always forgiven you because I've believed you were weak and couldn't help yourself. I've forgiven you because I love you above all else.' She looked at Rita's smirking face and her anger was tenfold. 'But you kept this from me. You didn't have the courage to tell me you'd got her with child. That much I can't . . . won't . . . forgive.'

'What difference does it make?' He had never seen her like this and he was destroyed. 'I don't want her, and I don't want the child.' He scowled at Rita, not noticing how the colour had drained from her face. 'Besides, how do I know it's mine? It could be anybody's.'

Maria was indignant. 'Oh, it's yours all right,' she said. 'I know when a woman's telling the truth about such a thing.' He went to touch her but she recoiled. 'Get her out of here. Pack your things and go with her. And don't ever come back.'

'No, Maria. You don't know what you're saying!'

'Do as I ask, or when David comes back I'll ask him to throw you out.'

'I thought we'd agreed you would never say anything to him?'

'That was before I knew she was carrying your child.' She had no intention of sharing his shame with David, but it wouldn't hurt to let Owen suffer for his sins.

'But why should her carrying my child make any difference?'

'You wouldn't understand.' There was a great sadness in her voice. 'Only a woman could understand.'

'All right, Maria, I'll go.' He saw no point in arguing now; he was arrogant enough to believe that when Rita was out of the way he would make Maria see sense. 'But only until the morning. Once you've had a chance to think about this, you'll be sorry, I know.'

She laughed softly and he saw a side to her he never knew existed. 'No, Owen. It's *you* who'll be sorry.' Turning away, she sat in the chair where only a short while ago they had made love. Softly she began to rock herself, back and forth, her arms crossed and her sorry gaze directed towards the dying flames in the firegrate.

'There's no talking to you like this,' he protested. 'Think what you're doing to us, Maria. I'll be back in the morning. We'll talk then.'

After collecting his hat and coat from the nail on the door, he dressed for the night air. 'You'd best be on your way,' he told Rita in a sour voice. 'You've caused enough trouble here, damn your eyes.'

Maria heard the front door close, but she didn't move. She was too filled with pain and shame.

'You *are* coming with me, aren't you?' Leaning against the wall of the house, Rita studied his face in the moonlight. She felt exhilarated, yet just a little afraid. 'It's what we wanted, isn't it?' she urged. 'You and me . . . and the child?'

Rounding on her, he snarled, 'It might be what *you* wanted, but it was never my intention to break up with Maria.' Clenching his fist he slammed it against the wall. 'What possessed you to do it? Why did you come here?'

'I came for you.'

Ignoring her remark, he groaned, 'I hope to God I can put right what you've done this night.' Catching hold of her arm, he propelled her away from the house. 'I'm taking you home.'

Struggling, she argued, 'I don't want to go home. I want to go with you.'

'That's out of the question, and you know it!' The very thought of it made him quicken his steps. 'You really are mad.' Convinced he must get her home and confess all to Frank Blackthorn, he dragged her at a smarter pace down the lane.

Rita argued all the way. 'I have money put away . . . enough to keep us in a grand style. The child will be a boy, I know it will.' She wanted to seduce him, she longed for it to be like it was before. The very thought of resuming some sort of existence in Frank Blackthorn's house left her cold. 'The child will be a son, Owen . . . a son for you and me. We'll have a fine life, and we'll be happy together, you'll see.' The faster he rushed her, the more breathless she became. She was in pain, dazed and confused. The wound on her head was throbbing and the blood was gushing out; she could feel it warm and sticky on her neck.

Incensed by her ceaseless argument, he suddenly stopped and shook her hard, his fingers digging into her shoulders and making her cry out. 'STOP IT!' he yelled. 'FOR GOD'S SAKE, LEAVE IT BE!' Slamming her against the trunk of a tree, he pushed his face close to hers. All need of her was gone. Only a sense of desperation remained. 'Listen to me,' he pleaded. 'As far as I'm concerned, we had nothing special. We had a fling . . . slept together. A bit of fun, that's all.' Shaking her again, he demanded, 'Do you hear what I'm saying? You were nothing more than a bit of fun. If I had my way I'd put an end to you and the brat here and now.' Pressing his fist to her stomach, he snarled, 'If it hadn't been for this, Maria would have forgiven me. Now I'm not so sure, damn you!'

Through a haze she saw the hatred in his face. It kindled a kind of love in her, and something else, some strange feeling she could not control. Slowly she slid from his grasp, and as she fell, the moonlight faded, her senses reeled, and she knew she was close to losing consciousness.

'Rita!' He fell to his knees beside her. It was then he realised how ill she was, how pale and racked with pain. The blood from her head wound trickled down her neck; it stuck to his hand and frightened him. 'I'll get you home,' he told her in a kinder voice. 'Don't worry, I'll get you home.'

To his surprise she pushed him away. 'I don't need you to take me home!' she protested. 'Get back to your wife.'

'I'm sorry,' he said penitently, moving away.

'Oh, you will be,' she promised. 'You *will* be sorry for what you've done to me.' Struggling to her feet, she stumbled away. Twice he attempted to help, and each time she threw him off, screaming abuses and lashing out.

'All right. If that's the way you want it.' Dejected, he took another direction.

The journey to Blackthorn House seemed to take forever. Driven on by rage and a burning need for revenge, Rita was only a few steps from the house when a figure lurched from the shadows and struck her, again and again, each time harder than before. In the moonlight she saw the silhouette of her attacker. She saw the face and she knew it well. The next time she was hit, her senses darkened and she slithered to the ground.

It was morning before Rita Blackthorn was found. Ruby wasn't certain whether what she saw was a figure or a poacher's sack. When she realised it was the mistress, badly hurt or even dead, she ran screaming into the house, going straight to the study where Frank was sleeping across his desk.

When some time later Rita was gently carried into the doctor's carriage, he climbed in beside her. Margaret was there, with Cathy and Ruby. They watched in shocked silence as he closed the doors.

Still deeply affected by what had happened earlier between herself and Jack, Cathy could hardly take it in. 'Will she die?' she asked, and Margaret's heart went out to her.

'All we can do is pray,' she said.

Aware that Cathy was in a state of shock, Margaret talked to her all the way back to the house. Behind them, Ruby sniffled loudly into her handkerchief. As for Jack, he seemed unusually preoccupied, kicking at the ground with his boot and planning his next move.

At the Infirmary, Rita was quickly taken to a room where the doctors attended her without delay. But there was little they could do. Frank sat by her side, watching helplessly as she drifted in and out of consciousness, her green eyes silently pleading with him but her mind dwelling on Owen and his wife. 'Who did it, sweetheart?' he pleaded through a blur of tears. 'Who hurt you like this?'

When she became agitated, he called the doctor, who gave her laudanum. 'She'll rest now,' he told Frank. 'But you can stay if you like.'

He was inconsolable. 'Have the police arrived yet?' he demanded. When told they had not, he rolled his eyes and looked at Rita's face once more. 'Who could do such a thing?' he pleaded.

Both men were startled when she answered, '*He* did it.' The doctor would have quietened her, but she was frantic. In a broken voice she confessed, 'The child . . . it's . . . Owen Leyton's. He wanted me . . . dead.'

In that moment she looked radiant. As she raised her eyes to the ceiling her voice was almost inaudible. 'Forgive me, Owen,' she whispered. 'But I can't leave without you.'

When Rita Blackthorn died two days later, she took her lover with her, just as surely as if she had stabbed him through the heart.

On her accusation he was instantly arrested. Spots of blood were found on the Leytons' hearth. Maria Leyton, still smarting from the confrontation, herself gave an account of how her husband was Rita's lover, and that she was carrying his child. She revealed how Owen and Rita had quarrelled on the night of the attack. She told how Owen went with Rita from the house, and of how she had heard them outside, shouting at each other, with Owen threatening to 'put an end to you and the brat'. She said all that in a surge of terrible rage. Then, when it was all too late, she regretted every shocking word.

Owen Leyton was charged with murder. At his trial the jury swiftly returned a verdict of guilty. The judge donned his black cap and pronounced that Owen Leyton would be hanged by the neck until he was dead.

The courtroom was packed. Frank did not attend. Since Rita's death he seemed to have lost his purpose in life. While Owen Leyton was standing trial, Frank was standing at Rita's graveside. Before that he had drunk himself insensible, as he had done every day and night since that awful day.

When the sentence was delivered, Maria's cry echoed from the walls and, gazing at her, Owen desperately pleaded his innocence.

Their two children stood close by: Teresa cold and unmoved; David tall and strong, but inwardly broken. As he left the court, his face was set like granite, his gaze fixed straight ahead. He was aware that Cathy was only an arm's reach away but dared not look up. The precious love they had shared was now lost to him forever. He could never go to her. Not now. Not when his own father had murdered her mother.

Though it was hard to realise her mother was gone, Cathy's heart went out to David in his grief. She followed him with sad lonely eyes, aching to go to him but knowing he must turn her away. 'Now, he will never want to know me, will he?' she said when Margaret came to her side.

'I think it's best if you put him out of your mind,' came the quiet reply. 'Put it *all* out of your mind.'

Jack was arrogant as ever, appearing untouched by all that had happened. Overhearing what Cathy had said, he remarked sourly, 'The Leytons aren't worth *that*!' Raising his hand he clicked his fingers and gave a small laugh, becoming instantly silent when Margaret glared at him.

Cathy's answer was to stare at him hard and long. 'I think I told you once before . . . David Leyton is worth *ten* of you!' she said menacingly. The dark anger in his face was all the satisfaction she needed. One day he would pay dearly for what he had done to her. One day, in the future, he would get his just punishment.

CHAPTER EIGHT

The hanging of Owen Leyton sent ripples of reaction through the whole of Lancashire. A month after the event, people still gathered on street corners and whispered of it; boozy men sat in dark corners of ale-houses, grinning and making snide comments about how they wouldn't have minded 'laying bare-arsed' across the beautiful Rita Blackthorn. Every man jack who knew the tale spread it far and wide; Frank Blackthorn became a figure of fun while Maria Leyton drew a mixture of pity and scorn, considering that, in her testimony to the authorities, she had helped her wretched husband on his way just as surely as if she had put the rope round his neck with her own two hands.

One bright spring morning, Cathy rose early from her bed. 'Is Aunt Margaret up yet?' she asked as Ruby came bustling out of the kitchen.

'Not yet, dear.' Ruby had on a new pinafore, a gaudy thing with a pattern of huge red roses and forget-me-nots all over. Her hair was meticulously curled and she had a certain look in her eye; the kind of look that made Cathy suspect she might have a suitor. 'There's neither your aunt nor your father out of their beds yet,' Ruby pronounced sternly. 'As for that surly young fella Jack – well, since your father doesn't keep an eye on him any more, he just seems to get lazier.'

Even the mention of Jack's name turned Cathy's stomach. The memory of a certain night was too alive in her, too bitter. Ignoring Ruby's comment, she said, 'I suppose you know my father was drunk when he came in last night?' It saddened her to see how little life meant to him since losing his beloved wife.

Ruby's face dropped. 'I'm sorry, dearie,' she said quietly. 'I know how hard it must be for you. But I'm sure he'll pull round. People suffer grief in different ways, and he was devoted to her as you know better than I do.' Her face brightened. 'It'll come right, you'll see. Nature has a habit of mending even the sorest wounds.'

Cathy was hopeful too. 'Bless you for that, Ruby,' she said, on impulse leaning down to kiss the dear soul on the cheek. 'I honestly don't know what we'd do without you.'

'Same as we've all got to do without our Queen Victoria,' Ruby said. 'We soldier on, that's what.' The news of Queen Victoria's passing had shocked and saddened the nation. 'For them as are left behind, life has to go on. As for you, Cathy Blackthorn, you've got enough of your own troubles to contend with, but you're made of the right stuff to carry you through.'

She looked at Cathy now and in that instant realised she had matured into a real beauty; her shining fair hair spilled over her shoulders in deep waves, and her stunning green eyes were deep with warmth and compassion. Lovely in looks, lovely in nature, Ruby mused. And made to suffer things not of her making. Since she was a bairn in arms, Cathy had forever captured a little corner of Ruby's heart.

Ruby seemed full of the joys of spring. Winking naughtily at Cathy, she said brightly, 'I was hoping everyone would be up and about early, so I could get the table cleared and everything spick and span before the ten o'clock tram into Blackburn.'

'What? Are you off shopping then, Ruby?'

'No, no, dear,' she replied guardedly. 'I'm just going to see a friend.' She blushed again, and Cathy thought better of pursuing the matter.

'Now then, young lady, I expect you're hungry?' Chattering all the way, Ruby hurried off to the kitchen. 'I'll have your breakfast on the table before you can bat an eyelid. It's all but ready.'

In a matter of minutes the aroma of sizzling bacon had filled the house. 'Will you mind very much if I don't have any breakfast, Ruby?' Cathy's stomach was turning somersaults at the very thought of food. She had lain awake until the early hours, waiting for her father to come home from the ale-house. A few minutes after he went into his study she crept down and opened the door; he was lying on the floor, blind drunk and raving incomprehensibly. The experience of these past weeks had taught her it was no use trying to move him, so she made him as comfortable as possible, put a pillow beneath his head, laid a blanket over him, and left him to sleep it off.

Even then she had hardly slept a wink, going downstairs at regular intervals to check on him. Now, all she wanted was a breath of fresh air. The sun was shining outside and the garden called. 'I need a walk, that's all,' she explained. 'To blow the cobwebs away.'

Too many 'cobwebs' clung to her. Darling Nan and her mother, the way those two had met with their awful end... her father's inconsolable grief and the insatiable drinking that would ruin them all... the way Jack had defiled her. And David. Oh, David! How she missed his tender affection and the warmth of his smile. Every day she loved and needed him a little more. Every day she wondered how she could mend the terrible rift that had grown between them. But it was not to be. He was lost to her, and she must learn to live with that; just as she must learn to live with all the other misfortunes that had touched her life. Such bad memories, yet in a strange way they were still very much alive, living and breathing, each a burden in its own way. Cobwebs, clinging shadowy cobwebs, which little by little threatened to suffocate her.

After drinking the cup of tea Ruby insisted on brewing for her, Cathy went out into the garden. Though the sun was shining, the air carried a cutting chill, but wrapped up in a long coat and scarf she felt cosy and warm.

The garden was pitifully overgrown. Weeds and brambles had invaded the lawns, the shrubs were tangled and the path that led to the rustic bench was made narrower by the encroachment of creeping foliage. Seating herself on the bench, Cathy took stock of all that surrounded her. 'When the weather breaks, I'll get Aunt Margaret to help me clear this mess away,' she murmured.

Just for a moment she turned her thoughts to Ruby's comments regarding Queen Victoria. It did seem strange though, for that grand lady had been Queen for all of Cathy's life and many long years before. She also realised that, no matter how grand or humble a person was, they all had to face the same God one day.

Margaret appeared at the other end of the garden. 'Mind if

I join you?' she called. When Cathy's answer was to shift along the bench, she came and sat beside her. Shivering, Margaret pulled her scarf tighter round her shoulders. 'Isn't it too cold for you to be sitting out here?'

'I just had to get out of the house.' Cathy had never been really happy there, and lately the walls felt as though they were closing in on her.

'You should have woken me,' Margaret chided.

Cathy chuckled at that. 'Don't think I wasn't tempted,' she teased. However, she knew Margaret was also having sleepless nights. On three occasions this past week when Cathy couldn't sleep and sought refuge in the kitchen, she had found Margaret already there. Each time the two of them had sat until dawn, sipping tea and talking.

Margaret settled back in her seat, the damp wood chilling her bones. 'How long do you mean to stay out here?' Folding her arms, she hugged herself. 'Ruby said you didn't want any breakfast. Why's that?' Lately, she had been concerned about Cathy. She suspected that something very secret was preying on her mind. And it wasn't only the sequence of tragedies that had overtaken this family.

Cathy answered two questions in one. 'I don't seem to have any appetite this morning. I had a bad night and thought a few minutes in the open air would do me good.' Afraid that Margaret meant to quiz her further, she quickly added, 'Give me half an hour, then I'll be ready to come with you to the churchyard.'

'Well now, that's why I came to find you.' Shifting in her seat so she could look into Cathy's curious eyes, she paused, wondering how to impart the news she had heard from the solicitor. 'Yesterday I had a very important letter. I needed to discuss it with your father then, but he was never in the house for more than two minutes at a time.'

Something in Margaret's voice alarmed Cathy. 'Is anything wrong?' she asked anxiously.

'Oh, I'm sure it's something and nothing. But the sooner I speak with your father, the better.' She took a great gulp of fresh air and slowly breathed it out while appearing to think hard, then she patted Cathy's hand and smilingly reassured her.

'There's nothing for you to worry about. And anyway, it should only take half an hour at the very most.'

Cathy was not altogether convinced. 'Can I ask you who the letter was from?' she enquired softly.

Loath to explain how the solicitor's letter had warned her of sales that had been made by Frank without her knowledge, Margaret answered, 'It's to do with our land and property.'

'Does Father know you want to talk with him?'

'Not yet, but I hope he's up to it.' Margaret wore a wry expression. 'He emerged from the study as I came out, and from the look of him, I wonder if he's in a fit state to talk about *anything* at the minute.'

'While he's still drunk. Isn't that what you mean?' There was a deal of sadness in Cathy's voice, but resignation too. She had long stopped fooling herself where her father was concerned.

Cursing herself for being so insensitive, Margaret lowered her gaze. 'I'm sorry,' she murmured. 'But, yes, that is what I meant.'

'It's all right. I'm old enough not to be shocked any more.'

'I know.' Margaret looked into Cathy's troubled eyes and was ashamed. 'That's something else I'm sorry about. I also know it must have been you who covered him over and made him comfortable.' She shook her head angrily. 'Oh, Cathy! Your father goes from bad to worse. Why can't he bear his grief with dignity?'

Cathy's voice was cold. 'Because he's a weakling.'

Margaret was shocked. Usually, Cathy sprang to her father's defence, yet here she was condemning him. 'He misses Rita dreadfully,' she said, summoning a little compassion for Frank. 'I suppose we'll just have to be patient with him.'

'What did the letter say?'

'What letter?' She pretended to have forgotten that important issue.

Cathy stared at her in disbelief. 'The letter you mentioned just now . . . the one about our land and property. Is it very serious?'

Margaret gave a small embarrassed laugh. 'Oh! *That* letter?' She was sorry she had ever mentioned it. 'It's just one of those irritating letters that remind you of your responsibilities, that's all,' she said casually. In fact the letter was very disturbing.

'Oh.' Cathy sensed it was more than that. Margaret was

193

worried and it showed. 'Do you want me to wait for you?'

'It seems a shame for you to hang about.' Worried that Cathy might overhear the imminent argument between herself and Frank, Margaret decided, 'No. You go ahead. I need to stretch my legs. I'll go for a little walk round the house before I disturb your father ... give myself time to think.'

'Are you sure?' Cathy sensed the letter meant more than Margaret was saying. Just now she had complained about the cold and here she was, talking about going for a walk. 'I can wait for you.'

'No. I'd rather you went on, sweetheart. I'll follow as soon as I've talked with your father.'

It was agreed. Margaret set out for her few quiet minutes in which to prepare for what she assumed would be a confrontation with Frank, while Cathy made her way back to the house.

In the kitchen Ruby was waiting to get ready the flowers. 'I've had them standing in water, so they're still nice and fresh,' she told Cathy. 'It's the wrong time of year for a colourful show, but these daffodils are long-lasting and should keep well.'

Taking the bright yellow flowers out of the jug, she separated them into two bunches and wrapped them in greaseproof paper. 'There you are,' she said, laying them on the draining board. 'And while you're at the church, I'd be grateful if you'd light a penny candle for me old dad. Been gone these past thirty years he has ... a miserable, spiteful old sod he were, so I reckon he still needs to be shown the way to heaven!'

Taking two copper pennies out of her purse, she laid them on the table. 'Happen you'd better light *two* candles, eh?' she chuckled.

Cathy was intrigued. 'I've never heard you talk about your father before. But I'll light the candles, of course I will.' She reached out to collect the coppers and was surprised when Ruby snatched them back.

'On second thoughts,' she said, dropping the coins into her purse, 'if he ain't got to heaven by now, there ain't much chance of him getting there at all, is there, eh?' That said she took off her pinnie and put on her hat and coat. 'Being Sunday there's only a skeleton tram service, so I'd best get a move on.' Ushering Cathy out of the kitchen, she suggested, 'You can walk me to the end of the lane and see me on the tram if you like.'

'Yes, I will,' Cathy agreed. 'First I'll just go and see if Father's all right.'

'He's gone back into his study,' Ruby told her. 'If you ask me he should be in his bed.' As far as she was concerned, Frank Blackthorn was beyond saving.

First Cathy knocked on the study door. When there was no answer, she knocked again and was told in a gruff voice to 'Enter'.

Going into the study, she was struck by the smell: stale alcohol and sweat. The window was tightly shut and her father was seated at his desk, his body leaning forward and his arms stretched across the polished top. 'What is it? I'm not in the mood for visitors.' Looking up with bleary eyes he peered at her face as if he had never seen it before. 'Is that you, Cathy?'

'Yes, Father.' In spite of his neglect of her all these years, it broke her heart to see him like this.

'What do you want?' As he spoke he slammed his fist on the desk.

'I've just come to see if you're all right.'

'Hmph! Do I *look* all right?' In fact he looked shocking. With swollen bloodshot eyes and a face that hadn't seen a razor for many days, he resembled the worst kind of vagabond. 'Do I look like Rita Blackthorn's husband?' he asked with a leer.

'No. Neither do you look like my father.' There was condemnation in Cathy's expression. 'You've changed, and not for the better.'

He sat up at that, his eyes wider and his whole countenance ready to pounce. 'Oh? And you don't like what you see, is that what you're saying?' he demanded.

'I don't like what you're doing to yourself.' She came to the desk and stood before him, like a criminal before a magistrate. But he was shamed and she was dignified. 'If I don't like what I see, it's only because I love you.'

'Well, I don't ... love ... you,' he said cruelly, the words issuing slowly and spitefully.

'I know you don't.' It cost Cathy dearly to say what was in her heart. 'I believe you've *never* loved me.'

'Does it matter?'

'There was a time when it mattered more than anything in the whole world.'

'Your mother loved you even less.'

Cathy gave no answer to that. But she had to know. 'Why does it please you to hurt me, Father?'

'Because you're not her, and you can't take her place.' Suddenly he was crying. 'She's not gone, you know,' he muttered. 'She's still here.'

He gazed round the room. 'She's all around ... everywhere I look. But don't you see? It's worse. It's agony because I can see her but not hold her. She's with me all the time, but when I reach out to touch her she moves away.' He gave a strangled laugh. 'It's always been like that between me and your mother.' He bent his head over the desk and cried, great racking sobs that shook his frame.

Cathy came forward and touched his head with great tenderness. 'Please, Father, don't punish yourself so.' It was awful to see him like this. 'If only you'd let me help, I know things could be better.'

With one mighty swipe he sent her staggering backwards across the room. 'I DON'T WANT YOUR HELP!' Standing now, he glowered at her from behind his desk, clinging to its edge for support. 'Your mother hated you, and so do I,' he hissed. 'Now get out!'

Shocked to the core, she turned away, glancing at him from the door before quietly departing. She wanted to cry but couldn't. Instead a cold, hard feeling came over her. Something changed in that moment; something which had once been very precious was now gone forever. It may have been the last hope clinging on from childhood ... or the desperate need of a young woman to be loved by her parents; it may have been the helpless sense of belonging that had existed even when she was never sure they wanted her. She couldn't tell what it was exactly. All she knew was that her feelings could never be the same again.

'Put you out on your ear, has he?' Jack's harsh voice infiltrated her thoughts. 'Still, I don't care. The more he hates you, the more money he'll leave to me when he goes to hell.'

She looked up to see him smirking at her, lolling against the banister in that lazy manner he had. She recalled Ruby's words:

'Since your father's been neglecting him, he seems to get lazier.' In fact he was hardly ever in the house; his shirt was in need of a wash, his hands were filthy and his thick fair hair was unkempt. Yet when his small hazel eyes smiled on her, he was still as arrogant and self-important as ever.

Cathy knew he was waiting for her to make a comment. But she had no intention of saying anything. With head held high and her expression giving nothing away she walked straight past him, towards the kitchen where Ruby was waiting. 'It won't be long now!' he shouted after her. 'The way the old man's going, he'll soon be rotting in the ground with *her*! If it were me, I'd be glad to be shut of her. When all's said an' done she never wanted him . . . went to the grave with another man's brat inside her, didn't she, eh?'

Enraged, Cathy swung round. But he was gone. Ruby came out to meet her. 'I heard what he said,' she murmured. 'I only hope the master didn't.' Her nervous gaze flickered towards the study. But all was still.

The silence was broken by Margaret's footsteps. Totally unaware of what had just taken place and surprised to see Cathy, she asked, 'Still here? I thought you would have been gone by now.'

Cathy's bright smile and quick answer belied the turmoil inside her. 'I wanted to see Father before I went.'

'Oh? And where did you find him?'

'In the study.'

'Is he in a better mood?'

Cathy hesitated. Ever since she was a little girl she had shared her most secret thoughts with Margaret, but now she found herself suppressing those deeper feelings as she answered, 'You might say he's the same as usual.' Rushing towards the kitchen, she explained, 'I'd best be off. Ruby's kept the flowers fresh and they should make a lovely show in the vases.'

As she hurried away she fought to keep the tears down. Her whole world was falling apart, with only Margaret and Ruby keeping it together. What she felt for them could never be expressed in mere words. They were like candles in the dark, warm and glowing, keeping her sane.

Margaret made her way to Frank's study, while Ruby and Cathy

197

went away from the house. At the bottom of the lane they parted company; Ruby to the tram-stop, and Cathy to take the narrow footpath that led to the church of St Peter. 'Mind how you go now,' Ruby warned. 'Make sure you stay close by the church so your aunt can find you.'

'Stop worrying,' Cathy gently chided. 'You just go and enjoy yourself.'

Ruby saw the glint in Cathy's eye and blushed a fierce shade of pink. 'Whatever do you mean?'

'You've been blushing all morning, you're dressed up in your very best clothes, and you've curled your hair. You look pretty enough to meet a gentleman, that's what I mean.'

Ruby blushed again. 'Cheeky young madam!' she muttered. But she didn't deny it and, when she went at a faster trot down the lane, suddenly burst out singing one of her favourite Irish ditties; all of which only served to convince Cathy that Ruby did have a suitor after all.

As she neared the church, Cathy's heart grew lighter. The walk to St Peter's was a delight in any weather, but on a day like today when the sun was shining, there was a timelessness about the scene that took her breath away.

She came through the spinney and out into the open again. At the top of the rise, she stood and looked out over the landscape. Immediately in front of her the bracken, shrubs and heather were already budding up. The fields stretched beyond as far as the eye could see, a huge magnificent patchwork quilt . . . green and gold, brown and russet, trimmed with hedges and low stone walls. Horses grazed contentedly, with curious hares standing bolt upright at a distance, watching the proceedings before leaping away, with ears pricked high and powerful hind legs driving them along. Heavily pregnant sheep dotted the open fields, heads down as they munched at the grass. In the distance the church bells could be heard calling the community to Sunday Mass, and above it all the birds twittered and sang in the treetops.

On such a day, there was something uniquely peaceful about God's earth. Just being part of it brought a soothing calm to Cathy's turbulent spirit. Lighter of heart, she went on her way, her steps more leisurely now. By the time she got to the church the worshippers would have gone home. Somehow she didn't feel able to mingle with a crowd. Not today.

Having arranged the first bunch of flowers in the stone vase, Cathy said a little prayer over Nan Foster's grave. She told her how much she still missed her, and promised, 'I'll never forget you.' Then, with tears in her eyes, she got up from her knees and walked to the other side of the churchyard, where her mother lay.

It was not hard to talk to Nan; to say all the things that were close to Cathy's heart. But here, with her mother not six feet beneath where she stood, Cathy always found herself afraid. Afraid to let her mother know what she was thinking, afraid she had been too harsh in her judgement, too condemnatory, too selfish and greedy in ever wanting Rita to cherish her. As a small child, rejected and unloved, she'd yearned so much for a 'real' mother, someone who would sit in the firelight with her and share those things that mother and daughter share; someone who would sing her to sleep or tell her a story, filling her world with dreams and wonderful things, someone who would smile and hold her when she was hurt. Most of all, someone who, when childhood was slipping away, could explain all the things that were constantly changing. This was what Cathy had yearned for.

Now, as a young woman, she saw it all in a different light. 'Some things are meant to be, and some are not,' she murmured. 'I can't understand why you couldn't love me, Mother, but I can't hate you for that.' She dropped to her knees and busied herself in arranging the flowers. 'Father is so unhappy,' she whispered. 'He misses you so, I'm afraid he'll kill himself with all the drinking.'

She remained on her knees a little longer, imagining her mother alive, so beautiful, so magnificent, even in the blackest mood. 'If ever I marry and have a child, whether it's a boy or a girl, I must never make the same mistake,' she whispered. 'I will love it with all my heart.'

Stepping back she looked on the grey granite headstone, a splendid thing, the best money could buy, with letters engraved in gold and an angel standing guard at its base.

There was nothing more to say. Without a backward glance,

she went across the lawn, down the gravel footpath and into the church. Here she dropped four pennies into the money box. Taking up four tiny candles, she wedged them into the wrought-iron stands and, striking a match, touched the wicks one after the other, until all four were throwing out a warm bright flame. Kneeling behind a pew, she folded her hands and closed her eyes, softly murmuring, 'One for Mother, one for Nan, one for Ruby's father . . . though Ruby might not approve,' she whispered with a little smile. 'And another for any poor soul who hasn't yet found its way to heaven.'

Three times she went to the gate to see whether Margaret was in sight. When on the third attempt there was no sign of her, Cathy returned to the churchyard, where she wandered at will, occasionally reading the interesting inscriptions on the headstones; on one ancient granite cross it told how a young woman by the name of Elizabeth Arnam had died in childbirth at the age of nineteen. Close to the church door, in the same spot for a hundred years, stood a tall and beautiful statue of the Sacred Heart; this was the last resting place of an entire family: 'Slain by a madman on this very spot'. But the one that saddened Cathy above all others was that of a small child by the name of Lucy Lane, who had been 'Caught between the wheels of a wagon'. In the same place lay Lucy's mother who, by all accounts, had 'Died of a broken heart'.

Seated on the bench, watching the horizon for Margaret's familiar figure and with her face warmed by the sun, Cathy thought on brighter things, like who was Ruby's suitor, and why she was being so secretive. The idea of Ruby strolling arm in arm with a man, looking up at him with shy, shining eyes, brought a smile to her face. 'I hope you've found a partner, Ruby,' she whispered. 'Nobody deserves one more than you.'

The joy that had flooded her heart at thinking Ruby might have found someone to love was suddenly swamped by thoughts of David. She wondered what he was doing now, right this very minute. Was he tending the horses? Perhaps he was logging in the spinney, or maybe walking the fields . . . or he might be heading for the spot near the brook where he always found comfort. He had taken Cathy there, and she thought it the most beautiful place on God's earth. 'Where are you, David?' she murmured. Leaning back, she lifted her face to the sun and closed her eyes to think of him.

With a jolt she sat up straight, her heart lurching as she remembered, 'It's tomorrow! Tomorrow you'll be leaving and I'll never see you again.' The thought was too awful to contemplate, so she tried to shut it from her mind. But it wouldn't be denied. Tomorrow, David would be gone from these parts, he and his family; with the exception of his beloved father who was buried somewhere in the prison grounds. Cathy had half expected him to be gone before now, but it was almost as though he could not bear to wrench himself away.

Agitated, Cathy went once more to see whether Margaret was on her way. There was still no sign of her. But Cathy was both astonished and thrilled when she saw two other familiar figures approaching. She recognised them straight away as David and his sister Teresa.

Cathy only had eyes for David. He looked wretched, just as he had looked on leaving the court after his father was sentenced. His face was thinner, almost gaunt; the dark eyes that had so often smiled at her, turning her heart inside out, now stared straight ahead. He seemed older somehow, not a boy but a man. Each footstep brought him closer; his long strides purposeful as ever. But there was a loneliness about him that struck her deep. In him she saw a kindred spirit and, more than ever, she wanted to be with him.

His sister walked alongside, sometimes running to keep up with him. She had a willow stick in her hand and with it she slashed at the trees. Her face was hard but not grief-stricken. Occasionally she would laugh and expect David to laugh with her. When he merely nodded, she kicked at the ground like a sulky child. She seemed impatient, angry, appearing to have come along only to guard him, just as she had always guarded him.

Keeping out of sight, Cathy waited until they had gone by. At one point David was so close she could have reached out and touched him. Somehow he sensed her presence, pausing for a moment and looking round before going on.

When Cathy emerged from her hiding place, it was to see him going through the great oak doors which led into the church. 'Of course ... you've come to talk with your father,' she said softly. 'I can understand that.' Staring at the doors she somehow believed that David would come out again and things would be the same as before, but of course that couldn't be.

She felt uneasy, deeply disturbed and torn in so many ways. She wanted to go to him but dare not. She wanted to leave but could not. There must be something left between us, she told herself angrily. What happened was not your fault, David, nor was it mine. She paced the grounds and all the time her gaze was focused on the doors of the church. If he was to come out now, what would you do? she asked herself. Could you face him after all that has happened? The thought was paralysing.

Without even realising, she found she had walked along the path to the church, and now here she was standing inside the porch, with only the great oak doors between herself and her love. She was trembling, cold with fear. What would he say? How would he greet her? Her heart told her one thing, her head another. Yet she must know! Before he left forever, she must know whether he really hated her.

With shaking hands, she reached up and closed her fingers over the door-knob. Ever so slowly she eased the door open. When it creaked and groaned she held it still for a second, her heart wildly beating. When, after what seemed an age, she had the door open wide enough for her to peer inside, she saw him there; he was kneeling in the pew closest to the altar, his dark eyes raised and his hands clasped together in prayer. He looked a sad lonely figure, so very different from the carefree laughing youth she had known.

Slowly, as though he was bearing a great weight on his broad shoulders, he stood up and strode towards the wrought-iron stand where Cathy's four candles still brightly burned. Here, he dropped a penny into the tin and collected a candle from the box. Reaching out he actually lit the candle from one of Cathy's before easing it into a nearby space. That done, he looked up at the face of the Virgin Mary; he didn't pray, nor did he move for almost a full minute, just gazed on that peaceful loving face, lost in thought. He was a man in deep pain, a man confused and desperately hurt by the loss of his beloved father.

Summoning every ounce of courage, Cathy took a step forward, hesitating when a harsh voice spoke out behind her. It was Teresa.

'I wouldn't go in there if I were you.' Pushing herself in front of Cathy, she quietly closed the door. 'I think you should know he hasn't forgiven you.'

Cathy looked at her, at the hard face that rarely smiled. 'What happened between your father and my mother was no more my fault than yours,' she replied calmly. 'Hating me won't change anything. I want David to know that.'

'He won't listen.'

'I have to try.'

'And deepen his grief?' Teresa played her part well. 'One way or another your family have ruined us. Oh, I know it was your mother who was murdered and they say my father did it. But, to tell you the truth, I'll never believe that, and neither will David. The real truth is your mother pursued my father. She came to the house and caused a terrible scene. Yes, they'd had an affair, but it was over. She couldn't see it that way though. Whichever way you look at it, a good man lies buried in the prison yard. Your mother's here, beneath the trees and surrounded by flowers. *She's* the guilty one, yet the man she used lies in a cold forbidding place. I don't care what sentence was passed on him, Owen Leyton was innocent! But he can't even be buried in consecrated ground. No wonder David wants to get out of this place as quick as he can!'

'If I could make amends, I would. You have to believe that.'

'No! It's too late. Leave him be. Let him leave without further trouble.' The last thing Teresa wanted was for these two to meet up, for she knew that if they did David would take Cathy in his arms and she would be on the outside again. All the time Cathy Blackthorn and David were finding happiness with each other, *she* could only watch and envy. The thought drove her almost crazy. 'Go away and leave us alone!' she hissed. 'Surely you can understand why David never wants to set eyes on you again?'

'I think I can. Only I don't want to believe we can't talk about what's happened. David and I have always been able to talk things through.'

Taking a chance, Teresa stepped aside. 'All right! Go in! Destroy him a little more. Cause a terrible scene in the church!

If that's what you want, then go in.'

Fighting all manner of emotions, Cathy hesitated. 'I never wanted him to hate me,' she said. 'If we must part I'd like it to be as friends. Is that so impossible now?'

Teresa was delighted to see she had set the doubts in Cathy's mind. '*I* don't hate you,' she lied, 'but David is a different matter. He hates like only a man can hate. It's been the devil's own job keeping him away from Blackthorn House ... from burning it to the ground and all of you inside.' Straightening her back, she took a deep breath. '*That's* how much he hates. Go on. Go inside ... let him tell you himself. He misses his father every minute of every day. Who knows? He might just strangle you and then he could be laid to rest in the prison yard, reunited with the father he adored.'

It seemed an age before Cathy answered. Every word uttered by Teresa had been like a stab to the heart. She didn't realise he could hate that much. How could she approach him now? How could she lay him open to such pain? And in God's house? Of course he missed his father. No one ever loved his father as much as David loved Owen; no son ever had such a wonderful relationship with his father as David had enjoyed. Of course he hated the woman who had brought it on them. And the family of that woman, because wasn't it true what Teresa had said, that in one way or another the Blackthorn family had ruined them?

In a quiet voice Cathy answered, 'I *can* understand David's reasons for hating me. I wish it didn't have to be this way, but things have happened, awful painful things, which affect all our lives. I wish I could turn the clock back, but none of us can.'

'Like I say, *I* don't hate you.'

'Thank you for that.' Cathy had no reason to disbelieve her. Glancing at the great oak door which was now firmly closed between her and David, she murmured before leaving, 'I hope your family can find happiness and peace wherever you are.' She doubted whether, without David, she herself would ever find real happiness.

Setting off in the direction of Blackthorn House, Cathy could think of nothing but what Teresa Leyton had said. The words spilled from her lips as she walked. 'He hates like a man ... the devil's own job to keep him from Blackthorn House ...

from burning it to the ground and all of you inside.' The tears fell then, hot scalding tears that tumbled down her face and made long meandering streaks dried by the sun. 'You'll never know it, David,' she murmured, 'but however much you hate me, it won't stop me from loving you.'

Somehow the thought of that love, the memory of his strong handsome face and the laughter they had shared before events had destroyed their happiness, brought a rush of immense joy. His memory was all she had now. And it would have to last her a long, long time.

While Cathy made her way home, Teresa waited for her brother to emerge from the church. She was impatient to put a distance between them and Cathy Blackthorn, who could still be seen walking along the footpath. 'I thought you were taking up residence in there,' she said when David appeared. 'Can we go now?'

Thrusting his hands in his pockets, he flexed his shoulders and took a deep invigorating breath of air. The church was cold and damp inside, and he felt a chill clinging. 'Aren't you going into the church?' His dark eyes were quizzical. 'I thought that was why you came with me.' Gazing over the fields, he felt a kind of peace settle on him. But it was an uneasy, short-lived peace. 'Go in if you want,' he urged. 'Like I say, I'm in no hurry to leave.'

Teresa was frantic. If *he* wasn't in a hurry to leave, she certainly was. Casting a cursory glance towards the church doors, she replied sullenly, 'I won't go in if it's all the same to you. There's nothing for me in there.'

He saw how distressed she was and misunderstood the real reason; he wasn't to know about the exchange between her and Cathy. Putting a brotherly arm round her shoulders, he said warmly, 'You can find peace, Teresa, if only you'll let yourself believe that.' Yet, except for a fleeting moment when he emerged from God's house, he had not found peace. Without Cathy, he was a lost man.

'I just want to go. There's still a lot to do.' She glanced worriedly at Cathy's retreating figure, grateful that he had not seen it. 'If you must know I can't wait to see the back of this damned place . . . the house, the barns, everything!'

'I understand.' Kissing her lightly on the forehead, he acknowledged, 'We'd best get back. Like you say, there's still a lot to do, and Mam will be getting anxious.'

Aware that Cathy was still in full view, Teresa began walking away in the opposite direction, following the route that had brought them here. 'Come on, David,' she pleaded. 'Like you say, Mam will be waiting, eager to start packing. I don't want her to be lifting things . . . she's still not strong enough.' The truth was, it didn't matter to her whether her mam hurt herself or not. If Maria Leyton was to die tomorrow, it would be an inconvenience that was all. In fact, Teresa often dreamed of there being only her and David. The idea was very pleasing indeed.

David turned to make sure the church doors were closed. As he swung round, he raised his eyes to the horizon. Recognising Cathy's tall graceful figure, he gasped aloud, 'Has Cathy been *here*?'

Teresa knew there was no use denying it. That footpath led almost directly from Blackthorn House and ended at the church. Feverishly she searched her mind and came up with the same devious lie that had separated her brother and his sweetheart from the very start; the same wicked idea that had *kept* them apart ever since and, if she had her way, would keep them apart for all time. 'I didn't tell you because it was too painful.' She even managed to sound tearful. 'Please don't blame me, David. I didn't tell you because I think you've been hurt enough.'

'What are you saying?' Bent over her, staring at her with dark pained eyes, he could not see the evil in her. 'You should have told me. You know I'd give my right arm for the chance to make amends to Cathy.'

'If she was prepared to give you that chance, or even if she could show the same gentleness you have for her, I *would* have told you.' A superb liar, she wounded him with every cruel, carefully calculated word. 'But Cathy Leyton is not forgiving like you, David. She's changed. I don't think even you could care for her any more.'

'For God's sake, Teresa! Don't tell me how I feel.' Believing he was venting his anger on an innocent, he raised his face to the sky and calmed himself. In a softer voice he told her, 'If only I'd known she was here. You should have told me!'

Wiping away pretend tears, she implored him, 'You know I would have told you. But she said the most awful things.' She bent her head. 'Terrible things that don't bear repeating. And I won't tell you.'

'I want to know!' He had his hands on her shoulders, his fingers bruising her flesh. 'Out with it, Teresa! What awful things did she say?'

She paused, looked up and paused again, seeming afraid to go on. Then, after taking a deep breath, she wiped away another pretend tear, whispering in a shaking voice, 'She said she hated you . . . hated me and Mam. She said we should *all* have been hanged.' Gulping hard and rubbing her hands over her face, she went on, 'She swore that, as long as she lived here, she would never forgive the man who had murdered her mother . . . or his family, and that we couldn't be gone soon enough for her.'

Having spilled out her poison, she paused to let it sink in; her conscience hardened against the look of pain on his face. 'I'm sorry, David,' she lied, pressing herself close to him. 'Now you know why I didn't want to say anything.'

Bitter and hurt, he stroked her shoulders where only a minute ago he had held her in a vicious grip. 'It's all right,' he assured her. 'I know you didn't want to tell me, but now I know, and it's just as well.' He dropped his hands from her shoulders, looked into her eyes and murmured, 'If Cathy Blackthorn wants us gone from her father's land, then we'd better get back. Like you say, there's still a lot to be done.'

As they made their way back, an uncomfortable silence descended over them. Teresa was hoping David would never discover how she had deceived him. As for David, he realised that the last remaining hope he had had of ever reconciling himself with Cathy was now an impossible dream. He felt her anguish and her anger and, because of it, he loved her all the more.

Drunk and insensible, Frank pushed away his chair and struggled to stand. 'What do you want with me? I didn't ask you to come into my study, so I'd be obliged if you'd get out!'

Margaret stood her ground. 'I'll get out when you've answered my questions and not before.' She came closer, throwing out her arms and pointing to him. 'Look at you, Frank! You're dirty and unkempt. Ever since Rita died, you've let yourself go. There's hardly a day goes by without you're drunk, or gallivanting into Blackburn... gambling and doing goodness knows what else.'

'I'll do what I please, damn it! I don't want you or anybody else telling me how to run my life.' With a cry he fell heavily into the chair.

'Well, whether you want it or not, *I* mean to tell you a few home truths.' Placing her two hands on the desk she leaned forward, eyes blazing as she went on, 'I appreciate you miss her. I know how much you loved her, and if I could bring her back for you, you know I would.'

'GET OUT!' He hit out with clenched fist, but his co-ordination was dulled by booze and the fist merely flailed in the air before falling to the desk with a thud. 'I'll swing for the bastards, you see if I don't.'

'They'll be gone soon enough.'

'I should have seen it,' he cried out as though in great pain. 'I could have put a stop to it, and now it's too late.' Rising in his chair he pulled at the roots of his hair. 'I should have seen it. They must have known all along. They're laughing at me. I want them out now... today. I want them off my land.'

'It's not them I'm worried about. They'll be leaving tomorrow, and besides, they have their own grief to cope with.' She looked at him now and it struck her that he was losing his mind. 'Frank, you have to realise it wasn't your fault. You didn't know what was going on between Rita and Owen Leyton. Nobody knew.'

'*They* knew.'

'Listen to me, Frank. It's *you* I'm concerned about now. I've pleaded with you and I've done my best to make you see what you're doing to yourself and to this family, but you wouldn't listen. Now you've come so far down you're almost in the gutter. No decency, no sense of dignity. And what about Cathy? Have you conveniently forgotten you have a daughter? Have you stopped to wonder whether she might need help? That she might just be missing her mother?'

'You take care of her, like you've always done.'

Her manner changed then. Placing the letter on the desk, she told him cynically, 'I'd be happy to do that, Frank, but I'm not sure whether you won't put us all in the workhouse first.'

He stared up at her, then at the letter, his bleary eyes narrowing to concentrate. Gingerly touching it, he asked impatiently, 'What's this? I'm in no mood for reading.'

Relieved to have gained his attention, she told him harshly, 'It's a letter from our solicitor. He claims you've been selling land and property . . . a great deal of land, Frank . . . and the cottage too. Tell me it isn't true?' She prayed there might be some sort of explanation. 'Tell me you haven't sold nearly all of our holdings?' Her hopes were dashed by his reply.

'And if I have, what do you intend to do about it?' Suddenly he seemed sober. Fear had a way of sobering a drunken man.

Trembling with anger, she composed herself and pulled up a chair. Sitting down straight-backed, she met his frightened stare with accusing eyes. 'I think you had better explain, don't you?' Folding her hands on the desk, she waited for him to tell her the worst.

It was more damaging than she had thought. When he had finished blurting out the details, she was ashen with shock. 'Are you telling me that all we have left is this house and the Leyton place?'

There was no remorse, no sign of regret for what he had done. 'Don't be ungrateful, my dear,' he said arrogantly. 'I was shrewd enough to keep a small amount of land with each property, and when we find a new tenant for the Leyton place, there will still be a modest income.'

'What have you done with the money you got from the sales?'

He actually smiled. 'Gone, my dear . . . every last penny.'

'Then you've all but ruined us.' Her voice shook, but she remained seated, stiff and straight, her eyes boring into his.

'Come, that's rather a harsh thing to say. We still have a roof over our heads, and I'm sure it won't be long before we secure a good tenant for the Leyton place.'

'I think you've lost your mind. If all our capital is gone we have nothing to fall back on. It could be months before we find a good tenant, and even when we do, the rent won't bring in enough to feed and clothe five people.'

He outstared her. 'There won't be five, my dear. There'll be you, me and the girl.'

'And what of Jack? And Ruby?'

'Ruby will have to go. I'm sure you and the girl can take up her duties. As for Jack, he must return to the streets where I found him.'

Her mouth fell open with astonishment. 'You really *have* lost your mind!' Taking up Ruby's duties would be no real hardship, but it wasn't as simple as that. There was Ruby herself to consider. Cathy too.

'What I do is no concern of yours.' Growing bold, he sat back, his fingers curled over the arms of the chair and a smug little smile on his face. 'I'm glad we've got it all out in the open,' he said. 'Now, if there is nothing else, I would prefer to be left alone.' Taking the letter, he screwed it up in his fist and dropped it into the wastepaper basket.

'Give me the letter, Frank.'

Something about her manner and voice made him retrieve the letter. After straightening it out he handed it back to her. 'Really, there's nothing you can do. The deals are signed and sealed, and the money has gone forever.' He chuckled. 'Regrets won't help. Not that I have any.'

'Oh, *I* have, Frank,' she informed him bitterly. 'I deeply regret not instructing the solicitor to make certain that all legal papers should bear *both* our signatures, not just yours. But that is now rectified, so thank God your hands are tied. Most of all, I am mortally ashamed that I allowed you to squander Cathy's inheritance.'

'It's done, I tell you.' Crashing out of the chair, he thumped both fists on the desk. 'You'll find a way to take care of the girl. Ruby will be one less mouth to feed, and tomorrow, when that wretched family leave, Jack can be sent on his way too. Oh don't worry, he's lived on his wits before. The young bugger's too cunning to starve, and I'll be sure to find him a few trinkets before he goes.' Dismissing her anxieties with a flick of his hand, he explained, 'I haven't plundered the family silver yet . . . nor the porcelain.' His eyes glazed over. 'Rita did so enjoy that. She always enjoyed nice things.' In a burst of renewed energy he went on, 'Of coure there are her beautiful jewels. But I shall never let them go. Never!' Drawing himself up to his full height he told her sternly, 'You may hate me for what I've done, but I would like you to know that I am penning a letter to cut Jack out of my will so that, in the event of my demise, whatever remains of this estate will come to you.' Swallowing hard, he wiped his hands over his face. 'Now, please get out and leave me to my thoughts.'

Even before she was halfway across the room he had fallen into the chair and thrown himself across the desk in a stupor. 'In spite of what you've done, I can't help but pity you,' she murmured, reflecting on their conversation. 'But it will be a long time before I ever forgive you.'

Outside the door, Jack kept his ear pressed to the panel. He had heard the entire conversation and was shocked to the core. 'After all I've done, you must be out of your mind if you think I'd leave empty handed,' he muttered. 'I would never have done what I've done if I didn't think there'd be a pot o' gold at the end. And now you say I'm to be sent on me way! What's it all been for, eh?'

His face was dark with rage as he planned a suitable vengeance. All the bad things rose in him ... latent murderous instincts at having been denied what he had come to believe was rightfully his.

CHAPTER NINE

'My! You're down early.' Ruby hated being caught unawares. 'It's only six o'clock. I've the firegrates to clean out yet, and umpteen other little jobs to do afore I start the breakfast.'

She was in the throes of cleaning the pantry shelves when Cathy came into the kitchen. 'These days I can't seem to catch me own tail,' she chuckled. Fetching an armful of half-empty jars out of the pantry, she set them down on the table. 'I must be getting old,' she said wistfully. 'Once upon a time I'd have had the whole house sparkling by six of a morning, and be enjoying a leisurely brew afore the family came down for their breakfast.' Sinking into the chair, she looked up at Cathy with mischievous eyes. 'Serve me right for staying out late of a night, don't it, eh?' she said with a little smile.

'I wondered about that,' Cathy admitted, her green eyes shining.

'Oh? And what else did you wonder about?'

'Whether you had got yourself a suitor.' Cathy made herself comfortable in the chair opposite, her arms stretched out and her hands covering Ruby's. 'Oh, Ruby! *Have* you got one?'

'Happen I have, and happen I haven't.'

'You'd rather not talk about it, is that it?' She was angry with herself for having pried. 'I'm sorry, Ruby, only I really would be delighted if you had found someone of your very own ... a good man who could take care of you.'

Ruby put a finger to her mouth to silence her. 'I know you would,' she said. 'And there *is* someone. But I'm afeared to count on it in case it all melts away and I'm on me own again.' She winked. 'I promise, if anything comes of it, you and Miss Margaret will be the first to know, but just now I'd rather keep

213

it to meself. You do understand, don't you?'

Cathy was quick to reassure her. 'Of course I do. I had no right in asking you about it in the first place.' She felt a peace offering was called for. 'Now you sit there while I make you a brew of tea.'

Ruby was horrified. 'You'll do no such thing!' she cried, scrambling out of the chair. But Cathy was already round the table and pressing the little woman back. 'Now then, Ruby!' she gently chided. 'Didn't you just say you missed the days when you were able to enjoy a nice leisurely brew before the family came down?'

'That was *then*, young 'un. Them days are long gone, more's the pity.'

'Then we'll turn the clock back.' Before Ruby could protest again, Cathy had put on the kettle and laid a pretty tray. In less than no time the kettle was puffing out steam and the tea was made. Setting the tray in the centre of the table, she asked in a rather grand manner, 'Would you mind if I joined you?' She didn't sit down until Ruby replied.

'It would be a pleasure, m'lady.' Smiling profusely, Ruby did a servile little bow from the waist. 'Would "modom" like to pour?'

'Why, how kind!' Cathy declared. And the tea was poured.

Twice more the rose china cups were filled, and the two women chatted like old friends. 'It don't seem right though,' Ruby commented thoughtfully.

'What doesn't seem right, Ruby?'

'You and me ... lady and servant ... seated together at the kitchen table and sharing the same teapot.'

Cathy smiled at that. 'Shame on you, Ruby,' she said. 'Since when did we ever worry about things like that?'

Ruby nodded. 'Aye, you're right,' she acknowledged. 'You and Miss Margaret have allus been like family to me, and I love you for it.' Her eyes grew round and fearful as she stared at the door. 'All the same, there are them as would take a very dim view of it. Certainly if the master was to walk in this very minute, he'd have summat to say an' no mistake!'

'As long as he doesn't want to share our teapot.' Cathy had seen Ruby was nervous, and wanted to put her at ease.

Ruby threw back her head and laughed with relief. 'Cathy Blackthorn, you're a scamp!' she said, her whole body shaking with mirth. After another cup of tea, she tidied the crockery on to the tray, telling Cathy with affection, 'You're a ray of sunshine to an old fool, that's what you are.'

'You're not an old fool,' Cathy reprimanded her. 'You're a friend.'

'Well, if I am, I'm glad of it,' Ruby answered softly. 'Lord knows you need all the friends you can get in this cruel world.'

Cathy sipped at her tea, a faraway look in her eyes. 'Friends are very special, aren't they, Ruby?' she asked. 'I've been lucky. You, Nan and Aunt Margaret have always been my friends.' It almost choked her to say it, but it fell from the tip of her tongue. 'David too. He was a very special friend.'

Ruby knew Cathy must have suffered a bad night, because of the dark shadows under her eyes, and because she had risen so early. 'Will it help to talk about it?'

'I don't think so, but thank you, all the same.' The things she felt were not for others to know; not Ruby, not even Margaret. But she was grateful for Ruby's concern. 'I'm fine now,' she lied.

The lie was written on her face. 'I might not be able to help, but I'm a good listener,' Ruby gently insisted. 'What's troubling you? Is it the fact you've lost your mam?'

Cathy put a great deal of thought into her answer. 'I'm sorry she had to die, but I don't miss her as much as I thought I might.' Suddenly ashamed, she leaned forward on the table and asked in a hushed voice, 'Oh, Ruby! Is that such a terrible thing to say?'

'No, it isn't. It would only be terrible if you lied to yourself. Shameful though it is, we both know Rita Blackthorn could have been a better mother to you.'

'I didn't understand, but I won't condemn her for that.'

'That's because you've a good, kind heart.'

Cathy would always regret the way it had been between her and her mother. 'I don't know how to explain it,' she confessed, 'but I don't miss her as much as I miss the love we never shared.' She couldn't explain, and didn't really want to. 'It wasn't my mother I was thinking about. It was someone else.'

Ruby smiled knowingly. 'You're pining for David, aren't you?'

Cathy felt a surge of relief. 'I can't hide anything from you, can I?'

Shaking her head slowly from side to side, Ruby quietly

regarded the younger woman. 'He'll be gone soon. If you're ever again to have peace of mind, you must accept that.'

'I have accepted it.' In a way she had, but it didn't ease the agony of losing him. She glanced up and her eyes were dull with pain. 'I'm sorry. I shouldn't be burdening you.'

'I only wish I could help. It seems such a shame that the two of you couldn't make amends.'

Something occurred to Cathy then, and she dared not tell Ruby. But if she was to act it must be quickly. 'I think I'll go back to bed.' She had no intention of going back but Ruby mustn't know that or she might rouse Margaret.

'I think that's a very good idea, young lady. Come down nearer eight o'clock and I'll have breakfast all ready.' Pushing her chair back Ruby cleared away the tray. From the cupboard beneath the sink she took out a box filled with polishing rags and half-used tins of blacklead. 'Meanwhile, there's umpteen jobs to be done.' Bursting into a tuneful melody, she ambled from the room. 'You get your beauty sleep while you've a chance!' she called over her shoulder. 'When you get to my age you'll be glad of every wink.' Laughing, she went into the drawing room and shut the door.

Cathy moved quickly, up the stairs and into her room where she hurriedly washed and dressed, choosing a brown dress and dark boots, and a long coat. Flicking her long corn-coloured hair outside the coat-collar, she ran down the stairs and out through the front door. She didn't stop running until she reached the footpath, where she slowed to a fast walking pace. The thought of seeing David spurred her on. She didn't want to miss him. Even now, she still hoped David might have a change of heart.

The bitter cold wind howled round her ears. It made her face raw and froze her fingertips, but still she pushed on. She recalled a conversation she'd had with Margaret only the night before. Her aunt had asked, 'Do you know where David might be headed?' And she had answered, 'No, but I wish I was going with him.'

She wished it now, then in the same breath was ashamed. Ashamed because of what had happened between her mother and David's father; ashamed of the outcome; ashamed because it seemed a harsh thing to say when Margaret needed her more than it appeared David did. And yet, she would gladly have walked barefoot behind the cart if it meant she could be with him.

Even while she was thinking these things, a sense of outrage welled up in her, spilling over until she cried out, 'Don't cheapen yourself, Cathy Blackthorn! If he doesn't want you, then to hell with him!' But words themselves were cheap, and it cost her nothing to say that. It cost her more to let him go without making that one last try. She adored Margaret. But it was a different kind of love she felt for David; the kind that grew in your heart, only to break it.

Margaret had said something else too. She had told Cathy, 'In teaching him to read, you've given David something he must cherish forever.'

Cathy thought about that now, and it warmed her heart. All in a moment it came rushing back: the long precious hours she and David had leaned over their books together; the way he laughed whenever he mastered a word; the closeness of his body, the smell of newly mown hay after he'd been out in the fields, and the shining black dampness of his hair when he washed it under the pump.

She remembered it all as though it was only yesterday, and her spirit was both drained and elated. 'David had a quick and clever mind,' she murmured aloud. 'Whatever he chooses to do when he leaves here, I know he'll be a great success.' Silent for the remainder of the journey, she was glad to lose herself in bitter-sweet memories. Even now it was hard to accept that he had turned against her with such loathing.

As he harnessed the horse to the wagon, David's thoughts were very close to Cathy's. 'I thought there'd come a day when she and I would be man and wife,' he told the sad-eyed horse, 'but it wasn't to be.' Pausing for a minute, he stroked the horse's head and nuzzled his face against its nose. 'I'm lost without her,' he whispered. 'What can I do? I love her with all my heart, and she won't have anything to do with me.'

Teresa stepped out of the shadows. 'Talking to yourself is a dangerous thing. Folks will be thinking you've gone out of your mind.'

He laughed at that. 'Happen I have.'

'Not you. You're too strong-minded.'

'Do you think I should go and see Cathy before we leave?'

'Only if you want to hurt her more.'

'The things she said . . . at the church. Do you think she said them in the heat of anger?'

Teresa had to scheme carefully if she was going to stop him from going to Blackthorn House. 'When she said those things to me, she was deadly calm. Believe me, David, going to her now would only make things worse.' Crossing the stable, she linked her arm with his. 'If I thought there was the slightest chance that she'd welcome you, I'd say go on, make one last try to make amends. But I know it would only make matters worse. I saw her face when she said those things, and I promise you . . . she meant every word.'

He glanced down and realised she still seemed upset by what had happened. 'Sorry, sis,' he said bitterly. 'That's what comes of a man like me hankering after someone like Cathy.'

'It's all in the past now,' she said hopefully.

'Best get finished and away,' he said abruptly. 'We're late as it is. I meant to be on the road before the cock crowed.'

'You're sorry to be leaving, aren't you?'

'It's like losing my right arm.' Cathy. Always Cathy. Without her, life was cold and empty.

'I'm not sorry to be going.'

'Well then, take yourself inside and help Mam pack the last few bits and pieces. It'll be a few minutes before I back the cart to the front door. If everything's ready for me to load we can be away in no time.' With that he bent to his task and left Teresa to run back inside and work with a frenzy. 'We're leaving, and the sooner we go the better,' he muttered. But Cathy would go with him wherever he went.

Some fifteen minutes later, the last items were being packed on to the cart. 'Don't damage my sideboard, son,' Maria pleaded. She watched as he wrapped his arms round the oaken bulk and slid it to the edge of the cart. 'Help him, Teresa,' she urged. 'Steady it.' She ran back and forth, nervously biting her handkerchief and issuing instructions.

'Stand back!' David warned as Teresa moved closer. 'If this thing goes it'll slice your toes clean off.'

He inched the heavy article on to the cart, keeping it well balanced and supporting the weight with both arms. The sweat ran down his face and his back ached, but he knew it was safer for him alone to handle it. 'There!' At last it was safely tied to the inside of the cart. 'I don't blame you for being concerned,' he told his mam. 'It's a lovely thing and no mistake.' Taking a moment to admire the oak sideboard, he marvelled at the intricate carving on the doors and panels; the deep fret along the top was edged with sprays of woodland flowers, and each straight sturdy leg culminated in a square foot.

'Your father bought that the day before we were wed,' Maria reminded him. 'And as long as I live, I'll never part with it.'

The box of crockery was last to go on. David wedged it between the eiderdowns, before covering the whole lot over with a canvas to protect it from the weather. 'Ready when you are,' he said. 'I'll just check the barn, while you two take a look inside the house and make sure we've got everything.'

'I'm not setting foot inside that house ever again,' Teresa declared. Climbing on to the back of the cart, she said under her breath, 'As long as I've got all *my* stuff out, that's all I care.'

Maria stood at the door of the house for what seemed an age. Her weary eyes travelled the empty room; where there had been rugs there were now bare floorboards; the walls were stark where once had hung squares of embroidery and small pictures. The huge open hearth was blackened by the many cheery fires that had burned there, but there was no cheery fire now, only dead ashes. 'I should curse you to hell for what you've done to this family, Owen Leyton,' she whispered. 'But, God forgive me, I can't.' On slow tortuous steps, she went into the room, and the memories were overwhelming.

David went to the house to find his mother. She was seated on the hearth, her head bent and her heart breaking. 'How did it all go wrong, son?' she asked, looking up with tear-filled eyes. 'One day we were a family ... the next we're torn apart. I daren't think what will happen to us now.'

Taking her in his arms, he promised, 'We'll be fine.'

'But we've no money, and nowhere to live. I'm frightened,

son. I can't help but be frightened.'

He felt her shudder in his arms and his determination was tenfold. 'Like I said, Mam, we'll be fine. While I've got a broad back and a pair of strong arms, you'll want for nothing.'

His words soothed her. 'You're a good man,' she said, and when he led her away from the place which had been her home she had great faith that all would come right in the end. Where Teresa was concerned, she had no illusions; besides inheriting some of her father's weak traits, the girl had a tendency towards greed and cruelty. But with her son beside her Maria believed she need not fear the future.

Soon she was seated up on the cart. One last look round, then, 'Let's away from here, son.' Her smile was warm and loving. 'Me and the girl... we're in your hands now.' There were no regrets in her voice. Only resignation, and a sense of relief.

Slapping the reins against the horse's rump, David too was impatient to be gone. His dark eyes were turned to the horizon, to the rising sun and the promise of a better day. 'You're wrong, Mam,' he said softly. 'We're in the Good Lord's hands. It's him we'll have to look to before this day ends.' He had an idea where he might find work, and with it a place for them to live. But he wasn't certain. Things changed so quickly, he must be prepared for disappointment.

As the cart rumbled slowly across the uneven ground, Teresa sat on the back, her legs dangling over the side and her brain feverish with mischief. She was elated to be leaving, thrilled at having come between Cathy and David, and now desperate to punish Frank Blackthorn for evicting them from their home. As the idea presented herself, she chuckled with delight.

While David and her mother quietly talked, she slid from the wagon and ran back to the house. Here, she collected a sack of debris which had been swept from the house and left outside. She took it into the parlour and emptied it in the centre of the floor. Next, she went to the kitchen and collected some of the papers left over from her mother's packing. Rolling them into a long thick stick, she dug in her pocket and drew out a box of matches. After striking one against the wall, she put it to the end of the paper torch and waited for it to take hold.

When it was blazing, she dropped it into the pile of debris and watched while the flames leapt high.

Satisfied, she went from the house, secured the door behind her and ran after the cart which was already turning out of the lane. Panting and excited, she silently slipped back on to it, her spiteful eyes fixed on the house until at last it was gone from sight.

At the top of the rise, Cathy paused for breath. But she couldn't stop long. Time was precious. Pressing on, she went over the rise and down the other side, half running, half stumbling, her heart beating like a wild thing's. In the distance she could see the rooftop of the Leyton house. It seemed a million miles away. Her eyes were drawn to the chimney. The sky was clear above it, and she knew what that meant. If there was no fire in the hearth, the family were not there. David was always about before dawn. The first thing he did was to light a fire. So many times she had asked him to describe his day, and she knew what it meant if there was no smoke rising from the chimney. 'He's gone! Please don't let him be gone!' Spurred on, she was oblivious of the sharp thorny bushes and the way they tore at her clothes and face.

Hastening her steps, she ran and ran until her chest was so tight that she could hardly breathe. As she neared the lane she could hear the rumble of wagon wheels. 'David!' Stumbling out of the hedgerow, she could see nothing. The lane was empty, but the sound of wagon wheels was not far off. Going at speed, she followed the lane up and out of the hollow. At the top she saw it; the wagon was a long way ahead and going at a smart pace.

Desperate now, she chased after it, calling again and again, 'DAVID! David, come back. We have to talk.' But the wind drowned her voice and the wagon was soon lost from sight. Dejected and heartbroken, she fell to the ground, and there she lay for some long time, her body racked with sobs.

She was still softly crying when she came to the top of the rise again. Searching the horizon with weary eyes, she realised he was gone and would never be back. About to turn away, she caught sight of a bright flickering light low in the sky. Curious, she shielded her eyes with the palms of her hands and peered closer. The light was a fire, and the flames licked at the air like giant tongues. In an instant it dawned on her. 'It's the Leytons' house!' She couldn't believe what her eyes were telling her. 'It's burning! The house is burning!'

Frantic, she took to her heels. Making straight for Blackthorn House, she ignored the lane and went straight across the fields, her eyes skimming the way ahead, searching for someone, anyone who might help. But there was no one. In that vast and empty place, she was all alone.

Ten minutes later, as she covered the short distance between the house and the rise, Margaret saw her approaching. Filled with relief, she ran to meet her. 'Where on earth have you been?' she cried angrily. 'I've been searching everywhere for you.' And then she saw Cathy's appearance; the torn clothes and deep scratches across her face. 'Good God! Look at you!' Clutching Cathy in her arms, she suddenly recalled how Jack had also left the house earlier, and feared the worst. 'What's happened to you?' she demanded gently, cradling Cathy close to her breast. 'Was it Jack? I need to know. Was it Jack who did this to you?' All her latent suspicions regarding that young man came to the fore.

Cathy caught her breath as the words came out in a rush. 'There's a fire! I saw it as I made my way back . . . it's the Leyton house, I'm sure of it.' Drawing away from Margaret she pleaded, 'Leave me . . . get help. You must get help!'

'It's you I'm concerned about. If the house was ablaze as you say, there's little to be done to save it now.'

'*Try!* Please try!' Pushing her away, Cathy promised, 'I'm not hurt. Please . . . get help.'

Margaret saw the distress in her eyes and realised that the house was all she had left of David. 'I'll be back for you,' she promised. Then she went at a run down the bank and across the field, calling reassurances as she went.

Sinking to the grass, Cathy took great gulps of air. Her lungs felt close to bursting as she followed Margaret's progress. Soon the familiar figure had gone over the horizon and was lost to sight. 'God speed,' Cathy murmured. Getting to her feet, she began following at a steadier pace. In her heart, she knew

Margaret was probably right. There was small hope now of saving the house.

When some short time later the fire wagon clattered through the street of Langho, its bells loudly ringing, the children followed. Raggy-arsed and barefooted, they shouted and laughed, some clinging to the wheels, others hanging from the tail-gate and a few running behind, occasionally cutting across the fields to keep up. This was a treat they couldn't miss, for a real fire in Langho was a rare event.

The house was beyond saving. By the time the firemen arrived, the flames had taken hold and were licking the sky. 'We might have stood a chance if we'd got here earlier,' said one weary man to another, his face streaked with soot and his red eyes weeping from the effects of acrid smoke. The other man shook his head and replied solemnly, 'It was a losing battle. The old place was laden with too much rotten timber.'

It was almost dark when the last man left. The fire was checked and the building gutted. There was nothing else to do but leave the blackened shell to the elements.

Frank was beside himself with rage. 'We're ruined!' Jutting out his chin, he paced up and down the drawing room, hands clenched behind his back. 'I'll have him for it though!' His shifty eyes flicked from Margaret to Cathy. 'Owen Leyton's son did this, and by God I'll make him pay!'

Cathy had heard enough. After being summoned here with Margaret, she had expected to hear some kind of constructive plans for the future. Instead of which her father had strutted about, blaming everyone else for his own misfortune and now threatening to set the law on David. It was the last straw. Springing out of her chair, she faced him with a look as furious as his own. 'I didn't want to attend this meeting in the first place,' she confessed, 'but I came here with my aunt because I thought you might have something useful to say. I was foolish enough to believe you might have found a way of salvaging something out of what we have left. But I was wrong. As I've always been wrong about you. You care for no one but yourself, isn't that the truth?' Now the anger was high in her she couldn't easily suppress it. 'As for David starting that fire, how can you be so sure? How do you know it wasn't just a dreadful accident?'

Momentarily astonished by her outburst, he stared at her with pink bulbous eyes. When he spoke, it was in a low guttural voice that betrayed his dislike of her. 'I know because he's made of the same rotten stuff Owen Leyton was made of. I know, because it's his way of getting back at me for having his father hanged.'

Defiantly, she told him, 'You're wrong about David. I can't defend what his father did, but I can tell you that David Leyton is a fine young man. I know him, and he would never stoop to such a level.'

He laughed at that. 'Oh, I'm quite sure you know him . . . just as your dear mother knew his father. In fact I shouldn't be at all surprised if he hasn't already bedded you, made you with child, like his father made your mother with child.' As the awful words left his lips, his eyes misted over and the tears rolled down his podgy face. 'It's plain enough how he forced himself on her. My Rita would never have betrayed me of her own accord. But *you!* Your poor mother was right about you after all, wasn't she? There's a badness in you . . . just as there's a badness in Owen Leyton's son. He set fire to that house right enough. No doubt the pair of you have been rolling about in the hay, laughing at me. Isn't that the truth, eh?' Taking her by the shoulders, he shook her hard. 'I SAID, ISN'T THAT THE TRUTH?'

Struck silent by the viciousness of his words, Cathy could only stare at him. When Margaret took hold of her, urging, 'He didn't mean it. Can't you see he's crazed with grief?' Cathy shook her off. In a move that took everyone by surprise, she darted forward. Pressing her hands over her father's arms she pinned them to his sides. 'It isn't me and David that's bad,' she told him. 'It's *you!*'

'Take your filthy hands off.' Amazed by her strength, he tried to shake her off but couldn't.

Cathy was relentless. 'There was a time when I loved and respected you. Not any more though. How can I respect a man who doesn't even respect himself? How can a daughter look up to her father when he's lower than the worms in the ground? You spend your life shut away in the study . . . drunk most of the time . . . not caring what goes on around you. You talk about

David and his father. But what about you, eh? What about the shocking things *you've* done?'

'What do you mean?' Now he was on the defensive, looking at her with a glint of fear in his eyes.

'I know what you did! The land ... the cottage ... how you sold it all without Aunt Margaret's knowledge.' She had listened with shame and disbelief when, after the Leyton house had burned to the ground, Margaret felt the time was right for her to know the state of things. 'I'm afraid it must affect us badly,' she had said, and Cathy realised that the dear woman was beside herself with worry.

Frank was unrepentant. 'That is none of your concern!'

'Of course it's my concern. You expected to get a handsome rent from the house, didn't you? Enough to keep the wolf from the door, you told Aunt Margaret. What do you intend to do now? The house is a shell. There will be no rent. You've spent every penny got from the sale of other assets, and all that's left is this house. You have cheated your own sister, and still you feel no shame.'

'I'm not her keeper!'

'And I'm sure she wouldn't want you to be. But I can promise you she will come to no harm. Not while I am young enough to find a way of earning a living. Aunt Margaret has been everything to me all these years. She was there for me when you and Mother were not. And I shall always be there for her.' A tide of emotion washed through her, a mighty wave of relief that seemed to release a dam inside. 'You can't hurt me any more. Remember that, Father, when you're filling yourself with drink and shutting out those who might have cherished you ... you can't hurt *either* of us any more.' Shaking and close to tears but keeping them in check, she snatched herself away. With a dignity that made her tower above him, she walked across the room and out of the door.

Once outside she leaned against the wall, strengthened by the depth of her own feelings and astonished that she had found the courage to say what had needed saying for too long.

'Well, now!' Jack's cunning face appeared before her. 'I heard what you said in there, and I reckon it took real guts to turn on him like that.'

Her first instinct was to move away. The very nearness of him turned her stomach. But she was still fired up. 'Be careful, Jack,' she warned in a quiet voice. 'Or I might turn on *you* next.' With that, she went to her bedroom, secure in the knowledge that Margaret would come and talk with her before the night was over.

Jack waited outside the drawing room. The door was open as Cathy had left it, and Margaret was urging Frank, 'Please, you must take stock of yourself. It still isn't too late to win Cathy's affection. The three of us could move away, make a fresh start. Perhaps that would be best for all of us, Frank. Won't you at least think on it?' The scene between father and daughter had upset her, yet she knew it had been a long time in coming, and wasn't all that surprised when it erupted.

'I want nothing from her, and even less from you.' Frank could see no further than his hatred for the Leyton family. 'As for that young dog, David Leyton, I mean to see him punished for what he's done.'

'As Cathy said, how can you be so sure it was David who set fire to the house?'

'I'm sure enough, damn it.' He began pacing the floor again. 'I had it all worked out. The rent from that house would have saved us, and now ...'

'And now?' Margaret prompted.

For the first time he appeared to be concerned. Coming to the chair he eased himself into it like an old, old man. He didn't look at her, but his voice was broken when he muttered, 'Some of the things she said ... awful to hear.' When, by her silence, she condoned what Cathy had said, he glanced up, his eyes ugly to look on. 'In answer to your question, Margaret ... about what might happen now ... I'm afraid things are out of my hands.'

'What do you mean?'

'I mean, with that wretched house burned down, and with it the prospect of a handsome rent, I can't see which way to turn. As you know, the money is all spent.'

'You still have Rita's jewellery. You said yourself it's very valuable.'

'It's sold!' he lied. 'Every last piece ... sold!' He eyed her like a cat might a mouse.

'Sold?' She'd never believed he could do that. 'So you've sunk even lower than the few principles you had left? No matter. We still have this house. By all accounts you raised a considerable sum of money from the sale of the cottage and land with it. This place is much grander and should fetch enough to keep us all comfortable. We can find a smaller property, I'm sure. As long as you give up the drink and make yourself useful, and are determined to live more modestly, we'll manage well enough.'

His silence was somehow encouraging, making her feel there might be hope for them after all. It was only when he looked up and she saw his expression that the fear was rekindled. 'There's something you're not telling me,' she said anxiously. 'What is it, Frank? This is no time to be keeping secrets.'

Like the coward he was, he couldn't bear to look at her. Dropping his gaze to the floor, he mumbled, 'It's worse than you think.'

'For God's sake, how can it be worse?'

'I took out a loan against the security of this house, and they're threatening to evict us.'

Margaret's senses swam. For a moment she was unable to answer. She sat in the chair and pressed her hands to her face. She thought of Cathy and of how they would manage.

'It's no use crying over spilt milk,' he said callously.

Her face was stern as she replied, 'I wonder if I can ever forgive you. What you have done would be beyond any decent man.'

'I am my own man, and I will do as I please.'

'Not any more you won't! You have me and Cathy to consider now,' she reminded him. 'And you mustn't forget Jack. After all, you brought the boy here, and now he's your responsibility.'

'He's going back where he came from. I've an idea he might be better off with his own kind.' It was on the tip of his tongue to admit that Jack was his own flesh and blood, but it would serve no purpose. 'Anyway, I've already told you I won't send him away empty-handed.'

'Has he been told of your plans?'

'Not yet.'

'You mean you haven't the courage to tell him.'

'All in good time, my dear.'

'I mean it, Frank. From now on, *I* make the decisions. This house must be put on the market at once. With luck there might be money left after the debt is settled . . . enough for us to make a fresh start.'

'There won't be.'

'For all our sakes, I hope you're wrong.' Regarding him with disdain, she remarked angrily, 'It's a great pity you sold Rita's jewellery, because that might have salvaged at least some future for all of us.'

'Are you after my blood, is that it? Do you think to put me through the grinder for my sins?' Having got the worst off his chest, his arrogance was returning. 'I've confessed everything to you. I've been insulted by my own daughter. The boy is being sent packing, just as you've always wanted, and the changing of my will is in hand. Surely that is enough to satisfy you?'

Margaret was cynical. 'The changing of your will is in hand, you say? I suppose that means instead of leaving your debts to Jack, you'll be leaving them to me? Am I supposed to be grateful for that?' She shook her head forlornly. 'Really, Frank. You never cease to amaze me.'

'It isn't all bad news,' he reminded her. 'Before the day comes when I lie in my grave, you may find a way to restore our fortunes.'

'I believe you really have lost your senses!' Exasperated, she pointed out, 'There is no way I can possibly restore our fortunes, as you put it. As far as I can tell, we have no money and precious little to fall back on. What we have left is this house with one acre of land – both of which are mortgaged.' Looking him straight in the eye, she demanded in a frosty voice, 'I know the house was valued last year for the sum of one hundred guineas. How much is owed on it? And don't fob me off with lies. I want the truth, Frank, however damning.'

'I'm telling you nothing more. You will find out soon enough, I expect.' With each word his chest seemed to expand and his chin jutted out a little further. 'It might be wise for you to bear in mind that I am still head of this household. Now, if you please, I want to go to my study.'

'As you say, Frank, I will find out soon enough what depths you have lowered us all to.' With that she departed the room, leaving him to return to his study and his bottle.

As Margaret made her way up to Cathy, Jack crept out of hiding. Going into the study, he put on a smile and sat himself in the chair before the desk. 'By! What a tartar that one is,' he chuckled. It was an effort not to spring at Frank's throat and throttle the life out of him. Flicking his thumb towards the door, he said admiringly, 'I reckon you handled her very well.'

Surprised and irritated at his intrusion, Frank rounded the desk and took hold of him by the lapels. 'You were not asked to come in here,' he snarled. 'What's more, I don't want your useless opinions.'

Jack's smile grew crafty. 'That's no way to treat me, now is it?' he said, shrugging Frank off. 'I've come in here to talk about my future.'

'Explain.'

'Oh, I thought it might be *you* who'd explain. I heard you meant to send me back where I come from. Is that right? Do you mean to throw me out on me ear?'

Frank's face fell. 'If you heard that, you will also have heard that I don't mean to send you away empty-handed.'

'So you *are* throwing me out on me ear?'

'You never belonged here anyway.'

Jack stared at him for a moment, hatred alive in his face. Then, without another word, he turned away and left.

Frank's next visitor was Ruby. 'Miss Margaret has asked for a supper tray to be served in the drawing room,' she explained. 'I wondered if you might join them?'

'Leave me.'

'Can I bring you a bite to eat? A pot of tea, maybe?'

'I want nothing.' Looking up, he watched as she opened the door to leave. 'Ruby!'

'Yes, sir?'

'Did you post my letter?'

'Yes, sir.'

He gave a deep sigh. 'Very well. Now leave me.'

It was gone midnight when Frank finally climbed the stairs. But he didn't go to his bed. Instead he went to Rita's dressing table where he pulled out the top drawer. Setting it on the floor, he then reached into a hidden cavity. From here he withdrew a small mother-of-pearl cabinet. Placing it on top of the dressing table, he took a key from his waistcoat pocket and unlocked the cabinet. For a long moment he gazed inside, reluctant to let the gems see daylight. 'See here, Rita,' he muttered, looking round the room and pointing to the cabinet, 'I've kept them safe. They think I've sold them, but I could never do that.'

One by one he took out the gems, caressing each one as though it was flesh and blood. Soon they were laid out on the dressing-table top, fourteen pieces in all, glittering and shimmering, and all bought by an adoring husband for a wily ungrateful woman.

He stared at them and touched them, he smiled and he cried, recalling each occasion he had given a piece to Rita, and how she had rewarded him with nights of lovemaking he would never forget.

After a while he fell asleep beside them, his arms folded protectively over them, and his head laid between them; when he lapsed into a deeper slumber, the tears were still damp on his face.

The footsteps came silently into the room. Swamped with alcohol and unconscious with grief, Frank heard not a sound. The footsteps paused by the dressing table, quick practised fingers reached out to stroke the gems. Avaricious eyes devoured their beauty before they were dropped into a small dark bag and thrust into a deeper pocket. The same grubby fingers shook out a rag and pressed it ever so gently over Frank's nose. Asleep with his beloved Rita, he knew nothing. He felt nothing. All too soon it was over, the cabinet was removed and the drawer returned, and all was as before. One more look, making sure there was no trace of what had taken place here, and the footsteps hurried away.

It was Ruby who found him. The night had long gone and a new day had begun, but not for Frank. The news spread far and wide: Frank Blackthorn had died of his terrible grief. There was no mention of murder or robbery. Frank's lies about having sold Rita's jewellery had unwittingly protected his own executioner.

At precisely nine o'clock one morning in February 1901 the solicitor arrived at Blackthorn House. A short balding man with the air of a giant and the voice of a sergeant-major, Mr Reginald Dalton inspired both awe and respect in his many clients.

Cathy let him in. 'Good morning, Mr Dalton,' she said, inviting him through to the dining room where Margaret was already waiting. 'You'll join me and my aunt in a cup of tea, won't you?' As they walked, the grandfather clock in the hall chimed out the hours. The days had been long since David had left, and still she ached for him. But time stands still for no one, she thought.

At Cathy's invitation to accept a cup of tea, Mr Dalton merely nodded but made no verbal reply. She took the nod as being an acceptance. 'I've already asked Ruby to fetch a tray,' she explained politely. 'Your reputation for liking a good cup of tea goes before you.' Her smile was friendly and encouraging, but when he continued to remain silent she began to feel just the slightest bit uncomfortable. 'Aunt Margaret thought we might be more comfortable round the table in the dining room.' Opening the door, she ushered him inside.

Margaret was on her feet. 'Mr Dalton, punctual as usual,' she remarked, offering him her hand.

'I would be no kind of solicitor if I arrived late for the reading of a client's will,' he reprimanded.

Seeing Margaret embarrassed, Cathy chipped in, 'And it's all to your credit, Mr Dalton!' She showed him to the head of the table where he lost no time in laying down his briefcase. Once the women were seated, he settled himself comfortably. 'It's a sorry day,' he said sombrely, glancing first at Margaret and then at Cathy. He saw Jack seated on a chair beneath the window, but took little notice of him. 'Shall we begin?' His question was directed at the two women.

Both nodded, so he opened the briefcase and took out a sheaf of papers. At that moment, there came a knock on the door. It was Ruby. 'I've brought the tray you ordered,' she told Cathy.

'Thank you, Ruby.' She gestured to the end of the table. 'Just set it down there. I'll see to it.' As Ruby put the tray to the table, Cathy noticed that the older woman's hands were trembling, causing the cups and saucers to rattle. 'Are you all right, Ruby?' she asked with concern.

'I'm sorry,' Ruby whispered, casting an anxious glance at Margaret and the solicitor, who were taking this opportunity to discuss other matters. 'Only I'm all at sixes and sevens this morning.'

'You're obviously ailing for something.' Cathy was concerned about her. For days now, Ruby had not been her usual self. She was pale and nervous, seeming to have a great weight on her mind. 'Let the work wait ... go and sit down awhile,' Cathy said gently. 'You don't look at all well.'

'Oh, you mustn't fret about me,' Ruby chided, putting on a little smile. 'You have enough to worry about without me adding to your troubles.'

'It will be a sad day when I don't worry about you,' Cathy told her with a grin. 'Please, Ruby ... do as I ask. Put your feet up and pamper yourself for once.' Taking hold of the work-worn fingers, she gave them an encouraging little squeeze. 'I'll be along to see you when we've finished here.'

'All right, but you will send for me if I'm needed?'

'You won't be needed. Now, do as you're told.'

When the door closed behind Ruby, the short preliminary conversation between Margaret and the solicitor ended. 'If you're all ready now,' he announced, looking from one to the other and saving his most ferocious glare for Jack, 'I'll make a start.'

It was as Margaret and Cathy feared. All their assets had gone, with the exception of the charred remains of the Leyton house and the land on which it stood, and Blackthorn House and contents, all of which were at risk because of money loaned against them. 'The sum owing is quite considerable, I'm afraid,' the solicitor said and mentioned an amount that had his audience gasping.

'Almost its entire worth,' Margaret murmured, and from the look on her face Cathy realised how serious the situation had become.

In conclusion, Mr Dalton announced, 'The new will was received by me on the very day of Frank Blackthorn's death. In it he leaves everything to his sister Margaret. Unfortunately, with the main assets already stripped from the estate, there is much to be done if any monies are to be salvaged. If the debt against the estate is not repaid in full by one month from today, the house and its contents will be seized by the creditors.' Looking over his spectacles, he addressed himself to Cathy. 'It will rest with you and your good aunt to decide on a suitable course of action.'

Her gaze was equally stern. 'I understand,' she assured him. Then, sliding her hand over Margaret's, added in a softer voice, 'We *both* understand.'

Margaret was heartened by Cathy's response. 'We have been prepared for the worst,' she revealed. 'Whatever happens now, we're ready to face it head on.'

'Good! Good!' Beaming from ear to ear, he actually smiled. 'And I'm quite sure you won't mind my making a suggestion?' He took a deep breath and went on, 'Blackthorn House is a very desirable residence. I have a client who would pay a handsome sum of money for such a property... the entire estate, I mean... this house and land, together with the remains of the burned-out property and surrounding land.' Pleased with himself and sensing a favourable response, he added, 'Of course, he would want the contents and furniture included in the price. But you have my word... I will negotiate a handsome sum on your behalf. One that would allow you to leave here with some dignity, together with the ability to set up home elsewhere.' It was to Margaret he now addressed himself. 'In the circumstances, I will of course waive my own professional fee. So can I take it you are you in favour of such an agreement?'

Margaret did seem to be in favour. 'I must admit I haven't relished the thought of seeking a buyer. Certainly your idea has merit.'

'Ah! Then I can make a start?'

Cathy had listened, and not without an inkling of suspicion. Before Margaret could answer, she asked, 'This client of yours... may I ask who he is?'

Mr Dalton was obviously embarrassed. He hummed and hawed and blew his nose into his handkerchief, before saying with an air of indignation, 'At this point in time there is nothing to be served by revealing his identity.'

Cathy was not satisfied. 'Is it *you*, Mr Dalton?' she demanded. 'Are *you* the one who wants to get his hands on Blackthorn House?'

Again he hummed and hawed and glanced at Margaret, who was intent on the conversation. 'Does it matter who the buyer is?' he asked her nervously.

Here Margaret intervened. First she asked Jack to leave the room. When he left in a sulk, she turned on Mr Dalton. 'I believe it is our right to know who the potential buyer is. Also what sum of money we might be talking about. As yet you haven't divulged that very important fact, and I am made to wonder, like Cathy, why all the secrecy?'

'What do you imply by that?' The room was cool, but the sweat was running down his face. Fishing out a clean white handkerchief from his waistcoat pocket, he feverishly dabbed at himself. 'Are you suggesting I intend to acquire the property by devious means?'

It was Cathy who replied. 'What my aunt means, Mr Dalton, is this . . . first of all, why couldn't you say it was you who was hoping to buy the property? And secondly, if you are not prepared to name a figure here and now, we can only be made suspicious. Now, if you would please explain exactly what you mean when you say a "handsome sum"?'

'As I have already explained, after settlement of all debts, the remaining monies will allow you and your aunt to retire in some degree of comfort.'

'But what *sum*, Mr Dalton?' Like a dog with a bone, Cathy would not let go. Looking on, Margaret realised that all the recent trials and disappointments had somehow given her niece a deeper determination.

'I thought . . . one hundred and seventy guineas.' By now his face was shiny and bright pink. 'The sum owed is one hundred and forty . . . leaving you and your aunt with thirty guineas. You can buy a modest house and arrange for a small income with such a sum.'

Cathy's face was set like stone. Pushing away her chair she told him in a hard voice, 'I do believe my aunt would like you to leave now.' She gave a sideways look at Margaret. who was clearly shocked by what amounted to deception by their own trusted solicitor.

Margaret came to stand by Cathy. When she spoke, it was to reiterate what Cathy had already said. 'Yes, I would like you to leave.'

'But what about Blackthorn House, and the remainder?' He saw his mistake and was eager to rectify it. 'I must apologise for not naming myself as the possible buyer ... it's just that I didn't want you to get the wrong idea. And now you have, and I'm embarrassed.'

Cathy gave no quarter. 'So you should be,' she snapped. 'A man in your profession should know better than to deceive the clients who place their trust in you.'

'I am sorry you feel this way, but I have to advise that the figure I offer is a good one, and you'll not get better elsewhere.'

Margaret considered this while Cathy saw him to the door. 'You are wrong about our not being able to get a better price elsewhere,' she informed him. 'Rather than let it go under market value, my aunt and I will consider putting it all to auction.'

He was appalled. 'Do that and you'll be throwing yourselves to the wolves.'

'Maybe. But you have already seen that Blackthorn House is a desirable property. There must be many more who think the same way. Wolves they may be. But if these same wolves are prepared to fight each other for what they want, that can only drive the price up.' Smiling as she closed the door on him, she added softly, 'You obviously thought to be handed everything on a plate. Well, now you can fight for what you want too ... just as my aunt and I must do.'

Margaret was intrigued by Cathy's idea. 'But how will we go about it? I don't know the first thing about auctions ... apart from the fact that Longdon Place went to auction last year and raised more than was expected.'

'There you are then! We have to do it. What we don't know we can find out. Besides, once we put it all in the hands of a reputable auctioneer, we just need to follow the proceedings.'

Excited by the prospect, she urged, 'What do you think? Shall we make some enquiries?'

It was agreed. Margaret, however, placed the burden on Cathy's shoulders, with the plea, 'Forgive me, sweetheart, but I feel drained by it all. Would you mind very much if I returned to my bed?'

Cathy was understanding. 'It's not surprising you feel drained,' she said, going with Margaret to the foot of the stairs. 'First Mother, and all the shocking things that came out about her and Owen Leyton. Nan . . . the Leyton house being burned down . . . and now Father. And on top of it all, this awful business of having to sell up and pay off enormous debts. It's too much for anyone to bear.'

Margaret smiled at that. 'It isn't too much for you though. And in losing David, you have lost the most precious thing of all.' She shook her head and wondered at Cathy's determination in all of this. 'You're a Godsend to me,' she whispered. 'Where you get your strength from, I will never know.'

'From you,' Cathy assured her. 'I get my strength from you. Whatever I can do to help now will never be enough to thank you for all the years of love you have shown me.'

'Are you sure you'll be all right going to see the auctioneer on your own? Won't you wait until the morning, when I'm sure I'll be able to face it in a better frame of mind?'

'Let me do this. Please.'

'All right. But I don't like you wandering about these auction yards by yourself.'

'We may have to face much harder ordeals before all this is over. There is no one else to do it for us.'

'You're right. Do what you can. I know I can leave it safely in your hands.'

Delighted to be trusted with something so important, Cathy got herself ready. When she came into Ruby's kitchen she looked every inch a businesswoman. Dressed in a straight brown skirt, high-necked blouse and small-heeled boots, with her long grey coat over the top and an official-looking folder tucked under her arm, she took Ruby by surprise. 'Goodness me! You look like you're all set to do battle,' Ruby declared, dropping her paring knife on to the vegetables. 'It's to do with the official gentleman who was just here, is it?'

'That was Mr Dalton, the solicitor,' Cathy explained. 'And yes, in a roundabout way it is to do with him.'

'I didn't take to him at all . . . he had shifty eyes.'

Cathy laughed. 'You always were a good judge of character.'

They chatted for a minute, during which time Cathy asked after Ruby's health, and she said she was feeling much better. Cathy was not altogether convinced and said she would come and sit awhile with Ruby on her return. 'Meantime, would you keep an eye on Aunt Margaret? I think the strain's beginning to tell on her.'

Ruby assured her she most certainly would, and Cathy went on her way with an easier mind.

Margaret came down to the kitchen and told Ruby how she had begged off going to the auctioneers because, 'I feel Cathy would deal with it much better than I ever could. She's making a fine young woman, and appears to have a splendid head for business.'

'Then she takes after you.'

Margaret shook her head in disagreement. 'You're wrong, Ruby,' she murmured. 'If I had been more aware of what was going on . . . if I had kept a closer eye on the business of this estate, we would never have come to this awful predicament. I'm afraid I have a great deal to learn, whereas Cathy has a natural talent for it.' She chuckled. 'It was Cathy who saw right through Mr Dalton's ploy to acquire Blackthorn House at a price advantageous to himself. It was she who virtually threw him out, and it was she who then suggested going to an auctioneer.'

'Oh, she has her head screwed on and no mistake.'

'That she has, Ruby. And I'm afraid from now on it may be a case of me leaning on her.'

'The lass's shoulders are broad enough,' Ruby said gently. 'She's young and strong, and has the heart of a lion.' She laughed aloud. 'In fact, just now she went out of here like a young warrior.'

They both laughed as Margaret said, 'I know what you mean. And in her present mood, I defy anyone to take advantage of her.'

James Armitage was the man everyone turned to when they

had need of an auction. He sold anything and everything, from sticks of furniture to industrial machines, and no one was more astute than he at driving a hard bargain. Small and 'wick', with big white teeth and a mass of ginger hair, he employed twelve good men and had never yet been the subject of complaint.

As was his way when dealing with women, he was charming and efficient. After paying the closest attention to what Cathy had to say, he told her, 'I'm confident we can find any number of well-heeled citizens who would be more than interested in owning such a place as Blackthorn House.'

'How do you mean to present it?' She had thought long and hard about how it should best be done.

'Why, I shall visit the site and value it,' he announced. 'Then, I shall have a catalogue drawn up and distribute it far and wide, together with the usual advertising.'

'I want everyone to know for miles round... even as far as London.'

He was deeply offended. 'Be assured I will leave no stone unturned to get you the very best price possible. After all, I have my good name and reputation to think of.'

'And a fine commission, I'll be bound! But we can discuss that in a moment. Also, I wasn't questioning your ability. My aunt and I have a great deal to lose if it goes wrong, so with all due respect to your good self, I do have a few thoughts of my own on how it might be handled.'

'I'm listening.'

'First of all, I wouldn't want the entire estate to be sold as one lot.'

'Really?'

'I believe we could raise a better price if we did it another way.'

'Go on.' He had never met such a forthright young lady, and was fascinated that she had put so much thought into what would be for most women a fearsome matter.

'I believe we should sell Blackthorn House with half an acre as one lot, the other half an acre on its own... which will attract not only those who want Blackthorn House, but also the adjoining farmers and any small landowner who wants to increase his holdings. Another parcel would be the burned-out shell and the land on which it stands. Then the furniture as a separate item.'

'Bearing in mind, of course, that you may wish to keep some of the furniture yourself?'

The very thought made Cathy cringe. 'We want nothing from the house.' She and Margaret had already agreed on this. 'That way we can increase the competition and raise the stakes. Are you in agreement?'

Inspired by her enthusiasm and sharp mind, he commented quietly, 'You are a very unusual young woman.'

'I'm sorry if you think I'm trying to tell you how to do your job, but I must look out for my aunt. You are probably too polite to say so, but I feel you must already know the whole story surrounding Blackthorn House and the family. My aunt has taken it all with great courage and now she needs peace of mind. The monies got from this sale will be all we shall have, so you do understand why I am so concerned to do the best I can? I owe it to my aunt, and to myself.'

He gazed at her before saying warmly, 'Yes, I do know the whole story surrounding Blackthorn House, and I fully understand your need to secure the best price you can for the estate.'

'You think my ideas are workable then? About splitting the estate into four different lots?'

He laughed. 'Do I think your ideas are workable?' He gazed at her again, and the laughter in his eyes became a look of compassion. 'I'll tell you what I think. I think your aunt is in good hands with you to look out for her. I think I should be ashamed I didn't think to split the estate in such a way, and yes, it may well fetch a better price under these circumstances. Rest assured you'll not get a better service from any other auctioneer.'

'Then I'm ready to talk terms.'

The commission he wanted was not acceptable to Cathy, so he reduced it a little. Still it was not acceptable, so he reduced it a little more. And eventually the terms were agreed. 'You will put it all in writing to my aunt,' Cathy instructed as she prepared to leave.

'Of course.' Rarely had he met such a forceful personality, and he was filled with admiration. He saw her out of the office door and led the way to the outer yard. 'Goodbye, Miss Blackthorn,' he said, shaking her by the hand. He had expected her hand to be light and delicate, like a feather in his own. But Cathy gripped his fingers and squeezed with remarkable determination.

'Miss Blackthorn?'

She turned to look at him. 'Yes?'

'I admire your courage.'

'When needs must, we all have to find a certain amount of courage.'

'But you ... so young, losing both parents in such a short time ... and in such circumstances. Now, taking on the responsibility for all this ... for your aunt.' Momentarily choked for words, he smiled encouragingly. 'You really are an exceptional young lady.'

'Thank you.' Cathy didn't know what else to say, although she might have told him how she owed her courage to another 'exceptional' lady. Margaret had taught her to be strong when she had most needed strength. That teaching would serve Cathy all her life.

He bade her good day but before she departed told her solemnly, 'I have two sons, but neither of them has your gumption. If the day should ever come when you need a profession, I would be proud to have you work alongside me.' He chuckled then. 'You might even be able to teach an old dog new tricks.'

Cathy returned his smile. 'I'm flattered by your kind offer. Who knows when our paths may cross again? For now, though, I want the best price for the estate. And be warned, I shall be watching every move you make.'

'I don't doubt that for a minute.'

'You will write to my aunt this very day?'

'The minute you're gone, I promise.'

Inclining her head, she said politely, 'Good day then, Mr Armitage.'

'Good day, Miss Blackthorn.' He watched her go, and wondered why it was that he had begot two layabouts, while a weakling like Frank Blackthorn had spawned such a proud and capable creature.

Margaret listened with interest. 'I'm proud of you,' she declared.

'I knew I was right to leave it all in your hands.'

On the way home, Cathy had entertained her first doubts. 'I hope I've done the right thing in persuading you to go to auction,' she said. 'Perhaps I've been too hasty.'

'While you've been gone, I've been thinking, and I believe you're right. An auction is a splendid idea, and as for suggesting to Mr Armitage that he should split the whole into four lots, well, that was ingenious.'

'I don't know about ingenious, but it seemed to me that some people might want the smaller parcel of land, while others would want only the big house. Then you might have other people who would want neither house nor land, but be glad to buy the furniture.' To give the auctioneer his due, she added, 'I'm certain it would have occurred to Mr Armitage at some point. He is very experienced after all.'

'Perhaps. But it was you who thought of it, and I'm glad you did.' Margaret was feeling a little stronger after her short rest, ready now to face Ruby with the full facts. 'Could you ask Ruby to come in now?' she requested. 'Jack, too . . . if you can find him. It's time they were both put in the picture.'

Jack was in the kitchen stuffing his face with apple pie while Ruby gave him a piece of her mind for not wiping his boots at the back door. 'You're an ungrateful scoundrel!' she told him. 'Not once have you shown any compassion for Miss Margaret or Miss Cathy, and you know how hard it has been for them.' She looked up as Cathy came through the door. 'Oh! I'm sorry,' she said. 'I didn't hear you coming.'

Cathy felt Jack's eyes on her but didn't look at him. Instead she addressed Ruby. 'You're wanted in the drawing room . . . you and . . .' She still couldn't bring herself to look at him, nor could she say his name. 'If you could both make your way there now, my aunt is waiting.'

With Cathy back beside her, Margaret was ready to begin. 'Jack, I would prefer you to sit over here,' she said, shifting her gaze to the window-seat where he sat slouched and surly. 'What I have to say affects us all.'

'I can hear well enough from here.' He glared at her. 'Besides, I've heard enough to know I've been thrown on the slag heap.'

'Very well. Stay where you are if that's the way you want it.' She had no patience with him. 'But I have considered how

241

harshly you've been treated, and I hope I might be able to make some amends for my brother's thoughtlessness.' At once he was across the room and settling himself on a nearby chair. 'That's better.' Margaret gave him a half-hearted smile. 'Now please sit still and pay attention to what I have to say.'

She then went on to explain that the estate was deep in debt. 'There is nothing to be done but to sell it lock, stock and barrel. At the end of it all, I can only hope we raise enough to pay off the debts and have a little left over with which to start again. In a more modest way, of course.'

Jack was the first to respond. 'What's coming to me then? You said you might be able to make amends for the way I've been treated.'

'I can make no promises,' Margaret replied sternly. 'To be honest, I never wanted you in this house, and I shall be glad to see the back of you. But, however misguided and for whatever reason, my brother took it upon himself to bring you here, and now I am taking it on myself to send you on your way with a token gesture ... hoping, of course, that it might keep you off the streets, at least until you find work and a permanent roof over your head.'

He sat up straight, his eyes gleaming. 'A token gesture, eh? I thought you said you were penniless?'

'No, I did not say that. However, things are very difficult at this moment in time. The house and what remains of the estate will be sold by auction. Until then we have no way of knowing what the outcome will be. That said, I intend to see the bank manager and request a favour ... a small favour that will compensate you for your time in this house, and allow you to leave it at the first opportunity.'

'Suits me.' He stretched his legs and stood up. 'But I hope the "favour" ain't too small. Don't forget I was led to believe I'd be well off ... then the old bastard goes and sells it all and changes his will so I can't even lay claim to what's left.'

Cathy stood up at his outburst. In a calm and dignified voice, she told him, 'Your colourful language cuts no ice here. If it was up to me, you'd be sent down the road without shoes or belongings. We none of us want you, so you'd do well to get out now.'

'My! My! Ain't you the bold one, eh?' Shaken by her remarks, he couldn't help but admire her. It was on the tip of his tongue to say how she of all people should know he got what he wanted, because hadn't he already taken her against her will? Oh, yes! She of all people should know he wasn't to be got rid of that easily.

He might have said all this, and more. But something in Cathy's lovely face, in the cold hard stare from her proud green eyes, made him shrink inside. His admiration turned to anger. 'I'll go when I've had my pay-off and not before.' With a sneer, he strode out, but his presence was felt for a long time afterwards.

Though she could see Margaret's motive, Cathy had to voice her disapproval. 'I don't think you should pay him a penny piece.'

'It might make some amends for my brother's foolhardiness in bringing him here in the first place,' Margaret explained. 'It can't be much, I know, and I have never liked that young man. But I will start my new life with a better conscience if it's done. You do understand what I'm trying to say, don't you, Cathy?'

'I understand, but I would rather he was dragged out of here tied to a carriage and four.' Try as she might, she couldn't keep the bitterness out of her voice. He had viciously ravaged her, and she could not forgive him.

Margaret regarded her with curiosity. 'I didn't know your feelings against him ran so deep.'

'I'm sorry.' Realising she had betrayed too much, Cathy was quick to put things right. 'Of course I understand what you're trying to do, and I admire you for it, because I know you don't care for him either. But how can you promise him anything when we don't even know whether we'll have enough to live on when the debts are paid?'

'It will be a small gesture, but a gesture nevertheless.' She turned to Ruby. 'We have just one month before we must leave Blackthorn House forever. As Cathy said, when it's all done we may not even have enough to live on. Do you have any plans, Ruby?'

Ruby was torn two ways. Having been told the full facts, she sat quite still, her face downcast, wringing her hands. As Cathy and Margaret waited for her response, she fought to keep the emotion out of her voice. 'I saw it all coming,' she confessed. 'When that official-looking gentleman came this morning, I knew then . . . I knew you might not be able to stay here. I knew I might have to say goodbye to you . . . to everything.' Her eyes glittered with unshed tears.

Cathy came to sit beside her, to reiterate Margaret's query. 'But . . . do you have any plans, Ruby?'

She surprised them by chuckling. 'I had a man friend,' she revealed. 'A sweetheart, would you believe? I honestly thought he wanted me to wed him. But I were wrong.'

'How do you mean, Ruby?' Cathy recalled how secretive Ruby had been of late, and she could see it all now. Ruby had a sweetheart, and she didn't want the world to know.

'I'm just an old fool, sneaking about, meeting him whenever I had a minute to spare. At my age I should have known better than to think any man would fancy me. He's gone, d'you see? Upped and gone, like he were never here.'

Cathy took hold of the older woman's hand. 'Then he wasn't worthy of you,' she said softly.

'Aye, well, it's done now, and I'm left behind, and don't know what the future holds.'

Cathy turned to look at Margaret. 'If all goes well, we can keep Ruby with us, can't we?' she pleaded.

Margaret nodded her head. Smiling, she said to Ruby, 'If there is any way we can keep you with us, you know we will, don't you?'

Ruby's whole countenance brightened. 'I know that, and I'm very grateful,' she answered. 'But you and Miss Cathy here . . . you've yourselves to think about now. You can't be burdened with an old mare like me.'

Cathy laughed at that. 'It's us that's been a burden to you these many years. But if you're trying to say you don't want to be with us, then say it, Ruby.' She knew that tack might work, and it did.

Ruby was bristling. 'Fancy you saying a thing like that, Cathy Blackthorn!' she chided. 'Don't want to be with you indeed! Where else would I want to be, tell me that?'

Laughing, Cathy hugged her, and soon the three of them were

enjoying the little deceit. 'You're a scoundrel, that's what you are,' Ruby told Cathy. 'You always were a cheeky madam.' Addressing Margaret, she said firmly, 'If there's a way you can keep me, I'm yours for the rest of me days.' Something else occurred to her. 'What's more, I've no need of fancy wages. I've saved a little nest egg, and now it ain't needed to feather me own nest, it's yours if you want it.'

'Take your hard-earned wages?' Margaret's features hardened to disbelief. 'Never!' But she assured Ruby, 'Cathy and I have no idea where we might end up, but wherever it is, and if it can be done, we do want you with us.'

'Bless you for that. It's all I can hope for. Till then, I'd best get on with me chores.' Ruby gave her thanks and excused herself.

'She's upset,' Cathy said. 'We have to find a way to keep her with us.'

'And we will.' Margaret also excused herself. 'First, I want rid of Jack. That means a talk with the bank manager. After that, you and I will just have to bide our time and pray things go well at the auction.'

'Do you want me to come with you?'

'Heaven forbid! He's a great pudding of a man, with a history of bronchitis. If I let you loose on him, he's likely to suffer a heart attack.'

Cathy's eyes twinkled. '*Then* where would we get a loan?'

'Shame on you.' Margaret was still smiling when she hurried from the room to get herself ready. 'I'll not be long,' she called, going out of the door. 'Pray he's in a benevolent mood, for if he turns us down, I don't know where next to turn.'

Two hours later, Margaret was back with the news. 'It seems the whole of Lancashire knows the predicament we're in. According to the bank manager, we are now a financial risk. Unlike you and me, Cathy, he does not envisage any profit from the auction.'

'Then he's a fool.' Cathy was up in arms. 'If there was that much of a risk, why is it the lenders have sanctioned the auction? If they were of the same mind as your bank manager, they would have moved heaven and earth to take control. Oh,

I know they are closely monitoring it, but they know full well they'll get their pound of flesh.'

'That's because they have us legally bound to repay the debt within a month.'

'And we will . . . and we'll get more besides, I know it.'

'Meanwhile, what do we do? How do we live?'

'We sell one of the silver ornaments. Leave it to me, eh?' Cathy was already on her feet and heading for the door. 'I know the very one . . . that large statuette in Father's study.'

Margaret agreed, and the very next morning Cathy took the statuette into town. Jake Montague, at the jeweller's, examined it through his eye-piece. 'Very nice,' he muttered, scratching the stubble on his long chin. 'Worth half a guinea.'

Cathy gave him one of her most disapproving stares. '*Three* guineas,' she said coldly. 'I know the value of that statuette as well as you.' She didn't, but it was worth a try.

He placed the statuette on the counter and touched it reverently with the tip of his fingers. Apart from its considerable monetary value, he had taken a liking to it and had no real intention of letting it go. '*One* guinea. That's my final offer.'

'Two guineas, or I take it away and sell it to someone who appreciates beautiful things.' Collecting it up, she began wrapping it in the brown paper.

His hand darted out to grab it back. 'All right,' he groaned. '*Two* guineas.'

Cathy's smile displayed her relief. 'Very wise,' she said. 'Even at that, you know you've got a bargain.'

'Hmph! Been robbed more like.' He paid over the money and grunted, 'I should have waited for the auction. Happen I'd have got it for half the price.'

'And you might have had to pay twice as much.' Cathy was satisfied though. 'Anyway, what makes you think my aunt planned to put it in the auction?'

A look of embarrassment crossed his face. Shrugging, he told her, 'It's common knowledge how you and your aunt have been left penniless. Moreover, I know the auctioneer well, and he reckons every stick and ornament will be included in the sale.' Fearing he had offended her, he apologised. 'I suppose he ought not to be discussing such things with me.'

Cathy was not offended. 'On the contrary. Mr Armitage promised to advertise far and wide, and I'm pleased he appears to be doing his job.'

'He'll do his best by you, there's no two ways about that.'

Her parting words made him bless his own good fortune. 'Think about this, Mr Montague,' she urged. 'If you had waited for the sale to acquire that statue, you might well have been bidding against several other would-be buyers. Like as not, you would have been made to pay four times as much as you've got it for today. You've taken advantage of two ladies in dire straits,' she added indignantly. 'Aren't you ashamed?'

He was so ashamed he gave her the three guineas she had at first requested, and she went on her way with a spring in her step.

Ruby came back into the kitchen. When she saw Jack seated at the table stuffing his face with the remains of the muffins, she grabbed the large wooden spoon and smacked him round the ear with it. 'You ungrateful bugger!' she screeched. 'You know very well I were saving them muffins for supper. It's getting harder and harder to make ends meet since the master went. There ain't no money coming in, and them good ladies is living hand to mouth.' She swiped at him again, but he dodged her and ran behind the table. 'You don't belong here, in a fine house with fine ladies. You're scum, that's what you are! Scum!'

Revelling in her distress, he teased, 'Scum I might be, you old ratbag. But I ain't moving till I get what's coming to me.'

'Well now, you might be interested to know that the bank turned Miss Margaret down. There ain't nothing coming from that direction, so you'd best be off and leave us alone.' Hurrying to the dresser, she dropped the wooden spoon and took down the largest meat cleaver she could lay hands on. 'If you ain't out of this house afore I've counted to ten, I'll have the head off your shoulders,' she threatened. And from the look on her face, she meant every word. 'ONE...' As she counted, she came towards him, the cleaver raised high in the air. 'TWO...'

'What? Yer mean she can't get no money to be rid of me? Yer lying buggers, the lot of yer!'

'THREE...' She was so close now he could see the whites of her eyes. 'FOUR...'

'You're bleedin' mad!'

'FIVE...'

'If yer think I'm going empty-handed, yer can think again.'

'SIX...'

Fear erupted in a giggle. 'You don't scare me, yer old trollop.'

'SEVEN...'

'If yer throw me out, I'll only come back and set fire to the place, then yer fine ladies will be in the same boat as me.'

Ruby was stopped in her tracks. 'You little bastard! It were *you* who set fire to the Leyton house, weren't it? WEREN'T IT?'

'NO! I swear to God it weren't me.'

Advancing, she began counting again, this time quicker. 'EIGHT... NINE.' She was only a hand's reach from him.

'I'M TELLING YER, I DIDN'T SET FIRE TO NOTHING!' He was yelling now, terrified like the coward he was. 'GIVE ME ENOUGH MONEY TO GET TO LONDON TOWN AN' I SWEAR YER'LL NEVER SET EYES ON ME AGAIN!' When there came no reply, he crouched, waiting for the blow that would sever the head from his miserable body.

'How much?' Ruby had the cleaver raised, her beady eyes boring into him as he stared up at her. 'How much to get you back to London?'

'To get me there and see I've a roof over me head for long enough to feel me feet... I'll need at least two guineas.'

'How much?'

'Less than that ain't enough to keep body and soul together!'

'How much?'

'Yer don't want me starving in the street, do yer?'

'I don't reckon I'd lose any sleep over that.'

'Give me what you've got, yer old bugger! If it's enough, you'll not see hide nor hair of me ever again.'

Taking the cleaver with her and keeping her eyes on him, Ruby went to the dresser. From here she took out her bag, and from the bag she took out a purse, and from the purse she withdrew a handful of silver coins and threw them one at a time on to the table. 'That's every penny I've got. Now piss off and be damned to you!' Stepping back, she waited until he had collected the coins, then she chased him out of the kitchen, through the door and away from the house. 'If that ain't enough, you'll have to sell the clothes on your back, won't you?' she called after him. 'I dare say you've done that an' all afore today.'

She was laughing out loud as she went back into the kitchen. 'Oh, Ruby Adams! Fancy using language that would make the vicar blush!' she chastised herself. 'Still, the rascal's gone, and it did me heart good to see him haring down the lane as though the very devil was at his heels.'

When the tale was related to Margaret and Cathy, the three of them laughed until they cried. 'That should teach him to mess with you,' Cathy said. And, against Ruby's protests, Margaret promised to replace that good woman's savings as soon as ever the opportunity arrived. 'We've sold one statuette and thanks to Cathy got a good price for it. If needs be, we'll sell another piece of silver before the auction.' Ruby would not hear of it, and the matter was left unresolved.

That night, Cathy lay in her bed, dreaming of David one minute and in the next wondering what the future might hold. 'It won't be much of a future without him near,' she thought aloud. Musing on him, seeing his face in her mind and reliving the special times they had together, she settled down to sleep.

As she lay there in the dark with her brooding thoughts, she eventually allowed herself to think of Jack. Glad beyond words to know he was gone, she dared not speculate any further. These past few weeks, she had felt strange within herself, poorly one day and disgustingly healthy the next. Something was different and she wasn't altogether certain what. Yet now the hideous prospect had crept up on her and she was made to face a shocking possibility. The impulse was so strong that she had to get out of her bed and put on the light.

Standing before the mirror, she pressed her hands over her nightgown, drawing the material tight across her stomach. As always it was flat and hard, with no outward sign to confirm her haunting suspicions. But inside she was alive with the memory of that night when he had brutally assaulted her. 'Jack may be gone, but I'm so afraid.' The fear lit her eyes. The whisper seemed to echo from every wall. 'Dear God, don't let me be with child!' Even now, when it seemed more plausible with every passing day, Cathy dared not, *would not*, allow herself to contemplate such a terrible thing.

249

Unable to sleep now, she went to the window and watched the night sky for a time. The night was beautiful, the stars high in the heavens and the gentle breeze created a melody in the overhanging branches close to her window. Soon the need for sleep came over her. Climbing back into bed, she closed her eyes and thought of David once more. Her thoughts became dreams and her dreams were sweet.

In the thickness of night, Jack approached the house from the rear. Pausing to look up at the window behind which Ruby was slumbering, he softly chuckled. 'Yer might have thought I were miles away by now, but y'see how wrong yer can be?' Coming forward on tiptoe, he made his entry through the pantry window. Ruby had made a rabbit pie for tomorrow's dinner, and the delicious aroma teased his nostrils. In the half light that trickled through the window he spied the pie and his stomach rumbled. 'I didn't come back for no pie,' he muttered, still smiling, 'but there ain't no reason why I shouldn't help meself.' Scooping it from the plate, he held it in both hands, ramming it into his mouth and licking the spilt gravy as it ran through his fingers. 'I'll say this for yer, Ruby yer old sod,' he muttered through a huge mouthful, 'there ain't nobody can bake a better pie than you.'

With his stomach filled to bursting, he replaced the half-eaten pie. Seeing a hessian sack filled with potatoes, he tipped it upside down, emptying them on to the pantry floor. That done, he tucked the sack under his arm and made his way out of the pantry. On tiptoe and keeping alert to every sound, he went along the dimly lit hall until he came to the drawing room. Here, he softly entered. Closing the door, he struck a match on the sole of his boot, losing no time before going round the room collecting all the silver and porcelain pieces. The smaller ornaments went into his pockets, the larger ones into the hessian sack.

Satisfied, he went back the way he had come, and was soon out of the house, lost in the night, congratulating himself on having had the last laugh. 'This little lot should fetch a pretty penny,' he told himself. 'Happen it'll be them in the streets and me with a better roof over me head. Still, it's no more than I deserve. I ain't never been one to carp, so I'm happy enough to cut me losses.' Pausing long enough to look back at the house, his eyes were drawn to one particular upstairs window. 'I ain't sorry about what I did, Cathy,' he said. 'I'm only sorry I couldn't get you to feel the same way about me.' He stood there for more than a full minute, the bulk of his thieving weighing him down. 'I've only got what's mine,' he grumbled. 'But I ain't such a bastard I can't wish yer well with the auction.'

Swinging the sack carefully on to his shoulder, he turned away, a crafty smile on his face. 'I'd like to see the old bugger Ruby's face in the morning, when she finds her precious pie half gone. Still, I did leave 'em a bite or two, didn't I, eh? I could 'ave took the lot, but I didn't. Generous to a fault, that's what I am!' He was still laughing when he ran through the spinney and across the open fields.

The pie was of no importance, but when it was discovered that a thief had removed almost all of the porcelain and silver, Margaret took it badly. 'I've no one but myself to blame,' she declared. 'I should have taken it all to the bank and put it on deposit . . . or given it into the keeping of the auctioneer. Now it's gone, and with it the prospect of making enough to set up elsewhere.'

'You're not to blame yourself.' Cathy had been aware her aunt was coming to the end of her tether and was anxious to protect her. 'I could have suggested putting it in safe keeping but, like you, I believed there was no real need. Now it's gone, as you say, but we mustn't let it drag us down. We *will* have enough to start again, you must believe that.' Her own hopes had been shattered when Ruby ran up to tell them a burglar had struck in the night. Now, though, she was determined they would come through somehow.

At her words, Ruby stopped crying, and Margaret looked up with admiration. 'You make me feel ashamed,' she told Cathy. 'I ought to be looking after you. Yet at every turn it's you, not me, who refuses to be beaten. You don't seem to know the meaning of fear . . . you tend to see the future in a way I cannot.'

'No, you're wrong,' Cathy corrected her. 'I *am* afraid. But no, I will not be beaten by some cowardly thief in the night.' A great rage took hold of her. 'I only wish I'd been downstairs. He might have wished he'd never set foot in this house!'

'Or wished he'd never been born?' Margaret said with the

glimmering of a smile. She was thankful that Cathy had not set eyes on the person who had violated their home. 'We'll have to let the police know. Maybe they can catch him before he sells everything.'

Ruby hurried away to inform the authorities. When some time later two constables arrived, they went over the house with a fine-tooth comb and took statements from them all. Finally they concluded, 'The thief is probably long gone by now. However . . . the list you've given of the stolen items will be circulated, and we shall certainly do our best, but we can't promise we will ever recover them. In cases like this we find the stolen goods are taken right out of the area . . . the silver could be melted down, and then there's no way of tracing it.'

Cathy was shocked. 'You seem to be giving up before you've even started.'

'I'm sorry, Miss, but we've had the bigger houses round here burgled before, and it's never easy to track down the stolen items.' He wisely changed tack. 'Have you any idea who it might have been? Did someone bear a grudge against you?' His questions were directed at Margaret.

'I can't think of anyone who would do such a thing,' she answered. Jack's name had been on the tip of her tongue but she bit it back.

Cathy was not so reluctant. 'I can think of someone,' she offered. She then told them about Jack, and how he had been sent on his way without the inheritance he had come to expect. 'If you find him, I'm certain you will find everything that's gone missing.'

'He's a bad 'un!' Ruby couldn't resist giving her opinion.

'I see.' The constable asked a few more questions concerning Jack, and wrote all the details in his little book. 'It's something to go on,' he said, and left soon after.

Half an hour later the auctioneer arrived with his foreman. They strolled round the house, through every room, with Mr Armitage also making notes in his little book. 'It's like a circus!' Ruby complained, fetching a tray of tea and toast.

Margaret preferred to sip her tea and await the auctioneer's return while, much to his dismay, Cathy dogged his footsteps. 'Have you had much interest?' she wanted to know.

'I'm delighted to say we've had more than a little.'

'Wealthy people, are they?'

'They need to be.' He cast an appreciative glance round the study. 'You do have some very valuable pieces here.' He was staring at the grand walnut desk. 'That alone should fetch a pretty penny.' His gaze went to the shelves. They were stuffed with leather-bound volumes, some of them quite rare. On the dresser stood a silver tray, displaying two handsome silver and crystal decanters with four tumblers to match. 'I have to say, your father had expensive tastes. He certainly liked to surround himself with the best of everything.' He was reluctantly growing to admire a man who'd lived life as he saw fit, and to hell with everyone else.

Cathy was not impressed. 'Not all of these things were my father's,' she said bitterly. In fact the tray and decanters had only recently been brought out from the dark recesses of a cupboard. 'So! I can look forward to a very successful auction, isn't that so?'

'I have high hopes.' He glanced at her and saw the determination in her face. He knew if he didn't promise his best she was quite capable even now of taking her business elsewhere. In that moment he saw his fat commission disappearing and was prompted to assure her, 'As you say, Miss Blackthorn . . . by rights, we should have a very successful auction.'

On the day of the auction they came from far and wide. Hopefuls who saw the opportunity of picking up an expensive piece at half the price; old women who had taken a fancy to Ruby's pine dresser and table; young men who fancied themselves in Frank Blackthorn's leather and oak swivel chair; and hard-faced dealers who thought to buy everything in for a song and sell it out again for a fortune. They crammed into the auction room, catalogues in hand, sparing a smile for one another while secretly lining up for battle. Much to Cathy's delight.

As requested, the auctioneer had arranged for three chairs to be set in the centre of the front row, and here sat the three women from Blackthorn House – three women who had much to lose if the amount raised fell below their expectations. Throughout the auction, Mr Armitage was made nervous by the fact that Cathy's eyes never once left him; vigilantly she watched his every move.

The bidding began with the house itself. After that came the articles of furniture, which were offered with all the atmosphere of a carnival. Item number one was the desk. 'A taster for what's to come,' Mr Armitage told Margaret. 'It'll whet their appetites and persuade them to open their wallets.' And he was right. At first the crowd played a cat and mouse game, waiting for someone else to start the bidding and carry the price towards what they were prepared to pay. When the price climbed and excitement grew to fever pitch, it was everyone for himself.

The lots went quickly, with every piece greedily sought after. 'Oh, Cathy!' Margaret's eyes shone. 'I really think we'll be all right.'

Cathy took hold of her aunt's hand. 'I told you there was nothing to worry about.' She had been mentally calculating, and by her reckoning they would have enough to repay the debts and still have a reasonable sum left over for their own needs.

She proved to be right. 'It was the best attended auction I've ever had,' Mr Armitage proudly declared.

Cathy wandered about then, watching as successful bidders took away their prizes. She didn't feel sad to see the familiar things being removed. She felt oddly regretful that a whole chapter of her life was over forever, but she didn't feel sad.

'Penny for them.' Ruby had come up behind her.

'It's strange, isn't it?' Cathy's attention was drawn to a rather large and well-dressed gentleman who was pawing Frank Black-thorn's desk. He reverently opened every drawer and stroked his hands over the top as though it was a desirable woman. 'I look at my father's desk and I see him seated behind it, just as he always was.' She smiled wryly. 'Whenever I was called to his study, it was to be reprimanded for something or other. Even before I was tall enough to see over the top of it, that desk was like a huge barrier between us, he on one side and I the other.' Memories flooded back. 'When mother was murdered, he took solace in hiding behind it . . . drinking and sleeping . . . always hiding behind that desk.'

'Aw, lass!' Deeply moved and awash with her own memories of those early days, Ruby put a chubby arm round Cathy's waist and hugged her close. 'It's only a piece of wood, carved and polished to make it look something grand ... but for all that it's still no more than a piece of wood. If your father chose to derive comfort from that instead of turning to you and your aunt, then we have to feel sorry for him.'

Sensing some other emotion in Ruby's voice, Cathy asked gently, 'You loved my father, didn't you?'

Overcome by all that had happened, Ruby felt the need to sit herself in an armchair close by. Taking out a small white handkerchief, she surreptitiously dabbed at her eyes while pretending to blow her nose. 'Aye, lass. I did have a soft spot for your faither, I'll not deny it. He were a weak man and happen I shouldn't be talking like this, but even though he idolised the very ground she walked on, your mother brought him little happiness.'

'Do you think they're together now, Ruby?' She had often thought about that.

'Who knows, lass?' Ruby had to chuckle at the idea. 'One thing's for sure ... if they *are* together, there'll be sparks flying and no mistake!'

Intent on each other, Ruby and Cathy didn't see the two men rushing towards them. 'Excuse me, Missus,' the thin, moustached fellow addressed Ruby, 'but I've just bought that chair and unless you want a ride to Wigan I should get yer arse out of it!'

Cheeky as ever, she retaliated, 'Well now, young man, I reckon my arse might enjoy a ride to Wigan. But it would take a better man than you or your mate here to entertain a fine lady such as meself. Besides, I'm particular about the company I keep.' With that she struggled out of the chair and, linking her arm with Cathy's, drew her away.

'You bad old thing,' Cathy laughed. 'Did you see the look on his face?'

'Not a very handsome bloke, was he? If I had a mind to go to Wigan, or anywhere else come to that, it wouldn't be with a fella who had a face like the back of a tram.'

Stifling her laughter, Cathy discreetly turned to glance at the man in question. Tall and thin with a straggly moustache and a face deeply scored with wrinkles, she saw what Ruby meant. In that instant the man glared at her and she had to look away.

'Whatever am I going to do with you, Ruby Adams?' she said, laughing aloud.

It did Ruby's heart good to see Cathy laughing. 'There y'are lass. Memories might hurt, but there'll allus be summat to make you chuckle.'

'Ruby?'

'Yes, lass?'

'Oh, it's nothing.' Cathy had been about to ask her whether she had got over the man who had deserted her. But now she could have bitten out her own tongue.

'It's all right. I know what's on your mind, and no . . . I'm not pining for the bugger who left me. I'll not deny I spent a few miserable nights, and if I'd have got me hands on him there's no telling what I might have done. But now I've had time to think straight, I reckon it's good riddance to him.'

'Sorry, Ruby. You should tell me to mind my own business.'

'What! Then you might tell me the same when I'm being nosy about what *you're* up to.'

'I'm not up to anything.' Terrified that wily old Ruby might have guessed Jack had probably left her with child, Cathy trembled inside.

Pausing to look up at her, Ruby sought for the right words. 'If ever there's anything on your mind, you know I'm a good listener.'

'I know, and thank you, Ruby.' Maybe in the not-so-distant future she might have need of someone to confide in, but for now Cathy knew she must keep her worries to herself. There could just be an outside chance that she was worrying for nothing.

Margaret had good news for them. 'Because he sympathises with our predicament, Mr Armitage says he can settle with me by noon tomorrow, instead of our having to wait the usual week. Apparently most bidders paid cash, and those who paid by other means are known to him.'

Cathy was pleased but surprised. 'I would never have thought he was the kind of businessman to let his heart rule his head.' She regarded Margaret with a mischievous twinkle in her eye. 'He could have his sights set on you, though? *That* would explain it.'

'Mind yer backs!' A great mountain of a woman barged past. 'Make way!' she called out, thrusting herself forward and forging a path for her dutiful husband. The poor little fellow was bow-legged beneath a pile of ladder-back chairs.

As he passed Cathy and the others he winked and sighed. 'She thinks I'm a bloody donkey!' he said wistfully. In fact, with his large head and long ears, he did bear an uncanny resemblance to one.

'Makes you wonder, don't it?' Ruby said with wide eyes as he passed.

Not quite sure what she meant, Cathy concentrated on more mundane matters. 'If Mr Armitage is settling up tomorrow, that means we can settle Father's debts and start looking for a house.'

For the first time in days Margaret appeared relaxed. 'That's something I'm looking forward to,' she said. 'The house and furniture are gone. We'll stay at the hotel in Blackburn as arranged, and then, when things are clearer, we can start looking for a house.'

Cathy agreed, pointing out, 'The rooms at the hotel are costing money we can ill afford, so the sooner we find a new home the better.'

That evening, the three women booked into the hotel. Margaret and Cathy carried a small portmanteau each, while Ruby arrived with two bulging tapestry bags. 'I'm not going nowhere without me precious knick-knacks,' she declared. The day before, when she and Cathy were deciding what to take and what to leave, Cathy vowed she would, 'Leave behind all but the clothes I stand up in, one outfit to change into, and all my underwear.' Margaret felt the same. It was as though each needed to cleanse herself of memories that might cling.

The rooms were clean and pleasantly furnished. In order to save money, Cathy was prepared to share, but Margaret would not hear of it. 'We've all been through a lot,' she explained. 'I think we all deserve some quiet time to ourselves.' Cathy would have preferred to have Margaret with her, but said nothing, thinking it her duty to respect her aunt's views.

The three rooms were on the same floor, though Ruby had

argued, 'I've no right being in a room alongside me employers, and I insist you do not repay the money I gave to that scoundrel Jack and use it instead to pay for me accommodation.' Seated in the small front room, they took a few moments to drink the tea which had been brought up for them by the housemaid. Ruby was adamant. 'I know it's a sorry situation that's brought us all together like this but it ain't right, and I don't feel comfortable, and you might as well know it.'

Margaret told her she would do no such thing as use Ruby's money to pay for the room. 'That money you gave to Jack was your hard-earned savings, and you shall have it back as soon as our debts are paid,' she insisted. Cathy upheld that decision and Ruby was made to concede gratefully.

'All the same,' she persisted, 'once you've found a house, I want me proper place . . . a room alongside the kitchen, or one at the back of the house where servants belong. If yer refuse, I'll find work elsewhere, 'cause I want *my* privacy an' all!' Put that way, neither Margaret nor Cathy could find an argument against it. Satisfied, Ruby went to her bed.

Too tired to talk, Margaret soon retired, and a short time later Cathy went to her own room.

After undressing and strip-washing at the basin, she put on her nightgown, brushed her hair and lay on the bed. Her thoughts wandered gently. 'The house is gone . . . everything's gone,' she murmured with some astonishment. It had all happened with such frightening speed that it seemed unreal. She thought of her mother, and father, and ached with regrets. She thought of David and her heart was like a lead weight inside her. 'Oh, David! David!' Just the taste of his name on her lips brought a sad kind of joy.

The joy was soon swamped by anguish when her thoughts turned to Jack. 'Please God, don't let me be with child,' she prayed, and with that awful thought shadowing her mind, fell into a slumber plagued with nightmares.

The next day was filled with sunshine, and life didn't seem so bad. 'After breakfast, I shall meet Mr Armitage,' Margaret announced. 'Then it's on to the bank where I intend to arrange payments of all our debts. Once that's achieved, it's round to the agent's to find out what houses are available.' Smiling at Cathy, she said, 'We'll find something to suit us, I know.'

Cathy was delighted to see her aunt seeming much brighter after her night's sleep. It was as though a great weight had fallen from her shoulders. 'If you like, Ruby and I could make a start on the house-hunting while you tie up the legal end. What do you say?'

'I need you with me . . . if that's all right?'

'Yes, if that's what you want.'

'And what about me?' Ruby needed to feel useful. 'What can I do?'

Cathy answered, 'You put your feet up and be waited on for a change, Ruby. We shouldn't be too long.'

It was arranged that Cathy and Margaret would meet Mr Armitage before going to the bank and organising payment of the debts. When that was all done, they would return to the hotel and collect Ruby. Cathy would search for a house in one direction, and Ruby would search with Margaret in another. 'Between the three of us, I'm certain we'll find what we're looking for,' Cathy said hopefully.

Unfortunately it wasn't that easy. Over the next few days, they trudged the streets of Blackburn and visited the few agents available. They went in and out of all manner of buildings . . . three-floored tenements and rundown terraced houses, shops with rooms over and smarter dwellings along the embankment. But there was nothing to match their needs, or their purse.

'It's no good.' Margaret was weary, and her spirits flagging. 'We've walked miles and seen nothing that could even begin to look like it might make a decent home.' The three of them were gathered in her room, where she sat huddled in a chair with a blanket across her knees suffering from a streaming cold that had taken all of her strength. 'I'm beginning to think we'll never find anything.'

Cathy recalled one particular house which she had visited along Preston New Road. 'It's the only one that has any potential,' she said. 'Is there no way we can afford it?'

Margaret had gone over the finances time and again, and each time the answer was the same. 'Not unless we lived on dry bread and went in rags for a year.'

'Then we'll just have to keep trying. In fact, we might have to lower our sights.'

'I've been thinking the very same,' Margaret admitted. 'Every penny we pay out at this hotel could be going into a home of our own.'

'Right then!' Cathy saw nothing else for it. 'I'll just have to redouble my efforts.'

'What do you mean... *you* will have to redouble your efforts?'

'I mean you look worn out and you're full of cold. I think you should take things easy for a while.'

'I'll not deny I'm bone tired.'

'That's settled then!' Collecting her bag, she asked Ruby to stay and look after her mistress, 'While I have a scout round the streets nearer to the market square. We've been in every direction but that one.'

'I think you should take Ruby with you,' Margaret suggested. But Cathy ruled that out. 'Right now you need her with you,' she answered, and went out of the door before either of them could change her mind for her.

Boarding the tram, Cathy swept right to the front. From here she could see both sides of the road more clearly, and if there were any empty properties along the route she couldn't possibly miss them. 'Return ticket, please,' she told the conductor. 'To the market square.'

He rang up the ticket on his machine, and gave her a penny change. 'Lovely day,' he said, and Cathy made it all the more lovely by her wide easy smile.

Ten minutes later she climbed off the tram and took a moment to look around. In the warm late-spring sunshine she looked a picture. The straight dark skirt and waist-fitting jacket showed her trim curves to advantage. Her fair hair was brushed to a deep shine and her green eyes sparkled with vitality. Something about her caused many a passerby to glance admiringly in her direction. But, unaware of their attention, she concentrated her mind on the task she had set herself for that day. It was a daunting one: to find a place that could be made into a home; a place they could easily afford; one that wasn't too far from the everyday hustle and bustle, yet far enough to afford them a little quiet when the mood demanded.

'Right, Cathy!' she muttered, straightening her coat and stiffening her shoulders. 'It's do or die. Today is the day when you'll find what you're looking for . . . and you're not to stop searching until you've found it . . . even if it means walking the streets until midnight.'

Her heart swelling with determination, she started across the cobbled market; there were a few stalls erected, and a bevy of vendors shouting the merits of their goods. Dogs chased each other in and out, and the chatter of passersby created a low hum that gave her a sense of belonging. Blackburn was a grand place, filled with warmhearted folk and teeming with life. 'This is where I want to be,' she murmured. 'Here, where people live out their ordinary lives without fuss or bother.'

Pausing to watch a young couple strolling hand in hand, her heart turned somersaults. Into her mind came a picture of her and David. But she pushed it away. It was still too painful.

As she made her way across the market square and down towards the main street where there was an estate agent's office, Cathy couldn't help but reflect on how she had come to be here, homeless and lonely; for, even with Margaret and Ruby waiting back at the hotel, she felt strangely isolated, almost as though, without even realising it, she had become another person. And, in a way, that was exactly what had happened, because like any one of us Cathy had been shaped by circumstances over which she had no control. When her mother was murdered, she had been just a girl; then later, when her father also was taken, that girl was lost. Something inside her matured and blossomed.

After all the chaos following the will and the ultimate sale of everything familiar to her, Cathy had emerged a woman, a beautiful and accomplished one with ambitions and dreams, some of which might never be fulfilled. She was alive, she could feel the blood coursing through her veins; the sun was warm on her face and the breeze gently ruffled her hair. All of these things told her she was lucky in so many ways. But beneath it all was David, the young man who had awakened something wonderful in her, the young man she had lost, her first and only love.

Now, when memories threatened to overwhelm her, she thrust them from her mind, to concentrate on the task in hand. A few more steps and she was outside the estate agent's. A quick glance in the window showed nothing different from the day before, or the day before that. The announcements were the same; the same expensive houses and the same tatty rundown places that were fit only to be demolished. But she was still hopeful. 'Have you taken on anything new in the past twenty-four hours?' she asked the girl behind the counter ... the same girl who had been there on the four previous visits Cathy had made: a smart creature with rolled-up dark hair and tiny spectacles that perched on the end of her nose.

Looking over her spectacles at Cathy, the girl shook her head. 'Nothing you would be interested in, I'm sorry.'

'But you have taken something new on?'

The girl gestured towards the back office. 'Mr Clegg is dealing with it now ... but, like I say, it's nothing you would be interested in.'

'Might I be the judge of that?' Through the inner office window, Cathy could see Mr Clegg, the manager, and with him was a younger man, aged about thirty, tall and slightly stooped, wearing a suit that looked as if it might have cost a pretty penny. He appeared to be giving instructions while Mr Clegg was hastily writing in his ledger. 'What exactly is it you're taking on?' Cathy could not afford to leave any stone unturned.

The girl came to stand beside her, and together they peered through the window. 'That's Tony Manners,' she said. 'He owns any number of properties across Blackburn ... houses, shops, anything he can make money on. He buys rundown properties ... charges rents that have already put many a family in the workhouse, then he tarts the houses up and sells them on at a profit.' Grimacing, she muttered, 'Tony Manners is a slimy character. I don't know anybody who likes him.' She obviously didn't.

'And what is he selling that I would not be interested in?' Against her better judgement, Cathy was intrigued.

'He's just bought a derelict club in Higher Audley ... means

to turn it into some kind of hostel, I shouldn't wonder. Though
he might have got a licence to reopen it as a night-club of sorts.'
Glancing at Cathy, she went on in a low voice, 'To find the
money he needs, he's instructing Mr Clegg to sell three of
his houses.'

'Oh? And what makes you think I might not be interested in
one of them?'

The girl's eyes grew wide with shock. 'You could *never* want
one of Tony Manners' places!' she hissed. 'He's had riff-raff in
them ... folks who can work but don't want to ... women who
entertain, if you know what I mean? The houses are filthy. It
wouldn't surprise me if they weren't ridden with rats and swarm-
ing with cockroaches!'

She might have gone on, but the office door opened and out
came the two men. 'Goodbye, Mr Manners.' The older man
shook the other by the hand. 'You can rely on me to find
a buyer.'

Tony Manners gave no reply. He had caught sight of Cathy
and couldn't take his eyes off her. 'You're not looking for a
house by any chance, are you?' he asked boldly. Taking off his
trilby he swung it back and forth in his hand. 'I've just instructed
Mr Clegg here to sell three of my properties.'

Before Cathy could reply, the girl spoke for her. 'Miss
Blackthorn requires a different type of property.' If looks could
kill, he would have dropped stone dead to the floor.

Her hostility made no impact on him. Instead he continued
to stare at Cathy. 'Miss Blackthorn, eh?' he murmured. Looking
her up and down, he came to the conclusion that she was a
lady born and bred. It only intrigued him further. 'Yes, I can
see you might be looking for something more ... respectable,
shall we say?'

Cathy's smile was cold. Like the girl, she had taken a deep
dislike to this arrogant man. 'You may say what you like,' she
replied politely, 'but it will not make my business any of yours.'
With that she turned away and made conversation with the girl,
who pretended to be showing her details of other properties;
ones which Cathy had already seen and rejected because of
the price.

While she listened to the girl, Cathy could feel Tony Manners' eyes on her. But she totally ignored him, and soon he was on his way out. 'Good day, Miss Blackthorn,' he called. 'I hope you find what you're looking for.'

Hearing the door close, Cathy straightened up and glanced round. Mr Clegg was still standing there, so she addressed her remarks to him. 'These houses you've been instructed to sell, might I have the details?'

The girl was horrified. 'You're never going to look at *them*?'

She lapsed into a sulky silence when Mr Clegg reminded her she was here to sell properties – 'Not to make disparaging remarks about the properties we sell, nor to offer personal opinions on our clients... who I might add... indirectly pay your wages!'

Cathy stepped forward. 'Mr Clegg, my aunt and I are also your clients, and as you know have searched far and wide for a suitable house. You have houses to sell, and we have cash waiting. Now... as to Mr Manners' properties, have you any objection to my having the details?'

'None whatsoever. Unlike my assistant here, I make no judgements... about persons or properties. However, as yet there are no written details. All I can tell you is that the houses are adjacent to one other, situated on William Henry Street, and being offered at sixty pounds each.' He gave a little snigger. 'If I remember rightly, your good aunt mentioned a sum of forty pounds? A shortfall, I think.'

Cathy was quick to reply, 'I'm sure Mr Manners would be prepared to negotiate.'

'I doubt that. But in any case, you haven't even seen the properties.'

'That's what I'm here for, Mr Clegg. You *are* in the business of selling houses, aren't you?' she asked cheekily.

'I haven't even seen them myself.'

'Then perhaps we can see them together?'

'When?' He had eaten and drunk too much the night before and was suffering from a burning pain in his chest. He was in no mood for playing the gentleman.

'Now if you please.'

'As a rule I like to visit the site before allowing clients in.'

Cathy smiled at that. 'Rules were made to be broken, Mr

Clegg.' She walked slowly towards the door. 'Is William Henry Street within walking distance?'

'Five minutes beyond the market square.' Flustered by Cathy's insistence, and feeling quite ill, he snapped at the girl, 'I shall be gone about half an hour. Mind you treat the customers with respect in my absence.'

'Yes, Mr Clegg.'

'Now fetch my hat, girl, and get a move on!'

'Yes, Mr Clegg.' Rushing through to the inner office, she collected his trilby from the hat stand and brought it to him.

Ramming the hat on his head, he muttered out of Cathy's hearing, 'Damned nuisance this! She'll waste my precious time, and run a mile when she sees William Henry Street.'

'Yes, Mr Clegg.'

Sighing at the girl's dumb insolence, he waved her away. 'Come along then, Miss Blackthorn,' he urged, opening wide the door and waiting for her to pass through it. 'As you so rightly pointed out, I am in the business of selling houses after all.' It was just as well he didn't see the grimace the girl made behind his back, or she might have gone out the door and not been allowed back in. But Cathy saw it, and it gave her cause to smile.

They went at a smart pace, along Ainsworth Street, down the entire length of Penny Street and over the bridge to William Henry Street. 'There you are.' Mr Clegg paused for breath at the top of the street. 'Not quite the area you're used to, I'll be bound,' he said smugly.

Cathy chose to ignore his bad temper. Stepping towards the edge of the pavement, she looked down the street and was both shocked and surprised. The cobbled street was teeming with children: little girls in mucky frocks playing with hoops, toddlers climbing in and out of the gutters, and young lads sitting cross-legged on the pavement, throwing five-stones; rolling about on the cobbles a pair of scruffy urchins were knocking hell out of each other, and only two doors from where Cathy stood two women sat breast-feeding, shouting and cackling as each told the other a saucy tale.

The sights and sounds did Cathy's heart good. 'You're wrong, Mr Clegg,' she said softly. 'My aunt and I used to visit families in a street very much like this one.' Warm recollections came to mind of how she and Margaret had struggled that day, arms laden with towels and linen; she recalled the homely woman who had an army of children, and all at once she felt at home. 'Show me the houses you have for sale,' she said, smiling at his astonishment as he led her down the street.

'If you're sure,' he answered, seeming shocked when she stopped to chat with one of the bare-breasted women. His smile never wavered though, because suddenly he had a glimpse of a sale. His step became much brisker. 'These houses were built for the gentry,' he bragged. 'Solid from the foundations up ... made to last, they were.' Filled with hope, he sang their praises. 'I shouldn't think they'll be on my books for long. They're a snip at sixty pounds.'

'Changed your tune, haven't you?' she remarked. In fact it amused her to see he was now desperate to convince her she would be missing out on a real bargain if she didn't buy one of Tony Manners' houses.

Striding down the street, he came to rest outside the last three houses. 'Like I said ... built for the gentry.' He stood, hands on hips, his trilby tipped back at a jaunty angle while he stared admiringly at the properties.

Cathy took stock of the houses. In all three, every window was broken. The door of the middle one was flung wide open to display a narrow dark passage littered with debris. The staircase had been robbed of several steps, probably for firewood to keep body and soul warm, and, even from where she stood, Cathy could see the dark stains where condensation had run down the walls.

The middle house, like the one to its left, had three floors, while the one on the very end of the row had only two. Obviously ravaged by the elements, the cornerstones were black with damp, and part of the chimney was collapsing to one side.

'If you want my opinion, you'll avoid the one on the end,' Mr Clegg advised, 'because it catches a northerly breeze and might be prone to damp.' The thought of sixty pounds going through his hands put a smile on his face. 'The other two, though ... now you could make a decent place of either of them.'

Cathy gave him a look that silenced him. 'As far as I can see, all three houses are unfit for human habitation. I'm surprised Mr Manners has not been reported for renting out such dilapidated dwellings.'

'Dilapidated?' Though he might have agreed, he merely stared at her with feigned amazement. 'You obviously don't know how difficult it is to get good accommodation in the heart of Blackburn town. These houses are large enough for a sizeable family, and I have never known anyone to complain.'

'Well, of course not! Mr Manners is not likely to broadcast his tenants' grudges. In fact he probably throws them out on their ear if they dare to speak out.' Out of the corner of her eye she could see the neighbours peeking at her. 'These people need a champion, I think.'

The implication appalled him. 'Good heavens! You're surely not considering taking on such a task?' Lowering his voice, he turned away from the inquisitive inhabitants. 'Mr Manners is a powerful force in this town, and by all accounts he makes a very formidable enemy.'

Cathy was not impressed. 'I'm sure he does.' Going towards the end house, she took a moment or two to survey the outside. Something about it drew her attention; it had a grandness, a certain style that bore out what Mr Clegg had said about the houses being originally built for the gentry. The stone mullions that framed the windows were intact, and above the thick panelled door was the prettiest lead-lighted window. Three deep wide steps led up to the door. To the right of the house, a narrow flight of steps went from the pavement to the cellar. These were surrounded by black-painted railings of wrought iron, and enclosed at the top with a little gate. 'How many rooms did you say the house has?' Before he could answer, Cathy was already on her way up the steps to the front door.

'Be careful!' Rushing after her, Mr Clegg put the big iron key in the lock and swung open the door. 'Don't hold me responsible if you harm yourself in there.'

Turning, Cathy flashed him a mischievous smile. 'I thought you had your eyes on a fat commission?' she teased. 'Or are you afraid if the roof caved in on me I might sue you for everything you have?'

Red-faced and anxious, he pushed his way in front of her. 'Follow me,' he urged, 'I'll test the floors.' Going gingerly forward, he stretched out his toes, feeling his way along the floor, terrified he might disappear into the cellar at any minute.

As Mr Clegg tiptoed into the parlour, Cathy went straight on, up the stairs and across the landing. It was a full minute before he realised she was missing, then his frantic voice sailed up the stairs. 'Miss Blackthorn? Are you up there? Oh, dear . . . I should never have taken these properties on . . . they'll be the end of me, they will!' At that moment Cathy stepped on a loose floorboard; it gave out a slow tortuous creak and Mr Clegg below was convinced she had fallen into some terrible black abyss. He started up the stairs, then climbed back down. Staring up from the bottom, he cried at the top of his voice, 'MISS BLACKTHORN, ARE YOU ALL RIGHT?'

'My word, you do panic.' Peeking over the banister, Cathy shook her head in reproof. 'What a coward you are, Mr Clegg,' she teased.

Shamed yet relieved, he went up the stairs at a careful pace. 'This house isn't for you. Come back to the office. I'm certain we'll find another more suitable.' Afraid for his life, it was all he could do not to run down the stairs and out into the street. 'Please . . . it's best if we leave now,' he pleaded. All thoughts of his commission had fled. All he could think about was her innocent teasing with regard to suing him for compensation.

Leaving him at the top of the stairs, Cathy went through each bedroom; there were four in all, two at the front and two at the back, the largest being at the end of the corridor with its own little staircase and far enough away from the others almost to be self-contained. 'A place for Ruby to call her own!' Cathy was delighted.

The rooms were all of good size, and each with a large enough window to let the daylight flood in. The big back room had a washbasin installed, and halfway along the corridor Cathy found a small bathroom and in it a rusty old tub. 'That must have been a real luxury when it was installed,' she called out. Mr Clegg was skulking by the stairs, holding on to the handrail as if it was a lifeline. 'Not many houses have a room with a bath.'

'I told you,' he called back, 'these houses were built for the

gentry . . . solicitors and the like. As they prospered, they moved
to fancier houses on Preston New Road and sold these properties to money-grabbing landlords.' He gave a funny little scream
when a bird came tumbling down the chimney and flew past
him out of the door. 'PLEASE! I think we should go now.'

'You go if you like,' Cathy told him as she swept by, 'I haven't
seen the downstairs yet.'

Downstairs, she went from room to room. She thought the
front parlour was the nicest room she had ever seen, although
the walls were blackened by soot from the fireplace, and the
wallpaper was peeling off at every corner. It had the prettiest
cast-iron fireplace, with flowered tiles running down either side
of the surround, and a pretty carved mantelpiece with a mirror
over. On the wall hung a lovely amber-coloured gas mantle that
simply begged to be cleaned and polished. The window-sill was
deep enough to make a seat where a body could sit and enjoy
seeing the children at play outside the window, and at that hour
of the day the sun shone right in through the window to light
the whole room.

The back parlour was the heart of the house. 'Whoever left
here must have gone in a hurry,' Cathy declared. 'Look.' Pointing above the big old range, she drew his attention to the
mantelpiece and the green chenille cloth that covered it from
end to end. 'I can't imagine anyone leaving behind such a pretty
cloth unless they were made to depart in a rush.' Going to the
mantelpiece she fingered the long silk tassels that dangled from
the cloth. As she touched them they released a shower of dust,
and fell apart in her fingers. 'Fit for nothing now,' she murmured sadly.

The kitchen was large and airy, with a flight of steps running
down to the yard. At the foot of the steps were two doors; one
leading into the lavatory, and the other into a vast cellar. A
ten-foot-high wall surrounded the yard; even so, the sun found
a way in, and from a treetop close by the sound of bird-song
filled the air. 'Surprisingly pleasant, don't you think?' Mr Clegg
remarked; though he would have considered it beneath himself
to reside in such an area.

Cathy was secretly excited, but kept her voice cool and disin-
terested. 'I don't know about that,' she answered, giving a little

grimace that dashed his hopes. 'As you so rightly pointed out, William Henry Street is very noisy, and the houses in a terrible state of dilapidation.' She shook her head and looked around her with feigned disgust. 'You say you're pleasantly surprised? Well, I can only say *I'm* surprised this house and others like it have not been put under a demolition order.' With that she departed, smiling to herself when he followed at a run, muttering something about how it might be possible to negotiate a more favourable price with Mr Manners: 'Though he is a hard man to deal with, and I can't promise anything.'

Outside, Cathy waited while he locked the door behind them. 'A more favourable price, you say?' She smiled. 'I'm afraid Mr Manners would have to more than *halve* his price, and even then I doubt whether I could persuade my aunt to step foot inside.' She pointed to a roof tile which was hanging dangerously over the guttering. 'A body could be killed!' she said. 'Besides . . . even *you* were afraid the whole place could come falling about your ears.'

He grinned. 'Perhaps I was a little hasty,' he suggested. 'Yes! I'm sure I was a little hasty.'

At the top of the street they parted company, he returning to his office and Cathy making for the tram-stop. 'Should I tell Mr Manners you might be interested?' Taking a huge white handkerchief from his waistcoat pocket, Mr Clegg mopped his brow. It had been an unnerving experience, and this young lady was a trial all by herself.

Deliberately taking her time in answering, Cathy appeared to be deep in thought. Presently she said, 'It isn't what we're looking for, and it does need a great deal of work doing. My aunt and I aren't wealthy. We hadn't counted on buying a place that needed money spent on it.' Sighing, she said wearily, 'But I have to admit we're not having much luck, and this house isn't suitable either . . . far from it!' She couldn't let him believe he had a keen buyer, or he wouldn't bring the price down one shilling, let alone by half.

'Not even if I could persuade Mr Manners to drop his price?'

Feigning impatience she said, 'No, Mr Clegg. Not even then.' Bidding him goodbye, she made to cross the road.

'We have your address, so if anything else should come up, we'll be in touch.'

'I doubt if my aunt will want to be bothered,' she replied. 'Not if the best you can offer is a house that needs more spent on it than it's worth!'

All the way back to the hotel, Cathy could hardly contain herself. That house was the one they had been searching for, and oh, she had so much to tell Margaret! Today of all days, though, the short tram journey seemed to take an age.

Margaret was not convinced. 'From what you say, the house needs a lot of improvement, and we simply don't have the money.'

'We will have ... if I can get Mr Manners to halve the price.'

Ruby chuckled. 'He's not likely to do that now, is he?'

Cathy was hopeful. 'He might.' Taking hold of Margaret's hands, she gently shook them. 'At least come and have a look at it. If you don't like the house, I'll forget about it and keep on searching.' When Margaret agreed to view it from the outside, Cathy gave a little whoop. 'You'll love it,' she cried. 'I know you will!'

The following morning, all three went along to William Henry Street.

'Well, I never!' The woman was white-stoning her front doorstep when she noticed Cathy. 'I never thought we'd clap eyes on you again!' she declared. 'It ain't often we get ladies strolling down this 'ere street.' She chuckled and passed a few minutes with them, watching with curiosity when they went down the street to the end house where all three stood looking up, talking about it and wondering whether this was the home they had been looking for. 'What do you think?' Cathy asked. 'Don't you think it has potential?'

Ruby stepped back a pace and regarded the house through narrowed eyes. She hummed and hawed and scratched the end of her nose; she coughed a little and glanced up and down the street, then she looked at Cathy, then she looked at Margaret, and scratched her nose again. 'Could be,' she muttered. 'Aye. Could be.'

Cathy waited patiently while Margaret went down the cellar steps and up again; she went up the front steps to the door and peered through the letter-box, and balanced on the edge of the step, but still couldn't see into the front parlour. 'It might have helped if you'd got the keys so we could go inside,' she said, exasperated.

'I didn't want Mr Clegg to know I'd persuaded you to come here.'

'If we can't get inside, how am I to say whether I like it or not?'

'Do you like the *outside*?' She had expected Margaret to take one look and turn tail and run. When she didn't, Cathy dared to hope. 'Apparently this street once housed the gentry.'

Ruby glared at her. 'Well, aren't *you* the gentry?' she demanded indignantly.

There was a world of pride in Cathy's voice when she answered softly, 'No, Ruby. I don't think so.'

Margaret's remark made them both turn round. 'Yes! I *do* like the outside. I only wish I could see the inside as well.'

Another voice intervened. 'If yer want, *I* can get yer inside, missus.' It was the woman who had been breast-feeding her bairn the day before, and white-stoning her step just now. Without another word she went up the steps and, hooking the tips of her fingers through the letter-box, gave one almighty tug. The door clicked open. 'It's a knack,' she explained dryly.

Cathy led the way up the stairs then down again, and in every room Margaret spent a few minutes describing how she might arrange the furniture. Ruby commented how she would be: 'Well suited to that room upstairs . . . me own stairway to the kitchen, and out of everybody's way.'

As she listened to them, observing their faces as they discussed such things as curtains and carpets, Cathy knew they were home. She even shouted it to the four walls, and soon the three of them were laughing and hugging each other. 'We're home!' Cathy kept saying. 'We're home!'

Just for the briefest moment her excitement was overshadowed by thoughts of David. If only he would walk through that door and smile at her, her happiness would be complete.

Margaret was convinced. 'Well, you found the place, Cathy,' she said. 'Do you really believe you can get the price reduced?'

'*Halved!*' Cathy laughed. 'I'll get it halved.'

The next morning, just as she had predicted, Mr Clegg arrived at the hotel. 'I've come to tell you that I've argued your case with Mr Manners, and he has agreed to reduce the selling price.' He didn't look too pleased, because the lower the price, the lower his own commission. 'But the transaction must be completed swiftly or the house goes back on the market.'

He addressed his remarks to Margaret, but she requested that he direct them to Cathy, who wanted to know, 'Did you tell him we would only consider the house if the price was reduced by half?'

'I did. I also told him that in my opinion it needed far more repairs than he had led me to believe.'

'And has he agreed the price?'

'He has. The property is yours, at half the original asking price.'

Cathy had never really hoped he would agree, but he had, and it was all she could do not to yell for joy. Instead, with a calmness that belied her churning stomach, she glanced at Margaret who was seated bolt upright in the chair, unable to believe that everything had been agreed. 'The decision is my aunt's,' Cathy said coolly. Turning to Margaret, she enquired, 'What do you say? Are you interested?'

Nervously clearing her throat, Margaret answered, 'I think we have a deal, Mr Clegg.'

'Good!' He rubbed his hands and feverishly nodded his head. 'Then I would be obliged if you could instruct your solicitor and get things under way.' Handing her an envelope, he explained, 'Inside you will find all the details you require. Now, if you will please excuse me, I have matters to attend to.'

'And so have we!' After he'd gone, Cathy did a little jig on the spot.

Ruby hugged her, then Margaret. 'There's only one thing that worries me,' said her aunt.

'Oh?' Cathy wasn't worried at all. 'What's that?'

'This Tony Manners... from what you told me, he seems an undesirable character. I only hope he hasn't taken a fancy to you.'

'He can take a fancy to whoever he likes,' Cathy answered. 'It won't get him anything.'

'I should think not!' Ruby declared. But, like Margaret, she couldn't help wondering whether Tony Manners would be more trouble than he was worth.

CHAPTER TEN

Within weeks, the house on William Henry Street was transformed. Cathy was given the task of choosing curtains and carpets, while Margaret took Ruby with her to browse round the furniture shops. The first priority had been to save the money being spent on rooms at the hotel. 'If we all roll up our sleeves and get stuck in, we'll soon have it ship-shape,' Cathy said, though it was obvious they would have to pay for someone to mend the front door and change the locks, then a plumber to free the blockage in the water pipes, and a handyman to tack back the plasterboard that was hanging from the upstairs ceiling.

Margaret decided to leave the recruiting to Cathy. 'By the time you've finished, they'll likely be pleased to do the work for nothing,' she laughed. Ruby scowled and warned her to be careful who she trusted, and the name of Tony Manners rose to mind.

Cathy enquired among the neighbours and found two workmen who could do all they wanted at a very reasonable price. They were in and out in less than a week, and were every bit as good as Cathy had been told; the ceilings were as new, the plumbing was working smoothly, and all that remained was the scrubbing and cleaning, then the decorating, before the carpets were laid and the furniture delivered. 'Another week and we should be able to move in,' Margaret said with relief, and Ruby began counting the minutes.

The house was a hive of activity. 'Leave the back and front doors wide open to let the fresh air blow through,' Margaret advised, taking up her broom and sweeping every corner in every room.

In her element at having a kitchen at last, Ruby rushed in

and out, making tea to keep their spirits up, in between finding all manner of things to do. 'I've never seen so much muck under a sink before,' she declared, loudly tutting and slapping a wet cloth over the shelves.

Cathy spent the best part of a week on her knees. One Monday morning she was on them again, sleeves rolled up and a hessian sack tied round her waist as she scrubbed the living-room floor. 'Get up from there afore yer knees flatten like saucers!' Ruby argued. 'There's a pot o' tea made, an' some fresh Eccles cakes from the corner shop.' She tugged at Cathy's makeshift pinnie. 'I've called Miss Margaret an' she's on her way downstairs, so come on. Let's have yer!'

'Ruby Adams, you're a bully.' In fact, Cathy was ready to stop awhile.

'Mebbe. But you've been on yer knees for over an hour, an' it's time for a break.'

A few minutes later, with their hands washed and pinnies thrown aside, they all sat on upturned boxes, round the big tea chest that served as a table. 'Are you all right?' Margaret had been looking closely at Cathy and, not for the first time of late, wondered whether there was something very wrong.

'I'm quite well,' Cathy lied.

'You look tired.'

'I didn't sleep well last night ... nothing to worry about.'

The truth was, she knew now without doubt that she was with child. It tortured her to think she must tell Margaret soon.

'You're working too hard.'

'We're *all* working too hard,' Cathy gently reminded her. 'But we've broken the back of it now. If all goes well, we should be in by the end of the week.'

'Thank God for that!' Just as Cathy intended, Margaret's attention was diverted. 'Won't it be wonderful to sit in big soft armchairs, round our very own fireplace?'

In a softer voice filled with conviction, Cathy told her, 'It's no more than you deserve.'

Ruby had been quietly regarding the pair of them, and now she had her little say. 'It's no more than the *both* of you deserve,' she declared. 'Me an' all, because I've missed having me own kitchen, an' it's been far too long since I cooked a proper dinner.'

Cathy stood up. 'Thank you for the tea, Ruby. Now it's back to work, or it'll be a month of Sundays before you have your own kitchen again.'

Margaret resumed her window-cleaning upstairs, and Ruby went into the kitchen to wash the pots. After a while she returned to the living room where Cathy was hard at work. 'Have you got a minute, lass?' she asked, standing over her.

Cathy looked up and the dark circles beneath her eyes were more prominent. 'What is it, Ruby? Is something troubling you?' Wiping her hands on her pinnie, she rose to her feet.

'No, lass, there ain't nothing wrong with me,' Ruby answered softly. 'It's you I'm concerned about.'

'There's no need.' Every instinct in her aching body urged Cathy to confess her troubles. But she couldn't. She wanted to, but God help her, she couldn't bring herself to say the words: 'Jack violated me, and I'm having his baby.' It was too horrible. But sooner or later it would have to be said, and when the news broke it would shatter all their lives; Ruby's because she would be filled with such a rage that she might want to search Jack out and do away with him, and Margaret's because she had borne so much anguish already and, though she tried hard not to let it show, was still haunted by the awful events that had brought them here to William Henry Street.

Ruby suspected there was something Cathy wasn't telling her. She also knew that Cathy was strong-willed and independent, and that the best thing was to leave her be and let her decide when to share her troubles. 'All right, lass,' she said reluctantly. 'But I've told you afore an' I'll tell you again . . . I'm here if you want to talk. You an' Miss Margaret are like family to me, an' I'd be offended if summat were deeply troubling you an' you couldn't find the heart to trust old Ruby.'

For a long minute, Cathy was racked with guilt. 'I *do* trust you,' she whispered, 'but I'm well, really I am.' Her eyes swam with tears. It wasn't easy to lie to this dear old soul, but for now she had little choice. 'There's no need for you to worry about me.'

'Hmm.' Biting her tongue, Ruby returned to her kitchen, where she was soon clattering about; though every now and then she peeped out of the doorway to see whether Cathy was all right.

Two days later, the house was finished. The windows were sparkling, the long tapestry curtains were hung, and the floorboards were scrubbed until every line of grain could be seen. At half-past eleven on a Wednesday morning, the carpets and furniture arrived. All morning excitement had been mounting and, now that the moment had finally arrived, Margaret was running round in circles. 'Put the sideboard there,' she instructed the two delivery men. 'Oh, no, that doesn't look right . . . sorry . . . could you please set it against that wall instead?' Four times they shifted the sideboard, and each time Ruby and Cathy hid behind the kitchen door, stifling their giggles. 'If she don't make up her mind soon they'll take the damned thing away and drop it in the cut!' Ruby chuckled. They doubled up with laughter when one of the long-suffering delivery men threatened the very same.

It took a full hour for the furniture to be carted in, and another hour for them to put it all where it was wanted. 'Jesus, Mary and Joseph!' The sweat was teeming down the younger man's face. 'If I'd known the job was like this, I'd 'a gone into farming like me da afore me.'

His face lit up when Margaret gave him and his mate a shilling each. But it was to Cathy he addressed himself. 'I hope everything's to your liking?' he asked shyly, blushing to the roots of his hair when she smiled warmly and thanked the pair of them for their understanding.

'We've worked hard to get this place how we want it,' she explained. 'It's important to have the furniture exactly where it should be.'

As they went out the door, the elder man muttered, 'Hmph! A shilling each won't buy a fat lot over the pub counter.' He had a loud voice and his mutterings were heard by everyone there.

'Go on, yer ungrateful buggers!' Ruby called out. 'Anyway, yer shouldn't be spending yer hard-earned money over the pub counter!'

Shocked that he'd been overheard, the older man turned

round and fell arse over tip down the steps, while the young lad screeched with laughter and got a clip round the ear for his troubles.

'Oh, it's wonderful!' Cathy led the way from room to room. Margaret's bedroom was furnished much like the one she'd had at Blackthorn House in warm dark colours, with brown scatter rugs, a serviceable walnut dressing table and an eiderdown with flowers at each corner. 'I really couldn't wish for anything better,' she told Cathy.

Cathy's room was mainly pink, with cream-coloured rugs and lace eiderdown, and a landscape painting hanging on the wall. It showed a summer scene; in the distance a young couple sat on the grass, deep in conversation and obviously in love. 'It reminds me of David,' she said simply, and there was a world of regret in her voice.

Ruby had given strict instructions as to how she wanted her room furnished. 'Good solid stuff that'll last as long as I do!' She had a narrow bed with a chequered eiderdown, and a tall clothes press with deep drawers and round wooden knobs. The curtains were plain but pretty and at the side of her bed was a soft blue rug which she claimed would 'Tickle me toes'. Her face beamed from ear to ear when she surveyed it all. 'By! We'll be comfortable here an' no mistake,' she said grandly.

The front parlour held a piano, a horsehair settee and two matching chairs, and a small table for taking tea on. 'This can be kept for visitors,' Margaret announced.

'As long as it ain't that sly Mr Manners,' Ruby declared. When she got a stern look from Margaret she announced her intention of making a fresh pot of tea 'To christen our new home', then hurried into the kitchen, muttering all the way.

The following morning, they moved into the house. Neighbours came from everywhere. 'By! You've made it look grand!' Ada Snettleton observed. Fred Arlinton saw they hadn't got a coal-scuttle. 'You've got to have a coal-scuttle,' he instructed, 'else you'll be forever up and down to the cellar with yer shovel.' The woman from the corner shop fetched two big meat and tater pies; somebody else brought the plates. Ruby got a knife from the kitchen and sliced the pies into tiny segments; everybody said how good it was, wished health to their neighbours and washed the victuals down with a drop of Michael Bone's home-made ginger-ale.

Right in the middle of it, Tony Manners turned up and invited Cathy outside to see his new carriage. 'All it needs is a fine lady to grace it,' he said enticingly.

'Then you'd best find yourself one, hadn't you?' she replied.

'I think I've found one in you,' he murmured. Reaching inside the carriage he brought out a huge bunch of flowers.

'I hope you realise I'm proposing,' he said.

Before she could tell him where to go, he kissed her full on the mouth, hopped into the carriage and was gone from the street.

'Good grief!' Cathy gasped. 'And to think we've only just met!'

It was evening before they had the house to themselves again. 'I feel we'll be happy here,' Margaret said.

'Some more than others,' Ruby remarked, stealing a glance at Cathy. She had followed her and Tony Manners outside earlier, and what she saw only fuelled her worst fears.

Cathy didn't know *what* to say, so she remained quiet until Margaret asked her whether she was happy. 'As I'll ever be,' came the answer. Then, 'Yes, of course I am. We've got a home of our own, a full pantry, and good neighbours to drink our health. All in all, it's a perfect end to a perfect day.'

That night she stripped and stood before the mirror. The gentle curve of her stomach was more pronounced and her breasts slightly swollen, but if she breathed in and held herself taut she looked slim and flat as ever. 'Tony Manners would marry you and never know,' she whispered. The idea was both attractive and repugnant. 'What harm would it do?' she argued. 'The child would have a name. There would be no shame, no repercussions.' Torn between love and hate for the child she was carrying, and the bitterness she felt towards its father, she desperately searched for a way out. 'Is marrying Tony Manners the only thing to do?' she asked herself. 'Give yourself to him, and as long as you live you will never be free again.'

She bathed and thought of what it would mean to be tied to

a man like Tony. She put on her nightgown and mused over the prospect. She brushed her hair and thought about the future, and it loomed before her like a long dark tunnel. 'How could you ever marry another man when you still love David... when you will *always* love David?' It would be hard, perhaps impossible, to pretend. She would have to submit to her husband's demands, lie in bed with him, be a wife in every sense of the word. It was a daunting prospect. 'If you can't have David, what does it matter? Whether you want it or not, this child will be born. It must have a name, so why not the name of Manners? Margaret and Ruby need never know your shame and, by moving out, you will lessen the burden on Margaret.' It was not the ideal solution, but unfortunately it was the only one.

The next morning Cathy's mind was made up. She had spent another restless night, the shadows beneath her eyes had deepened, and when she touched her stomach she imagined she could feel movement inside. 'Don't be silly,' she argued with her image in the mirror. 'It hasn't been long enough.' But time was passing quickly and soon her condition would be apparent to everyone. 'Should I tell Tony the truth?' she asked herself. 'How could I hide the truth from him, even if I wanted to?' It was another dilemma, but: 'If Tony asks me outright to marry him, I'll say yes, and let the consequences take care of themselves.'

As it was, he didn't come anywhere near for several days. 'Good shuts to him,' Ruby said, and was reprimanded by Margaret. 'Like you I don't care much for the charming Mr Manners,' she said, 'but he's polite and friendly, and appears to be genuinely fond of Cathy, and God knows she needs someone to take her out of herself.'

'Ah!' Ruby had said nothing about her concern for Cathy, because she didn't want to worry Margaret unnecessarily, but now that Margaret had mentioned it, she would have her say. 'So you've noticed how unhappy Cathy seems to be of late?'

'Yes, I have noticed.'

'Have you asked her what's wrong?'

'Not yet. I was hoping she would confide in me of her own free will.'

'She won't. I've asked her time and again what's troubling her, but she won't say.' Plucking the clothes out of the dolly tub, she dropped them into the enamel bowl; the hot water made her wince when a trickle of it ran down her arm. Taking another bowl, she placed it under the tap at the bottom, and ran the water off. That done, she tipped the water down the big pot sink, filled it with clean water and rinsed out the newly-washed clothes. 'By! I reckon it would be just as quick to wash the whole blessed lot in the sink,' she complained. Turning to glance at Margaret, who was leaning on the door jamb to stare out of the back window, she enquired softly, 'Where's Cathy now?'

'Next door.'

Ruby wondered if she'd heard right. 'Next door!' Wringing the clothes out one by one, she placed them on the draining board. 'Whatever is she doing next door? The place is empty, ain't it? Dangerous, too, I shouldn't wonder.'

'*He's* with her.'

'Who?' Red-faced from the steam, Ruby wiped her eyes with the back of her hand. 'Surely you don't mean that Manners bloke?'

'Apparently he thinks it unwise to leave the house now we're living here, so he's looking to furnish the place and rent it out. He thinks Cathy has good taste and wants her advice, that's all.'

'Don't you believe it,' Ruby retorted. 'It's the lass herself he wants.' Leaning forward with her arms against the sink she regarded Margaret through red-rimmed eyes. 'Don't that worry you, Miss?'

'Yes, it worries me,' Margaret admitted. 'But I don't think it's right for me to interfere. I've already done her enough harm . . . what with persuading her not to go and see David before he left. I was wrong, Ruby. Those two were made for each other and I should have encouraged her to go and talk things through with him. Now he's God knows where, and Cathy will probably never see him again.'

'She'll never stop missing him neither.' Ruby had thought long and hard about it and now she was convinced. 'I reckon that's what's troubling her. Without that young man she's like a summer's day without sunshine.'

Cathy's interest had been aroused. 'I think you should have sensible furnishings . . . good solid furniture and curtains with a smooth surface so they won't hold the dust.' Reluctant at first, she was now caught up in the idea of transforming the derelict house next to their own. 'You're right,' she agreed with Tony Manners, 'it has possibilities.'

'I knew you would be the one to ask.' Regarding her from head to foot, he licked his lips like a dog about to be given a chop. 'Let's hear your ideas then, as long as it doesn't cost me a small fortune.'

'If you're going to renovate the house, you might as well do it properly.' Regarding him with a frown, Cathy roved the large empty room. Gingerly tapping at the loose floorboards with the tip of her toe, she remarked, 'Most of the floors are unsafe, so they'll need replacing.' She peeked at him. 'It just might cost you a small fortune after all.'

'The way you're smiling, anyone would think you liked the idea of me parting with my money!'

'I'm sure you don't want some poor unsuspecting soul to plunge through the floor and break his neck?'

He shrugged. 'All right. What's next?'

'The walls. I think they should be painted in soft light colours . . . to reflect sunshine into the room.' She half-smiled at a mental picture of how it might look once Tony Manners had dipped deep into his pocket.

Leaning against the fire-range he watched her moving about. He saw the light in her lovely green eyes and wanted her all to himself. 'Like you?' he murmured, coming forward.

'What did you say?' He was at one end of the room and she at the other, and he had spoken so low she could hardly hear him.

'Paint the walls soft and light, you said . . . so they can reflect sunshine into the room.' He was standing before her now, putting her on her guard. 'That's what *you* do, Cathy . . . reflect the sunshine into the room.'

Something in his manner made her nervous. 'I'd better be going now,' she replied, dashing his hopes. 'You asked for my ideas and I've given them. Whether you choose to use or ignore them is up to you.'

'Oh, I shall use them, of course.' She began to turn away but he caught hold of her hand. 'Have you been thinking about what I asked you the other day?'

'I can't recall your asking me anything.' She knew what he was referring to, but wanted him to spell it out.

He seemed astonished. 'You really can't remember?' Giving a small chuckle, he tugged her towards him. 'And here I was . . . thinking you'd been dreaming of me ever since.'

'Hardly!'

'It isn't every day I propose to a beautiful young woman.'

'I should hope not.'

'Well?'

'Well . . . what?'

'Was my proposal wasted?'

'Untimely, perhaps. I hardly know you.'

'We can rectify that here and now.' His voice was purring, his hands reaching out to undo the buttons of her dress. 'I've never wanted a woman like I want you.' Looking down on her, his eyes were like a cat's, yellow one minute, dark and seething the next. 'You're very beautiful.'

With her blouse undone and her breasts exposed, she felt like a hussy. When he bent his head to cover her nipple with his open mouth, her every instinct told her to throw him off and run from that place. But she was held by chains that could not be seen . . . human chains. The unborn child; Jack; a need to be needed, to belong for the first time in her life. She was angry, fused with a strange longing, yet burning with hate. So much confusion, so many emotions she couldn't explain. Her future was uncertain, yet here he was, offering her a lifeline she could ill afford to refuse. The truth was she desperately needed a father for her child.

She felt his hands move to her waist; a few deft movements, a determined tug, and the skirt fell to her ankles. He didn't stop there, and soon she was standing before him stark naked. The cold air struck like a damp cloth against her shivering skin. But it wasn't the cold air that made her tremble. It was shame. The same deep crippling shame that had stayed with her since Jack took her to himself. RUN CATHY, RUN! It was her own voice, persisting in her head. NOW. GO NOW, CATHY! Sorely tempted to grab up her clothes and cover her nakedness, she smothered the voice, thinking only of a greater shame that lay ahead if she didn't use Tony Manners the way Jack had used her. She was here, and he was touching her, and all she could think of was the price she must pay. Against all her better instincts, she made no move to stop him.

Discarding the last of his garments, Tony Manners fell to his knees before her. 'I knew you felt the same.' Pushing open her legs, he flicked his tongue, shocking her when the moist tip found its mark. 'You want me, don't you?' he moaned. 'Say it . . . say you want me!'

'NO!' Her voice rang out, startling him, startling her. Frantically she pulled away, desperate to be rid of him. 'I can't do this,' she whispered.

He looked up, eyes wide and his face contorted with passion. 'Yes, you can . . . it's what you want. It's what we *both* want.'

Disgust rippled through her. 'I must have been mad to let it go this far!'

She would have wrenched herself away but he held her fast. 'Don't play games with me,' he warned.

When she brought her gaze to him, he saw the revulsion in her eyes. 'If you try and force yourself on me,' she whispered hoarsely, 'I'll kill you.' Every word struck home.

Suddenly he was dressing, his voice laced with fury as he claimed, 'Women don't usually refuse me, and you . . . you led me to believe . . .'

'No!' Quickly pulling on her clothes, she couldn't look at him. 'You led *yourself* to believe.'

'I could give you everything money can buy.'

'There are some things money *can't* buy.'

'Do you know how much I want you?'

'I think so.' They were fully dressed now; he was flushed with passion, while she was pale with the agony she felt inside. 'I should have stopped you earlier. I'm sorry.' It was partly her fault, she knew that.

'I'm sorry too.' Secretly he hated her, but his craving to have her was stronger. He became arrogant, sure of himself, determined not to lose her.

Quickly, before he could detain her, she hurried down the passage to the front door.

Stealthily he followed, vain enough to believe she could not bring herself to walk out on him. When he called her name she paused to look back. He was standing only an arm's reach away. 'You don't have to go,' he pleaded softly. 'I don't want you to go.'

She turned away. 'I'm sorry. I can't stay here ... with you.' Reaching out, she clicked the key in the lock and swung open the door. 'Goodbye,' she whispered. 'Forgive me.'

Realising she meant to leave, that she really didn't want him, was too humiliating. 'Don't fool yourself,' he hissed. 'You're not going anywhere!' Darting forward, he grabbed her by the wrist.

Taken by surprise, Cathy felt herself being dragged away from the door and down the passage-way. Summoning every ounce of her strength she dug her heels into the frayed carpet and set herself against him. 'I don't think you heard me right,' she yelled angrily. 'I don't want you. I *never* wanted you!'

The two of them were struggling harder now, he intent on dragging her into the privacy of the back room, and Cathy equally determined he would not get the better of her. Another scene ran through her mind, of her and Jack. But this time she was stronger. This time she was ready. With one final surge of energy, she jabbed the heel of her shoe into his ankle.

'You bad bugger!' Gritting his teeth he bent to rub the flat of his hand over the broken skin. Taking the chance, Cathy ran. But he was quick. They both reached the door together. As she lunged forward he grabbed at her, causing the hem of her skirt to catch on the iron railings. As she tripped forward, he made another dash to grab her but it was too late. With a cry, she plunged down the steps, knocking her head as she fell. It all happened so quickly. One minute she was fighting him off, and the next she was lying crumpled at the foot of the steps, her face like marble and her body so still he believed she was dead. 'God above!' he muttered, over and over. He made no move to help her but leaned against the door, biting his nails and glancing up and down the street with a kind of animal terror. When he realised there had been no witnesses, he slunk off, keeping close to the wall as he went and glancing back just once to make sure he had not been seen.

It was a few minutes before Cathy was found. One of the neighbours had come out to sit in her chair on the pavement and smoke her pipe. At first she thought it was a bundle of rags lying at the foot of the steps. She came closer, gasping out loud when she saw Cathy's white face. In a minute she had run back to fetch Margaret. Ruby ran off to call for help, and in no time at all Cathy was being whisked to the Infirmary, with Margaret and Ruby beside her. They were both thinking of Tony Manners, and of his probable part in Cathy's 'accident', but neither voiced their suspicions. There'd be time enough for answers when Cathy was awake and well, please God.

She was still unconscious when they rushed her inside. Margaret and Ruby waited in the corridor. The nurse brought them a cup of tea, but it was left to grow cold. 'It's that Tony Manners!' Ruby could hold her tongue no longer. 'It were him who hurt her, an' nobody will tell me otherwise!'

'We don't know, Ruby.' Margaret looked ill. The two of them had waited for half an hour, and still there was no news. 'Until we find out what happened, we mustn't blame anyone.'

Glancing at Margaret, seeing how drawn and worried she looked, Ruby was angry with herself for speaking out of turn. 'You're right,' she said comfortingly. 'The only important thing is for Cathy to be well again.' After that, she kept her opinions to herself.

Another half an hour passed and still no one came to see them. 'What in God's name are they doing in there?' Getting out of her seat, Margaret waylaid a passing nurse. 'Cathy Blackthorn . . . what's happening to her? Is she all right? Why doesn't someone tell us?' She gripped the nurse's arm and wouldn't let her go. 'Please. Is she going to be all right?'

Before the nurse could answer, a plump grey-haired doctor intervened. 'Cathy will be fine,' he said, gesturing for the nurse to leave.

Passing her hand over her face, Margaret almost fell into his arms. 'Thank God!' she whispered. Ruby came to her side and Margaret leaned into her. 'She'll be fine, Ruby . . . Cathy will be fine.' She actually gave a little laugh, and Ruby did the same.

'There! What did I tell yer, eh?' Ruby was full of herself now. 'Didn't I tell yer Cathy were made of strong stuff?'

The doctor spoke softly. 'Your niece suffered a bad fall,' he explained. 'She's still concussed . . . and has two broken ribs.' He saw their expressions change and hesitated. 'But, as I've already told you, she's young and strong, and I'm confident she'll make a full recovery . . .' He took a deep breath. What he had to tell them next was not going to be easy.

Margaret stared at him, her voice quivering as she prompted, 'There's something else, isn't there? Cathy will make a full recovery . . . *but* . . .?' She could tell from his face that there was bad news to come.

The only way to tell it was straight out, without too much emotion but not without a degree of compassion. 'I'm afraid we couldn't save the unborn child.'

His words hung heavy in the ensuing silence. Both women looked at him in disbelief. It was a moment before Margaret spoke, and the word was a whisper. '*Child*?' She was slowly shaking her head from side to side, her confused gaze going from the doctor to Ruby and back again. Ruby too had been stunned by the news. Yet, in their hearts, both women knew there had been something troubling Cathy, something so deep she had not been able to tell them.

Ruby's voice came out in a croak. 'Come and sit down,' she said, leading Margaret to the chair.

The doctor followed. 'I'm sorry.' In cases like this he would rather be anything but a doctor. 'We did all we could, but it wasn't enough.'

Recovered now, Margaret asked, 'Does she know . . . that she's lost the child?'

He pursed his lips, thought for a while and smiled sadly. 'I think she knew even before we did.'

'Can we see her?'

'That would do her good. She hasn't spoken to any of us, and she needs to talk about her loss.' Indicating the double green doors, he led the way. 'However, she's still very weak. I can't let you stay too long.' He saw them to the sister's office, before going about his many duties.

'Just a short time,' the sister said. 'She's very tired.'

Cathy was lying on her side. 'By! She looks like a small child,' Ruby whispered as they came close. 'And she's no colour at all.' Cathy was sleeping, her face stark white and her long slim fingers clutched as though in spasm across her breast.

Leaning forward, Margaret gently touched the folded fingers.

'Once she's home again we'll soon put the colour back in her cheeks,' she said, thinking Ruby was right; Cathy did look like a child.

Hearing the voices of those she loved, she opened her eyes. One look at their faces told her. 'You know about the baby?'

Margaret wrapped her fingers around Cathy's. 'Yes, sweetheart, we know.' Her voice was soft and caressing, relaying all the love she felt. 'We can talk about it later . . . if you want to.'

Against the white skin, Cathy's green eyes looked like large emerald pools; incredibly beautiful, alive with pain. Tears trembled on the long dark lashes. 'I'm so sorry. I should have told you.'

'It doesn't matter,' Margaret said encouragingly. 'What matters now is *you* . . . getting you better so we can take you home.'

'I love you both.' Reaching up awkwardly, Cathy took hold of Ruby's hand. 'I should have told you.' Memories became almost too much to bear. 'I've been bad,' she whispered. 'I can't talk about it.'

'Whenever you're ready, sweetheart.'

'I don't *ever* want to talk about it.'

Sensing that they were getting into deep waters, Margaret assured her, 'It's for you to decide, but when you're better you might feel different.'

Cathy closed her eyes. She felt strange, incredibly tired. The doctor's words echoed in her mind. 'I have to tell you . . . you've lost the child.' In spite of the way it was conceived, she had never consciously wished it harm. It was an innocent, a victim like herself. How could she want it harmed? Yet in her deepest heart had she wanted rid of it? She could never be certain. And now she was beginning to wonder whether all of it was her fault. Had she been too friendly with Jack? Did he take her friendship to mean she felt something stronger for him? And what of Tony Manners? There was no doubt she had seen him as her salvation. She had smiled at him in such a way that he was made arrogantly sure of her. Was it any wonder he saw her as being easy, someone to satisfy his needs and pander to his every whim? A man was only a man after all, and could see no further than his animal desires. But, no! That wasn't true. One man was different from another, just as a woman was different from another. Jack and Tony Manners were two of a kind. David Leyton was another matter altogether. David was kind and good, and had never asked more of her than she was willing to give. If he was here now, she would give him everything she had. But he wasn't here. HE WASN'T HERE!

In all of her life she had never felt so devastated; with the child gone her body felt drained. With David gone there was little to live for. Oh, there was Margaret, and Ruby, and she would always love and need them. But her life was empty, finished. And all she could think of was the child, and David. David! David!

Suddenly she was crying, sobbing as though her heart would break. Margaret was holding her. 'That's right, sweetheart,' she was saying. 'That's right.' But it wasn't right. Cathy feared that nothing could ever be right again.

'Don't worry,' the nurse told Margaret. 'It's only natural she should be weepy after such a shock. On top of losing the child, she's still slightly concussed and the broken ribs will cause her a deal of pain. It's bound to take time, but she will be well again.' While she was talking, Cathy drifted in and out of consciousness, not caring whether she lived or died.

'We'll be there soon as ever they open the doors in the morning.' Intent on keeping Margaret's spirits up, Ruby chattered all the way home. 'It'll not be long afore she's home, then we'll soon get the colour back into her cheeks.'

A week later Cathy came home. Still very weak and in great pain from her broken ribs, she talked and smiled and ate the good broth that Ruby made. She slept well, and sat in the yard, letting the sun warm her face. She read, and she sewed, and just as Ruby had predicted, the roses came back to her cheeks. 'By! She's doing fine,' Ruby declared. Returning to the sitting room after taking Cathy a cup of tea in the yard, she grinned from ear to ear. 'The lass will soon be up to her old tricks . . . rushing about, bossing the pair of us and wanting to put the world to rights.'

'Do you really think she's mending, Ruby?'

'Aye, lass. Mending fast, I reckon.'

Margaret was not of the same mind. Going to the window

she gazed out. 'I'm worried about her,' she said softly. In the wicker chair that Margaret had bought at the market, Cathy was seated against the west wall. It was covered in trellis and pricked with the first blossom of an early-cropping apple-tree. Soon after they first moved into the house, Cathy had knocked the trellis to the wall, and helped Ruby to tie in the tree. 'I shall make some delicious apple pies from that,' Ruby had promised. But that was some time away yet. The blossom had not even begun to shoot.

'I don't know why you're worried about her,' Ruby remarked. 'The lass is eating well, and the pain in her ribs is lessening. The colour's back in her cheeks and her smile is bright as it ever was.'

'I know all that,' Margaret murmured. 'Somehow, though, I have the feeling she's only half alive.'

'By! That's a sorry thing to say.' Ruby had been smiling but now she was looking at Cathy in a different way.

'It's nothing physical, Ruby. Nothing you can put your finger on. It's a feeling, an instinct if you like.' She shivered. 'I don't know what it is, but ... I'm afraid.'

'Happen we're being too impatient. The lass has been through so much, and losing the child was a terrible thing. You heard what the doctor said ... it will take time to get over summat like that.'

'Has she spoken to *you* about that, Ruby?'

'Not a word.' Ruby's voice fell to a whisper. 'Lord knows I've given her ample opportunity ... without pressing her, you understand? But she's said not a word. Not about the bairn, nor about how she came to fall down them steps.'

'Nor to me. And since Tony Manners has made himself scarce, we can't ask him either.'

'That scoundrel has a lot to answer for, I'll be bound.'

'We still can't be sure of that.'

Ruby hesitated to raise the subject again. She and Margaret had discussed it briefly, but neither of them felt it was right to talk about it without Cathy's being present. Yet the burning question hung in the air like a cloud over their heads. 'Do you still think it were David Leyton as made her with child?'

Margaret never took her eyes off Cathy. 'Who else could it

291

be? David was the only young man she was ever close to. I always believed that Cathy and David would marry one day.' She recalled all those times when she had found them together, two young sweethearts shutting out the world. 'I don't honestly know *what* to believe.'

'If you're concerned about the lass, don't you think you ought to talk with the doctor?'

'No. It isn't a doctor Cathy needs.'

'Who then?' Ruby's eyes lit up. 'It's David, isn't it? You think she's pining for him?'

Still, Margaret kept her gaze on Cathy. 'Maybe. Maybe not. All I know is this . . . we're losing Cathy, and I can't seem to get through to her. She won't talk to you either, so the only other person I can think of is David.'

'Are you sure about all this?'

'I know her so well, Ruby. Think about it . . . she's eating, yes, and her health seems to be improving . . . but do you really believe that forlorn creature down there is the Cathy we know?'

Ruby had to concede, 'Happen you're right. Happen I'm seeing only the good signs and not seeing the truth. I've noticed her spirits are low, and it bothers me that she won't talk about the matters close to her heart.' Margaret's anxiety had conveyed itself to her. 'If you're right though, an' our Cathy *is* fretting inside, what's to be done? Tell me that, lass . . . what's to be done?'

'I wish I knew.' As she spoke, Cathy glanced up to see them there. Margaret thought she looked cold. 'She's been out there too long, Ruby. I'll fetch her in. You fill a nice hot bath.' With that she went smartly down the steps, leaving Ruby to go on her own way.

'You're an old fusspot.' Cathy would have stayed outside for a time, but Margaret was right. The sun had gone behind a cloud and the breeze had grown chilly. 'I bet you've got Ruby filling a hot bath for me, haven't you?' There was a smile on her face, but it didn't seem to touch her lovely green eyes.

'Don't be cheeky, young lady!' Margaret gently chided. 'Or I might leave you out here until you beg to be brought in.'

'I'm capable of bringing myself in.' In fact she was going up the steps on her own, when previously she'd had to lean heavily on Margaret. 'You see, I'm growing stronger by the day.' Her bright voice belied the trauma inside her. It was true she was growing stronger. But that was on the outside. Inside, where only she could see, something was slowly dying.

That evening, when Ruby was busying herself in the kitchen, Cathy and Margaret sat on the settee. Cathy was watching the sky through the window. 'Do you want to talk?' Margaret asked softly.

Cathy brought her gaze to the older woman. Her voice was soft and surprised. 'What about?'

'Oh, I don't know.' She kept her eyes on Cathy's troubled face. 'Tony Manners perhaps? Or the child? Or we could talk about . . . David.'

The mention of his name brought a glimmer to Cathy's eyes, but it only lasted for a second. 'David's gone,' she said, and the sadness was tenfold.

'You miss him terribly, don't you?' Now that she had got Cathy talking, Margaret didn't want to let the moment go.

Cathy's answer was a curt nod, but it spoke volumes.

'I imagine he's missing you too, sweetheart.'

'No.' How could he be missing her, when she had given him every chance to make amends and he had turned his back on her?

'Cathy, I have to ask . . . was David the father of your child?'

Cathy was shocked. Yet she reasoned it was only natural for Margaret to make such an assumption. 'No,' she answered softly, 'David and I . . . we never actually made love.'

Margaret was at a loss for words. For a long awkward minute she said nothing at all, and then she murmured, 'I didn't mean to pry, you know that.'

'I know.'

'But if David wasn't the father of your child . . .?'

Cathy had said too much already. David was gone. The father of her child was gone, and now so was the poor innocent child itself. There was nothing to be gained from raising the past. 'I'm tired now.' Getting up from the chair she bent to kiss Margaret on the forehead. 'Perhaps we can talk tomorrow?' Margaret made as if to stand up, but stayed put when Cathy

293

told her gratefully, 'I can manage. The stairs are easier for me now.'

It was like climbing a mountain, but Cathy was determined. Racked with pain she went doggedly up the stairs one at a time, pausing for breath after every step. At the top, she turned and smiled at Margaret. 'Good night, God bless.'

'Good night, God bless.' Though she was disappointed that Cathy had curtailed their little talk, Margaret believed she had made a breakthrough. At least now she could put away the idea that David had made Cathy with child. She told Ruby as much.

Ruby was astonished, 'If it ain't David, who the divil is it then?'

'I have my suspicions,' Margaret murmured.

'She might be trying to protect David.'

'It isn't like Cathy to lie.' In fact Margaret's thoughts had been along the same line as Ruby's. 'Mind you, she always had a very protective instinct towards David.'

'There you are then!'

'She misses him dreadfully.'

'Did she say that?'

'Not in so many words, but it was painfully obvious.'

'What about that Tony Manners? Did she say what happened between 'em?'

'She was tired, Ruby. Tomorrow, when she's had a good night's sleep, I'm sure she'll confide in me.'

Cathy didn't have a good night's sleep. At dawn she was still awake, seated by the window and looking at the sky outside, thinking about Margaret's question. Softly she gave the answer again, 'David and I never made love, and now we never will.' In the half-light her eyes glittered with tears. 'She's right though, David . . . I do miss you so.' A solitary tear spilled down her cheek. Wiping it away, she opened the window and braced herself against the rush of cold air.

Dawn peeped over the horizon, and Cathy thought she had never seen a sky more beautiful. Round its edges the golden hue spread like a creeping flame, splintering the silver and black at its heart. She couldn't take her eyes from it, and just for a while its breathtaking beauty brought her a deep sense of peace and contentment.

In the morning, Cathy slept like a child. She slept beyond breakfast time, and into the late morning hours. 'I don't want to wake her,' Margaret said. 'She looked so tired last night.'

At midday, she was still sleeping and Ruby asked, 'Is she unwell, do you think? It ain't like her to sleep such long hours.'

At two o'clock, Margaret woke her. 'You must have something to eat, sweetheart.' Ruby had prepared a tray and the aroma of freshly made tea and muffins filled the room.

Astonished that she had slept for so long, Cathy got out of bed. While Margaret waited she washed and dressed. 'I'm not really hungry,' she said, though on Margaret's insistence she did manage half a muffin and a cup of tea.

While Cathy brushed her hair, Margaret quietly regarded her. She was always shaken nowadays by Cathy's physical appearance; her arms were twig-like, and there was no vitality about her at all. 'How do you feel, sweetheart?' Coming to her side, she put one arm round Cathy's shoulder. 'Is the pain in your ribs lessening?'

'They're getting better. Stop worrying.' It wasn't so much the pain in her ribs that was debilitating. It was the pain in her heart; pain for everything she had lost; pain of a kind she could not explain. Right now, she felt incredibly low, physically drained. But she would overcome it, just as she had always done.

'Ruby wonders whether we should let the doctor see you?'

'I'm mending. There's no need for a doctor.' And to prove her point, she brushed a little rouge on to her cheekbones. 'There! I'm ready for anything now.'

Margaret tutted. 'Shameless hussy,' she said and, hugging each other, they laughed together like they used to.

It was to be a long time before Cathy would laugh like that again. With the assurance that she would follow in a minute, Margaret took the tray downstairs. 'By! Is that all she could manage?' Ruby asked, her manner brightening when she was told how much better Cathy seemed and that she was on her way down. 'Washed, dressed and painted in rouge, would you believe?'

They were still talking when they heard the bump from Cathy's bedroom. Margaret reached her first. 'Get the doctor, Ruby.' she cried. 'Quickly!' Ruby was already halfway down the stairs when Margaret tenderly lifted Cathy from the floor and laid her gently on the bed, shocked at how feather light the girl was in her arms.

The doctor was swift to arrive. He examined Cathy while Margaret and Ruby waited anxiously outside. When he emerged, Ruby went in with Cathy while Margaret accompanied the doctor to the sitting room. 'She's weak and anaemic. I'm not happy about the rate of her recovery.' Snapping his bag shut, he looked at her with an air of frustration. 'Unfortunately, I can't force her to be admitted to the Infirmary.'

Margaret stared at him in disbelief. 'You mean she's refusing?'

'Perhaps you can persuade her?'

Margaret tried but couldn't, and Ruby didn't even make the effort. 'I've come to think you're right,' she said. 'It ain't a doctor Cathy wants. It's someone to share her secrets with. Someone her own age ... someone she thinks to have lost for good.'

'You mean David?'

'Aye, that's who I mean.'

Over the following week, the doctor visited every day, and every day he said the same thing. 'See she takes her tablets, and try to get her eating more.' Cathy took her tablets, and Ruby stood over while she ate the good broth they'd made her. But Cathy grew weaker, and it was heartbreaking to see. 'Please, lass ... will you go to the Infirmary and let them get you well again?' Ruby pleaded. Margaret too sat by her bed and did her utmost to persuade Cathy that she should do as the doctor said.

'I won't get better in the Infirmary.' She was adamant. 'I want to be here, with you. I'll soon be up and about, you'll see.' She made them promise not to send her away, and they prayed they would not live to regret such a promise.

The days flew by, and still Cathy's recovery was painfully slow. 'She's not getting well, is she, Doctor?' Margaret was at her wit's end.

The doctor was truthful. 'She doesn't seem to *want* to get well. When that happens, I'm afraid there's very little we can do.'

'Well, there's something we can do!' Ruby declared when he'd gone. 'We can find David. Fetch him here and then you'll see that bonny lass grow stronger.'

'I've been wondering about that, Ruby.' Margaret was ready to try anything. 'It might work. Cathy has so much unhappiness inside her... pain and heartache that goes back a long long way... to when she was small.' Bowing her head, she covered her face with her hands, recalling how she alone had been both mother and father to that lonely little girl.

Suddenly she was pacing the room. 'We mustn't lose her.' Excited and hopeful, she began to make plans. 'There isn't much money left, but we'll manage. We'll get a private detective and find David at whatever cost. It may not be the answer; he may not want to know... after all, he did turn his back on her, didn't he?' She sat down on the sofa, jerking her head back and forth, desperately making herself believe. 'It's our only hope, Ruby. I'll hire a detective today... tell him all we know about David Leyton and his family. Oh, Ruby... Pray God we're making the right decision!'

Ruby had no doubts. 'If anybody can help her, you mark my words, it's that young man.' She took the liberty of seating herself right next to Margaret. 'But I don't think you should spend your remaining nest egg on a private detective. He'll take your last penny and might not find him anyway.'

Margaret was aware of that. 'But what else can we do?'

'You can send *me*!' Before Margaret could argue, she went on, 'I know what David Leyton looks like. I know what he and the lass meant to each other. When I find him, I can get to the bottom of why he turned his back on her. I've allus wondered about that.' She grinned mischievously. 'Besides, what would you want a private detective for? If anybody can find a needle in a haystack, it's ol' Ruby! What's more, it won't cost yer a farthing... except o' course, there'll be the cooking and such like to do.'

'That's no hardship. And it's a labour of love to look after Cathy.'

'I can go then?'

'With my heartfelt thanks, Ruby.'

A look passed between them that showed their love for Cathy, and for each other. 'I'll find him,' Ruby promised. 'What happens after that. I can't say.'

An hour later, she was ready to leave. Before she said her goodbyes to Margaret, she went up the stairs to Cathy's room.

Gazing down on the sleeping girl, she made a mental note of how thin and drawn that darling face had become; she touched the long fair hair and murmured a promise. 'David never stopped loving yer, lass . . . I know that. In your heart you must know it too. But he hurt yer, didn't he, eh? He hurt yer and he should stand afore yer to say why.' She bent to kiss the sleeping face. 'I'm off to fetch him, lass. If I have to search all the four corners of the earth, I promise you, I'll find him.' As she spoke, the tears ran down her face. 'I'll fetch the bugger back, you see if I don't!'

Margaret gave her enough money to see her all right for at least a week. 'It should be me going, not you,' she argued.

'And why's that?' Ruby asked indignantly. 'Reckon I'm too old, is that it?' Collecting her big tapestry bag, she put the wallet inside. 'I may be long in the tooth, but I can take care of meself, don't you worry about me.'

Margaret waved her off, and she knew she would worry every minute of every day until Ruby returned.

Upstairs, Cathy stirred. 'Ruby?' Hoisting herself on to one elbow, she looked round the room. 'Ruby, is that you?' When there was no answer, she fell back into the pillow and closed her eyes, but she could still hear Ruby's promise.

'Ruby's bringing David home,' Cathy whispered. And, for the first time in many long months, the burden began to lift from her heart.

PART TWO

1901

. . . Come True

CHAPTER ELEVEN

The heat was unbearable. From the first day of June, the sun had beaten down, parching the earth and singeing the crops. Since then, there had been no let up; no breeze, no flicker of clouds in the sky; all was still. Even the branches drooped.

Two men laboured in the field; one a man of about sixty, the other a strapping young fellow with thick dark hair and smiling black eyes. Stripped to the waist, his tanned shoulders glistened with sweat in the merciless sun. Since the early hours they had laboured in the field, layering the hedges and clearing the land beneath. It was hard back-breaking work, but when he stepped back to survey the end result, David was proud. 'That's a good job done, Ted,' he remarked, and the older man was quick to agree.

Taking off his cap to wipe the sweat from his eyes, David peered at the approaching figure. 'Looks like Barney,' he said.

The older man joined him. 'Aye, it's him right enough.'

David was puzzled. 'What's he doing right out here?' Barney was the gentleman farmer's runabout.

'Summat's up, I reckon.' A deep frown etched itself into his old weathered features. 'That bugger don't stir from the comfort of his office unless there's a good enough reason.'

Together they waited, anxious now, expecting the worst.

Barney Lent was a little man in every sense of the word; no more than five foot tall, with close-set eyes and thin brown hair, he puffed and panted, out of sorts and out of temper. 'I've been sent to fetch you,' he panted. 'The boss wants you back at the farm, and he wants you now!'

David grinned, his straight white teeth lighting up a face darkened with sweat and earth. 'You needn't have bothered

301

coming all the way out here,' he said. 'We're just about to pack up and make our way back.'

Barney's temper wasn't improved. 'Get on then!' he snapped. 'The boss is waiting, and you know what an impatient bugger he can be!' With that he swung away and began to retrace his steps through the rows of prime cabbages. 'Get on! Get on!' he called behind him. 'I've done what he asked and I can't do no more!'

David couldn't see rhyme nor reason in Barney's trudging all the way back when he could have a ride on the wagon. 'Get on the cart,' he yelled. 'We'll take you back with us in half the time.'

Barney was disgusted. 'What! Climb on that filthy contraption, and me in my decent clothes. Be buggered!'

His reply had the two men in fits of laughter. 'Oh, la de da!' spluttered the older man, his eyes round and mocking. 'Mustn't get our pretty clothes dirty . . . and we certainly mustn't sit aside two men covered with muck and sweat. Whatever next?'

David didn't care much for Barney, but he felt bad about mocking him. All the same, he couldn't help but laugh. 'Honest to God,' he remarked, watching the irate figure step daintily in and out of the market crop, 'it beats me how a fussy bloke like Barney ever came to work on a farm.'

''Course . . . being here only three months, you wouldn't know, would you?' queried the older man. 'When Mr Reed Barton bought the farm and moved into the big house, Barney came with him. Apparently he was butler to Reed Barton when they resided in the heart of London town.' He winked. 'Mind you, I reckon there were more to it than master and butler . . . have you seen the way them two look at each other?'

David was intrigued. 'Can't say I have.'

'Aye, well, that's because you live at the cottage some two mile away, and I live at the back of the big house.' He chuckled. 'There ain't much I miss, I can tell you.'

'Better not.'

'What you don't know you can't tell, eh?'

'Something like that.' David had wondered about the relationship between the boss and Barney Lent. But that was their business, not his. 'We'd best get back,' he said, slipping on his shirt.

'Aye,' the other man agreed sombrely. 'We wouldn't want Barney to get in trouble with his sweetheart.' He laughed out loud, and David couldn't help but smile. But beneath the smile was an aching heart as he thought of a sweetheart he once had. Time and again he had wondered about Cathy, about why she had turned against him the way she did. Surely to God she must have known he would have moved heaven and earth for things to have been different. What happened between their parents was no more his fault than it was Cathy's. One day, when he could trust himself not to grab her in his arms, he would seek her out and tell her that. Until then, he had to live without her, and never expect to hold her in his arms again.

As always when his heart was pained with memories of Cathy, he distracted himself with other things. Soon the wagon was loaded with the pitchforks and axes, and the two of them were seated up top. David slapped the reins and got the horses gently moving, and the older fellow quietly smoked his pipe. 'I wonder why the boss wants to see us?' David mused aloud. 'It must be important for Barney to be sent.'

'Summat and nothing, I expect.'

'No, I think it's more than that.' Coming towards the back of the house, David glanced at the other man. 'When have you ever known him to send Barney after us?'

'Never.' They were lost in thought, each with their own explanation, each with their own worries. 'You've got me wondering proper now.' Tapping out his pipe on the side of the wagon, Ted went on, 'Summat's always puzzled me about Reed Barton.'

'You've already said.'

'No. I don't mean about whether them two lie in the hay together.' The very idea was unnatural to him. 'If they want to tickle each other's fancy, that's up to them ... so long as they don't want to tickle *mine*!' His face hardened to a serious expression. 'What I'm saying is this ... why would a businessman ... a gent from the city ... why would he move to the outskirts of Ilford and buy a market gardening business? You have to admit, he doesn't know the first thing about farming. I mean, he relies on you for everything. I'm old and knackered, but he's latched on to you as his saviour. It's you as says what crops need planting, you as buys and sells, and he leans on you for every little thing. In the short time you've been here you've worked miracles. You've been to auction and bought his stallions, sorted the mares and found the finest hunters round here for miles. You plan his working diary . . . and all you get for your trouble is a labourer's wage and a three-bedroomed cottage.'

'It'll do me for now, Ted.' He had his ambitions though. One day he meant to have his own farm, and his own big house. One day . . .

'Can you explain why a gent like that should move out of the city and live in the country? It ain't natural. He's like a fish outta water. The man don't belong here. Any fool can see he's not happy.'

'Happen he's had enough of city life.'

'If that's the case, why is he there more than he is here?' Ted tapped David on the arm. 'Answer me that! If he's so fed up with city life, why is he allus popping back and leaving you in charge?'

'I don't know, and I'm not sure I want to.'

The old fellow leaned back in his seat and sighed. 'And I'm not sure I want to know why he's sent for us. I've been expecting him to pay me off. He knows I'm past my best. He wants rid, that's what'll it be . . . got some strapping young fella such as yourself to take my place.' His voice broke. 'I don't know what I'd do if he asked me to leave. I've lived in that cottage for over thirty years . . . me and the missus, till she passed on five year since.'

'So you weren't much older than me when you first came here?' It wasn't hard to imagine him as a young man. Ted was still broad of back and walked as upright as a man half his age. He had a strong craggy face, with twinkling blue eyes and a smile that revealed a kind happy nature.

'I were coming up twenty-nine, newly wed, and excited to be moving into our first real home.' His eyes misted over. 'We loved that cottage from first sight. The owners were a fair-minded couple, and they paid good wages. Oh, aye, apart from never having children, we had a good life, me and the missus. When the owners retired, Reed Barton bought this place with me as part of the fixtures and fittings.' He sighed deeply. 'I were a fitter man then. These days I'm a bloody old crock!'

'Don't belittle yourself, Ted.' David had grown fond of him. 'You might be a few years older and a bit slower, but you give a good day's work for a good day's pay. Besides, you know farming inside out, and he's well aware of that.' Playfully thumping him on the shoulder, David smiled encouragingly. 'Reed Barton won't get rid of you,' he told him confidently. 'Don't concern yourself about that.'

'You'd speak up for me, would you?'

There was a smile on David's lips as he glanced at him. 'I don't know about that . . .' he teased.

The old fella chuckled. 'You're a grand 'un!' he said. 'Salt of the earth.'

When they drew into the yard there was no sign of Barney. 'The bugger ain't fell down a rat'ole has he?' chuckled Ted. And the two of them were still chuckling as they reported to the office.

Barney Lent's office was a converted outbuilding at the back of the house. It was only a stone's throw from Ted's humble abode, though the two buildings were separated by a high laurel hedge that afforded Ted all the privacy he needed.

Mr Reed Barton was seated behind the desk. A huge man with staring eyes and an abundance of dark hair round his face and chin, he presented a formidable sight. 'Where's that fool Barney?' he demanded in a rasping voice. 'I want him here.'

It was David who answered. 'He's on his way.'

'Why the hell didn't he ride back on the wagon with the two of you?'

'You'll have to ask *him* that.' It was all David could do not to chuckle.

'Oh! I see.' The slightest hint of a smile lifted the corners of the big man's mouth. 'Too particular to ride with the peasants, eh?' He coughed and cleared his throat, and got out of the chair. 'We'll wait for the daft bugger!' he said.

Clutching his hands together behind his back, he walked to the window and looked out across the fields. Struggling towards the house was Barney. 'Here he is now,' he observed. He watched the door for Barney's entrance.

It was only a few minutes before he tumbled in, gasping and moaning, and swearing beneath his breath. 'Look at my boots!'

he grumbled, pointing to his mud-caked feet. The pungent smell of damp manure filled the air.

'Bugger your boots! You stink to high heaven!' The big man gestured for him to sit behind the desk. 'But take your boots off first and leave them far enough away so we won't be choked.' As Barney struggled to untie his laces, he added impatiently, 'It's beyond me how you managed to make such a mess of yourself when there hasn't been a drop of rain in over a week!'

It was hard for David to keep a straight face as he surmised, 'I expect he came by way of the onion beds. That ground is prone to dryness, so I fill in the trenches with horse manure ... helps keep the moisture in.' He bit his lip to stem the rising laughter, and beside him Ted choked as he too kept a straight face. 'Before the dry spell we had a deluge of rain as you know,' David explained. 'As the field slopes to the onion bed, I expect Barney sank in to his ankles.' He glanced at Barney, who was taking off the other boot. 'He might as well throw them away because they'll never be the same again.'

The big man followed David's glance, and when he saw Barney, barefoot and red in the face, he laughed out loud. 'Serves you right!' he cried. 'Next time you might be glad of a ride on the wagon.'

As suddenly as he had laughed, he became hard-faced. 'Get out of my sight. Come back when you smell a bit sweeter, damn you!' He waited until Barney had scuttled away then seated himself behind the desk once more, his staring eyes fixed on the two men. 'You're no doubt wondering why I've sent for you?' His question was addressed to David, who was also look-ing grim-faced.

'That's right.' Sensing there was bad news to come, he had no desire to prolong the inevitable.

'Right. Well ... I won't keep you in suspense,' he said. 'The truth is, I was never a farmer. Buying this place suited me at the time, but now I'm selling up.' Leaning back in the chair, he tucked the tips of his thumbs behind his broad leather braces. 'You shouldn't be too surprised,' he remarked harshly. 'You must have known I was out of my element.'

Ted grew bold. 'Will you be selling everything, sir?'

'Lock, stock and barrel.' Anticipating the next question, he looked from one to the other. 'I'm sorry, Ted . . . the cottages are included. *Both* of them.' He looked at David. 'You won't find it hard to get another job. I have nothing but praise for you.'

'Not much consolation though.' David had half expected this, but it was a bitter blow, especially coming when his mother was bedridden and with Teresa going off the rails.

The big man spoke to Ted. 'I can't promise anything,' he commented, 'and I won't make it a condition of sale, but I will have a word on your behalf with whoever buys this place.'

'If they chuck me off, sir, that'll be the end of me.' There were tears in his eyes. 'But I'd be grateful for anything you could do to let me keep my cottage.'

'Remember, I'm making no promises.'

'No, sir.'

'Now get off home.'

'There's the wagon and horses to see to first.' He sounded heart-weary.

David touched him on the shoulder. 'It's all right, Ted,' he said quietly. 'I'll see to the horses. You go and put your feet up.'

'Will you call in on your way home?'

'If you want me to.'

Ted nodded, excused himself to the boss, and shuffled out. David turned his attention to the man behind the desk. 'Losing his home means losing everything. He's no family, and all his memories are in that cottage.'

'Not my problem.'

'Then what you said to him . . . about having a word on his behalf? Just talk was it?'

'Nobody's going to keep Ted on.'

David's blood was boiling. 'You've no right to get his hopes up like that.'

'They'd keep *you* on though.'

'I dare say they would.'

'Do you want me to keep that in mind?'

'Maybe. Maybe not.'

David's quiet smile made him curious. 'You always were a deep bugger.' He got out of his chair and came round the desk. 'Got plans have you?'

'A man always has plans.' David had been careful with his

307

money, but for something like this farm it was nowhere near enough. 'Would you rent the farm to me?'

The big man shook his head, took out a cigar and chewed on it. 'Sorry. I need the money.'

'Would you rent the field . . . the one we keep for market-gardening?'

'Not even a handkerchief square.'

'Then there's no more to be said.' He could see he was wasting his time, and he had to get home. Teresa had stayed away again last night. She was causing their mother a deal of heartache, and it was time for a showdown. 'How long will it be before we're paid up?'

'You've got until I sell the property . . . could be a week, a month . . . a bit longer. It can't be soon enough for me.' Having got the worst over, he could afford to be arrogant. 'Ted will manage, so will you . . . especially you. You're young and strong, and you've a good head on your shoulders, and I dare say there'll come a day when it'll be *you* paying the wages. You're a man to be reckoned with, young Leyton!'

'You're right about that.' David's ambitions were strengthened by this setback.

Going to the door, the big man opened it wide. 'I expect you think I'm insane . . . giving up this place. But you see, I'm a city man bred and born. Once this lot's auctioned off, I'll pocket the money and be away, and you'll never set eyes on me again.'

Ted wasn't surprised to hear Reed Barton couldn't wait to get away. 'The city's where he belongs,' he said. 'Leave the country-side to them as loves it.'

'I'm sorry I said he wouldn't get rid of you. I had an idea he wouldn't stay too long round these parts, but I honestly didn't think he'd sell up so soon.'

'His sort come and go.' Ted had been rocking himself back-wards and forwards in the big wooden rocker that he had made with his own hands, but now he brought it to a halt. 'I've been so busy thinking about myself I never gave you and yours a thought. What with your mam and your sister, you've *three* to worry about. What will you do, son? Back on the road, is it?'

'Mebbe.' His answer was given in a soft thoughtful tone.

The older man was intrigued. 'You've summat up your sleeve, I can tell.'

'A dream, Ted.' David had never lost sight of his ambition of one day being his own master. 'I've always wanted my own land, and I shan't rest till I have it.'

Ted shook his head and sighed. 'By! There's no justice in the world. Reed Barton has no love for the land, yet he owns a farm that you'd give your right arm for.'

David smiled. 'I don't know about my right arm. What use would I be without that, eh?'

'I wish to God the farm were yours. I'd have a better chance of keeping this 'ere cottage then, wouldn't I, eh?'

'A man who works like you do? Goes without saying.'

'I don't suppose there's a way?' He was shaking his head even as he asked. 'No . . . that would be asking too much.'

David had been racking his brain. 'Nobody wishes more than I do that I could get hold of the farm,' he admitted. 'Or even the five-acre field we were working in today. That would be enough to get me started.' He took a deep invigorating breath, letting it out noisily through his nose. 'I can't see it happening though . . . not without a miracle, and that's not about to happen.' He was used to wanting things and not having them. Look how often he'd prayed that a miracle might fetch Cathy back to him. And he was still waiting.

'Happen he'll not find a buyer.' Ted brightened at the thought.

'Oh, he'll find a buyer right enough!' Striding to the door, David prepared to leave. 'I'll see you the morrow then?'

'Unless the good Lord decides otherwise.'

'He'd better not!' Going out of the door, David cheered him up. 'You tell him there's half a field of spuds to be bagged yet.'

'Get away home with you!'

As a rule David whistled as he walked home. But not tonight. Tonight he was too deep in thought. 'If there was a way to buy that field and the cottages, I'd walk through burning coals in my bare feet,' he muttered. But it took more than courage to buy land. It took money, and as yet he had none to speak of.

Maria had spent the last half hour watching through the bed-room window for her son to come home. When she saw him striding towards the house, she rattled the window with her stick, frantically waving at him when his attention was caught.

He came into the cottage at a run. 'Are you all right, Mam?' Rushing into the bedroom, he was relieved when she nodded her head and struggled to sit up. 'Here, lean on me.' Stretching out his arms, he pressed his shoulder to hers. 'I'm sorry to be late,' he apologised, thinking that was why she had panicked. 'I called in on Ted as I made my way home.' She seemed more settled now, so he sat in the rocking chair and regarded her more closely. Always a little woman, she seemed lately to have shrunk and, with her large pale eyes, looked like a little doll.

While she settled herself comfortably, he glanced curiously round the room. Something occurred to him. Just now, when he came through the cottage, there had been no sign of his sister. 'Where's Teresa?' Searching Maria's face he knew there was something wrong. 'She should have been home from work long since,' he said, looking at the bedside clock; it was ten minutes past five. 'She's always home soon after midday. The draper knows she has to be back for you... he never keeps her late.' He was on his feet now, angry that Maria had been left on her own for so long.

'It doesn't matter now, son.' She wanted no trouble. '*You're* home now. That's all as matters.'

'Where is she, Mam?' His dark eyes glittered angrily.

'She'll be back when she's ready, I dare say.'

'You knocked the window when you saw me coming... you've been waiting for me... wanting to tell me something. What, Mam? What is it you're worried about?'

'She won't listen.' Maria began crying. 'I've argued with her till I'm blue in the face, and she'll not listen to a word I say.'

'She'll listen to *me*, the bugger!' Taking a handkerchief from the bedside drawer, he tenderly wiped her eyes, afterwards putting the handkerchief into her hand. 'What the devil's she been up to now? Will she never give you any peace?'

Maria was loth to tell him, but she had to. Teresa was getting in over her head, and unless she came to her senses was bound to come to a bad end. If anybody could talk sense into her, it was David. 'You know she's been restless for weeks now?'

'Aye. Ever since she met that slimy bloke from the City.'

David was listening intently. 'Go on, Mam . . . what's happened?'

'She didn't go to work this morning. When I asked her why, she flew into a temper . . . said she'd packed the work in . . . said she was sick to death of living hand to mouth, and wanted something more glamorous than being a draper's assistant.' She rolled her eyes. 'That Manners fella told her she had a good singing voice . . . said he could make her rich.'

'She's gone to London, is that it?' He was angry with himself, 'I should have seen it coming.'

Maria shook her head. 'Teresa has a mind of her own, and she's always been devious. I honestly thought she'd seen the badness in that fella, but I was wrong, because that's where she's gone right enough. Packed her bag and left early this morning.' Turning on her side she winced, her blue eyes closing in agony. 'Right bloody man about town that Manners bloke – apparently he has his fingers in all kinds of deals, North *and* South.'

'God Almighty! You've been on your own all day!'

Maria forced a smile. 'I've come to no harm,' she assured him. 'But I'm glad you're home now, son.' She hesitated to ask, especially when she knew he'd been working on the land since early light. She looked at his face, such a strong handsome face. He never talked about Cathy, but Maria knew he would never forget her. She thought it sad that the girl had blamed David for all that happened. 'I'm sorry,' she murmured. 'Your sister and I are a great burden to you.'

'You're never that, Mam. As for Teresa, she's headstrong and easily led. She has to grow up, and the sooner the better.'

He lapsed into deep thought, deciding what to do. 'Look at me, son,' Maria said softly, and he raised his dark eyes to hers. 'Will you fetch her?' she asked. 'Will you go to the city and fetch our Teresa home?'

The dark eyes smiled, a deep-down smile that put her heart at ease. 'Oh, I'll fetch her, don't you worry about that,' he promised. The tension was over. 'There's time enough. I expect she'll be in that club where I found her once before . . . it's less than a half hour away, so I've time to get us both something to eat. After I'm washed and changed, I'll backtrack and fetch Ted . . . he'll be glad to keep you company while I'm gone.' His

311

jaw worked angrily. 'I'm not leaving you on your own again.'

It was settled. In no time at all, David had sliced the ham, boiled four eggs, made the tea, and set it all out on two trays, with a large chunk of bread for himself and a smaller one for Maria. 'It's too much for me,' she complained, but she ate both eggs and half the bread. After that she swallowed two cups of tea and asked for another.

Washed and changed into a clean blue shirt and dark trousers, David was gone less than ten minutes before he returned with Ted. 'The two of you can keep each other company,' he told Maria, and she urged him to make tracks and find his sister. She also reminded him, 'You don't know how long it'll take for you to find her. Late evening can get chilly, so you'd best take your jacket.'

Kissing her fleetingly, he took his leave. 'Hopefully I'll be back before dark,' he told them. Whether or not he would have Teresa with him was another matter altogether. She had a way of losing herself when it suited her.

Tony Manners sat in the darkest corner, tapping his feet to the music and wondering whether he had done the right thing in getting tangled up with the Leyton woman. He said as much to his colleague, a red-headed fellow with stubble on his chin and a down-turned mouth that betrayed his surly nature. 'Women is nothing but trouble!' the fellow drawled. 'Take my woman . . . you've seen her in here, ain't yer?'

'Maggie, isn't it?' He'd seen her time and again; a slim-built creature with big sad eyes, and no wonder when she was kept little more than a beggar, and stayed beholden to a man who beat her till she was black and blue. But then, women did that to a man; they had a habit of bringing the worst out in even the mildest of chaps. Look how Cathy Blackthorn had led him on and then caused him to run. And now, because of her, he had to keep his distance from Blackburn . . . William Henry Street in particular. Still, though he might be a rogue and a coward, and only just managed to stay on the right side of the law, he didn't see himself as being as rotten as this fellow beside him. If it wasn't for the fact that he did a lot of underhand deals with the foul-smelling scoundrel, he'd tell him to piss off.

The last thing he wanted was to sit here and pass precious time with him. They had already done their business for the night, and now he had an urge to take Teresa upstairs.

The other fellow eyed him suspiciously. 'I'm surprised you remembered her name. But you're right, it is Maggie.' He tested Tony further. 'Hey! You've not got a hankering for her, 'ave yer?'

Tony Manners pointed to Teresa, who was preparing to sing. 'I've got my own entertainment,' he chuckled. 'Why would I hanker after anyone else's?'

The surly fellow turned his attention on Teresa. 'You know how to pick 'em, I'll say that for yer. She's a good looker an' no mistake.' Eyeing her up and down, he fancied her himself; a big girl in every respect, she had the most striking blue eyes, long brown hair that shone like silk in the hazy half-light, and a personality that drew every man's eyes to her. He sniggered. 'Good between the sheets, is she?'

'Wouldn't entertain her if she weren't.'

'Sings like a bird too. By all accounts, she'd do it for nothing more than the attention it gets her.' He tapped the side of his nose and winked. 'Clever of you to wheedle a paypacket out of the proprietor here. As a rule, he wouldn't part with the drippings of his nose.'

'She sings ... he pays. You don't get nothing for nothing.'

'He pays and you pocket it, eh?'

'None of your business.'

'All right, matey! Just being friendly.' Settling back in his seat, he made the snide comment, 'All the same, fancy you remembering Maggie's name.' He didn't want her, but he would cut the heart out of any man who thought he could take her from him.

'Don't make such a thing out of it,' Tony Manners warned. 'I've a good head for names, that's all. You can ask me the name of every man jack in this room, and I dare say I could tell you.' In the shady business of 'buying and selling', he had to know whose company he was keeping.

The other fellow seemed satisfied, but secretly he vowed to question Maggie about it later. 'There was a time when she was a raving beauty, but not now. Gone to seed she has.' He guffawed so loud everyone turned to glare at him, but they quickly averted their attention when he glared back. 'Fit for nothing now she is,' he continued. 'Can't seem to keep me satisfied no more. Yer can't blame a man for wandering, can yer, eh?' Drawing deeply on his cigar he exhaled the smoke over the man on his other side, but the man didn't complain. He didn't fancy being left for dead in the alley one dark night.

'Wander a lot, do you?'

'Every chance I get, matey.' Leaning sideways, he whispered, 'Being a man of the world yerself, you must have had yer fair share?'

'I'm not complaining.'

'Like me, I expect you've suffered for the sake of making a profit?'

'I don't follow.'

'What I mean is ... sometimes you have to butter a woman up, however much you'd rather put a bag over her head.' He sighed impatiently and took another drag on his cigar. 'There were this woman, d'yer see? Ruby I think 'er name were.' He coughed and spluttered and laughed through his words. 'Some bloody Ruby! You'd think with a name like that she'd be hot to the touch and raring to go. Not this one! This partic'lar Ruby were sixty if she were a day, and well past 'er prime.'

'So why would you want to butter her up?' In spite of himself he was intrigued.

'Use your brains, man! I found meself out in the country, stalking a young bugger who thought he could get one over on me. The housekeeper were a means to an end, weren't she? She worked in this big house ... had access to silver and the like. Through her, I got inside information, didn't I, eh? The silly old cow thought we'd be wed. She couldn't see I were using 'er.' He smiled from ear to ear. 'Trusting she were ... lonely and trusting. When they're like that, they tell yer things they don't even know they're telling yer.'

'I thought *I* were bad enough.'

'You've a long way to go afore you catch up wi' me.' His dirty face shone with pride.

The music softened and the order was given, 'Quiet now, men! Let the young lady sing.' The compère stepped back and

Teresa came into the spotlight. Her voice rang out loud and clear, vibrant and filled with emotion. All eyes were on her, and for a time you could have heard a pin drop.

Tony Manners congratulated himself on having acquired such a prize. On top of that, she doted on him. It couldn't be easier. With her voice and his shrewd business acumen, he believed he would be a richer man in no time. His temper shortened when the burly fellow interrupted. 'Never met Maggie's son, 'ave yer?'

'Can't say I have.' Picking up his glass, he took a long gulp of whisky. 'He's not *your* son, then?'

'She says he is, but there's times when I wonder.' A murderous look came into his face. 'Them two's as thick as thieves. Some time back he cleared off.' A dark satisfaction came into his face. 'He thought I couldn't find out where he were . . . hadn't reckoned on somebody being as artful as himself, the cocky bastard! But I never once let him know I were on to him. Oh no! I let him go on thinking he were getting one over on me, when all the time I were closer than his bleedin' shadow.'

'Watching him, were you?'

'Oh, I were doing much more than that.' He licked his lips. 'Anyway, after a while . . . back he comes, large as life, and his pockets bulging.' He groaned as though in pain. 'He never shared it with me though, the crafty bugger! Took off, he did, an' I ain't seen hide nor hair of him since.' Ramming the cigar into his mouth, he narrowed his eyes and spoke around it. 'If he knows what's good for him, he'll stay outta my way altogether.' There was menace in his voice, and madness in his eyes. 'I've an idea his mam knows where her precious Jack is. But if the pair of 'em think to cheat me out of my share, they'd best think again.'

'And you reckon this Jack might not be yours, eh?' Sniggering, Tony observed cunningly, 'Sounds to me like he's a chip off the old block.'

'Happen he's mine, and happen he ain't, but there's no two ways about it . . . Jack is a bad bugger all right.' He got a deal of satisfaction out of adding spitefully, 'Maggie thinks the sun shines out of his arse, but I keep telling her, one o' these fine days he'll swing from the end of a rope.'

'That's what people say about you.' Tony was taking his life into his hands, but thought himself a match for this clumsy bag of wind.

The burly fellow roared with laughter. 'Oh, an' they'd be right an' all!' he cried, much to the irritation of a nearby group who were intent on listening to Teresa sing. 'What the bloody hell are yer staring at, eh?' he yelled. 'Keep yer eyes frontard where they belong... less yer want 'em gouged outta yer head!' He laughed again when they turned away. But the music had stopped and Teresa was coming towards them. From the look on her face it was plain she did not like being upstaged.

'You might have the bloody decency to listen when I put myself out for you!' With her hands on her hips she stood in front of them, staring from one to the other and saving her most withering look for Tony Manners.

In a minute he was at her side, charming as ever, mentally calculating whether he should still demand payment from the proprietor. 'What makes you think I wasn't listening?' he coaxed. 'There might be some who don't appreciate you, my love, but not me.' He glanced scathingly at the burly fellow. 'I *know* a true songbird when I hear one.'

'Let's get out of here.' Sidling closer to him, she murmured in his ear, 'You and me on our own, eh? We could go back to your flat. You've been promising for ages to show me your place, but you never have.' It was a bone of contention with her. Before Tony came along, the only man in her life was her brother David. 'You know I worship the ground you walk on, but don't make a fool of me,' she muttered. 'I can be all the things you want, but one thing I *won't* be is a plaything you can use and throw away.'

He didn't like the tone of her voice, and he didn't care much for being threatened by any woman, yet he had to tread carefully, because though she talked like a navvy, she had the voice of an angel and *that* was what attracted him, nothing else. Still, he could play her game if that's what she wanted. 'I told you I'd take you to my place, and I will,' he told her. 'First things first, my beauty.'

Propelling her back-stage, he urged, 'Finish your song or we won't get paid, and if we don't get paid, how am I expected to provide a little love nest, eh?' He was a master of charm and deception.

'Put like that, how can I refuse?' Kissing him brazenly, she followed like a dog.

A few minutes later, she was on stage again; this time the house was quiet and her mentor had moved to a table far away from interruptions. He had made an investment in Teresa Leyton, and he was counting on a high return for his time and effort.

When she finished singing, the house erupted into applause. She bowed and smiled, and kept her beady eyes on the man who had brought her. 'I've done what you wanted,' she reminded him later. 'Now it's time you did what I want.' She put on her coat and wouldn't take no for an answer. As they passed him on their way out, the burly fellow winked obscenely. 'If you don't want her, I'll take her off your hands,' he offered in a slurred voice. When Teresa replied she would rather sleep with a hairy monkey, he fell back in his seat and howled with laughter.

He was still laughing a short time later when David came through the door. Convinced he had seen David before, he engaged him in conversation. 'Ain't you the brother of the one who sings here?' Recalling how she had snapped at him, he went on to describe her as 'the songbird with a sharp beak.' David ignored him, so he persisted, 'If I remember rightly, you and 'er boyfriend almost came to blows.' He thought it was an opportunity missed because he loved a good punch-up, but the cowardly Tony Manners took off rather than have his face put out of shape.

Not recognising the fellow, David didn't pay him much mind until he heard him sneer, 'You've missed the buggers this time, matey. They were 'ere one minute and gone the next.'

Peering through the rising clouds of tobacco smoke, David made certain Teresa was nowhere to be seen. Reluctantly, he asked the burly fellow, 'Was she with Tony Manners?'

'All over him.' He grinned meaningfully.

'Mind your mouth!' David stood over him, his dark eyes smouldering and fists clenched. 'I'm in no mood for your filthy jokes.'

The burly fellow sat up straight, his boozy features drooping to a scowl. He didn't take kindly to being spoken to like that. However, he took careful stock of this young man; the strong broad shoulders and the upright stance . . . the look of determination in the dark eyes. He knew he'd met his match. 'Get a move on, and you might catch 'em,' he grumbled. 'They ain't been gone above five minutes.'

David gave no answer. He left then, searching the dim-lit streets outside, looking for the familiar figure of his sister.

Seeing a likely chance, Maggie stepped forward from the alley where she'd been talking with her son, Jack. 'Got a spare coin for a poor lady?' Stretching out her hand she stared solemnly at David, smiling her gratitude when he thrust his hand into his trouser pocket and dropped a shilling into her palm. 'Thank you, sir,' she murmured, and would have slipped away if he hadn't called her back.

'Have you seen a couple come out of there in the last few minutes?' he asked anxiously. 'The man looks a slimy devil . . . you couldn't mistake him.' Pointing to the club, he explained, 'The young woman sings here occasionally . . . long brown hair . . . taller than you.'

Maggie laughed. 'Every woman in London must be taller than me!' she said. She saw how he was frantically searching up and down the street, and was sorry she couldn't help. 'I've only just come along meself,' she explained. 'Me and my son 'ere.' Turning, she called out, 'You ain't seen no couple come out o' the club, 'ave yer?' Only silence greeted her. 'Musta gone.' She smiled. 'I'll say good night, young fella, though I hope you find who you're looking for.'

'Thank you.' He didn't hear her reply. He was already making his way to the driver of a cab waiting nearby.

Maggie searched the alley. 'Jack!' All was quiet. Only the plaintive mewing of a cat disturbed the silence. 'Jack, you ignorant sod! Where are you?' She nearly jumped out of her skin when he stepped out of a doorway. 'Good God above! What the devil d'you think you're playing at?'

His crafty face leered at her under the lamplight. 'I might ask you the same thing, mother dear,' he mocked.

'What d'you mean?'

'Well! Darting out like that . . . begging for a copper. I've already told you we can set our sights higher now.'

'Bad habits die hard, our Jack.'

'We can take time to think what to do now.' He jutted out

his chin and smiled knowingly. 'Now that we've got summat tucked away . . . where *he'll* never find it.' He jerked a thumb in the direction of the club. When he looked at Maggie again she had a guilty expression on her face. 'Hey!' He took her by the shoulders and shook her. 'You've not told him, have you? Because if you have, I'm off, and this time I won't be back!'

'No.' Pushing him away she answered truthfully, 'I promised you I wouldn't tell, and I won't.' She lowered her head and stared at the ground. 'It's just that I'm frightened he'll find out somehow.' She raised her sad eyes. 'He knows you've come home flush . . . he don't know about the silver and such but he knows summat.'

'Let him think what he likes. He'll not find out. There's only you and me know what's stashed away.' Bunching his fists together, he hissed, 'It's all this bloody waiting! I want to get rid of the stuff *now* . . . any of the fences would turn it over for me. Tony Manners would give me a good price for it. But I daren't put the word out. Not yet. Not until the rozzers have given up on it.'

'Do you think they're on to you?'

'Naw, I don't think that. But they must be searching far and wide.' He glanced to the end of the alley. 'That bloke . . . the one you spoke to just now . . .'

'What about him?'

'He could be looking for me.'

'Why should he be looking for you? Anyway, you're wrong. He was asking after a couple.'

'Tricks! They're up to all manner o' tricks.' Lowering his voice he confided, 'That bloke knows the family I stole from. I fancied my chances with a young beauty called Cathy, but that bugger there scotched any hope o' that!' The memory of the night he took her against her will brought a flush of delight to his face. 'But I got to taste her afore I took off.'

Maggie grabbed him by the coat collar, her voice gruff as she told him, 'I hope you don't mean what I think you mean! If you're going the same way as him in there, I'll disown you, so help me I will!' She too had been taken against her will many times, and loathed the idea that her own son could cause another woman the pain and humiliation she herself had to suffer.

319

Pointing to her neck, she bared a long jagged scar. 'That great bully nearly did for me,' she grumbled. 'I don't want you ending up like him, d'you hear?'

'Get your paws off me!' Shaking her loose, he stepped back a pace. 'I don't know what I'm saying, that's all,' he lied. 'Seeing that bloke has put me right off me stride. His name's David Leyton.' Instinctively he stroked his face, momentarily feeling the crunch of David's fist. 'Him and me ... we had a bad run-in. One sniff that I'm here, an' he'll keep after me like a dog with a bone.'

'So that's why you hid just now?'

'Huh! Don't go away with the wrong idea. I didn't hide because I'm scared of the bugger. It's just that there's no sense looking for trouble, is there, eh?'

'You're right, son.' Glancing furtively about, she suggested, 'You'd best make tracks, but keep outta sight.' Glancing anxiously behind her, she hissed, 'I'd best be off. If I don't go inside now, he'll be out looking for me.'

Together they walked to the end of the alley. Long after Maggie had gone inside, Jack remained, his eyes turned towards the top of the street where David stood talking to the cab-driver.

'Want a fare, matey?' The driver was seated up top, warmly wrapped against the evening and enjoying his clay pipe.

'Not yet,' David answered. He explained he was looking for a couple; the young woman was his sister and he had to find her. When the cab-driver shook his head and said he'd been taking a nap while he waited, David thanked him. 'I'll walk the length of the street and ask in a few of the cafés,' he decided. 'But I've a feeling I'll not find her tonight.'

'The city's a big place. If you want the advice of them as knows, you'd do better to get off home and start again in the daylight.'

'I reckon you're right. But I can't give up so easily.' He glanced back at the club. 'Wait here,' he said. 'I'll only be a minute'

'I'll wait half the night as long as you pay me,' came the chirpy retort.

Inside the club, David sought out the proprietor. 'Sorry, but I can't help you.' Beads of sweat ran down the podgy face as he blatantly lied to the young man who had caused trouble here once before. 'I've no idea where Tony Manners might have gone with your sister.'

'Do you know where he lives?'

'Not a clue!'

'Are they likely to come back tonight?'

'Naw. She's done her singing for the evening. Mr Manners didn't book her in again.' He smiled cunningly. 'Happen he's got her booked in at the Palladium,' he jeered. 'Manners has his sights set higher than a flea-pit like this. He's got the push and she's got the voice. It wouldn't surprise me if he didn't get her right to the top.' He lowered his voice. 'From what I'm told, he owns properties in the North. Happen he's taken her there?'

'And happen you're trying to send me on a wild-goose chase!' David had taken an instant dislike to this greasy fellow. 'Another Manners in the making,' he muttered as he returned to the cab. 'You're right,' he admitted to the cab-driver, 'I'll not find her tonight. The rat's returned to his hole and he's taken her with him, but he's bound to show his face again, and when he does, I'll be waiting.' With that he gave directions and settled back in his seat. 'Property in the North, eh?' he mused aloud. 'I wonder?' It could be a ruse as he suspected. He didn't doubt that Manners owned properties everywhere. Scavengers like that made good by climbing on the backs of others. Manners was a bad lot and, one way or another, David had to make Teresa see that.

Maria took the news well. 'You've done your best,' she said. 'You can't do no more.'

'I'll make another search tomorrow night,' he promised.

Maria wouldn't hear of it. 'No! I've been giving it some thought, and I've decided she's caused us both enough heartache. Now she can get on with it. She'll come home of her own accord, you'll see. When she realises what a bad 'un she's got mixed up with, she'll run home with her tail between her legs. Till then, we'll leave her to her own devices. She'll not listen to anything we say; so let her learn the hard way.' She was adamant, and nothing David could say would convince her otherwise.

The runner fell against the wall, gasping for breath, his feet aching, and his heart pounding. 'Must want my head tested!' he groaned. 'Who the hell would want to run round Whitechapel at this time of night – and all for a bleedin' shilling!' Looking up at the big old building, he was just thankful he had the right place. The derelict warehouse had been turned into a tenement, with each room rented out to make the owner a fortune. 'Shouldn't be surprised if Manners don't own *this* place an' all,' he grumbled, going inside.

At the top of the stairs, he took out the note which the proprietor had given him. After reading it, he glanced along the doors and smiled when his eyes alighted on the right one. 'Number four,' he muttered, quickening his steps towards it. 'That's the one!'

He knocked on the door for a third time, and still there was no answer. Gingerly, he pushed open the door and poked his head inside. 'Mr Tony Manners?' He knew this fellow's reputation and didn't want to get on the wrong side of him. 'Anybody there?' he called. From the adjoining room came a series of grunts and strange noises. 'Hello?' He came into the room, shouted again, then went carefully towards the second door. It was slightly open, so he bent his head to peep inside. What he saw brought a smile to his face and held him mesmerised.

Teresa was lying on top of the bed with her legs wide open, and in between them lay Tony Manners, feverishly working up and down, his hands clutching her breasts. 'GO ON!' she was crying. 'NOW! NOW!' The two of them were rocking the bed until the floorboards bounced.

'Bleedin' hell! They'll be through the floor next!' The more they worked themselves into a frenzy, the wider grew the runner's eyes, until they were all but popping from his head.

Excited to fever pitch himself, he made a noise that caused Tony Manners to jerk round. 'We've got a Peeping Tom.' Teresa just giggled.

Manners jumped off the bed and ran across the room. The onlooker was slow to move, his attention held by Manners' erect penis as he rushed towards him. The next thing he felt was a fist in his face.

When he awoke again Manners was standing over him, fully

322

dressed and bursting with rage. 'You'd best explain yourself!' he snapped. 'Well? I'm waiting!'

Teresa was waiting too; lounging on the bed and smiling at him with wicked eyes. He had the feeling she was ready for more, and she didn't care who mounted her.

Struggling to his feet, the runner gasped, 'I've come from the club . . . the boss sent me.' Quickly, before he could get another smack in the mouth, he grabbed the crumpled letter from his pocket and thrust it at Manners.

After reading the letter, he ordered the runner out, kicking his arse as he went. 'Tell your boss he's lucky I didn't have your head from your shoulders!' he yelled. But the runner was long gone, down the stairs, away up the street, and looking for a woman, *any* woman. What he'd seen was enough to send a man crazy!

'What does it say?' Teresa watched as Manners read the letter again.

'He's persistent, I'll say that for him.' He flung the letter at her. 'I might have to go to drastic lengths to keep your brother off my back.'

She scanned the letter and dropped it to the floor. 'You'll not lay a finger on him,' she warned. Getting up from the bed she came and stood before him. Opening her robe to show her nakedness, she invited brazenly, 'Ready to finish, are you?'

His hands shot out and grabbed her by the throat. 'Don't *ever* tell me who I can and can't lay a finger on.' His fingers tightened. When she began to choke, he took one hand away and fetched it so hard across her mouth that she was thrown to the bed. Then he stripped off, got on top of her, and the two of them were soon once again finding delight in each other.

Afterwards he fell asleep. She went to the mirror and examined herself; her throat was still red-raw, a trickle of blood had dried on her mouth, and her face was badly bruised. 'This is *your* fault, Mam!' she muttered. 'Yours and David's . . . To hell with the pair of you!' With that she splashed her face with cold water from the bowl, then climbed back into bed and snuggled up to her man. 'It wasn't your fault,' she murmured. 'I don't blame you, sweetheart.' She hugged him closer when he stirred. He slyly smiled, and planned how he might use her.

Maria was right. The week after David haunted the nightspots of London looking for her, Teresa turned up. Late on Saturday afternoon, in a blistering heatwave, she got out of a cab in the village and started across the fields. It was quite a walk and, still weak from yet another fierce beating at the hands of Tony Manners, she stopped several times for a rest. 'Bloody place!' she grumbled. 'Only rabbits and vermin live this far away from civilisation.' Three times she tripped over molehills, and once she stepped on an ants' nest. She rested, and swore, rested again and strode out; until at last, though it was still a good way off, she had the cottage in sight.

Hot and tired, with her best shoes covered in a film of dust and the hem of her skirt knitted with bracken, she was itching for a fight ... with her mam ... with David ... it didn't matter. She blamed them both for her dilemma and she was here to let them know it.

David arrived home at twenty minutes to five; he had been at work since quarter to six that morning, and was glad to be back under his own roof. 'Your mam's asleep,' said Nancy Proctor, a dear old soul who lived on a nearby farm. Taken on by David to look after his mam while he was out at work, she was strong as an ox, trustworthy, and used to ruling the roost. 'I've a nice rabbit stew cooking,' she announced, giving him a wrinkly smile. 'It'll be on the table in half an hour. Time enough for you to wash and change.'

'Smells wonderful!' David replied enthusiastically. He hadn't the heart to say he would have preferred a cold pie or a hank of bacon and some fresh baked bread.

A peek into Maria's room showed she was still asleep, so he quietly closed the door and went upstairs to his room. Here he sat on the bed edge, his head in his hands and his mind far away. Since leaving Cathy behind there had been days when he questioned the purpose of what he was doing; days when he thought he couldn't go on without her. Today had been such a day. 'Oh, Cathy! Cathy! Without you, nothing seems worthwhile any more.' He let the wonderful memories flow through him, before shaking her from his thoughts.

Washed and changed, he went back downstairs. He was making his way to Maria's room when Nancy Proctor's voice gently called out, 'Don't disturb her. She's still fast and hard asleep. Time enough to wake her when the dinner's ready.'

Feeling a little lost, he wandered outside. The sun was still hot, and there was no breeze whatsoever. Rolling up the sleeves of his shirt, he went to the pump and filled the two buckets there. Taking them to the kitchen, he was told, 'Your mam's awake now. Fetch her to the table if you like. So long as she's well supported, it'll do her good.'

Maria was thrilled. 'I like it when the two of us sit down together,' she said, smiling up at him as he tucked her safely into the carver. 'It'll be like old times.'

They talked, and laughed, and for a while Teresa was forgotten. Mrs Proctor washed and dried the dishes and quietly left when her husband came to fetch her on the cart. David and his mam remained at the table, talking about this and that; mainly about when David would likely lose his job, and what they might do when the time came. 'Don't you worry your head about it,' he insisted. 'Happen it'll be a blessing in disguise.'

'You're up to summat,' she answered. 'Come on, out with it.'

'When the auction comes up, I mean to be there,' he confessed. 'I mean to buy the field for market gardening, and the two cottages with it.'

Maria was astounded, but she didn't dash his hopes altogether. 'It's all very well wanting to be a property owner, son,' she said kindly, 'and I don't doubt that one day you'll get what you're after. But, well . . . where would you ever get that kind of money?'

'I've been working every hour God sends, and though it probably isn't enough, I've saved a fair bit.' His smile was that of a confident man. 'I may never get another chance like this, Mam,' he said softly. The smile dropped away and his face was set with determination. 'Trust me. I'll have the money on the day because, by one means or another, I intend to have that field, this cottage, and Ted's as well. He's a good man, and he'll be invaluable when I start up my own market-gardening business.'

Teresa's voice cut through the air, startling them. 'Why don't you ask Tony Manners to lend you the money? He'll deal with *anyone*, even you.' There was malice in her face. But it wasn't the malice David saw. It was the dark bruises on her cheekbone, and the angry wound to the top of her neck.

Springing to his feet, he took hold of her by the shoulders, his dark eyes examining the marks. 'He did this to you, didn't he?' he demanded angrily. 'The cowardly bastard! Well, now he'll get a taste of his own medicine. Where is he? Where's he hiding?' If he had Tony Manners here he wouldn't be able to control himself. 'You might as well tell me where he's hiding, because however long it takes, I'll find him anyway.'

Twisting from his grasp, Teresa faced him with hostility. 'Search from one end of London to the other, you won't find him.'

'Oh, I'll find him all right, and when I do, it'll be a long time before he beats a woman again.'

'He's gone away . . . on business.'

Maria had remained silent until now. When she spoke it was to Teresa, and in a voice that her daughter didn't easily recognise. 'Answer me one thing,' she asked harshly. 'Do you mean to go back to the fella as did this to you?'

Teresa laughed out loud. 'If he'll have me, yes.'

'Then you should be ashamed of yourself.'

'Well, I'm not!'

David couldn't believe his ears. 'Then it's *us* who should be ashamed of you.' His dark gaze raked her. 'Do you really mean to take up with him again?'

'Just as soon as I'm able.' She narrowed her eyes. 'If you come between us, I'll hate you for as long as I live.'

Something in her manner touched him deep down. 'Don't worry,' he answered stiffly. 'I won't stain my hands with him. If you still want the coward after he's done that to you . . .' – he raised his hand and gestured angrily to her face— 'then I reckon the two of you deserve each other.' That said, he lifted Maria from the seat and carried her back to her bed as though she weighed no more than a child.

'She's her own worst enemy,' Maria murmured sadly. 'She'll break our hearts, and I'd still have to love her.'

On 8 June Cathy took a turn for the better. For days she had

been delirious with a fever that even the doctor didn't understand, and had at last been taken to the Infirmary. At one
stage he warned Margaret to: 'Prepare yourself for the worst.'
Margaret stayed by her bedside and prayed through the night.
'Don't leave me, sweetheart,' she whispered, and slowly but
surely Cathy fought her way back. They told Margaret a deep
infection had invaded Cathy's body. Margaret listened but was
convinced it was not Cathy's body that had been invaded but
her heart and soul.

'You want me to see a *priest*?' Cathy was sitting up now,
allowed out of her bed for two hours at a time when she would
sit for a while in the chair or take a gentle walk down the ward
on Margaret's arm. 'Why would I want to see a priest?' She
smiled and her face was lit with a special kind of beauty. 'Unless
you think I should confess my sins?' she said. It struck her then,
that she did have sins to confess. Sins that had weighed her
down until she was crippled. Yet she wasn't ready to talk about
the things that remained hidden deep down inside her. Maybe
she never would be.

'I'm not suggesting you have sins to confess,' Margaret
explained. 'And I thank God that you are getting stronger by
the day. But I won't rest until you shed the pain inside. There
are things you've never talked about, Cathy ... things that
almost took you from me. Awful things that you keep so deep
inside that they grow and fester.' Taking Cathy's hands in hers,
she pleaded, 'Please, sweetheart. If you can't talk to me about
it, then talk to a man of God ... let *him* help you come to
terms with what troubles you.'

Cathy raised her eyes, soft green pools that shone with love
for this woman who had given her everything. She didn't speak.
Instead she met Margaret's gaze until the tears spilled over her
lashes and trickled down her nightgown. There was so much
pain that it tore at her like a claw. All the years of her young
life she had lived every minute, every hour, every day, always
yearning for what she could never have. She had weathered the
storms and dismissed her mother's hatred, making herself
believe it didn't really matter; after all, she had Margaret, and
that was enough. She told herself these things, not fully realising that the yearning to be loved and wanted by her own mother
would never really go away. And later so many awful things, all

adding to that hard knot that grew daily inside her ... the child she had lost, the love she would never have. The grieving, the disappointments and the broken dreams, all suppressed. Maybe it was time to let them out, to destroy them before they destroyed her.

'You don't need to say anything,' Margaret assured her. 'Not now. Wait until you're feeling a little stronger, then maybe we'll talk again ... if you want to?'

Cathy clung to her. 'I want to,' she promised, and just admitting her need seemed to lighten the burden a little.

Hopeful now, and knowing that Cathy would think about what she had said, Margaret told her, 'I had a letter from Ruby this morning.' Anticipating Cathy's next question, she went on, 'Apparently she's traced David as far as Cambridge, where he worked on a farm for a while. But he's moved on ... gone nearer to London.'

'I'm not sure she should be tramping the roads like that.' Since Margaret had confirmed that Ruby had indeed promised to bring David back, Cathy had fretted over her. 'I think you should ask her to come home. Even if she finds David, he won't want to see me. When he left he was filled with loathing. Nothing has happened to change that.'

Margaret was coy. 'Are you saying you never want to see him again?'

'Not if he still hates me.'

'You don't know that. After he left, he may have realised how much he misses you.'

Cathy smiled a sad smile. 'I don't think so, otherwise he would have come back. And don't say he wouldn't know where to start looking, because if he wanted to find me badly enough, he would leave no stone unturned.' Like I would, she thought. If I believed for one minute that he loved me, I would spend my life searching the four corners of the earth. 'Bring Ruby home,' she pleaded. 'I miss her.'

'If that's what you really want?'

'It is.'

'All right.' In a strange way, Margaret was relieved. 'I'll put pen to paper and post a letter this very evening.'

'You mustn't worry about me now,' Cathy told her. 'I'm

stronger in myself, and the doctor says it won't be too long before I'm home.' Kissing her goodbye, she said quietly, 'About . . . the priest. I promise I'll keep in mind what you said.'

'That's all I ask, sweetheart.' Margaret left then, and Cathy thought about their conversation. One thing was certain. 'Ruby's coming home. And David really has gone for good.' She must come to terms with it, in the same way she must learn to come to terms with everything else that had shaped her life. Since losing the child, and then suffering the illness that had sapped her will to live, she had seen nowhere to turn. She would talk to the priest, and ask God's forgiveness for letting the badness grow inside her.

True to her word, Margaret wrote to Ruby at the address she had been given in the last correspondence:

Dear Ruby,
    It's time you came home. Like Cathy, I feel you have done more than was expected of you.
    Cathy believes David can't love her, and now I believe she may be right. She wants you home, and so do I. We miss you.
    Love from us both.
    Margaret

CHAPTER TWELVE

Ruby thanked the blacksmith. 'Morton Farm, you say? You're certain it's a Mr David Leyton who works there?'

'The very same.' Taking a rag from his apron pocket, he blew his nose; a surprisingly small nose for a giant of a man. 'Him and Ted fetch the shires in regular ... loves his animals, does David.' He blew his nose again. 'It's a pity the farm's being sold off next month. By rights a man like that should have his own land.'

After all her searching, Ruby had to be sure. 'What does he look like?'

The blacksmith chuckled. 'It's your man all right,' he declared. 'David Leyton by name ... tall and built like a young bull, brown-eyed with a mop of dark hair.' He thought for a minute before saying cautiously, 'He always has a smile and a cheery word, but I get the feeling he has troubles he keeps to himself.'

'What kind of troubles?'

'Who knows what troubles a man has? Money troubles ... woman troubles. All I know is he's got troubles of a family kind, what with his mam being old and frail, and that sister of his coming and going all the time. But if you ask me it has nothing at all to do with any of that. Oh, no. It's summat he doesn't talk about, and who can blame him? Sometimes a man has secrets he doesn't want spread about.'

'If you'll kindly point me in the right direction, I'll be on my way.' Ruby was relieved and delighted to have found him at last, though she was faintly apprehensive about the reception she might receive. According to Cathy, David had left with feelings of animosity towards her. Maybe he still felt the same. But, for Cathy's sake, she had to find out once and for all.

'I'll take you there if you like?' he offered. 'I've a quiet morning for a change . . . first cob not arriving till mid-morning, and only two fillies to shoe after that.'

The cart was surprisingly comfortable. The bench was padded, and the springs had been treated so they easily rode the bumps. 'Built this myself,' the blacksmith told her. 'Took me nigh on a year.' He stroked it like a baby. Ruby broadened his smile by saying she thought it was the grandest cart she had ever ridden on.

Inside the cottage, Maria was demanding the answers to a few questions. 'What makes you want to stay with a man who could treat you like that?'

Teresa's temper had not improved in the few days she had spent here. 'I don't pry into your personal life!' she snapped.

'That's because I don't have one,' came the swift reply.

'Just leave me alone.' She had been brushing her hair but threw the brush across the room. 'I'll not trouble you any longer than I have to,' she snarled. 'Matter of fact, I'll be glad to see the back of you . . . nag nag nag! That's all you've done since I got here.'

Maria reached out of bed to collect the brush from the floor where it had landed. 'If you can't behave in a civilised manner, I'll be glad to see the back of *you* an' all,' she declared.

Walking across the room, Teresa remained defiant but a little subdued. 'I hate it here,' she moaned. 'I've got used to the bright lights. That's where I want to be. In the heart of London's night-life.'

In spite of everything, Maria loved her daughter, and it showed in her voice as she said softly, 'With *him*? After what he did to you?'

'I'd rather be with him than with anyone . . . even you.'

Maria's eyes clouded over. 'You know how to hurt your mam,' she said. 'But I won't always be here, so you must do what you feel right for yourself.'

'Oh, I will.' Collecting the brush from Maria's hand she moved away, standing before the mirror, attending to her hair and examining the fading bruises on her neck and face. 'I think I've been here long enough to teach the bugger a lesson. Come tomorrow, I'll be on my way.'

'Will we see you again?'

'Not if I can help it.'

'Don't be cruel, our Teresa,' Maria pleaded. 'I'll always love you, you know that.' She hated the rift her daughter had caused. 'It would do my heart good if you could make it up with David. He loves you too ... in spite of everything.' When Teresa gave no answer, she went on, 'While we have a roof over our heads, you'll always be welcome, you know that.'

Smiling slyly, Teresa taunted, 'Seems to me it's a good job I can take care of myself, because as far as I can see, once the farm's sold, *I* might be the only one with a roof over my head.'

'You're a wicked little bugger!'

'But you love me, eh?' She counted on it.

'God help me for it.' Maria was angry with herself. 'But I'm still your mam when all's said and done.'

Leaning on the cupboard, Teresa regarded her mother with a thoughtful expression. 'I seem to remember you always saved for a rainy day,' she said coaxingly. 'Have you got anything hidden away?'

'I might have.' Maria could read her mind, but she feigned ignorance. 'Why?'

'I need to borrow a few shillings ... enough to get me back to London. Come to think of it, a guinea would suit me fine.'

Maria laughed. 'I expect it would,' she replied. 'But you'll not get a guinea from me, my girl!'

'A few shillings then?'

'We'll see.'

'I could find your money and take it. You couldn't stop me.'

'You'd better think again!' Reaching down under the bed-clothes, Maria drew out the long sturdy stick which David had made for her. Pointing it at Teresa she said coldly, 'Try taking what ain't yours, and you might be sorry.'

Knowing she would have to change her approach if she was to get what she needed, Teresa laughed out loud. 'I was only fooling,' she lied, 'I would never take what wasn't mine.'

Not altogether satisfied, Maria nodded. Putting the stick away, she was surprised to hear a knock on the front door. 'Whoever's that?' she queried, craning her neck to see through the window. 'We don't usually get visitors out here.'

'Happen it's Tony ... full of remorse and come to find me!'

Rushing out of the room, she ran to the front door. As she opened it, her mouth fell open when she saw who it was. For a split second she hadn't been certain, but then it all came flooding back . . . her father's affair with the wife of his landlord . . . Rita Blackthorn's murder . . . the hanging . . . and more than that, she recalled David's fondness for Cathy Blackthorn, a fondness that had deepened to love.

Her first instinct urged her to strike out, to send Ruby flying into the mud, but she hadn't forgotten her own part in it all . . . the deception that split her brother from his sweetheart . . . the deliberate firing of the cottage. Her mind raced ahead. She must play it clever, like before. Fear cautioned her, sweetening her tongue. 'It's Ruby Adams, isn't it?'

In spite of Teresa's smile, Ruby had the feeling she wasn't welcome. 'For a minute there, I thought you might have forgotten me.'

Ignoring her comment, Teresa remarked, 'You're a long way from home. What's brought you here . . . to *this* house?' All kinds of possibilities flew through her guilty mind. 'What is it you want with us?'

'I've come to see your brother.'

'He's not home.' She was more than curious. 'Can I help?'

'I don't think so. I've come on a delicate matter.' Ruby spoke softly. 'It's to do with Cathy. She had an unfortunate accident.' It was on the tip of her tongue to explain that Cathy had lost the child because of her fall, but something stopped her. That kind of information was not for everyone's ears. 'She's very ill. Her aunt and I feel it would help her if David could spare the time to come and see her. They parted on such bad terms, you see.' Before Teresa could take it all in, she went on, 'The big house was sold soon after you left the area. We're living in Blackburn town now . . . William Henry Street.'

Teresa's fears heightened. If David should ever find out how she'd come between him and Cathy, he might seek his revenge by doing the same with her and Tony. She had to think fast. 'I'm sorry to hear about Cathy Blackthorn,' she lied convincingly. 'But I have to tell you, your journey has been wasted.'

'Oh?' Ruby had feared as much. 'Why is that?'

Convinced she would get away with her lies, Teresa actually

334

invited Ruby in, but was glad when the invitation was gratefully declined. 'David's feelings haven't changed,' she went on. 'He has never forgiven Cathy or her family for what happened to our dad. We've made a good life out here. David has a new love now. She's carrying his child, and they're due to be wed soon.' She looked dejected. 'I'm so sorry,' she sighed. 'David can be stubborn when he puts his mind to it. He was closer to our dad than anyone, and now he'll never forget or forgive. He's trying to put it all behind him. If you have any thought for him at all, you'll leave us be.' Inwardly panic-stricken, she reached out to touch Ruby's hand. 'Please,' she begged. 'You must see it's all for the best?'

Ruby was devastated. Her journey was all for nothing. She was hurt to think that David could not find it in his heart to forgive, and she might have said as much, but there was no point. It would not mend things between Cathy and David, though it might easily deepen his bitterness. 'A bairn on the way, and soon to be wed, eh?' she murmured, and her heart went out to Cathy.

Secretly gloating, Teresa dared to insist that she come in for a cup of tea. 'You look like you could do with one.'

Ruby shook her head. 'No. You're very kind, but I must be on my way home now.' Half-turning, she said, 'Happen it'll be best if you don't mention it to David that I've been here. As you say, if he still harbours bad feeling, there'll be nothing gained by him knowing of my visit.' As an afterthought she said kindly, 'I hope he'll be happy with his new love. Good day to you now.'

When the cart had rumbled away, taking Ruby with it, Maria called out to Teresa. She sat bolt upright in her bed and demanded to know, 'Why did you tell her such a pack of lies?'

'You heard then?' She was unrepentant, concerned only that Maria might tell David what had taken place here.

'I should have called out ... told the poor woman what a liar you are!'

'Then what? Think what you're saying, you old fool!' Threateningly, she came towards the bed. 'David has no thought for any other woman but Cathy Blackthorn. If he knew how I'd deceived him before – well, like as not he'd strangle me with his bare hands. And if he were to find out she's ill and asking for him, he would move heaven and earth to be with her. Don't imagine for one minute that he'd give *you* a second thought. Especially when I tell him how *you* are as much to blame for letting him believe Cathy wanted no truck with him!'

The awful words tumbled from her mouth to frighten her mother half out of her wits. 'What! He'd be gone, and you'd be left here on your own, because *I* don't intend to stay around a minute longer than I have to.' She bent her head to stare Maria in the face. 'Is that what you want, Mam? To have him flay me alive, and then to be left on your own?' Maria huddled into herself, more afraid than she had ever been in her life. 'Answer me! Is that what you want?'

The whisper was barely audible. 'I won't tell him.'

'Of course you won't, Mam.' Teresa was smiling again, pleased with herself. 'Now, about that guinea?' Holding out her palm, she waited.

Maria had no intention of letting her see where she kept her cash. 'Later,' she said, 'I'll find you a guinea later.' Then she fell back into the bed and lay with her eyes wide open and her breathing irregular. 'You'll be the death of me yet,' she muttered.

'Not till I've got my guinea.' Teresa left the room giggling. This time tomorrow she would be back with Tony. The thought of it made her burst into song.

Having eavesdropped on the conversation between Ruby and the young woman, the blacksmith turned it all over in his mind as they travelled back to Ilford. After a long silence, he decided to speak his mind. 'You can say it's none of my business,' he began, 'but I told you I had an idea there was something troubling that young fella . . .'

Ruby wasn't paying much attention. Instead she was thinking of Margaret and Cathy. 'Sorry, what were you saying?'

Drawing into the kerb, he climbed down and proceeded to help Ruby off the cart. 'I was just saying how I had an idea there was something troubling him.' He cocked his head and grinned at having learned a secret. 'All the same, I would never have guessed he was about to become husband and father all at the same time.'

'What do I owe you?' Now that it was over, she couldn't wait to get home to those she loved.

'Nothing at all.' Before she could offer him a fare he quickly drove the equipage away, geeing up the old horse as he went.

That very evening, Ruby was given a letter that had been forwarded from her previous boarding house. 'I hope it isn't bad news, my dear,' the kindly landlady said.

It wasn't bad news. Margaret was calling her home. 'It's me who'll be carrying bad news to you,' Ruby murmured as she packed her bag. Cathy had been right. David may have adored her once, but that was a lifetime ago.

CHAPTER THIRTEEN

Cathy was adamant. Seated in the chair at her hospital bedside, she looked first at Ruby, then Margaret. 'I expect you've found David,' she said calmly. 'He isn't here, so I can only think he wants nothing to do with me.'

Margaret quietly regarded her niece, and for the first time in her life came close to deception. Cathy was still very poorly. It was true she had recovered from the infection that nearly took her from them, and it was true that with every day she grew a little stronger. But she was painfully thin, and her face was white as chalk. Her lovely green eyes still held a deep secret agony, and Margaret was afraid for her. 'Ruby's home with us now,' she said evasively. 'Soon you'll be home as well, and the three of us can start rebuilding our lives. Isn't that enough for now?'

Cathy remained calm, her hands gripping the chair-arms, the need to know overriding everything else. 'Please. I have to know what he said.'

Uncomfortable beneath Cathy's intent gaze and knowing how she was bound to be hurt, Margaret hesitated. Lowering her gaze to the floor, she wondered how she might soften the blow.

Cathy sensed her dilemma. 'I know he's never coming back to me,' she said, and just for a second her voice broke on a sob. When she spoke again, it was with great dignity. There was no trace of anguish in her face. Looking at Ruby, she said softly, 'When I realised you had gone to search for David, I was angry and hurt. But I know you did it because you love me, and I'm deeply grateful for that.'

More than once since her return, Ruby had regretted ever having gone; she regretted it now. 'It was wrong of me,' she answered. 'But I thought I were doing it for the best.'

Putting out her hand to hold Ruby's, Cathy told her honestly, 'I know that, Ruby, and I love you for it.' Returning her attention to Margaret, she said, 'I know you were both thinking of me. Now, though, if you want me to rebuild my life, I have to know everything. How was David? Where is he working? What did he say?' Hardening her heart against him was difficult, but she had to do it if she was ever to grow away from him. 'Please . . . I need to know.'

Margaret pondered. There was no way to soften the truth, and so she came right out with it. 'David is about to be wed.' She took a deep breath, waiting for Cathy's reaction, waiting to comfort her. She had deliberately kept back the fact that David was also about to become a father. Margaret had not forgotten it was losing the child that had almost pushed Cathy over the edge. For reassurance, she glanced at Ruby, visibly relaxing when Ruby gave her a nod.

Reeling inside from the news that David had found himself a new love, a woman he was about to make his wife, Cathy fought with the turmoil of emotions that threatened to overwhelm her. She remembered every word he had ever said to her, every gesture, every promise. He had told her lovingly that one day he would make *her* his wife. It had been the dream that carried her into womanhood, and now it was gone. The dream was over, and he was making a life with someone else.

'I'm sorry, sweetheart.' Margaret knew the news must have shaken Cathy to her soul. She was angry too. 'If he could hate you for what someone else did, then he isn't worth a second thought. Put him out of your mind.'

Cathy had seen the look that passed between her aunt and Ruby. She knew them of old. 'There's something you're not telling me,' she persisted. 'I need to know *everything*.'

This time it was Ruby who answered, and it was in the softest of voices. 'What your aunt says is right, child,' she remarked. 'A man who could turn his back on you like that . . . well, he ain't worth spit.' She wrinkled her face in disgust.

'You *are* keeping something from me, Ruby? What is it?'

She hesitated. It was obvious Cathy would not be satisfied until she knew it all. 'You allus did know what were going on in ol' Ruby's mind,' she admitted with a helpless smile. 'You're right. There *is* summat else.' Taking a deep breath she went on, 'David is getting wed right enough. He's also on his way to being a father.' Like Margaret she feared what the news might do to Cathy. After all she'd been through, it was one more blow.

'Thank you for telling me.' Cathy sat back in her seat, her hands fiercely gripping the chair-arms and her eyes closed. It had all come as a shock, yet in one way she was not surprised. 'It's only natural that David should make a new life,' she said presently. 'He's a handsome hard-working man, with a good kind heart.' Before they could question such a statement, she went on, 'I don't blame him for feeling the way he did ... and for wanting to make a fresh start.'

Margaret was not so forgiving. 'All the same, he had no call to blame you.'

Sitting up straight, she looked at Margaret, her smile warm and reassuring. 'I know,' she admitted simply. 'I could never harbour any hatred for him, but we all have to deal with loss in our own way. He was always close to his father, so his loss was greater than mine.' In her heart she had always understood David's bitterness about his father's hanging. 'I wish him well,' she went on. 'I'm glad he's found a new love. In fact, I'm grateful for it, because now I can put him behind me and look forward to a new life of my own.'

'By! You never fail to amaze me, child.' Shaking her head slowly from side to side, Ruby admired her determination. She had seen this lovely young woman suffer one crisis after another, and each time Cathy had found the strength to overcome it.

Margaret said nothing but got out of her chair and came to where her niece sat. Putting an arm round her shoulders, she hugged her close and for a precious moment the two of them remembered how it all used to be. Ruby's eyes swam with tears; she murmured her goodbyes, and tactfully left them alone.

Some moments later, when Margaret joined her outside, she asked worriedly, 'Do you reckon the lass'll be all right?'

'I think so, Ruby. It won't be easy for her, but now she knows David is out of her reach, she has little choice but to forget he ever existed.'

'What about the child she lost? That's summat else that's preyed on her mind.'

'Like I said, Ruby, it won't be easy.' Margaret had one hope

341

above all else. 'Just now, she promised to see the priest when she comes home. I feel he can help.'

'D'you think she'll tell him who fathered the child?'

'I don't know. For her own sake, I pray she'll tell him everything.'

Waiting on the side of the road for the wagons and carriages to pass, Ruby had a dreadful thought. 'If she's to start afresh, I hope it isn't with that awful Tony Manners!'

Margaret had no time to reply because suddenly there was a gap in the traffic and the two of them ran across the road. All the way home, she considered Ruby's comment, and it raised all manner of anxieties in her mind.

'I see your visitors have gone?' The nurse, with her big blue eyes and masses of fair hair spilling from beneath her cap, had a waist that was no bigger than a child's. She tidied the bed and smiled like nurses do, then hurried away.

Cathy sat in the chair for what seemed an age. Supper came and went. She was ushered into bed and soon afterwards the lights were put out for the night. From her bed she watched the nurses change shift, and smiled when the auxiliary dropped the contents of a bedpan all over the floor.

After a while all was quiet. She thought about Margaret and Ruby, and vowed never again to do anything that would make them worry about her. She thought about David and his new love and her heart was like a lead weight inside her. 'Be happy, David,' she murmured. She smiled at the memories, and her eyes clouded when she thought about the way it had all gone wrong.

Suddenly her love for him was like a great rushing tide inside her; regrets, emotions and lost dreams, all mingled together, washing everything else before them. Steeling herself against the feelings that threatened to destroy her, she buried her head in the pillow. Then the sobs came, long aching sobs that racked her body and carried her to a restless nightmare-haunted slumber. She would be strong. She would be all that Margaret and Ruby wanted. But she could not be happy. Never again could she be truly happy without him.

On 1 July, Cathy went into Blackburn market for the first time in months. Margaret insisted on accompanying her. 'You may be well, thank God,' she argued, 'but you're still not strong enough to be out on your own.'

'All right,' Cathy conceded. 'But only if we can walk all the way.'

At the kitchen doorway, Ruby stood beaming with delight. She and Margaret had worried about Cathy, but the lass was good as her word; she got up in the morning with a smile on her face, and she spent the day keeping herself busy. She had even taken on the task of teaching one of the street children to read. She laughed and chatted, and it was good to see how happy she was becoming.

'Let the lass walk,' Ruby called out. 'It's a grand day and the market ain't too far.' As they went out of the door, she ran after them. 'Fetch me some darning thread,' she instructed. 'I caught me stockings on the mangle and now there's a hole as big as a midden.' Taking a sixpence from her pinnie pocket, she put it into Cathy's hand. 'I'm that proud of you, lass,' she muttered, and with that she went at a run back into her kitchen. 'Me muffins!' she cried. 'The buggers'll be burnt to a crisp!'

As they went down the street, womenfolk stopped them to chat. 'Good to see you home again, young lady,' commented Ada Snettleton. One neighbour pointed out it was time the landlord found a buyer for the empty house. 'There'll be rats running round us feet next!' said Fred Arlinton. Lottie Barnett wanted to know why Tony Manners hadn't been to collect the rent himself. 'He sends a snotty-nosed lad round,' she complained. 'A nasty piece o' work in the making that one.' Her ma-in-law had taken a particular dislike to the young fellow in question. 'He wants dipping in the canal,' she grumbled through her toothless pink gums. 'Looks to me like he ain't had a wash in a month o' Sundays!'

Cathy was still chuckling as they came into the market square. 'I'm glad we moved to William Henry Street,' she said, and Margaret agreed.

They bought the darning thread and a basket load of fresh fruit. Afterwards, they wandered among the many colourful stalls, examining this and that but buying nothing else. Presently they made their way to the little café on the corner.

Here they sat and passed the time of day, and Margaret said warily, 'Have you given up the idea of talking with the priest?'

'I will go and see him,' promised Cathy. 'But not yet.' Somehow she still couldn't bring herself to talk about the things closest to her heart.

'Don't leave it too long, sweetheart,' Margaret advised gently. 'I know how hard you're trying to forget. But it's still there, isn't it? Still hurting as much as ever.'

For a moment it seemed as though Cathy might answer. But the moment passed and she was asking, 'See over there?' Pointing to the draper's stall, she suggested light-heartedly, 'Wouldn't Ruby be pleased if we took her a brand new pair of stockings?'

Margaret understood and chided herself for thinking she knew best. 'All right, sweetheart,' she apologised. 'In your own good time.'

CHAPTER FOURTEEN

It was Thursday, the night when revellers came from all over London to hear the band. By nine o'clock there wasn't a sober man in the place, come ten o'clock there wasn't even standing room, and by the time the musicians played their last melody of the first set, deals of all kinds were being done in every corner of the club.

'I'm no bloody fool!' The burly fellow kept the dainty jewel-box in the palm of his grubby hand. 'You'll have to give me a better price than that, or I'll take me business elsewhere.'

He would have put the box in his jacket pocket, but Tony Manners held out his hand. 'Let me see it again.'

Opening it up, the burly fellow took out a small picture of two infants. Showing it to the other man first, he then tore it into pieces and threw the pieces into the ash-tray. 'Pictures of kids is worth nothing,' he grumbled. Handing the box over, he said, 'If you want this, though, you're gonna have to pay for it.'

Tony Manners turned the box over and over in his palm. It was a beautiful thing; small and heart-shaped, made of platinum and gold, and encrusted with rubies. It was obvious that some-one had cherished it, someone from a grand house. 'A thing like this might be fitting for a lady,' he observed softly, and straightaway Cathy came to mind. 'I don't normally ask where you get your stuff,' he remarked, 'but this is different . . . better class than you usually fetch me.' Instinctively he stared round, looking for strange faces, anyone who might look suspicious. 'Look here, I don't want the rozzers on my back,' he said harshly.

The burly fellow laughed. 'Relax! Like I said, I'm no bloody fool. That box was taken months back. I've kept it hidden all this time, and you can take my word there'll be no rozzers on your back.'

'Straightforward burglary, was it?' Something about that box made his blood turn cold.

'That's my business.' He wasn't about to admit that he'd brutally murdered an old woman for it. Agitated by the sight of it, he snarled, 'Do you want it or don't you?'

'I want it.'

'Name your best offer?'

'Half a guinea?'

'To hell with that!' Snatching the box, he put it back in his pocket.

At that moment, Teresa returned from the dressing-room. 'He wants me to sing another number,' she explained. 'I told him I'd check with you first.'

'Tell him you'll do it, and that I'll expect to talk terms with him after closing.' Tony watched as she made her way back. When he turned he saw how the burly fellow was watching her too. 'Fancy her, do you?' he asked.

'Bursting out me pants, I am.'

'I should break your legs for that.'

'You could try.'

'How badly do you want her?'

The burly fellow stared at him in disbelief. 'Are you saying what I think you're saying?'

'The price I've offered . . . and *her*.'

'Jesus!' He started trembling. 'She won't do it . . .'

'She'll do as she's told.'

'It's a deal. But I'll hang on to the box for now.'

'I've another deal waiting.' Standing up, Tony said softly, 'I'll be back before she's finished singing.'

'I'll be waiting, matey.' Just then Teresa came on stage and went straight into a rendering of 'I'll take you home again, Kathleen'. The burly fellow watched, his eyes raking her body. 'Sing your heart out, my lovely,' he croaked hoarsely. 'Afterwards, I'll show you what a *real* man can do.'

Jack was getting nervous. 'Where the hell have you been?' he hissed as Tony Manners approached, and slunk back into the shadows. 'You know I don't want my old man to clap eyes on me.'

'Better get a move on then.' He was amused by the constant game of cat and mouse between the burly fellow and Jack. 'He's in there now, impatient for me to go back inside.'

Taking a small sack from beneath his coat, Jack opened it and took out a silver statuette. 'That's the last of the big ones,' he whispered, thrusting it into the older man's hands. 'Gimme the same as before and let me get out of here.'

While Tony Manners counted out the coins, a row erupted inside the club. 'Get a move on!' urged Jack. 'For God's sake, get a bloody move on!'

No sooner were the words out of his mouth than the club doors were flung open and out came a very irate Teresa, with the burly fellow hard on her heels. 'Tony, you bastard!' Rushing up the alley, she flung herself at him. 'Is it right what he says?' In the lamplight tears glittered in her eyes. 'Did you really tell him I'd sleep with him?' Her voice fell to a sob. 'You didn't say that, did you? Tell me you didn't say that.' She was plucking at his coat, desperate for him to deny it.

Angry that she had interrupted his deal, he glared at her. 'One night, that's all, you stupid cow! It's important to me, or I wouldn't ask.'

Suddenly all hell was let loose. Jack and the burly fellow caught sight of each other, and it was only seconds before they were rolling about on the ground, punching and gouging at each other. Somebody got excited and yelled, 'Garn! Teach the big bugger a lesson, Jack!' Another drunk shouted for the big fellow and soon the whole crowd was in turmoil, fists flying and blood spattering everywhere. The proprietor called for help, and the sound of a police whistle sent Tony Manners fleeing away down the alley, with Teresa in tow.

As he looked back, he saw a swarm of blue uniforms gathering round the crowd. 'Mindless fools!' he groaned. 'My money's scattered all over the alley and I've got bugger all to show for it. I've dropped the statuette, and thanks to you, I don't expect to clap eyes on that box again.' Raising his fist, he brought it down heavy over Teresa's face. 'Next time I make you part of a deal, you'd do well not to question it.'

As she fell to the ground he gave her a kick in the groin for good measure.

CHAPTER FIFTEEN

Maria sat up in bed and supped at the tea David had brought her. 'I do miss her, son,' she said. 'Bad as she is, she's still my lass.'

'I know that, Mam,' he acknowledged. 'And nobody prays harder than me that she'll come to her senses before too long.'

'I only wish she were more like you in nature.' After draining her cup she gave it to him and watched while he replaced it on the tray. 'You're a good man,' she told him softly. 'You don't deserve a sister like that . . . nor a silly old woman like me for a mother. There must be times when you wish you were miles away from the pair of us.'

Regarding her with dark smiling eyes, he asked softly, 'Do you really believe that?'

She shook her head and chuckled. 'Naw,' she confessed. 'But if I were you, I'd 'a dropped the pair of us long ago.'

'No, you wouldn't,' he chided. 'I may be stubborn, but I'll never see the day when I can match you.' With a wry smile he added in a regretful voice, 'Or Teresa, come to that.'

'Being stubborn isn't a good thing, son. It's being strong that counts, and we'll neither of us ever have the strength that was born in you.' She had been riddled with guilt since the day when Teresa turned Ruby away from the door with a pack of lies. Night and day it had rested uneasy on her conscience. Looking at him now, knowing how hard it had been for him to leave his Cathy behind, she was tempted to tell him and to hell with Teresa's threats. 'Son . . .?'

He was at the door now, ready to take the cob into Ilford. At the sound of her voice, he came back, 'What is it, Mam?'

Her courage deserted her. 'Nothing. Go on, be off with you.'

349

'Is there anything else you want before I go?'

'Is Ted coming to stay with me?'

'He's on his way.'

'Then I want for nothing.'

'I'll not be long. I should be back from Ilford by half-past seven . . . an hour to see the cob settled in his stable, and ten minutes across the field to home.' Grinning, he called behind him as he went from the cottage, 'Ask Nancy to have the kettle on for quarter to nine. I'll have a thirst on me like a fire.'

Outside the cob was restless. 'We'll soon have you a new set of shoes, you old devil.' Tickling it under the chin, he lifted himself on to its back. Gently squeezing his knees into its belly, he urged it on, away from the cottage and across the fields in the direction of Ilford town. He went slowly at first, then the cob broke into a trot, and the summer breeze strengthened. It was an exhilarating experience, riding on the strong broad back, across the hills and valleys with no hedge or fence to mar your path. 'Go on, boy! Go on!' As they crossed the stream the breeze played around them, spurring them on. David bent low over the cob's back, his eyes raw where the breeze whipped into them, and his dark hair spilling back from his forehead.

As they came nearer to town, he brought his mount back to a slower pace. Smacking it fondly on the neck, he confided, 'It'll be a sorry day when the farm's sold. There's no telling where either of us will end up.' He'd had time to mull over the changes ahead. 'If I can find my way to keep the field, I'll find a way to keep you an' all,' he promised. 'But it's a sad day all the same, when things have to change. Though change they must, and sometimes we have to part from them we've come to love.'

Cathy was always on his mind, always in his heart, but sometimes, as now when he was out in the fields with only nature around him, she crept right into his soul. 'I had a sweetheart once,' he told the cob. 'Her name was Cathy . . . and she was the loveliest creature on God's earth.' A great ache grew in his heart and, as he relived those precious times he'd spent with her, he felt as though his life was ended. 'She's gone now,' he whispered. 'Strange how easily her love died when mine never could.'

For the remainder of the journey, he thought about other

things: the old cob; the farm and when it might be auctioned; his mother and how he would do anything to avoid her having to move house and home again; Teresa and the way of life she was caught up in. All these thoughts washed through his mind, leaving him more determined than ever that he wouldn't take it all without a good fight.

He didn't have to think about Cathy. She was just there, not a thought or a memory but the very essence of his being. She was with him every minute of every day, and would be for the rest of his life.

The blacksmith was expecting him. 'You're the last of the day,' he said with a grateful sigh. 'The old back's playing me up again, sod it.'

Jumping down from the cob's back, David led it by the reins into the yard. 'You'll have to think about retiring soon,' he told the older man. 'I recall you telling me when I first came here that you were looking for someone to take over.'

'Aye, an' I were. But I've stopped looking now, because men who could do this job are few and far between.' Suddenly his eyes brightened and he stepped back to look at David's fine figure. '*You* could do it though,' he suggested hopefully. 'When the farm's closed you'll be looking for work.'

'True enough. But I'm hoping to be my own boss.'

'That takes money.'

'You don't have to tell me that.' Rubbing his hand reassuringly up and down the horse's shoulder he smiled knowingly, winking as he revealed confidently, 'I'll do it though. I don't know how yet, but I will do it.'

The blacksmith was impressed. David's determination only made him more persistent. 'I can see you've had enough of working for others, so how about if I offered you a share? How about if, instead of earning your wages, you worked for a share in the business with me?'

It was an offer out of the blue, and David didn't want to sound ungrateful, but blacksmithing wasn't for him. Holding out his hands, he said in a serious voice, 'See these?'

'Aye, and I can see they're strong and capable . . . you'd make a fine blacksmith.'

'What I'm trying to say is these hands are used to working

351

with God's good earth. Though I thank you kindly for your offer, I have to say no.'

'More's the pity.' Sighing, the blacksmith prepared to shoe the horse. 'It's a lonely job and no mistake,' he chattered on while David watched him turn the hot iron in the heat of the fire. 'Happen I should do as you say ... retire and find myself a woman.' He chuckled. 'A nice homely sort like the one as came to see you the other day.' His chuckling erupted into a full-bellied laugh. 'I don't mind telling you, I took a shine to that lady. Mind you, I tend to fancy every woman I clap eyes on. Trouble is, they don't fancy me.'

David thought the other fellow must be confused. 'You've got me mixed up with somebody else,' he said. 'I've had no lady visit me ... homely or otherwise.'

The blacksmith was affronted. 'I might have a bad back,' he said in an injured voice, 'but I ain't senile ... not yet I ain't!' Taking the hot iron to the cob, he raised its hoof and seared the shoe into place. 'I took her out to your place on the cart. She spoke to that sister o' yourn, and then I fetched her back again. I didn't charge her a penny. If I can't give a lift to a lady when it's needed, what kind of a gentleman am I, eh?'

David was paying more attention now. 'I wasn't told about this.' Suspicions of Teresa came into his mind. 'The visitor ... did she give her name?'

'Nope.'

'What did she look like?' His heart was racing. Somehow he dared to hope it might have to do with Cathy. But then, how could it?

The blacksmith looked up. 'I'd say she were in her late fifties, maybe a little older, but presentable if you know what I mean.' He frowned. 'I'll tell you what, though. She looked troubled ... didn't have much to say for herself. Deep in thought most of the time.'

David's mind was racing ahead. Why would a woman like that want to see *him*? 'So she never mentioned what her business was?'

'Oh, aye! Her business were *you*. She came here especially to see you ... asking after you she was. Knew your name, knew your family. On the way out to your place, she had a smile on her face. On the way back it was wiped off. Whatever your sister told her, it dampened the poor creature's spirits, that's for sure.' He thought it best not to mention how he'd overheard the conversation between Teresa and the visitor.

The blacksmith finished his work and tried his luck once more before David left. 'Are you sure you won't change your mind about coming into business with me?'

Now astride the cob's back, David was eager to get away, to ask his mam about this mysterious visitor. 'I'm not made for blacksmithing,' he declared. 'When a man's heart is in the soil, that's where his ambitions lie.'

'Good luck to you then.'

Hot and sweating from the race across the fields, David tethered the cob and ran into the cottage. Maria was awake. When she realised he knew about Ruby Adams calling, she lied with conviction. 'If she came here I must have been asleep, son, because I know nothing about a visitor.' Feigning tiredness, she yawned and slid beneath the sheets. 'Ted's just gone,' she said, desperately trying to turn his attention from the delicate issue. 'He's a grand neighbour . . . nothing's too much trouble for him.' Observing David out of the corner of her eye, she hated herself for deceiving him.

'Did Teresa say if she'd be coming home again?'

'You know what she's like, son. Here one minute an' gone the next. She can be gone weeks, or turn up when you least expect it.'

'Who do you reckon the visitor was, Mam?' Happen he was clutching at straws thinking it might be something to do with Cathy. There was no reason to think such a thing, yet he couldn't shake the feeling off.

'Some old gypsy woman, I expect. They're allus at the door, after one thing or another.'

'By all accounts it was no gypsy woman.' He recalled the blacksmith's very words. 'She asked for me by name. What do you make of that?'

'Somebody heard the farm were up for sale . . . sent her maid-servant to offer you work.'

'Teresa had no right not letting me know.'

'If it had been important, I'm sure she would have.'

'Happen I should make it my business to find out.'

A thought struck her then, making her sit up in her bed. 'You're never going to the city to find her? Good God! Look at you . . . you've worked yourself to a standstill. You've the cob to take back yet, and when you've trekked your way across the fields, I dare say it'll be gone midnight.' She tutted with frustration. 'You're never telling me you mean to go to the city at this time of a night? And what for, eh? To ask your sister about some poor old bugger who, for all we know, might have been looking for work herself?' She tutted again. 'And do you intend waking Ted from his bed, eh? Or are you gonna leave your old mam on her own at the mercy of every rambler?' Fear of his finding out the truth was evident in her voice.

Misinterpreting her fear, he was quick to assure her. 'Don't worry. You'll not be left alone, Mam, and I wouldn't be so callous as to wake Ted. You forget, I know how hard he works, so I know how much he needs his sleep.' Her arguments began to make sense. 'You're right. If it had been important Teresa would have let me know. When all's said and done, it might well have been somebody asking after work. It's no secret that I mean to raise the money for that field. It follows that folk might believe there'll be work going.' All the same, he couldn't help but be curious.

Settling his mam down, he told her, 'I'll stable the cob here in the shed for tonight. It won't hurt.'

All night long, Maria tossed and turned. Visions of Teresa haunted her dreams. Once, when the dreams became nightmares, she woke up screaming. In a minute David was by her side. 'Hush now,' he murmured. 'It's all right . . . I'm here. You're safe.'

The night hours lengthened into the dawn, and during the long vigil he patted her forehead with cold water, soothed her with a quiet voice, and wondered what had triggered such terrible nightmares. Even when she was awake, they seemed real. Twice she startled him by calling out Cathy's name. When she called out his father's, he thought she had been dreaming of the hanging. 'No, no, it's all over,' he coaxed. 'Everything's all right.' Yet he knew that for him it would never be all right again.

CHAPTER SIXTEEN

On Saturday mornings, Ruby had got into the habit of baking a dozen loaves. Cathy would put them in the oven when they were risen, and take them out again when they were baked and crusty. 'You'll soon be doing me out of a job,' Ruby complained, but secretly she was delighted to see Cathy coming back to full health.

When the bread was wrapped in muslin and placed in the deep wicker baskets, Cathy would take these and place them on the front doorstep; just as she did on this warm and pleasant Saturday afternoon. Half an hour later, she opened the door and took the empty baskets inside again. 'You were right about not taking the bread to their doors,' Margaret acknowledged as Cathy replaced the baskets in the cupboard. 'I would never have thought about doing that.'

'These folk are very proud,' Cathy acknowledged. 'They would much rather help themselves than have us take the bread to their doorsteps. It can't be easy for them to accept charity.'

'It's never easy,' Ruby answered from the kitchen doorway. 'Most of the menfolk down this street were in work when we first came here. Now every other household is finding it hard to scrape by.' She chuckled mischievously. 'It's funny though how the bread just vanishes like that, as though the fairies come out of their hidey-holes and whisper it away.' Winking, she declared, 'One o' these days I'm gonna peek out from behind the parlour curtain.'

Margaret clicked her tongue. 'You'll do no such thing, Ruby Adams,' she said. 'Besides, Cathy can tell you who has the bread, and who doesn't.'

'Oh?'

'It goes to those who need it most,' Cathy explained. 'When I asked Molly Turnbull to let it be known that the bread was there for anyone who needed it, she put the word round. She says it's going to the right folk . . . the poorer families, where the men have lost their work.' It was good to help, even if it wasn't enough. She was humbled by such God-fearing folk. 'Sometimes it's the children who come for the bread.' Pausing, she wondered about something Molly Turnbull had revealed. 'She told me how no one else would ever take the bread that was meant for these families. The ones who had enough for their own would never take from the mouths of others.'

'Good job we're among honest folk,' Ruby declared, wiping her hands on her pinnie. 'Else the baskets would be spirited away along with the bread. Then I'd be after strangling somebody, 'cause them baskets is me pride and joy!' That said, she ambled back into the kitchen and busied herself with the making of a plum duff.

Following Ruby into the kitchen, Cathy took the bucket to the tap and half filled it. 'What the divil d'you think *you're* doing?' Ruby swung round, showering Cathy with flour from her hands. 'I'm not having you cleaning them windows, my girl! You've not been out of the Infirmary five minutes, and you think you can do what you like.' She rubbed her nose and sneezed when it was covered in flour. 'Leave it to me, lass. I'll clean the windows when I've put the pudding on to steam.'

'You do too much already,' Cathy argued. 'Besides, I've got nothing else to do.'

Ruby glanced at the clock. It was gone two. 'Ah! So young Tommy Turnbull ain't turned up, is that it?'

Cathy tried to hide her disappointment. 'I'd best make a start on the window.'

'What you want is a nice quiet little pastime. Your aunt's embroidering. I'm sure you'd rather do that than clean the front window?' she asked hopefully. One look at Cathy's face told her otherwise, so she shook her head and smiled. 'Not for you, eh? Go on then, you young divil! Clean the blessed window. And don't dare leave a smear else I just might make you do it all over again.'

Cathy had cleaned only one corner of the window when she

was interrupted by Molly Turnbull's son, a big lad with a crippled foot and a smile that would light the blackest day. 'Hello, Mrs Cathy.' However much she told him she was not a 'Mrs', he insisted on addressing her in the same way. Holding up a small exercise book, he told her proudly, 'I've brought my book. And I learned that word just like you told me.'

Cathy clambered down the steps. 'Hello, Tommy.' She was delighted to see him. 'You had me worried. I thought you weren't coming to see me.' Taking the book, she opened it to the first page. Written down in big bold lettering was the word 'Blackburn'. 'Good boy,' she enthused, giving him a big hug. 'Come and sit beside me.' She patted the step and he sat alongside her. 'Do you remember how to say the word?'

Opening his mouth he formed the letters. It was a painfully slow procedure. 'Bl...ack...b...urn.' When he'd finished he clapped himself and Cathy clapped too. His smile broadened and he broke out in a fit of giggles.

'What does the word mean, Tommy?'

'It's where I live.'

'Is it the name of the street?'

He shook his head.

'What then?'

'It's...' He had to think for a minute, recalling what Cathy had told him. Suddenly he was grinning from ear to ear. 'It's the *town* where I live.'

'Right. Now then, get your pencil out and let me see you write your name again, and remember to say the letters as you write them down.'

'Aren't we going inside?'

'Do you want to?'

'Naw. I want to stay on the doorstep.'

'So do I,' she agreed. 'The sun's shining out here.' It was so good to feel the sun on her face, to feel the strength running back into her body.

Wondering why Cathy was so long, Ruby came to the door and peeped out. When she saw Cathy and the boy earnestly studying, she crept away and went to tell Margaret. 'It does my old heart good to see her teaching that lad,' she said brokenly. 'I don't mind telling you there was a time when I thought we'd lose that lass. God was good when he brought her back to us.'

Margaret put away her sewing and went to the front parlour. From the window there she had a clear view of Cathy and the boy. She gazed at her niece for a long time, thinking how well she had begun to look; her long fair hair shone in the sunlight, and her green eyes were dazzling as she laughed and giggled with the boy. But there was still a faraway look in those lovely eyes, a lost and lonely look that betrayed the truth beneath. 'You'll get over him, sweetheart,' she whispered, closing the curtains. As she wandered back to the sitting room, she sent up a little prayer that Cathy's extraordinary strength would carry her through.

Later that night, when Ruby had gone to her bed, Cathy made two mugs of hot cocoa; one for her and one for Margaret. 'Tommy's coming on a treat,' she said. While she spoke she stood by the window, absent-mindedly watching the trailing stars in a beautiful sky. 'He has a real thirst to learn.'

Margaret hoped she wasn't trespassing in matters best left alone when she asked softly. 'Teaching that lad ... it reminds you of David, doesn't it?'

At first Cathy didn't answer; it was as though she was searching for the right response, when of course there was only one answer. 'Yes.' Turning round, she came to the chair opposite Margaret. Sitting down, she placed her mug of cocoa in the hearth. '*Everything* reminds me of David,' she answered simply. 'Teaching Tommy to read and write ... the sunshine ... the night sky.' Her smile was wonderful. 'He's everywhere I turn.'

'I'm sorry.' Margaret had been afraid to open old wounds, and now she had. 'I should not have asked you such a question.'

'I'm glad you did.' With each passing day, Cathy knew she had to come to terms with all that happened. 'I think I'm learning to put it behind me.'

'You will. Oh, I'm not saying you will ever forget David because I know you won't. But, with God's help, there will come a day when you'll be able to remember without pain. You do believe that, don't you?'

'I have to.' Taking up her mug of cocoa she sipped at it, her mind wandering back to the past, and her heart warming. 'I did love him,' she murmured. 'I *do*.'

'Do you want to talk about the child?' She knew that until Cathy let go of the pain, she would never fully recover. 'Or the child's father? You know what they say . . . a trouble shared is a trouble halved.'

'Soon maybe. Not yet.' Visions of Jack tearing at her clothes assailed her. She visibly shivered. Since coming out of the Infirmary she had agonised over a certain promise she had made to Margaret. In that moment she made up her mind. 'Tomorrow morning, I mean to go and see the priest.'

'Oh, Cathy, if only you can open your heart to someone, I know it will all come right.'

The following morning, Cathy put on her best cream skirt and blue linen jacket. Her hair hung to her shoulders in a thick straight line, and for the first time in many a month she walked down the street with a spring in her step. Now that she had made the decision, she was actually looking forward to talking to the priest.

Two children swinging on a lamp-post stopped to stare at her as she went by. 'Cor, ain't she pretty?' cried the chubby girl with the egg-splattered smock. 'She ain't as pretty as my Auntie Pat!' yelled the buster of a boy. In a minute they were going at each other like a pair of dogs, with the girl astride the boy and the boy screaming for mercy.

After Cathy successfully intervened, she scolded the pair of them, explaining to the little girl, 'That wasn't a very ladylike way to behave.'

'That's 'cause she's a scruffpot!' snorted the lad, and if Cathy hadn't taken the girl home there might well have been blood spilled. When peace was restored, she went down the road, chuckling. Before she turned the corner at the bottom of William Henry Street, she could hear them going hammer and tongs at each other again.

The frantic knocking on the door sent Ruby up the passage at a run. 'Wait a minute, for heaven's sake!' As she flung open the door, she was shaken to see David standing there, taller, broader of shoulder, and more handsome than she remembered. 'You!' She stared open-mouthed. 'What the divil do *you* want?'

Margaret was equally shocked to see him. Having followed

Ruby to the door she was even more astonished when David pleaded, 'I have to see Cathy. Please . . . tell her I'm here.'

Ruby snapped at him. Believing he was here to cause Cathy more pain, she couldn't hide the hostility in her voice. 'She doesn't want you here. None of us do.'

He turned to Margaret. 'You have to let me see her!'

'Why should I?' Like Ruby, Margaret thought he would only cause Cathy a deal more heartache. 'From what I understand, you're due to be married. I believe double congratulations are in order . . . you're also about to become a father, isn't that right?'

David shook his head. 'No, it is not right.' Relieved that he had found the place where Cathy was, and sensing somehow that she must be in better health, his dark eyes melted into a smile. 'Look, I have to talk to her,' he told Margaret in a calmer voice. 'Teresa gave out a pack of lies. I'm not about to be wed, and there's no woman carrying my child.' He laughed wryly. 'The only woman I've ever wanted is Cathy.' Looking beyond the two women, he glanced down the passage. 'Please . . . tell her I'm here.'

Ruby and Margaret glanced at each other; the news he had brought was the best they could have heard. Ruby laughed out loud. 'You're not even courting?' Her laughter turned to tears, and she couldn't say another word. Instead she wiped her eyes on her pinnie and trembled all over.

Margaret felt the same, but managed to hide her emotions. After all, she had to be certain. 'You'd better come in,' she said, stepping aside for David to pass. 'Ruby, I'm sure a cup of tea and a slice of your fruit cake would be most welcome.' On her mistress's instructions, Ruby scuttled away.

David followed Margaret into the sitting room. 'I have to see Cathy,' he groaned. Realising he was being scrutinised, he grew agitated. 'I don't blame you for being suspicious, especially when Teresa also led you all to believe that I blamed Cathy for what her mother did.' Standing in the doorway, he ran his hands through his hair and bowed his head in despair. 'Don't you understand what I'm telling you?' he pleaded. 'I believed it was Cathy who loathed me! For some wicked reason that gave her pleasure, Teresa played us off against each other. She wanted to separate me and Cathy, and by God she did!' Turning his head he called up the stairs, 'CATHY!' His voice echoed in the silence. He couldn't see her, couldn't hear her. It was more than he could bear.

Margaret's calm voice broke in. 'It's no good your calling her, Cathy isn't here.'

His dark eyes widened with fear. 'Not here? Where then? For pity's sake! Where is she?'

If she'd had any doubts about his love for Cathy, they fell away in the face of his anguish. 'She isn't too far away,' she answered. 'She's well again, but ... she's missed you, David ... missed you like nothing on this earth.' Shaking her head, she invited, 'Sit down with me. Tell me everything, so I can understand.' Gesturing to the two armchairs by the fire-grate, she waited for him to accept. When he hesitated, she went and sat down, her eyes never leaving him for one moment.

'You won't tell me where she is until I do, will you?' He was quiet yet inwardly in turmoil, he knew how Margaret had always protected Cathy, and he admired her for that.

'I have to know Cathy won't be hurt again,' she explained. 'When we've talked, and I can be sure, *then* I'll tell you where to find her.'

Realising he had no choice, he walked across the room and sat in the chair opposite, his dark eyes filled with pain as he told her how he had found out about Ruby's visit from the blacksmith, and how, deep down, he'd sensed it might be something to do with Cathy. He couldn't let it go and so he found Teresa and she told him everything.

'The man she was with had a habit of beating her. But when he tried to force her into prostitution, she turned on him. I brought her home and she was filled with remorse at what she had done. She told me what Ruby had said ... how Cathy was ill and needed me.' When the tears welled up in his eyes, he paused to choke them back. 'You can't know what that did to me.' He paused again before going on, 'Teresa confessed how she had deliberately put poison between me and Cathy ... leading us to believe each loathed the other for what happened between our parents.' Taking a deep breath, he bowed his head and spoke in a quieter voice. 'I've been distraught,' he murmured. 'Now I just want to hold Cathy in my arms, to tell her how much I love and need her.'

When he lifted his gaze, Margaret was shocked by the depth of emotion in his face. 'I believe you,' she said.

Relief flowing through him, he closed his eyes and leaned back in the chair. In a moment he was standing beside her. 'I must go to Cathy now.' His voice was low and firm. The need for her was like a clenched fist inside him.

Realising the significance of the moment, Margaret stood up. 'I'll take you to her.'

As she went to fetch her jacket, she took a moment to think of Cathy. 'He's home, sweetheart,' she murmured. 'David has come home for you.'

Father Goldstone looked at Cathy with compassion. 'From what you've told me, life hasn't treated you too well. First your parents and their inability to love you as they should ... the young man you loved and lost ... the other young man, a wicked and cruel creature ... then the agony of losing that little innocent child.' His soft gaze enveloped her. 'I know how hard it can be, but you have to forgive. If you don't, you'll only succeed in destroying yourself.' He looked at her, at her lovely face and clear green eyes, and he saw the spirit beneath. 'It's only when we learn to forgive that we become strong enough to go on.'

'I understand that, Father.' Coming here had been the right thing to do. 'I am beginning to put it all behind me. The cruel things, the precious things I never had ... I can accept that now.' Her love for David was overwhelming. 'But I did have something very precious with David.' Her voice trembled. 'However hard I try, I can't seem to put that behind me.'

'When you experience a love such as you feel for your young man, you may *never* be able to put it behind you,' he answered honestly. 'But you still have to go on. There will be another love, I dare say.'

Cathy smiled wistfully. 'No, Father,' she whispered. 'There will never be another love for me.'

Outside, Margaret and David approached the church. 'I'll wait here,' she suggested. 'You go ahead.' She meant to stay just long enough to see them reunited, and then she would sneak away. The tower clock chimed ten. 'Cathy would have got here at about nine-thirty; I expect she'll be coming out at any minute now.'

Cathy opened the door and let herself out. In the fresh air she took a long deep breath. As she raised her eyes to the sunshine, a strange feeling came over her: that of being watched. Slowly, with beating heart, she turned her head. There was a young man making his way down the path towards her, a tall dark-haired young man. His long quick stride was oddly familiar. Suddenly he was running. Their eyes met and her breath caught in a gasp. '*David*?' The name came out in a whisper. She was shaking her head in disbelief, the tears streaming down her face as he called her name.

'CATHY! OH, CATHY!'

Before she could get her breath they were in each other's arms, crying and laughing, lost to everything but the joy of each other. An old couple smiled as they passed. 'Young lovers,' said the man to his wife, and as they looked on, they too were young again.

From a distance, Margaret watched the emotional reunion. She saw the radiance in Cathy's face. She heard the laughter as David swung her round again and again. She even cried a little. Then she went quietly away to tell Ruby the wonderful news.

All day Sunday, Cathy's head was in the clouds. In the afternoon she and David walked in the park, content in each other, she with her arm linked through his, and he walking tall and proud beside her. 'I don't think I'll ever forgive Teresa for what she did,' he said, leaning over the rail beside the lake. 'If it hadn't been for the blacksmith, I might never have known Ruby had come to find me.'

'I've thought hard about Teresa,' Cathy admitted. 'And about what the priest said.' Smiling up at him, she took pleasure in the warmth of his dark eyes, saying softly, 'If we don't forgive, we'll only destroy ourselves . . . it's only when we forgive that we find the strength to go on. That's what the priest said. And that's why we have to forgive Teresa.'

He gazed down on her, thinking what a lucky man he was to have found such a gem. 'I love you,' he said.

'No more than I love you,' she answered simply. When he bent to kiss her, a great warmth spread through her. She'd never thought to see this day and now it was here and she was in David's arms. Glimpsing the blue sky above she sent up a silent prayer of thanks.

CHAPTER SEVENTEEN

On 14 September 1901 Cathy and David were married, joined together in wedlock by the same priest to whom Cathy had turned in her greatest need. Margaret attended her. Dressed in a pale blue outfit and holding a small posy, she looked ten years younger.

Throughout the service, whenever Cathy glanced up at David, he was glancing down at her. Though she could feel his hand in hers and hear the priest giving his blessing, she still found it hard to believe that she was actually here in God's house, being married to the man she'd feared had gone from her life forever.

When the service was almost over and the words 'I pronounce you man and wife' were spoken, she looked up into David's dark eyes and saw her own deep emotion mirrored there. 'You look lovely, Mrs Leyton,' he murmured. They kissed for the first time as man and wife, and when they walked down the aisle – he looking smart and debonair in a dark suit, and she looking radiant in a white silk gown made by Margaret's own hands – there was never a couple better suited to each other.

As they passed the pews, all eyes turned towards them. Ted and Maria were there, Maria seated at the end of the pew in an old bathchair that Ted bought in a house sale. As Cathy brushed by, she reached out her hand to wrap her fingers round Maria's; in that briefest touch a lifelong friendship was forged. Teresa had promised to be here but was not. Ruby sniffled into her hankie until her nose looked like a ripe tomato, and in the back pews a number of neighbours and regular churchgoers broadly smiled and wished the couple well as they went by.

Afterwards they gathered in the house on William Henry

Street where Ruby and a few of the neighbours had laid out a spread fit for a king. They ate and chatted and danced to the tune of Mr Entwhistle's accordion. By two o'clock the party spilled on to the streets where the neighbours were having their own knees-up, and soon it was time for David and Cathy to leave.

'Enjoy yourselves!' shouted Ada Snettleton, wiping a snuffy dewdrop from her nose. 'God go with yer!' shouted the old drunk from the top house. As the carriage pulled away, Cathy fell into David's arms and the two of them laughed until they were out of sight of William Henry Street.

Once they were on the train going south, they spent the hours talking about their future. 'Are you sure you don't mind us living with my mam for a while?' David asked. He had other plans under way, but there was time enough for him to tell Cathy all about those later.

'As long as I'm with you, I don't really care where we are,' she assured him. 'As long as your mam doesn't mind.' All the same she had been giving it a great deal of thought. 'When the farm's sold, I expect we'll all have to move on . . . where will we go?'

'Don't worry your head about that,' he said. 'We're on our honeymoon . . . booked into a little country hotel with a whole week to enjoy each other.' He breathed a sigh of relief when she rested her head on his shoulder, closed her eyes and lightly slept.

The hotel was small but friendly. Though it was very late, the proprietor's wife served a delicious cold meal. 'Could you wake us early in the morning?' David asked the proprietor's wife. 'We have an important appointment.'

'What appointment?' In the privacy of their own room, Cathy was curious.

Taking her in his arms, he whispered in her ear, 'I'm going to get you the best wedding present in the whole world.'

She didn't reply because he was peeling off her clothes. 'Are you going to take advantage of me?' she asked coyly.

'I might . . . or don't you want me to?' He was teasing and she loved it.

'I want you to.' She spoke the words into his mouth as he pushed her gently on to the bed, kissing her with the tenderness of a lover.

First he gripped her hands and spread her arms out, then he licked her nipples with the tip of his tongue, and now he was stroking his fingers over the outline of her breast. 'You're beautiful,' he whispered hoarsely.

'Love me,' she coaxed, softly kissing him on the curve of his neck. 'Make love to me now.'

He rolled on top of her. Lying against her body, he kissed her all over, every now and then returning to kiss her passionately on the mouth, and all the while he murmured sweet endearments, taking his time in loving her, his heart bursting and the feel of her in his arms almost more than he could bear.

Cathy stroked his thick dark hair, whispering into his ear all the things she had never been able to tell him. She could sense his great love for her. Soon their passion rose and he eased open her legs. She felt the thickness of him hard against her thigh. Slowly at first, he entered her. Sighing with pleasure, she arched towards him, wrapping her arms around his back. Their bodies entangled and as he pushed in and out of her, caressing and wooing her, their passion was roused to fever pitch.

Filled with wonder, she gave herself to him, revelling in the touch of his bare flesh, clinging to him, needing him like she had never needed anything in the whole of her life. Too soon it was over. They held on to each other, breathless and fulfilled. 'I adore you, Mrs Leyton,' he murmured softly against her face. And she could only hold him as though she would never let him go.

The following morning they awoke early and made love again. Later, they enjoyed their breakfast before boarding a carriage. 'Where are you taking me?' Cathy wanted to know.

'Wait and see,' came the answer. 'If I tell you now it won't be a surprise, will it?'

When the carriage pulled into the farmyard, Cathy thought the driver had made a wrong turn. 'There's a sale going on,' she exclaimed, craning her neck to see the crowd of people surging round the auctioneer's rostrum.

Jumping out of the carriage, David offered a helping hand. 'Well, are you coming or not?'

There was a mischievous smile on his face that made her suspicious. 'Why would I want to watch a sale?' she asked cautiously.

'All right. Stay where you are.' He began striding away.

'No, wait!' Scrambling from her seat, Cathy ran after him. 'What are you up to, David Leyton?' she demanded.

Turning round, he put his hands on her shoulders and pushed her gently towards a hay bale. First he kissed her full on the mouth. 'I want you to trust me, Mrs Leyton,' he declared, kissing her again when she began to protest. 'I promised you the best wedding present ever, didn't I?'

'You did,' she retorted playfully. 'So where is it?'

Stretching his arms wide, he swung round, embracing all the land as far as the eye could see. 'This is it,' he said, and there was wonder in his voice.

Amazed, she followed his gaze; looking from the land to the outbuildings and then to the big farmhouse. 'This *farm*!' Her voice came out in a strange little croak. 'Are you saying this *farm* is my wedding present?'

Grabbing her by the hand, he ran her across the gravel yard to where the auctioneer was offering the farmhouse. 'Together with thirty acres of prime agricultural land.'

As the bidding began, David stood back, letting them take the price as far as they could; until one by one the bidders dropped out, each having reached his own financial limit. It was then that he put in his bid. Twice he had to raise it, and each time the other man stood against him. Anxious now, David put forward a bid of seven hundred guineas; that was as far as he could go. Feeling the sweat trickle down the back of his neck he nodded at the other man. The other man nodded back. It was a calculated game of bluff. David smiled confidently; the auctioneer asked the other man if he wanted to raise his bid. The man looked at David once more, took a moment to think it through, then shook his head and, disappointed, slunk quietly away. The hammer went down.

'SOLD TO MR DAVID LEYTON!'

A cheer went up and Cathy felt herself being lifted through

the air as David swung her high in his arms. 'We're landowners!' he cried, hugging her until she thought her bones would break. 'I have my Cathy, and now I have the land I've always dreamed of.' His dark eyes glowing, he murmured, 'What more could any man want?'

'A child,' she answered. David's child to complete her joy.

CHAPTER EIGHTEEN

Though David had saved a tidy sum of his own, it was the blacksmith who had made it possible for him to buy the farm. Because of his recurring back trouble and an urge to try another line of work, he had entered into a partnership with David. For five years David would pay the blacksmith a small income from the farm, together with regular payments to reduce the loan. It was a fair and satisfactory arrangement, releasing the blacksmith from the work that was crippling him, and giving David the opportunity to farm the land that would one day be his own.

Over the next five years, tended by David's strong hand and shrewd business mind, the farm prospered. Two days before the agreement ran out, he had repaid every penny to the blacksmith who then decided to become a trader and buy two shops in the heart of London town.

Teresa was never seen again in Ilford. She stayed with Tony Manners and went on to be a famous singer.

Jack was jailed for ten years after admitting a string of offences, including the theft of a quantity of silver and other valuables from the big house in Langho. His father, who claimed he was only looking after his son's interests, confessed to murdering two people... Nan Foster and Frank Blackthorn. He was duly sentenced to hang, but cheated the hangman when he died of gangrene before the day of execution.

Both men vehemently denied killing Rita Blackthorn. There were those who whispered that it was her own husband who had ended her life, rather than let her share it with another man. Over the years the rumours grew, for no one else was ever brought to answer for her murder.

The police were able to return most of the valuables stolen

from Blackthorn House. Margaret and Ruby remained in the house on William Henry Street, living modestly and contentedly; they lived to be very old.

Margaret never learned the truth about Nan; in the circumstances perhaps it was just as well. Sometimes more pain is caused by knowing than not knowing. Some things are best left to merge quietly with the past.

On 4 April 1902 Maria and Ted were married in a registrar's office. David made them a present of Ted's cottage, and they lived there happily for many years.

Two years after their marriage vows, Cathy and David were blessed with a son. Cathy was thrilled. 'He has your dark looks,' she observed, holding him close to his father's face.

The following July, she gave birth to a daughter, with fair hair and lovely green eyes. Cradling the tiny infant in her arms, she whispered a heartfelt promise: 'You and your brother will never want for love,' she said. 'Whenever you need me, I'll be here.' The tears rolled down her face as she remembered her own lonely childhood. But it was over. With her husband and their two lovely children, she had a wonderful future to look forward to. A future she had thought would never be hers.

'Come out here, sweetheart.' David's voice carried into the house. With their son cuddled against her shoulder, and the tiny girl tucked in her other arm, Cathy went to him. 'Look at that,' he said, his dark eyes encompassing the sun-kissed landscape. 'Did you ever dare to think that one day such a beautiful place would be ours?'

Cathy wasn't looking at the landscape. Her gaze was intent on his face; on that rich dark hair and those dark glowing eyes that could turn her heart over with one glance. 'I never dared to believe *you* would be mine,' she murmured softly. 'Can you ever know how much I love you?'

Slowly he turned his head and looked at her, and his heart was full. 'There will never be a single day in the whole of our lives when I don't know that,' he answered. 'How could I not know it, when I feel your every heartbeat?' Embracing his small son with one arm, he stretched out the other, drawing Cathy and their daughter close to his heart. 'What we have, my lovely,' he whispered in her ear, 'will last a lifetime.'

And it did.